W9-BEV-393

Sweet Revenge

NORTH INDIAN RIVER COUNTY LIBRARY
1001 SEBASTIAN BLVD. (C.R.512)
SEBASTIAN, FLORIDA 32958
PHONE: (772) 589-1355

ALSO BY DIANE MOTT DAVIDSON

Catering to Nobody

Dying for Chocolate

The Cereal Murders

The Last Suppers

Killer Pancake

The Main Corpse

The Grilling Season

Prime Cut

Tough Cookie

Sticks & Scones

Chopping Spree

Double Shot

Dark Tort

Sweet Revenge

Diane Mott Davidson

HARPER LUXE

An Imprint of HarperCollinsPublishers

NORTH INDIAN RIVER COUNTY LIBRARY

This book is a work of fiction. The characters, incidents, and dialogue are drawn from the author's imagination and are not to be construed as real. Any resemblance to actual events or persons, living or dead, is entirely coincidental.

SWEET REVENGE. Copyright © 2007 by Diane Mott Davidson. All rights reserved. Printed in the United States of America. No part of this book may be used or reproduced in any manner whatsoever without written permission except in the case of brief quotations embodied in critical articles and reviews. For information address HarperCollins Publishers, 10 East 53rd Street, New York, NY 10022.

HarperCollins books may be purchased for educational, business, or sales promotional use. For information please write: Special Markets Department, HarperCollins Publishers, 10 East 53rd Street, New York, NY 10022.

FIRST HARPERLUXE™ EDITION

HarperLuxe is a trademark of HarperCollins Publishers.

Library of Congress Cataloging-in-Publication Data

Davidson, Diane Mott.
  Sweet revenge / Diane Mott Davidson.—1st ed.
    p. cm.
  ISBN: 978-0-06-052733-4 (Hardcover)
  ISBN-10: 0-06-052733-1
  1. Bear, Goldy (Fictitious character)—Fiction. 2. Women in the food industry—Fiction. 3. Caterers and catering—Fiction. 4. Maps—Collectors and collecting—Fiction. 5. Cookery—Fiction. 6. Christmas—Fiction. 7. Colorado—Fiction. I. Title.
PS3554.A925S94 2007
813'.54—dc22
                                                        2007022130

ISBN: 978-0-06-136701-4 (Luxe)
ISBN-10: 0-06-136701-X

07 08 09 10 11 WBC / RRD 10 9 8 7 6 5 4 3 2 1

LP
F
Dav

To Katherine Goodwin Saideman,
with deep thanks for nineteen years of incisive comments
and affectionately rendered recommendations

They flee from me that sometime did me seek. . . .
—Sir Thomas Wyatt

What-the-Dickens Holiday Breakfast

—∞∞∞—

Great Expectations Grapefruit

Chuzzlewit Cheese Pie

Tale of Two Cities French Toast

Bleak House Bars

Hard Times Ham

Christmas Carol Coffee Cake

Butter, Syrup, Assorted Jams

Juices, Eggnog, Champagne

Coffee, Tea

—∞∞∞—

1

A month before Christmas, I saw a ghost.

This was not the ghost of Christmas past, present, or future. I didn't need to be reminded of bad things I'd done, nor, as far as I knew, of good things I ought to be doing. This wasn't, as my fifteen-year-old son, Arch, would say, any high woo-woo stuff either. I liked the past to stay in the past, thank you very much. Anything I hadn't handled well in my first thirty-four years I certainly didn't want to be reminded of in my busiest season, when I had twenty-five parties to cater between the first of December and the New Year.

Still, there had been that ghoul, that vision, that *whatever it was*.

The specter appeared on November 25, which fell on the Friday after Thanksgiving, when I was on my way to Smithfield and Hermie MacArthur's house to book two parties. I'd been looking forward to seeing the MacArthurs' place, because the events promised to fill my Christmas stocking with dough, and I didn't mean the kind I made into cinnamon rolls.

Hermie MacArthur had introduced herself to me at a church-women's luncheon I'd done earlier in the fall. In her midforties, with a much-powdered face, grayish-blond hair, and a commanding Southern accent, Hermie possessed an imposingly tall body that was shaped like a McIntosh apple—a hefty chest on stick legs. The luncheon speaker, a local woman named Patricia Ingersoll, headed a weight-loss group. Patricia had been droning on about how nobody should be consuming my gingerbread, made with unsalted butter and freshly grated ginger and—secret ingredient—freshly grated black pepper. I'd enjoyed catering Patricia's wedding reception four years ago. I also felt very sorry that she'd lost her relatively new husband to cancer in just the last year and a half. But I *did* wish she could have found another outlet for her energies besides telling people to stop eating.

The churchwomen had been shifting, murmuring, and whispering about regretting inviting Patricia. I'd escaped to my event center's kitchen, where I'd been wondering what I was going to do if nobody ate dessert.

Hermie MacArthur had followed me in, cornered me, and said, "Darlin', we need to talk." She'd fingered her multiple strands of pearls and diamonds while telling me that she and her husband had lived in Aspen Meadow's Regal Ridge Country Club area for only ten months, and she felt the holidays would just be a heavenly time to get to know her neighbors better. Yes, yes, I'd echoed as I reached for my calendar. Great idea. I was all for rich folks getting to know one another better.

We'd set up our November meeting date. But Hermie had been reluctant to leave the kitchen, and it wasn't because she couldn't stand to listen to Patricia anymore. I thought perhaps she wanted a second helping of something. Or an early piece of gingerbread? But no. Finally she confided that she was eager for the parties to go well, for her husband Smithfield's sake. It had been Smithfield who'd had the idea that they combine their holiday parties with a celebration of his hobby.

"And what is his hobby?" I'd asked with trepidation, fearing something to do with snakes.

"Why, darlin'," Hermie had replied, "it's map collecting!"

I'd almost choked as I imagined having to make a cake in the shape of North America, complete with squiggly lines for the rivers. But Hermie didn't mention a cake. I smiled and reminded myself that I'd had plenty of practice dealing with ultrawealthy people and their eccentricities. So if the MacArthurs wanted to haul out their Rand McNallys along with some mincemeat pies, who was I to complain?

I did tell Hermie that the one famous map of Aspen Meadow, with its maze of dirt and paved roads winding through the mountains, was *You Use'ta Couldn't Get There from Here!* She'd frowned. She said she was hoping I could do some reading on map collecting before I came, in case Smithfield wanted me to help with a slide, and I needed to reach for South Africa and not the South Bronx. Plus, Hermie went on, there would be at least two map dealers at the party, and one of them, Drew Wellington, was a former district attorney. Did I know Drew Wellington? she asked.

Yes, I said after a pause. I knew Mr. Wellington.

Hermie also wanted a touch of elegance, she said, and shook a ringed forefinger with a diamond the size of one of Arch's old marbles. Elegant was my middle name, I replied cheerily. Of course it wasn't, and my business, *Goldilocks' Catering, Where Everything Is Just Right!*, could be as low-down as a cowboy barbecue. But Hermie had seemed satisfied.

So there I was on November 25, tootling along Regal Road, the curving mountain byway that led past one of Arch's favorite snowboarding places and ended at the entrance to Regal Ridge Country Club, a relatively new fancy development built after Aspen Meadow Country Club had filled up. Hermie and I were set to make decisions on the menus for a dinner for eight to be held on Saturday, December 16, and a luncheon on Monday, the eighteenth. *Elegant* meant we weren't just talking soup to nuts. I was offering her crab dumplings in fresh herb broth to precede her first event, a curry dinner that would conclude with lime—not mincemeat, thank goodness—pie. For the Monday lunch, Hermie had asked for lamb and potatoes. I was going to propose lamb chops persillade and potatoes au gratin. The potatoes would be made memorable with fresh sage and caramelized onions. After we'd decided on the food, we'd hammer out the details of a preliminary contract. I would see how the MacArthurs' kitchen, dining, and living areas were set up. Then, most importantly from my point of view, Hermie would write a check for a down payment.

Accelerating up a steep hill, I felt *phat,* an expression of Arch's that he now told me was *so over. Phat* meant happy, not overweight, although I probably was that, too. I had a reason to feel good: the upcoming slew of holiday parties had, for the most part, been planned and paid for. Six weeks prior to the holidays was my cutoff date for booking events, but Hermie MacArthur had begged so earnestly that I'd agreed to take her on. For the rest of the affairs I was catering, the food had been ordered and the servers lined up. And I was especially happy that my event center by Aspen Meadow Lake had been cleaned and professionally decorated. Artificial trees and thousands of tiny colored lights had transformed the place into the proverbial winter wonderland.

I'd offered the center to Hermie. But she wanted to have their parties in their home. They had more maps than I had twinkling lights, she explained, and if they tried to move them, they had insurance concerns. I said I understood. Their residence wasn't a pretend mansion, I'd been told by Marla Korman, my best friend and the other ex-wife of our now-deceased ex-husband. It was an estate. In fact, Marla had said, the MacArthurs' home was an exceptionally fortified *palace* that had been built on one of the outcroppings of the Regal Ridge itself. According to Marla, the mansion commanded an impressive view of Denver, forty miles to the east. But the back side of the house perched on a sheer cliff overlooking a thousand-foot drop. It wasn't a place where herds of elk would ruin your garden, that was certain.

All this was okay with me, except for one thing: how you got to the MacArthurs' house. After you passed the snowboard area, the road narrowed. And even when you were driving below the speed limit, which I *was*, I later told my husband, Tom, the road presented problems. It was one of those two-lane Colorado byways that wind up the side of a mountain and are always losing their guardrails. If we were subject to a sudden snowstorm or one of the MacArthurs' guests had too much to drink, somebody could drive a Mercedes over the cliff, and no map was going to help you find those folks until the snow melted in springtime.

I tried not to think about all this as I slowed to negotiate a particularly nasty curve. When I got to the other side of the hill, the road dipped sharply before climbing again. I made sure I was slowing my van as I went down. Then I gave the gas pedal a gentle nudge to start back uphill.

And that's when I saw her.

Actually, I saw the approaching car's passenger first. She was young, fourteen or fifteen, I thought. She sat in the front seat, talking and waving her hands in the air. Something about her was sharply familiar. I took my foot off the gas and watched in fascination as she chatted up the driver of the car, a woman not much older, whose smiling face was in partial profile. The passenger, at that age between childhood and young womanhood, had bouncy shoulder-length dark brown hair. She was very lovely, but my memory stubbornly refused to give up a name or a family. A schoolmate of Arch's? Somebody from the church? Wherever that memory was, it was just out of reach. So I squinted at the driver. Was she having as good a time as her passenger? Was she just as lovely?

The driver turned her attention back to the road. Smiling, nodding, dark hair, pretty, *Wait a minute.* I knew that face. Okay, the hair was wrong. It was brown, not bleached blond, and it was pulled back in a ponytail. But I recognized her nonetheless.

Suddenly I was like a speeder who sees a state patrol car. I inadvertently smacked my brakes so hard they squealed, and my van skidded sideways. Trying to stop was a mistake, because then the driver of the other car hit *her* brakes, but only for a moment. When she glanced over, it was with the practiced, furtive movement of a criminal.

Am I in trouble? her look said. *Did somebody see me?*

The driver stopped smiling and tucked her chin. She spoke to her young passenger, zoomed around my crookedly stopped van, then raced up the hill I'd just come down. I eased my vehicle onto a narrow gravelly shoulder that was the only surface between me and a dented guardrail overlooking a very long plunge that ended on the interstate. In my confusion, I hadn't gotten a license plate. As I strained to catch a glimpse of the departing car, I couldn't even remember what kind of vehicle it was. A station wagon? An SUV? How about a color? I asked myself. All I could remember was that the vehicle had been dark.

But I *really* thought I knew that face, and the woman to whom it belonged. Maybe I was very much mistaken, and I could have been, I told Tom when we talked. Still, I was 99 percent sure that the driver of the car was named Alexandra, also known as Sandee, Brisbane—the woman who, six months earlier, had shot and killed my ex-husband.

In June of this year, Sandee Brisbane had confessed to the crime in front of me and a dozen others. Then she'd disappeared over a ledge into a raging forest fire that had, by the time it was put out, destroyed ten thousand acres of the Aspen Meadow Wildlife Preserve. Sandee had been only twenty-two.

She had perished, law enforcement had concluded. No one could have survived that inferno. Case closed.

Could Sandee not have died? I wondered as I sat in my van and tried to catch my breath. Could she be living in Aspen Meadow, half a year after she'd been declared dead? I shakily retrieved my cell and pressed the speed dial for Tom's office at the Furman County Sheriff's Department, where he was an investigator. After I blurted out what I'd seen, my husband said he just had one question.

When was the last time I'd been checked for glasses?

Very funny, I retorted as I stared up Regal Road and waited for my heart to resume its normal rhythm. I breathlessly repeated my description of Sandee and the teenager, then told Tom that I was sure Sandee had recognized me. She hadn't stopped to make sure I was all right, as most Colorado folks would have. Instead, she'd wrenched her car around my van and gunned her engine to speed away.

Whether or not Tom believed me, eventually he did realize how upset I was. He started taking me seriously, or he pretended to. In fact, he asked so many questions and paused so long while writing down the answers, I thought I was going to be late for my meeting with Hermie. I finally told him that I would see him that night. I resolved to put the apparition—the phantom? some inner voice asked—of Sandee Brisbane out of my head. I eased the van back onto the narrow road, and continued along to the stone gates marking the entry to the Regal Ridge Country Club area.

★   ★   ★

Marla had been right. Wending my way down a dead-end street, I passed two impressively massive homes, then reached the end of an enormous cul-de-sac, where the MacArthurs' house sat, a contemporary stone castle complete with a crenellated roof and turrets at either end. I smiled as I descended the steep driveway, then put on my professional face and demeanor as I ascended the staircase that led to the kitchen.

Working with "please call me Hermie, darlin'" to decide on the menus went reasonably well. I assured her that the first event, the curry dinner celebrating a recent acquisition Smithfield had made, would be fantastic. It was while Hermie and I were figuring out the flow of guests and times for serving that Smithfield MacArthur burst into the kitchen.

"Hermie!" he exploded. Like Hermie, he was quite tall and had thin gray hair. But what made my mouth drop open was that he had a very, very red face. Was he from Virginia, I wondered, and had his parents laughingly named him after a Smithfield ham? No, no, that would be too cruel. I closed my mouth and noted that like many megarich folks, Smithfield did not care a whit about his clothing. He wore a rumpled white shirt, much-creased khaki pants, and ancient, loose penny loafers that were literally coming apart at the seams. "Hermie!" he yelled again.

Hermie languidly lifted her wide, well-powdered chin and clacked her pearls together with her hand. "What, darlin'?"

Smithfield squinted and moved his head around wildly, as if he couldn't see the two of us seated at the black granite breakfast bar. He was perhaps ten years older than his wife, but that didn't stop him from acting as if he were her child. "Hermie!" he bawled for the third time. "What did you do with my glasses?"

"I put 'em on your head, darlin'," his wife patiently replied.

"Oh, for God's sake!" Smithfield cried. He reached up, nabbed his specs, and slid them into place. He thrust his jaw forward and demanded, "Are you sure you invited both Drew and Larry to the party?"

"We're plannin' the party right now."

"Is my caterer here?"

"She's sittin' right beside me, darlin'."

Smithfield thrust his scarlet face toward me. "Have you done your reading yet?" he bellowed.

"Reading?" I echoed.

"Oh, for God's sake, Hermie!" Smithfield shouted.

"I'll give her a copy of your book," Hermie promised.

"Make sure she pays for it," he grumbled.

Then he stomped out of the kitchen. Hermie sighed,
and I wondered if I could slip Smithfield one of Marla's
Valiums the night of the curry party.

Two hours later, I drove back up the MacArthurs'
long driveway with a copy of Smithfield's fat, self-
published volume, *Map Collecting Through the Ages*,
tucked against the passenger seat. Hermie had waved
her hand and said I could have it, no charge. And if I
could read it in my spare time—I almost choked with
laughter at that idea—then I could return it when I did
the curry dinner. Whoopee!

At the top of the drive, I came upon a gaggle of teenage girls playing lacrosse in the dead end. Since the
MacArthurs' house was right next to the cliff of Regal
Ridge, I wondered what happened when lacrosse balls
went over the edge. If it was your ball, you were out of
luck.

While I was stopped, the players parted slowly, a Red
Sea of masks, sticks, and sweatsuits. It had been several
hours since I'd passed the dark car with its two inhabit-
ants. Was one of the lacrosse players the girl I had seen
with Sandee, if indeed it was Sandee I had seen? I

scanned their faces and shook my head, then eased the van into the cul-de-sac and away.

With the winter solstice fast approaching, darkness fell over the mountains like smoke. I drove the winding road past the Regal Ridge Snow Sports Area, where man-made snow and bright spotlights were now allowing snowboarders to whiz down the hill until nine at night. Was Arch there now? I wondered. I couldn't remember, and frantically called his cell.

He was at home, he reminded me when he picked up, because I'd said he needed to work at least an hour decluttering his bookshelves before he could go to a sleepover. I exhaled in relief, then asked if he knew a fourteen- or fifteen-year-old girl with long brown hair.

"I know about fifty of them."

"Well, she's very pretty."

"Twenty-five, then. Are you going to let me work on these books?"

I told him to remember to pile them into boxes, then signed off and headed home. When I finally came through the front door, Tom gave me a long hug. He was handsome, brown-haired, and just enough taller than I was to make an embrace both comforting and exhilarating. I closed my eyes and happily let his mountain-man body encircle mine.

"Miss G.," he said when we parted, "you're beginning to worry me. You think you see things, and you call Arch because you forget where he is but he's home doing what you've been nagging him about all week. You need to get more rest. You've been working too much, and you're beginning to act like a nutcase."

"Never call a caterer a nutcase. We think it's something to eat."

"Exhaustion makes you see things," he reminded me.

"Right. So what you're saying is, I'm tired, I'm exhausted, I'm totally whipped? And therefore it follows that what I saw was a hallucination?"

"Is that whipped like potatoes?"

I tried to punch him. But he was too quick for me, and I missed. He laughed, but I didn't. I was still thinking of that ghost.

2

Well. Insofar as possible, I tried to put seeing Sandee—or whoever she was—out of my mind. But this did not prove easy. It wasn't that I fumbled with my work. The first two weeks of holiday events went off as planned. Under Tom's watchful eye, I began going to bed earlier—no later than midnight, unless a party ran over. When I did fall onto the mattress beside my warm husband, I'd be asleep before I landed.

But then . . . four hours later I would awaken in a sweat. Somehow I couldn't forget the vision of Sandee's surreptitious glance, of her quick move to avoid my van. Worry enveloped me like a miasma. Why was she back? What had she been doing on Regal Road, and who was the girl in the car? Would Sandee come after me the way she had John Richard, my ex-husband, because I'd seen her . . . and knew she was very much alive? What about Arch? Was *he* in danger?

I didn't have any answers. Tom sensed my distress and repeated to Arch that he was never, ever, to take a ride from someone he didn't know. Arch, with only the faintest band of freckles still running across his turned-up nose, nodded sagely and said, "I wouldn't, and I won't."

I went on working. Some parties brought in big money, others less. A shipment of oysters was lost somewhere between the Mississippi and the South Platte. A truck carrying beef tenderloins was hijacked. These things happened. Caterers coped.

But then there was the one celebration I was doing at cost, which basically meant at a loss, for the Aspen Meadow Library.

This proved *different*.

The library had contracted my business to do a holiday breakfast for their staff and volunteers. No one is immune to flattery, least of all yours truly. I suppose that was why I agreed to do the unprofitable, labor-intensive fete.

"We voted, and you were the *clear* winner," Roberta Krepinski, the ultrathin reference librarian, had gushed. When Roberta talked about how much she loved her work, her tightly curled carrot-colored ringlets all bounced at once. I worried about her, though, because I was always afraid she wasn't eating enough. *I* thought devouring books and chocolates should go together, but Roberta didn't like people to munch while they were reading *her* books, by which she meant the library's. I didn't argue, because I'd learned long ago you couldn't win an argument with a librarian.

Where I came into Roberta's line of sight revolved around the fact that she ran special events at the library. "And anyway," she'd burbled while working with me in October, "everyone is so sick of the usual Christmas potluck."

"So that's what you voted between?" I asked. "Me and potluck?"

A frown creased Roberta's brow. "No, Goldy. We wanted you."

So Roberta and I hammered out the details. First issue for discussion in the contract: Why was Roberta insisting on my doing a holiday *breakfast*? What were we going to have, rum toddies and toast? No, no, Roberta replied. This, too, was something the staff had voted on. With an early Saturday-morning event, everything could be cleaned up by nine-thirty, and the library could open on schedule at ten. The party would have a festive air, Roberta assured me, because volunteers already were plan-

ning on decking out the shelves with ropes of greenery
and a profusion of red bows. The breakfast itself would
be held in the library's high-ceilinged reading room.
There, a gas fire produced flames that looked so realistic,
the librarians sometimes caught kids trying to roast
marshmallows.

At the beginning of the second week of December,
despite my early-to-bed routine, Tom assessed me grimly
and said I looked horrible. Not only was he concerned
about the number of events I'd done, he told me I hadn't
been able to hide my insomnia. I said my bout of not
sleeping had been precipitated by the appearance of
Sandee, and if his department would do their job and
find her, I'd be able to drift off to Dreamland without a
care. He ignored this and urged me to cancel the library
event. He asked why I couldn't let them have their potluck after all. I pointed out to him that our town's librarians had put their hands on every single one of my
requests for out-of-print French cookbooks. I couldn't
abandon them at the last minute.

"You never say no," Tom said. "You're planning a
breakfast that morning, a lunch at noon, and a dinner
that evening. You'll never make it."

"Not true." From the oven, I pulled a test of the
cheese pie I was hoping to serve the librarians. "Julian
will be helping with the lunch and dinner," I went on,

referring to my enterprising twenty-two-year-old helper, who lived in Boulder. "And if I truly am out of the library before ten, I'll have plenty of time to skedaddle over to the conference center and get set up for the garden-club ladies."

"That's another group you should have let fend for themselves. Whoever heard of a cookie exchange where nobody makes cookies?"

Actually, I had, and was grateful for it. Unlike the library party, the lunch and cookie exchange for the Aspen Meadow Garden Club was going to he hugely profitable. All the cookies the ladies would be trading had been made by two people: Julian and me. To the garden-club ladies, *who* was actually making the cookies was a mere technicality. Like the library staff considering a potluck, the garden-club members had thought making their own cookies would ruin all the fun. I mean, who really wants to be hassled with rolling, shaping, baking, icing, and decorating mounds of sugar-cookie dough during the holidays?

Who indeed. Julian and I had spent hours happily cutting out reindeer, snowflakes, Santas, trees, wreaths, and bells, which we'd then frosted and frozen. Before the luncheon, I had one last baking chore to complete: the making of the gingerbread-house door prizes, to be given to three lucky ticket holders when things wrapped up. My other server had canceled, claiming her husband had surprised her with a ski trip. Julian had promised to look for a replacement. I doubted he would be successful. And if the weather turned suddenly frigid, I was worried about Julian's and my ability to zip around serving sixty women without anything getting cold. But we would manage, I reassured myself. We always did.

Still, the library event came first . . . chronologically, anyway. Roberta had said that the staff would love to have a Dickens-themed party to celebrate the end of another year of dealing with budget cuts, book damage, thefts of movies, and folks who had to be kicked out of the library for drinking pop, eating pizza, and being disruptive . . . usually when there was a fight over cell-phone usage.

So in the end we'd decided on several dishes: French toast, made in the library kitchen and kept warm in their oven. I'd also be offering the cheese pies, slices of coffee cake, chocolate cookie bars, bowls of fresh fruit, and for the meat lovers, spiral-cut ham. Roberta gave me free rein to use Dickens titles for the dishes. I said what I always did when clients wanted something: No problem!

To drink, I'd be serving coffee, tea, rum-laced eggnog, and champagne. At breakfast. On a workday. I had learned that librarians could be naughty, too.

Because I was going to be making the French toast and cheese pies fresh the morning of the event, Roberta and I had agreed that the evening before, she and a couple of staff members and volunteers would help me put out all the long tables, folding chairs, linen, and tableware. We were set to do this between four and five o'clock, which was closing time on Fridays. I'd been more than happy to do the afternoon setup, as I'd had an extremely busy week. That Friday evening, the one obligation of *Goldilocks' Catering* was a six-course vegetarian dinner for two that was paying more than a buffet for twenty. It was being ably handled by Julian.

Directly after the reading room was set up, I was looking forward to the night off. While I was involved with the tables, linens, and china, Arch, whose room was still a wreck, was going to study in a carrel at the library. Then he was spending the night with Todd Druckman, his best friend. Arch and Gus Vikarios, Arch's newly discovered half brother, had become very close over the last six months, and I'd been a bit worried about Todd feeling like a fifth wheel. But the three boys had bonded so well that I'd been pleased, if only because it meant we had one more set of drivers when it came to skating, snowboarding, and *staying* or *sleeping over*—the boys' term for *slumber parties,* an expression way too girlish for cool guys to use.

This sleepover was ostensibly for the boys to study together for their Latin exam, their last test before the holiday break. Todd's mother had offered to drive them to and from the exam. I was so grateful I could have kissed her, but instead I gave her several bags of frozen cookies. We had plenty.

Tom did not have any pressing investigations under way, and he had promised to come home Friday night and make a ragout "just for the two of us," which we would enjoy, he said, before a roaring fire—the real kind. The rest of the night, he'd warned, was also "just for the two of us." Maybe I wouldn't be going to sleep early. But we would be in *bed*. Yes!

I put Sandee, or whoever she was, out of my head . . . at least during the day. I ordered food, worked with clients, put on a flurry of parties, and looked forward to my husband's ragout . . . and whatever else he had in mind.

When Friday, December 15, finally rolled around, I was exhausted and wanted to get set up for the library breakfast as quickly as possible. Arch told me I should be careful. The Latin for "as quickly as possible" was *quam celerrime*. Julius Caesar, Arch explained, had been exceedingly fond of doing things *quam celerrime*—and look what had happened to *him*.

Was today the Ides of December? I asked as the van's tires crunched through the packed snow on Main Street.

It was not, Arch replied. The fifteenth of March, May, July, and October were the Ides. It was the thirteenth of every other month, including December. But he didn't think the teacher would ask that, he added, since their teacher had just explained it to them two days ago.

Well, at least we got *that* straightened out, I thought as I circled the packed library parking lot for the staff entrance. Unfortunately, that door was blocked by a library van and an SUV. Peeved, I did another two laps of the lot before someone finally backed out and I snagged a space. As Arch and I stepped out of my van, I took a deep breath. The air had turned cold and sharp, and the snow that had begun to swirl down in the early afternoon was now falling steadily, blown sideways by a frigid wind. At least Arch, who had a learner's permit, had not wanted to practice his driving skills by piloting the van through the white stuff. For this I was thankful.

Once Arch was seated at a carrel outside the big reading room, Roberta, two staff members, three volunteers, and I began our work. Roberta promised to ask the library van driver to hurry his unloading so I could back my own vehicle up to the staff entrance and off-load my supplies. The library was busy. Roberta's curls all bounced at once as she told me heightened activity on Friday afternoon was normal. Folks wanted to snag their books, CDs, and DVDs before the weekend began. With the return to standard time, the days shortening, and darkness falling earlier and earlier, folks were reading more. Of course, I was also aware that people were *eating* more, and for that I was grateful.

The trio of patrons in the reading room when Roberta and I started working were all men, all beavering away on laptops. Two were gray-haired and one, working in the area with wi-fi, was bald. They sat as far as possible from one another. It didn't look as if a single one of them was using library materials. These fellows were hunched over their keyboards, I surmised, because they were working on résumés. With their furrowed brows and secretive manner, I recognized the desperate look of the unemployed. I knew; I'd been there once myself. Sadly, Roberta whispered to me, once folks were dumped from their places of work, they often made the library their office.

When Roberta politely asked them to take their computers elsewhere so we could get ready for a staff breakfast, every one of the men balked. Even though there was less than an hour before the library closed, they didn't have time to move their . . . stuff, as they called it, and get set up again. They needed to use every minute, they insisted. After squabbling with Roberta for a moment, the bald one stalked out with his laptop under his arm. The obstinacy from the two remaining men melted when I offered them Christmas cookies, which they could take home. Inside my van, I *just* happened to have a couple of extra treat bags.

It never ceased to amaze me how useful food bribes could be.

I dutifully trooped with the two fellows to the parking lot, where I handed them their cookies. The profusion of thanks they gave me made me wish I could fix them dinner, too. I remembered thinking: Too bad that angry bald fellow hadn't stayed, so I could have offered him a treat.

But I had, as we say in food service, other fish to fry. Back in the library, Roberta, the staff, the volunteers, and I hustled around setting up. By four-fifteen, we had moved the chairs and end tables, plus the desks, out of the reading room. I raced back outside. The library van was gone from the staff entrance, but the clown with the SUV had parked it halfway between two places, and I had to maneuver and reverse, maneuver and reverse, just to get my van to a decent unloading position.

With ten minutes lost, the volunteers and I worked frantically to carry in all my dishes, linen, and serving paraphernalia. When the first warning came over the loudspeakers that the library would be closing in fifteen minutes, I jumped. Ominous blinks from the overhead fluorescents illuminated the fact that the reading room was not even close to being ready for the next morning. The workers and I waited until the announcement concluded and the library lighting returned to normal before cracking open the serving tables and covering them with tablecloths.

"Oh, dear, I thought you all would be further along by now." When Roberta spoke and nodded at the same time, all her hair's red ringlets bobbed in agreement. "I'd love to help you finish, but it's my job to go around and make sure patrons are aware we're shutting down."

"We'll manage while you round up the stragglers," I replied, although I sure couldn't understand why the blaring announcement and flashing lights weren't enough to scare any soul out of the stacks.

Roberta sensed my doubt and leaned forward to whisper conspiratorially. "I have to make sure people aren't ignoring us, and that we've allowed enough time to clean up. Last week at this time, somebody had brought in fried chicken, coleslaw, and beans, and spilled it all over one of the tables. Can you believe it? It took us an hour to make things presentable again." I nodded; I'd seen food messes—including ones spilled over books—that would have straightened Roberta's hair. "The single fear the food smugglers have is that a real human is coming around to chuck them out. That usually forces them to clean up their act." Her thin strawberry eyebrows climbed her pink forehead. "Still other folks are so soothed by the quiet and warmth of the library, they fall asleep. It can take the dozers the full fifteen minutes until we close to wake up. I keep threatening to buy an electric cattle prod, and use it to give the stragglers and secret eaters a *real* shock."

"Okeydoke," I replied, not wanting to conjure up that particular mental picture. The workers and I unfurled the first of the white tablecloths. "We'll be fine."

No sooner had Roberta left the reading room than a sudden shout split the air. "Hey!" a man yelled. This was followed by "Hey, shut *up!*"

"Would you please cool it?" Arch asked, a bit too loudly.

My skin prickled with gooseflesh. I raced out of the reading room and tried to remember the location of the carrel where I'd left Arch.

The man's voice rose. "Don't tell me what to do, kid! I'm on a very important call to an attorney!"

"I don't care!" Arch replied at the same volume. "You need to turn off your stupid cell phone!"

I looked around but felt disoriented. Where was Arch?

"Shut up, kid!"

"Cool it!"

Ahead I finally saw the cluster of carrels where I'd left my son . . . except he wasn't working. He was standing up, his jaw thrust in the direction of the bald fellow from the reading room, the one who'd stomped off when Roberta had first asked him to leave. He was large, stocky, and muscle-bound, and Arch looked short, slender, and wholly inadequate to hold his own in this fight.

"Hey, boy!" the man hollered. "I'll teach you what it means to be cool!" The bald man used his free hand to shove Arch's shoulder. Arch lost his balance, toppled back toward his carrel, but stood his ground. Furious, the man lifted the cell phone as if he planned to strike Arch with it.

The bald guy didn't see me coming. I whipped around to his side, mashed my hands together, and chopped them upward, dislodging the cell phone and sending it flying.

"Hey!" yelled the bald guy, diving for his phone, which had skittered under a bookshelf. "What the hell do you think you're doing, lady?"

I ignored him. "Arch, are you okay?"

Arch, still standing, looked a bit shocked. "I'm fine." His wide brown eyes implored me. "Mom, he was being rude! He was yakking away on his phone, and he was so loud I could hear him through my headphones. So I couldn't concentrate. Finally I asked him to hang up, and he yelled at me. Then suddenly everything got totally intense. Oops, look out."

The bald guy was back on his feet. "What have you done, woman?" he shrieked. "That was a very expensive phone! What is the matter—"

But he had no chance of finishing that thought because Roberta, bless her brave heart, interposed herself between him and me. "Sir," she said, her voice firm, "I'm going to have to ask you to leave the library *right now*—"

"What about my last fifteen minutes?" he demanded. "And what about *her*?" He used what was left of his phone to point in my direction.

"You pushed a defenseless boy," I said.

"Was I talking to you?" the man wanted to know. To Roberta, he said, "Make *her* leave the library ten minutes early."

"I will deal with her and her son," Roberta said quietly.

"You?" the man howled, incredulous. "How old are you? You don't look as if you could deal with a *poodle*, much less a *bitch*—"

"In the interim," Roberta interrupted firmly, "Hank here will accompany you to the door." One of the male volunteers, a wide, humpbacked fellow wearing a cow-boy hat, had appeared at Roberta's side.

"Git yer stuff," Hank's low voice rumbled. The bald fellow's eyes narrowed to slits. Arch, who had his arms folded, stood well away from him.

"I am not going anywhere!" the bald man cried. "Make *her* leave!"

Hank said, *"I'll* git yer stuff." He leaned over the car-rel and picked up the bald fellow's laptop.

"You take your hands off—" the bald man cried when he realized what Hank was doing. He hurtled toward Hank's back, but Hank expertly sidestepped him. The bald guy reeled into a bookshelf.

I wondered if there was anyone in the library who was still working.

Hank pulled the bald guy's laptop cord out of its out-let, closed the computer, and gathered up some stray pa-pers from the carrel. With his free hand, he gripped Baldy's upper arm. Hank, who clearly had studied at the Calvin Coolidge School of Communication, said, "C'mon."

The two of them made their awkward way toward the door, Baldy now subdued but still protesting, and Hank moving purposefully forward. Roberta caught me with a questioning glance. Arch, meanwhile, had put on his noise-canceling headphones and gone back to work.

"Shall I call the sheriff's department?" Roberta asked. "We don't want that man waiting for you and Arch out in the parking lot."

"We'll be fine," I replied. "Maybe Hank could place himself at the front door, in case Baldy tries to come back in." Roberta nodded. "Then if Hank could make sure Arch climbs into Mrs. Druckman's station wagon safely, and I get to my van, that would be super. I still have work to do."

Roberta spoke to a male volunteer. Then she turned, intent on her mission of clearing the library. The rest of the volunteers had vanished from the reading room, which was probably just as well, since I liked to ponder exactly where the silver and china should go. First I placed the silver holders for the serving dishes in strategic spots, bearing in mind that *how it looks* is the most important aspect of catering. I imagined the grapefruit halves next to the dish I'd dubbed Chuzzlewit Cheese Pies, then the Tale of Two Cities French toast—so people would see they had a choice of carbs—followed by the Bleak House Bars, just in case folks believed that chocolate was the perfect food for breakfast. This was the Christmas season, right?

I'm on a very important call to an attorney! Baldy's shouts suddenly echoed in my ears. If the call was so important, why hadn't he made it from his vehicle? And why had he shoved Arch?

Stop thinking about it, I ordered myself. I stared at the plates and silverware. The volunteers had wrapped individual knives, forks, and spoons in cloth napkins. I had just finished setting out the dishes for the buffet when I was distracted by a movement to my left.

Through the large reading-room windows, I could see that the snow was coming down more heavily. Since the reading room jutted out from the rear of the building, I could also see back into the east wing of the library, where another bank of windows gave a partial view of a corner seating area and the library's nonfiction stacks. Someone was moving stealthily behind the first set of shelves. The lights in the library flickered again, casting strobelike shadows on that secretive-seeming person, so that he or she appeared to creep along, only half visible beyond the row of books. I shivered.

Without thinking, I leaned over and snatched the knife we were going to use for the ham. But when I peered through the windows again, I couldn't spot anyone in the stacks at all. Had I been seeing things? Was I just, as Tom claimed, really, really tired? Maybe my mind, jangled by the argument with the bald man, was creating phantoms.

I put down the knife and rearranged the silverware. Periodically, I couldn't help looking over at the shelves where I thought I'd seen someone. An emergency exit sign shone above unoccupied easy chairs. Nothing seemed to move.

I blinked. Someone now stood near the windows opposite me, right next to the stacks. I could make out a face, in profile. The person was staring at the corner of the library, where the chairs were. It was a young woman. I inched closer to the reading-room windows. My skin turned cold. *Oh Lord,* I thought, *there she is again.*

And she's still supposed to be dead.

I stood, immobilized, as the woman slowly turned. She was no longer looking at the seating area. She was staring at me.

A child squealed outside the reading room, and I looked away. One of the staff members was speaking to someone in a sharp, frustrated voice. When I glanced back in the direction of the woman in the stacks, she had disappeared.

"Let me have it!" the child shrieked. "I want it!"

"Jamie, give that to me!" came a woman's voice, presumably the little boy's mother.

"It's time, folks." It was the staff person again, more loudly this time. "You need to pack up your stuff and throw away your trash."

Man, what was it with Friday closing time at the library? I figured the librarian had caught the kid eating cookies or drinking hot chocolate, and now the mother was trying to confiscate the contraband. I looked again at the bookshelves, but the ghost of Sandee Brisbane had not reappeared. Once more, I wasn't entirely sure of what I'd seen. Had the woman been Sandee? Was she also the person I'd noticed moving among the shelves?

With the library closing, I didn't have time to chase down phantoms, and I concentrated on getting the last of the breakfast dishes set out. A few minutes later, people were murmuring outside the reading room. Then a high whine went off—yet another warning? I'd never heard it before. Had someone tried to slip out the exit with a library book that hadn't been checked out?

A voice cried out for help. Was Arch all right? Worried, I quickstepped to his carrel, but he was pressing his hands on his headphones and concentrating on his Latin. The whine was louder outside the reading room, I noticed. At the reference desk, none of the staff was in sight.

"Oh, Christ!" someone yelled. It sounded like Roberta.

"Jamie!" the mom from before hollered. "Come here now!"

"Dammit!" Roberta shrieked.

"Jamie!"

"Mom!" the child cried. "I'm not done yet!"

"Jamie, come here when I call you!"

Jamie must really not want to leave the library, I thought as I walked quickly in the direction of the whine and the voices. Somehow, I didn't think Jamie's problems with his mother were what had Roberta so panicked.

"Somebody please help me!" Roberta shouted again. It sounded as if she was in the back of the library. This was the same area where I'd seen Sandee or whoever it was. So that was where I headed.

In my haste, I failed to notice a toddler race around a corner of the stacks. Clutching a huge stack of videos, he was bolting for the checkout desk.

"Jamie!" came the impatient cry from behind me. "You'll never be able to see all those in one weekend!"

As it turned out, Jamie couldn't see me either. When we collided, a goodly portion of the entirety of Disney's output caromed outward and landed on the floor. I lost my balance, and Jamie fell on his behind.

"*Oof.*"

"*Ack!*"

My knees smacked a library cart and I doubled over. Once I was back in a standing position, I rubbed my knees, blinked hard, and ascertained that Jamie was fine. He even told me he was sorry as he hastily nabbed his stash and began, once again, to scurry toward the check-out desk. I checked that he could make it without running into somebody else. As I turned, I caught a very angry glare from his mother. I shrugged and apologized. She warned that I should be more careful. What did she think I was supposed to do? I walked away. If I'd had the misfortune to be that woman's kid, I'd want to glue myself to the TV all weekend, too.

Over the nonstop whine, someone in the far corner of the library was moaning. Was that Roberta, too? Two librarians rushed past me. With my knees still recovering from the collision with Jamie, I limped after them.

Roberta was past the shelves and carrels, in the seating area I'd been able to half see through the windows. Arch had said once that the easy chairs there were the best and most comfy in the library. But Roberta didn't look comfy. She was crouched beside a figure in the corner, a big, blond fellow who looked as if he'd rolled forward in his chair. Roberta had her arm around him, as if she were trying to hoist him up.

"Can somebody help me?" Roberta pleaded. The other pair of librarians, too stunned to move, stood by. Maybe they'd seen a ghost, too. Roberta ordered them to go to her desk and call an ambulance. *Now!* They pivoted and stumbled past me.

Roberta looked up and caught my eye. All color had drained from her pretty face. "Goldy," she said, "please help me lift him. I thought he was sleeping, but he won't wake up. Please. Something's terribly wrong with him. Oh God, I thought he was sleeping."

I hustled forward and put my right arm around the man's shoulders. He was very heavy, and I could only get an awkward hold on him. "Lower him to the floor," I commanded. "Once he's down there, we can flip him over."

Working in tandem, we managed to get the man out of his chair. I felt his neck for a pulse, but couldn't find one.

On the floor next to him, a toppled thermos had spilled dark liquid all over the carpet. There was the smell of liquor mixed with coffee. Roberta kept saying, "I thought he was sleeping. I went to wake him up. Oh God."

She slumped against the wall. I tried to turn the man over, but I needed Roberta's help to get him into a position for CPR. Several other staff members came over to us, asking Roberta what they should do. Their questions seemed to galvanize her. She gulped back her distress and told them to keep everyone away from this area of the library. The three women quickly retreated, tumbling over one another and shouting for curiosity seekers to keep back.

I realized the freezing-cold sensation I felt wasn't just from fear, but from a frigid wind blowing into the library. I searched for its source. For crying out loud, the emergency exit was open; snow and winter air were pouring in. The exit was also the reason for the high whine. Now that I was right next to the door, the piercing sound was almost unbearable.

"We need to start CPR," Roberta called to me. Together we rolled the man onto his back, and I finally got a good look at his face. He didn't seem to be breathing. I moved aside as Roberta bent over him. Then I flipped open my cell phone and punched in the numbers for Tom. I was pretty sure that there beside me lay a man before whom Tom had appeared many times.

And now it was my job to tell my husband that former district attorney Drew Wellington appeared to be in very bad shape. Despite his crime-fighter reputation, Drew had lost the last election three years ago. There'd been some kind of scandal, of which I'd only caught a whiff. Something about drunk driving? I couldn't remember. Undaunted, Drew had gone ahead and turned his hobby, collecting high-end maps, into a wealth-producing machine. He was one of the people the Mac-Arthurs had invited to their party tomorrow night.

When I got Tom's voice mail, I left a message for him to call me *ASAP.*

I closed my phone and looked carefully around the area where Drew had been sitting. Besides the spilled thermos, there was an open briefcase and a spew of papers. Was that a silver flask in his briefcase? As in the kind you use for whiskey? I thought so.

Roberta worked patiently on Drew. She was better at CPR than I was. Still, Drew Wellington was not responding. It looked as if he'd had a heart attack, or stroke, or *something.* I glanced at the dark carpet. There seemed to be too much liquid to have come out of such a small thermos.

"Please tell me this isn't happening," I said aloud.

Roberta, pumping and counting, seemed not to hear me.

3

The sheriff's department had an out-
post, an office actually, that was next to the library, and
the skeleton staff that worked there—two men and one
woman—were still on duty on Friday at five in the evening. They hustled over as soon as a librarian sum-
moned them. Just the sight of their uniforms filled me
with a sense of calm. The female officer immediately
went to work trying to resuscitate Drew Wellington.

The two male officers secured the scene. I knew the
drill: members of law enforcement needed to make sure
there was no one with a weapon lurking in any corner of
the library, nor in the parking lot. When the duo returned from outside, they took down the names, ad-
dresses, and phone numbers of the remaining patrons.
Back when Roberta and I were working on Drew, I

should have thought to insist that no one leave the library, but I hadn't. There was only a handful of folks, who were quickly questioned and summarily hustled out to their cars. I took this to mean that no one had seen anything of import. Still, it was unlikely those two cops were going to tell *me* anything.

My friend Eileen Druckman arrived with her son, Todd, Arch's buddy. They'd come to pick up Arch for the sleepover, and the two cops agreed to question my son next. Since he was a minor, I stood beside him, but was cautioned not to say anything. Arch looked shaken as he related that he hadn't seen Mr. Wellington at any time, nor had he seen anything unusual. The exception, of course, was Arch's altercation with the bald man, whom he described. I wanted to clutch Arch tightly when he was telling the police officer his story. But my son gently shook off my arm when I put it around his shoulders. He was almost sixteen, I kept reminding myself, and no matter what the circumstances, sixteen-year-old boys did not want Mom giving them hugs in public.

Once Arch had left with the Druckmans, the two officers ordered me, the library staff, and the three male volunteers to stay. There was no sign of the female officer working on Drew. Hank and the other two fellows who'd been helping me and shelving books looked dismayed but resigned. It was still snowing hard, so one of the policemen told us which outside path to our vehicles we could use. A cursory glance out the emergency exit must have convinced them that if the crime-scene unit was called in, they'd need to pick up whatever they could from an area that now had at least two new inches of white stuff.

In the meantime, we were told, we needed to stand apart and not talk until sheriff's-department investigators assigned to the case had arrived. *Investigators*. The reason they needed us, the officers said more gently, was that we knew the layout of the library, the security system, and what belonged where. Unable to stand the tension, I hustled outside to the snowy sidewalk.

The night was already very dark and cold. Flakes fell in a ceaseless curtain.

After what seemed like an eternity but was probably only ten minutes, I heard the sirens. You always hear them before you see the lights. Julian, who loved physics, had explained the reason for this to me. Even though light travels faster—hence the delay between lightning and thunder—light doesn't bend. Sound does.

Why was I thinking about this? I wondered as Roberta and her colleagues joined me outside. Because Tom still hadn't called me back, and I didn't want to face what was happening.

The oncoming phalanx of law enforcement personnel didn't bother me nearly as much as the fact that if Drew Wellington was indeed dead, the media would swoop down on our small mountain town with less mercy than local red-tailed hawks showed to meadow mice. Even on a frigid December night like this, they would come. I looked back at our little library. Wind whipped the snow into the pines and aspens around the brick building and up the hill that ran behind it. I could just imagine the shrieking announcements: *It looks as if a former district attorney has met a mysterious end in the library . . .* It would be a TV, radio, and newspaper feeding frenzy. I didn't want to think about it.

Maybe Drew had just had a heart attack. It could be, I thought, that the cops from next door were only being careful in ordering us all apart. Perhaps Drew was going to make it. But I doubted it very much.

Roberta Krepinski stood not ten yards away from me. At least she'd had the forethought to don a puffy down jacket. In the light of the neon lamps that shone outside the entrance, her face appeared ghostly pale. Poor thing. Maybe because she looked so young and so thin, I felt motherly toward her. I made a mental note to ask the sheriff's guys to have all the staff and volunteers wrapped in the quilts that loving, unpaid workers sewed for the victims, families, and witnesses to accidents and violent crime.

I pulled my cell out of my apron pocket and tried Tom . . . again. The last few times I'd punched in the numbers, I'd received that rapid busy signal that told me either everybody and their brother was on a cell phone, or Tom was driving through one of those folds in the mountains into which no signal penetrated.

"Schulz," he answered on the first ring. That businesslike tone of his put the fear of God into criminals, and sometimes even me. I shuddered.

"Something bad has happened to Drew Wellington," I began without preamble. "Roberta found him . . ." My teeth were chattering and my ears felt frozen.

"Goldy." Now his voice was warm, comforting. "Tell me where you are."

"I'm at the library. The department is on its way."

"I know. My guys already called me. I should be there in fifteen minutes." He paused for a fraction of a second. "Did you . . . see anything?"

"No, but—" The wind whistled into my cell as I tried to talk.

"Goldy?"

"Sorry, it's just—" I wanted to tell him about seeing Sandee, or seeing a woman who looked a lot like Sandee, at the library.

"Why don't you wait in your van? You can come out and meet our guys when they get there."

"Some officers are already here. I mean, they were next door. We're supposed to wait."

"We?"

My mind whirled. "Sorry to be so out of it. I'm talking about all the library staff and the volunteers. Plus myself. They told us to hang around so we can talk to, you know, the investigators. Your guys." My teeth were chattering. "Plus then there'll be an ambulance, more cops—"

"Please do me a favor and get in your van. If anyone hassles you, tell them to call me."

"All right, all right," I promised as I walked toward my vehicle, which was exactly where I'd left it. The vehicle that had been parked so ineptly next to me was gone. I felt my shoulders sag.

"Tom, there was an SUV next to me, and now it's gone—"

"Miss G. Get in your van and lock the doors. Then you can tell me what's bothering you. Besides the missing car there. Something else happened, right?"

What something had happened, really? As I wrenched open the van's driver-side door, I tried to mentally rewind and replay those fifteen minutes before the library was supposed to close. I'd been setting up for an event. I'd seen that ghost again, this time near the shelves. Then everything had imploded.

"I thought I saw Sandee near where Drew was found. She may have been watching him."

"Sandee *Brisbane*? Again?"

"Yup. Then a few minutes later, Roberta Krepinski discovered Drew in a chair by the corner," I went on. "You know Roberta, the reference librarian?"

"I don't know her. But she found Drew Welling-ton?"

"Yes, Tom. She said she thought he was asleep, and went to wake him."

"You talked to her?" he asked, his tone tense. If this was a crime scene, was the implication, he wouldn't want me talking to anyone.

"She called for help when she found him, and I went to see what was wrong. She kept repeating, 'I thought he was sleeping.' I guess she feels responsible."

"But you didn't see Sandee, or someone who looks like her, still hanging around?"

"No, Tom. And you're right. I'm not even sure it was Sandee. You know her hair's different, or at least not the same as Sandee Brisbane's was six months ago. But I'm pretty sure it was the same woman I saw in the car last month, up on the road to Regal Ridge. You know? I thought that woman was Sandee, too." There was silence for such a long time on the line that I thought I'd lost the signal. "Tom?"

He took a deep breath. "How's Roberta doing now?"

"Not so hot." I didn't say what I suspected, that Roberta would be traumatized that her beloved library was now going to be invaded by law enforcement, and to receive more negative media attention than the *Hindenburg*.

"You're *sure* she was the one who first came across him, Miss G.?"

"Yes. No. The emergency exit was making this horrible noise, and I just heard Roberta moaning and crying, and I went over to help. We lowered Drew onto the floor—"

"Aw, jeez." Tom's tone said, *So much for the crime scene.*

"Tom! We thought he'd had a heart attack or maybe a stroke, I don't know. He looked awful. I felt his neck and there was no pulse." Almost as an afterthought, I said, "There might have been blood on the carpet."

"You didn't see a weapon anywhere, I take it?"

"Nope. Just a thermos of spilled coffee, and a, well, a silver flask inside his briefcase. And it was . . . cold over there. That emergency exit I mentioned? It had been opened. Plus, there was . . . the smell of booze, and coffee."

My phone beeped—call waiting. Could it be Arch, phoning to say he'd arrived at Todd's? Like Tom, Arch was a worrier.

"Tom, I have to go. This could be Arch."

"See you in ten."

Instead of Arch, my caller turned out to be good old Marla, who in addition to being my dear pal was the self-appointed Aspen Meadow Town Gossip.

"Tell me," she said breathlessly. "Drew Wellington? He's, uh, *been involved* with half the women in Furman County. And not all of them women his age, if you know what I mean."

"I don't know what you mean. And how did you hear so quickly about what was going on here?"

She cleared her throat. "A library patron who was allowed to leave gave me a buzz, thought I'd want to know what was happening."

I shook my head. "So what's this about Drew being a ladies' man?"

"Doesn't Tom let you in on anything?"

"Not on that kind of thing. Plus it's been a few years since Drew was D.A. The department is due here any minute, though—"

"Oh, *please*," she said, indignant. "The department is going to want to talk to *me*, when they try to figure out what happened."

"I'll send them right over. So," I said, thinking of twenty-two-year-old Sandee, "were these women all younger than Drew?"

"Some of them were," she said, then hesitated. "Actually, I'm not familiar with all the details. I'll check. Somebody could have been executing a vendetta, that kind of thing."

"We don't even know if what happened here was a crime."

"Uh-huh. Has law enforcement arrived?"

As if on cue, red, blue, and white lights cut through the darkness and falling snow. That shrill call of sirens approaching meant that all the regular folks out on the road had finally moved out of the way. I shivered inside the van, which I hadn't turned on while I was trying to talk on my cell.

"You're not saying anything," Marla prompted.

"They're almost here. You want to tell me something, or not?"

"He was involved with at least three women that I know of," she said quickly. "And he called them all problems. Topping the list was his ex-wife."

"What? Who describes his ex-wife as a problem?"

"Who doesn't?" Marla's voice was impatient. "I heard Elizabeth still hates Drew. Doesn't that make her a *problem*?"

The sirens' screaming was less that a block away. The police-car and ambulance lights flashed so brightly I had to turn away and face the hill that rose behind the library. "What other woman problems did he have?"

Marla sighed. "His girlfriend is Patricia Ingersoll."

"Patricia Ingersoll? The head of Losers?"

"The very one. I'm sure the head of a local weight-loss group hopes one day to put you, O lover of cream, out of business. Poor thing, it's only been a year and a half since cancer killed Frank. *I* think she's still on the rebound from losing him. Still, I heard Patricia had cheered up when she and Drew Wellington set a wedding date."

I wanted to say, *You heard that from whom?* But one of the sirens had stopped. The prowler lights flashing through the pines had also ceased their shaky forward movement. Two medics with their bags jumped out of the ambulance and raced into the library.

"I need to talk to you later," I told Marla. "But tell me quickly how you learned about Drew's love-life issues."

"A friend of mine, along with perhaps twenty other people, heard Drew Wellington making a cell-phone call at DIA, just before their flight to Salt Lake City. He said he had a problem with his ex-wife, and a problem with his girlfriends. That's *girlfriends,* plural. Then he laughed. And he yucked it up about his situation within earshot of all twenty folks."

"Problems with his *girlfriends*?" I echoed. "That's girlfriends with an *s*? Is that the third woman?"

Somebody tapped on my window and I jumped.

"Mrs. Schulz, is that you?" A round face with thick lips and pudgy cheeks was peering into the van. He wore a dark, scalp-hugging snow hat. "Goldy? It's Neil Tharp, Mr. Wellington's . . . business associate. Could we talk to you? Could you get out of your van for a minute, please?"

"Bye, Marla." I closed my phone and got out of the van.

"Miss G.?" Tom called from the front lawn of the library. Tom was here, finally. Thank God.

Neil Tharp glanced back at Tom and licked his lips. When someone from the crime-scene unit suddenly cried, "Schulz!" Tom had to go off in the opposite direction. Neil, sensing an opportunity, pulled off his hat, as if he were introducing himself, but he wasn't.

"We need to talk to you," he said urgently.

"What's that, the royal we? I'm not supposed to be talking to anyone until I've given a full statement to the police, Mr. Tharp."

He pulled his unhealthily pasty face into a scowl and countered with "Mrs. Wellington is very eager to talk to you." He motioned to a dark Jeep.

My shoulders sagged as Elizabeth Wellington barreled in the direction of my van. The former prosecutor's ex-wife was a professional fund-raiser. Short and top-heavy, she had narrow dark eyes, a steel-wool pad of blackish-brown hair, and a way of charging up to you that made you feel as if she was going to bowl you over. She always wanted donations for this or that, and she was very good at making you feel guilty if you politely declined to get out your checkbook. I'd catered for her a few times, for charity events, and we went to the same church, St. Luke's Episcopal. Even in the best of times, I hadn't found her to be the most pleasant of women. And this definitely was not a best time.

"What happened to Drew?" she demanded of me now.

"I don't know."

"Would you answer my question, please?"

"No, I don't think so."

"We heard you were with him," she argued. "You must tell us."

I looked at both Neil Tharp and Elizabeth Wellington. How did everyone in this town hear news so quickly? I said wearily, "I must *not.*"

Neil Tharp said, "We'll see what Investigator Schulz has to say about *that.*"

I almost laughed.

Neil politely told Elizabeth Wellington that it would be better if she waited in the Jeep. She charged away as quickly as she'd appeared. Neil, meanwhile, scooted toward me until his short, muscled body was uncomfortably close. I felt annoyed, because I wanted to see Tom, to talk to him, to be held by him. I did not want to visit with a man whose sparse black hair, now being snowed on, was held in its comb-over by something vaguely smelling of musk.

"You have to talk to me," Neil repeated.

I shook my head and stared at him. He squinted at me and did not move, as if we were in some kind of standoff. I turned aside, looked straight ahead, and did my best to ignore him. Meanwhile, Tom was taking forever with the crime-scene unit.

I knew Neil Tharp had worked for Drew Wellington in the map-selling business. These days, accumulating maps—or cartographic records and charts, as one church matron called them—had suddenly become very big, for both decoration and investment. Now that the family-crest and coat-of-arms fads had passed, these collectors, mostly nouveau riche folks like the MacArthurs, had an insatiable desire to make the interiors of their *new* mountain homes look respectably *old* by putting up maps with Latin words that nobody, except perhaps Arch, could read.

What was next, I wondered, tapestries of the Lady and the Unicorn?

Still, I'd watched with amused interest as Neil Tharp waddled around behind Drew during the coffee hour after the Sunday services at St. Luke's. Our rector, Father Pete, had specifically prohibited folks from trying to sell any kind of *stuff* at church. But Drew had ignored him and worked hard, and charmingly, on trying to enlighten parishioners as to what a *great* investment old maps were, how they dignified the living-room walls of *the very best homes.*

If Father Pete had frowned on Neil and Drew's practice of hustling business during the two church-service coffee hours, he had frowned even more severely when the two men started showing up with freshly baked doughnuts from the Aspen Meadow Pastry Shop. I, of course, knew well that there was nothing like free food to put people into a buying mood. Father Pete had tried to look stern, but two cream-filled chocolate-glazed Bismarcks was all it had taken to get him in line. But the next week, I hadn't been so sure of this. Father Pete had continued to watch Drew and Neil carefully . . . and after a while, he declined all doughnut inducements.

One time, when Drew had been uncharacteristically absent, I'd seen Neil's mouth moving as he sat in one of the pews before the liturgy. I had wondered if he was speaking in tongues. Turned out he'd been talking into his cell through an earpiece. At the time, I'd thought this showed profound disrespect for the Almighty. Like Roberta Krepinski wanting to correct folks at the library, I'd wished for an electrified cattle prod, turned to *zap*.

"Miss G.," Tom called out again finally. "I'm coming."

"Mrs. Schulz," Neil said quickly. "Here is Investigator Schulz. Now talk to me, please. I know you were supposed to be setting up for an event, so I would like to know exactly what happened in there, how someone in the *library* could have—"

"Uh, *excuse* me," said Tom as he placed his large left hand oh-so-gently on Neil's chest. "I need you not to talk to my wife at this time, please."

"Do you have any idea who I am?" Neil sputtered. "I *must* know what happened here, and if you do not allow me to talk to . . . to your wife, I will report your insubordination to your—"

"I know who you are." Once again, Tom's clipped speech sent chills of fear down my back, and he wasn't even talking to me. I had no idea how Neil Tharp's spine was doing. I know that Neil was pushing his chest up against Tom's hand, and Tom was pressing hard right back. "Let's see. Insubordination? Okay, I got it. I need you not to talk to my wife at this time, please, *sir.*"

"But you don't understand," Neil wheedled. "Mr. Wellington had some very, very valuable pieces with him—"

"Pieces of what?" Tom asked.

"I'm not going to talk to you now," Neil Tharp said with a sudden sniff. "I will reserve my comments for the sheriff only. Meanwhile, I am leaving." He abruptly turned on the thick heel of one of his black leather shoes and marched off in the opposite direction. Tom pointed to one of his investigators, then to Neil. One thing was certain: Neil wasn't going anywhere.

"Oh, that was smart, Tom. He reports you to the sheriff, then what? You're always telling *me* to be more agreeable—"

Tom leaned over furtively and pecked my cheek. I wanted to kiss him back, but I was suddenly aware that the team of cops unrolling crime-scene tape around the library parking lot had stopped moving.

I murmured, "Thanks. But really. What's going to happen if Neil Tharp reports you to the sheriff?"

"Oh, that." Tom gazed off in the direction of Drew Wellington's assistant, who was being questioned by an investigator. "Was Neil Tharp in the library this afternoon? I mean, did you see him?"

"No."

"And you don't know how he got here so quickly."

"No to that, too."

"Trust me, we'll deal with him later. Now"—his green eyes penetrated mine—"how are you doing?"

"I'm cold," I said, suddenly realizing I was freezing.

"Why didn't you stay in the van and turn on your engine, get yourself warmed up?" he scolded.

"Because I was trying to talk on my cell, and my engine isn't all that quiet. And then Neil Tharp came over and started peppering me with questions." I couldn't seem to help the note of hysteria that was creeping into my voice. "He was so demanding!" Without my willing it, my voice rose. "And then, you saw him, he was practically pushing his way into my face—"

"Stop talking for a sec." Tom cocked his head toward the team of curious cops, who pretended to be working diligently to finish the unwinding of the crime-scene tape. "Everybody's listening very hard."

The coroner's van pulled up. So. Drew Wellington hadn't made it.

Two investigators I knew, Sergeants Boyd and Armstrong, separated themselves from the crowd and came over to join us. Once we were all sitting in the van's cold seats, I turned the engine on and clicked the heat over to high. We were rewarded with a blast of frigid air.

"Before you say anything," I began, "could you arrange for quilts to be brought to the library staff who had to deal with this?"

"Absolutely," said Boyd. "'To deal with this,' she says." He paused, then said, "My, my, my." He withdrew his notebook from inside his sheriff's-department jacket. "Trouble just follows you around, Mrs. Schulz, doesn't it?"

4

Boyd regarded me with his black eyes. When he shifted his barrel-shaped body, the back-seat squeaked. I switched on the van's interior lights. Boyd's scalp glistened beneath his unfashionable crew cut, and his carrot-shaped fingers clasped a ballpoint pen, poised over his notebook. "Not meaning any disrespect," he said with a half grin.

"Don't worry," Tom interjected. "She's used to it. Trouble, I mean."

Sergeant Armstrong, whose short wisps of strawberry-blond hair fell forward as his lean body tried to get comfortable, said, "All right, Mrs. Schulz, you know the drill. Start with when you woke up this morning, and take us up to where we are now."

I closed my eyes and thought back. There had been Arch's mad dash about the house as he'd tried to find, and then gather up, the index cards he needed for the review his Latin class had planned this morning. He hadn't been able to find his Latin textbook, and had pawed through every pile of stuff in his room to find it. He'd gone through the same drill trying to locate his thick notebook. For reasons unknown to me, Arch loved Latin. Still, the exasperation and frustration he'd exhibited trying to find his school materials resulted in him being extremely nervous and stressed out. The chaos he now lived in, I believed, was to blame. I'd been perplexed that he'd changed from being a neatnik child to a teenager who lived in a muddle of litter and confusion—a muddle he refused to allow me to clean up. That was why I was insisting *he* organize the mess as soon as the exam was finished.

But I didn't tell the investigators all that. I only told them about getting Arch out the door with Tom, then spending time on the telephone with clients as I figured out the work for the day. I still had those gingerbreads to make. As I worked packing up the paraphernalia for the library gig, I'd talked on the phone to my assistant, Julian Teller, about the vegetarian dinner over in Boulder. We'd also discussed two other parties, the ones we were doing for the MacArthurs tomorrow night and Monday. "Drew Wellington was supposed to be at the first one," I added. "It is going to be, or was going to be, a very big deal, celebrating an acquisition the MacArthurs had made."

Armstrong whistled through his teeth. "Okay. Tell us about the MacArthurs and where they live."

"They're at 202 Wild Bill Way, over in Regal Ridge Country Club—"

"That big new development south of the interstate, near the ski area?" Armstrong interjected. "Looking at the houses on those cliffs just gives me the shakes."

"Tell me about it," I said, thinking of my first run-in with maybe-Sandee. "Anyway, Smithfield MacArthur was very anxious that Drew and somebody named Larry were going to be invited to the party."

"Spell these people's names for me," Boyd ordered. This I did. Then he said, "Why did he want Drew at the party?"

"Hermie MacArthur said the party was to celebrate map collecting. Drew was their dealer, I think."

Armstrong snorted. "Their *dealer.*"

I felt a chilly wash of fatigue, as if all the day's energy, and the adrenaline rush from the mess I'd witnessed at Roberta's side, were suddenly receding. I was desperate to head back to our place, to be with Tom in our own environment.

"The sooner you can go on about your day," Tom said gently, "the earlier we can get home." It wasn't the first time he'd read my mind.

I told the three of them about how I'd packed up the van, because of needing to set up for the library breakfast the next morning. They asked me if I knew Roberta Krepinski, and I gave them a quick summary of my visits with the reference librarian. Then I briefed them on the interchange between Arch and the bald guy.

"This guy have a name?" Boyd asked.

"I'm sure he did, but we didn't get to introductions. Arch related what happened to another investigator already. We both gave a description of the guy."

"And this man was aggressive," Tom said. "Threatening? He shoved Arch?"

"He did."

"What happened to him, do you know?"

I told them about laconic Hank forcibly leading the protesting bald fellow out of the library. I then pointed out my van window at Hank, who was being questioned by two detectives. With their pens poised over their clipboards, they seemed to be waiting for longer answers than what they were getting.

"After Hank, what?"

"Well," I said, pausing, "the library was closing."

They waited.

"Then I saw something, or someone," I went on, still hesitant, "through the windows of the reading room. It was a person hanging around over by the stacks, near where Roberta and I eventually found Drew Wellington."

When I didn't elaborate, Boyd finally said, "Okay, Mrs. Schulz. Who was it?"

"Please call me Goldy," I prompted.

"Mrs. Schulz," Boyd continued, "was this a person you *recognized*?"

"I thought so. She was acting suspicious, anyway, and that's what caught my eye. She wasn't looking for any books. I think I also saw her a little earlier, walking through the stacks. It was almost as if she was stalking someone—"

"Oh, for God's sake, Goldy," Tom said, "tell them."

"Sorry. I thought it was Sandee. You know, also known as Alexandra Brisbane, the woman who killed my ex-husband—"

"What?" said Armstrong. "Are we talking about the Sandee Brisbane who confessed in front of a slew of firefighters and law enforcement personnel—"

"And me," I interjected.

"And you," Armstrong went on, "and then jumped off a boulder into an out-of-control forest fire that claimed several lives, including hers?"

I kept my voice quiet. "Except they—you—never found her body. Or her skeleton, or anything."

"We found her locket," Boyd interjected. "Her body could have, you know, ended up some place we haven't looked yet."

"Did she have something against Drew Wellington?" I asked.

Boyd shook his head. "I can't believe I'm having this conversation. Maybe Jimmy Hoffa and Drew Wellington had a falling-out, too, and Jimmy came back to whack him. Schulz? We got any issues with teamsters in this county?"

"Beats me," my husband said. Behind us, Boyd and Armstrong began to chuckle. Tom went on: "You should tell them you saw a woman who looked like Sandee a couple of weeks ago. Three weeks ago, to be exact."

"Yes, I did." I tried to keep the defensiveness out of my voice. "This woman was the image of Sandee, only with brown hair. This woman seemed to know me, too. I slammed on my brakes when I saw her, and then she gunned her car around me—"

"And where was this?" Armstrong asked.

"It was when I was on my way to the MacArthurs', to book this party I just told you about."

Neither one of them was writing anything down.

"Mrs. Schulz," said Boyd, his tone indulgent. "There's no way that Sandee Blue Calhoun Brisbane, or whatever name she was using six months ago, could have survived that fire."

I said, "Sandee was a member of Aspen Meadow Explorers and knew her way around that wildlife preserve the way some people know their yards. Plus, the rescue workers found two bodies, both of them confirmed to be missing hikers." But even a part of me was doubtful. I thought, *That fire was just too hot, too omnipresent, for her to have escaped. Maybe she just burned up, her body vaporized by the heat. Maybe she drowned in Cottonwood Creek, and they'll find her corpse when the spring snowmelt drains into Aspen Meadow Lake—*

I exhaled. I'd been worrying myself sick for three weeks. Had the woman I'd seen been Sandee? Was she back? If so, why? And why had she been at the library this afternoon, right before Drew Wellington had turned up dead?

"Okay, so you thought you saw Sandee," Armstrong said, in a let's-get-on-with-it tone. "Then what?"

I told them about hearing the high whining noise, and then Roberta, about running into Jamie the toddler and his impatient mother, and then about finding Drew Wellington. There'd been confusion trying to get an ambulance, the frigid air sweeping in from the opened emergency exit, and finally, attempting to keep curiosity seekers away from Drew. At some point, one of the staff had gone next door and called in the three sheriff's-department officers on duty. We'd all ended up outside. Neil Tharp, Drew's partner, and Elizabeth Wellington, Drew's ex-wife, had approached me and demanded to know what had happened.

Following Boyd's instruction, I spelled Neil Tharp's name, and told them about how he and Drew had hustled rich folks during the coffee hours at St. Luke's.

"Hustled rich folks for what?" Armstrong pressed.

"Sorry," I said, again aware of fatigue creeping up my bones. "For their business, Mile-High Maps." I paused. "There's one other thing. When I was unloading, there was an SUV pulled up by the library's rear door." I thought back. "At least I thought it was an SUV. It might have been one of those big station wagons with four-wheel drive. When I came out later, after we found Drew, the vehicle was gone. And before you ask, no, I didn't get a license plate. Sorry. I can't even remember what kind of car it was. That's all I know."

The only noise in my van was the engine and the whirring of the fan, which was finally bringing warmth to the four of us.

"Think they'll cancel?" Boyd asked out of nowhere. "The library staff having the party, I mean?"

"Why?" I demanded, confused.

" 'Cuz I'm getting *damned hungry*," he replied, his tone indignant.

I turned in my seat and lifted my chin, indicating a plastic-wrapped platter that was right behind him. "Those are the platters and things I was going to put into the staff lunchroom refrigerator tonight. Storing food at the place where you are going to be doing an event can help, as long as nobody's there to get sticky fingers."

Boyd said, "Is it lucky for us that you didn't have time to get it into the staff refrigerator?"

I couldn't help it; in spite of everything, I laughed. "Why don't you reach around and bring out that first tray? We can have some chocolate-raspberry cookies. They're called Bleak House Bars—"

"Forget it!" When Armstrong bellowed, he sounded like a foghorn.

"Why?" Boyd whined. "I haven't eaten since this morning."

"Because it's a bribe," Armstrong said. "You know the captain would have a conniption if he knew you were taking food from a witness."

"I'm not a witness," I protested. "I just helped the librarian bring Drew Wellington down to the floor."

"That's enough for me," said Boyd. He stretched around and grasped the tray. Under the plastic wrap, four dozen bar cookies glistened in the van's light. My stomach growled.

"The captain smells that on your notes, he's going to have your hide," Armstrong warned.

"Fellas, fellas." Tom's voice was soothing. "We're friends here. Let's all have something to eat."

With this permission from their boss, Boyd and Armstrong lost no time ripping the plastic off the platter. While the crinkling paper occupied them, I gave Tom a puzzled look. But his eyes were hooded, so I knew something else was going on. If *we all had something to eat,* would we find out what two Furman County investigators thought of Drew Wellington, former district attorney?

I didn't know. In addition to being tired, I, too, was hungry. I sank my teeth into one of the Bleak House Bars, then swooned over the combination of chocolate, raspberry, cream cheese, and toasted pecans.

Boyd licked his fingers and picked up his notebook. "Anything else you can tell us? Such as whether you recognized anyone in the library, besides Sandee Brisbane, that is," he said, trying to sound serious. I thought again and said I wasn't sure. I would have to ponder that one. Something was niggling at the back of my brain, but I couldn't think of what it was.

"You remember what kind of noise Roberta Krepinski made when she found Drew Wellington?" Boyd asked, casting a regretful glance back at the tray of Bleak House Bars.

"She was moaning and calling for help. Loudly." I described finding Roberta and then following her lead by helping the limp Drew Wellington to the floor. Suddenly I felt dizzy.

"Wrap it up, guys," Tom told the sergeants. He was gazing at me. Apparently, the two investigators weren't going to divulge their opinions of Drew Wellington. Wait—now I remembered what had been bothering me. Should I tell Boyd and Armstrong about Marla hearing somebody else tell her about overhearing . . . Drew Wellington's cell-phone conversation at DIA?

"Hey, Goldy, look me in the eyes, would you?" Sergeant Armstrong commanded. I obliged. "Anything you know about the former district attorney that we might not?"

What, was Armstrong reading my mind, too?

"You're hesitating," Boyd prompted me.

"Sorry." I could hear the guilt in my voice. Could they? Best to come clean. "It's just that my best friend, Marla Korman, shared some things with me about Drew Wellington. Unsubstantiated things." When nobody said anything, I reluctantly went on. "Marla said that he was involved with Patricia—"

"Ingersoll," said Armstrong. "Yeah, we're aware of her."

"Marla also told me Drew preferred women who were younger than he was. She mentioned a cell-phone conversation Drew Wellington had at DIA that a bunch of folks overheard." I told them about the former district attorney's complaints concerning the women in his life. "That's it, guys. That's all I know."

"Mrs. Schulz, I want to hear what else you know," Armstrong ordered me, not as nicely this time.

I glanced at Tom, waiting for support, direction, I knew not what. But he was looking at his large hands. What was going on here? I glared at Armstrong. "What?"

"You're *sure* you saw Sandee Brisbane?" he asked mildly. "Watching, stalking, from the stacks? Right near where Drew Wellington was sitting?"

"Why are we coming back to this?" I asked, my tone brusque. "So your guys can laugh at me again?"

Boyd was rubbing his hands together. "Well, maybe you've heard something from the supposed killer of your ex-husband—"

"*Supposed?*" I interjected. "I was right there when she confessed. As were half a dozen firefighters, who just happened to be able to confirm the story. Besides, you all just *said* she was dead."

"Right, right." Armstrong again. "We do all know that Sandee Brisbane confessed to killing your ex right before she disappeared over the ledge into the Aspen Meadow Wildlife Preserve, which was on fire."

"She did," I insisted. Why wasn't Tom saying anything? I looked to him for confirmation. Why was he still staring at his hands?

"You guys need to tell me what you're saying," I said firmly. "And what this has to do with Drew Wellington." *And why you're asking me about it,* I wanted to add, but thought better of it.

Armstrong inhaled loudly. "We're not saying she's alive. But if you saw her near Drew Wellington, well, that might be a different story."

When he didn't say more, I rubbed my forehead and looked out at the crime-scene unit, which had set up bright lights around their large van. The cop cars' flashing lights lit the night. How soon would I be able to go home? I wondered.

"What I tell you stays in this car, okay, Goldy?" Boyd asked.

"Sure."

"Drew Wellington," he went on, "recently received three threatening e-mails. Very graphic threatening e-mails, saying the former D.A. needs to keep his pecker in his pocket and move. Move away from Aspen Meadow, that is, *or else.* The person sending the e-mails says she's a woman who knows what to do if her words aren't taken seriously. The whole department has been alerted, and we're supposed to be on the lookout for her."

"Be on the lookout for whom?" I asked. "A woman you say is dead?"

Nobody said anything for a minute. "All we have," Armstrong reluctantly said, "is a partial view from a security camera. Maybe a woman, maybe sort of young, wearing a sweatsuit with the hood up. You didn't see anybody like that, did you?"

"That's too general a description, I think. What security camera are you talking about?" I asked.

"Not a very good one," Boyd interjected. "But that's 'cuz all the threatening e-mails have been sent from within the Furman County Library System, and each library only has one surveillance camera near the main entrance."

Great, I thought.

Tom, Boyd, and Armstrong were all called away briefly to look at something inside the library. I sat quietly with the engine running. Threatening e-mails from inside the libraries? What had this woman, or this man posing as a woman, been threatening to do to Drew Wellington? And why had the innuendos been, ah, sexual in nature? Why had Wellington been told to move from our town?

When Tom and the two sergeants returned, they looked unusually weary.

"What is it?" I asked. Tom shook his head. I asked the sergeants about the nature of the threats against Drew Wellington.

Armstrong and Boyd exchanged a glance. "*Not* that she was going to kill him," Boyd finally said. "And we've told all the librarians to look out for this young brown-haired woman that you thought you saw, and to give us a call *stat* if they see her."

"When were these three threatening e-mails sent?" I asked, my turn to be accusatory.

"Over the last month," said Tom, whose ability to display composure never ceased to amaze me.

I said, "And no one got a good enough look to be able to give a reasonable description of this person."

"Nope," replied Boyd. "Whoever she or he is, they're pretty handy with disguises."

"And at routing e-mail," Armstrong said.

I was thinking that the Furman County Library System needed a new surveillance system, or maybe even to replace their computers, if it was proving so hard to find a phantom Internet user who wore disguises but managed to send threats to a former district attorney, without being detected.

I looked out the windshield. Snow was still coming down steadily, and the glass was blanketed with crystals. Poor Drew Wellington. He probably had thought he was safe at the library. I mean, who wouldn't?

Also—if the person I'd seen was indeed Sandee, then had she been there to deliver a threat, or perhaps to deliver *on* a threat?

I said, "*Why* would someone be sending threatening e-mails to Wellington at this point in his life?"

"We don't know, Miss G.," Tom said. "But now that he's dead, you can bet we're going to get our intel guys on it. They might be able to figure out something more than a woman in a hoodie. Plus, you know what we're going to be doing. Tracking Wellington's movements, seeing who his enemies were, that kind of thing."

"Could all this have to do with his work as a D.A.? Some criminal he sent away, somebody who threatened him in court, is now out, and wants revenge? Or maybe a disgruntled voter is holding a grudge. Why was Drew defeated in the election three years ago?" I asked, trying to sound innocent.

The cops cleared their throats. "Matter of public record," Boyd said. "Wellington got a DUI, and he tried to have it hushed up."

"That's it?" I asked.

Boyd sighed. "Goldy, we have work we have to do. As your husband said, we're going to try to find out who Wellington's enemies were."

Tom reached for my hand and squeezed it. When I glanced at him, he raised his eyebrows and gave me a warning look: *Don't press this now.*

Boyd, Armstrong, and Tom talked in quiet tones about when the county pathologist was going to do the autopsy. I tried not to listen to their conversation, because I preferred not to think about what actually happened during an autopsy.

Instead, I focused on what else, besides the death of Drew Wellington, I could bring to mind. There was the library event, *my* library event, a breakfast party I'd been due to put on in the morning. Would the librarians change the venue? Would they cancel? If they changed the location for their party, I would have a lot more transporting to do . . . and this would push me back on doing the luncheon for the garden-club people. This, in turn, would make me late doing the MacArthurs' dinner . . .

Suddenly I saw all my Christmas bookings collapsing backward, like so many dominoes, and *Goldilocks' Catering, Where Everything Is Just Right!* getting squished under an enormous oblong of blackness.

Boyd's cell buzzed. When he answered it, Tom reached out and squeezed my hand again.

"You okay, Miss G.? I mean, these circumstances notwithstanding."

I bit my lip and gave a quick shake of my head. "I've been trying *not* to reflect on how much this mess with Drew Wellington is going to impact mundane business issues. But I'm not having much luck. I'm also trying *not* to worry about the fact that the temperature is dropping very, very quickly. I have foods in the back that don't take too well to freezing."

"Everything will be okay," Tom whispered.

"My van's about to run out of gas."

Tom kept hold of my hand, but turned to his deputies. "Let's finish up here, guys. I need to get Miss G. home."

Armstrong opened his door. Boyd hung up his cell, looked at me, and let out an unmistakably self-pitying sigh.

"Sergeant Boyd," I said as I retrieved a pair of zip-type freezer bags from behind my seat. "Hand me that tray of Bleak House Bars, and I'll send you and your partner away happy."

5

On the way home, the snowfall thickened. Once Tom and I were in our kitchen, we called the Druckmans to make sure they'd arrived safely. They had, and their party had increased: Arch had begged for Eileen to pick up Gus that night, too. Arch and Todd had argued that the three boys could do Latin review better together—uh-huh. Gus lived with his grandparents, and according to Arch, they had given an enthusiastic thumbs-up. Since Eileen drove a brand-new Hummer, the Vikarioses had reportedly said they would love for her to take Gus down to Christian Brothers High School for his last exam.

"Who'll be doing the driving?" I asked, remembering some car catastrophes Arch had had in October.

Arch sighed. "Don't worry, Mrs. Druckman is doing it." He hesitated. "Is that guy at the library going to be okay?"

"I don't think so, hon. The police are there now."

In the background, the boys called for Arch, and he signed off. It was good to have company when you needed it.

I needed it, too, which Tom seemed to know. He expertly built a fire with one hand while using the thumb of his opposite hand to punch in digits on his cell. I could only glean a fourth of what was being said. That is, I picked up on half of Tom's half of the conversation, because I was making trips to the van. But that was enough to garner some interesting tidbits.

It seemed that the investigative team was going to meet at the sheriff's department at nine *that night* to pool information. As I traipsed in with box after box, I wondered whether getting everybody together in the middle of a snowstorm wasn't excessive. I doubted very much that the county pathologist would drop everything to come do an autopsy. And without an autopsy—or weapon, as I certainly hadn't seen a knife, or gun with a silencer on it, anywhere near Drew Wellington—how could they have anything to discuss?

It didn't matter, I mused as I stamped through the thick snow sifting down, since nobody was asking me.

Still, try as I might, I couldn't get the image of Roberta trying to revive Drew Wellington out of my mind. What had happened? Why had Sandee—or whoever she was—been there, seeming to be watching Drew Wellington? And why was the sheriff gathering everybody to the department at night?

I became chilled bringing in the first few loads of food, so I fixed myself a hot chocolate. Tom was still on the phone, so I told myself to think. The victim, Drew Wellington, was technically a member of law enforcement, even if he hadn't been reelected. For most of his tenure, he'd been a charismatic district attorney, and his supporters and friends would be calling for the sheriff's head if the case wasn't solved quickly. Add to that the fact that the media would be scrutinizing the department's every move. Pressure coming down from the governor, the county commissioners, and who knew who else would be unparalleled. Given all these factors, I thought as I drank the last of the cocoa, it made sense that the pathologist would be called that night and the staff assembled. Damn the torpedoes. The sheriff's department was going full speed ahead.

I washed my cup and told myself that I still needed to bring in the grapefruit and coffee cakes. And then another problem occurred to me.

As mundane as it sounded, who was going to take responsibility to call the librarians who had *not* witnessed Drew Wellington coming out of the library in a body bag, to tell them their holiday breakfast would not be held in the reading room? Would the rest of the staff show up early the next morning, only to find their beloved book sanctuary ribboned off by police investigators? I shook my head. No matter what, it didn't seem quite right to ring up Roberta Krepinski right after she'd handled a corpse. *Hey, Roberta! What'm I supposed to do with these cheese pies?* I knew folks who could be insensitive; as far as I knew, I wasn't one of them.

With the phone tucked under his ear, Tom came out to the kitchen. He brushed log dust off his hands and whispered, "If you'll just wait, I'll bring the rest of your stuff in for you."

I mouthed the words *I'm okay,* and proceeded back to the van for my last load. The wind rammed a wave of frigid air through the pines. I balanced the tray of grapefruit on top of the coffee cake, then carefully wended my way down the flagstone path that Tom had placed over my old dirt-worn trail between the freestanding garage and our deck.

Tom had opened the pet-containment area, and now Scout the cat streaked through my legs as I came through the back door. I grabbed the tray before a dozen grapefruits went bouncing across the kitchen floor. Jake, our bloodhound, proved no less a distraction, because he was extremely eager to see me. He let the neighborhood and Tom know the fact through an enthusiastic bout of howling. I stowed the food, held the door open, and yelled for him over the wind. He reluctantly lumbered inside, then tried to knock the ham off the counter.

I stashed the last of the food in the walk-in, fed the animals, and let them back out. When I called them a few minutes later, the wind had picked up even more force. Temperatures were dropping by the minute, so this time both pets raced back inside. Tom was still on his cell phone; he rolled his eyes at me and wrote me a note: *Off soon.* He herded the pets to the living room. I closed the kitchen doors, washed my hands, and sat down again at our little oak table.

Almost immediately, memories of the calamitous events I'd witnessed rose up. I heard Roberta's groans and cries for help. I felt myself running toward her, but the sensation was like swimming through lead. I saw Roberta trying to lower Drew Wellington to the floor. His heavy chest rose up to greet me.

Okay, that did it. I had to cook.

The chicken breasts for the garden club's Chicken Divine—much lighter than the classic Chicken Divan— was already brining in a buttermilk bath, and I would bake them off just before the lunch. The day after Thanksgiving, Julian had thrown his energy into making and freezing hundreds of potato gnocchi, which he would cook and slather in melted butter once we got to the conference center. He'd also be steaming baby artichokes and asparagus, if he could find some of the latter in Boulder after he picked up ganache-topped chocolate cupcakes from his favorite bakery. The strawberries were trimmed and the dressing made; we'd do the avocados just before serving. The cookies were, so to speak, in the bag. In many bags, as a matter of fact. I still had to bake the gingerbread door prizes. But first, I had to figure out that night's meal for Tom and me, a meal I would have to prepare quickly, as he'd be heading out the door no later than half past seven. So much for our ragout and relaxing evening together.

The walk-in yielded half a dozen fresh chicken thighs that Tom had picked up, put in a zip plastic bag, and helpfully labeled "Ours!" I mixed up a simple buttermilk brine to tenderize the chicken. I then donned the surgical gloves required by the state for poultry handling—even though this was going to be a meal for our family, I'd developed the glove habit and was loath to break it—rinsed off the thighs, and plopped them into the solution. I set a big pot of water on to boil, scrubbed a batch of fingerling potatoes Tom had man-

aged to hide from me, stirred up a champagne vinaigrette, and lightly rinsed a bunch of baby arugula,
another find of Tom's. Where did he get these delica-
cies, I often wondered, and how much did he pay for
them? I didn't care. He loved to surprise me . . . although he would be the one surprised, since he was getting them for dinner that night.

I set the table and located our stash of candles, in
case things briefly turned romantic . . . or the power
went out. Then I brought out a bowl of bread dough
that I'd made that morning. When I'd baked one into a
roll to test the recipe, I'd tasted it and decided it was
too tangy for the garden club. Frozen homemade rolls
would do for them, and we could use the sour-tasting
dough for something, I reasoned. I just didn't know
what.

As I punched down the dough and began to knead it,
I thought about Drew Wellington. Like so many folks in
Colorado, he'd insisted on immediate familiarity, even
though he'd invariably seemed to be looking over my
shoulder, to see if there was someone more important he
should be talking to. "Just call me Drew," he'd said
vaguely when Tom had introduced him to me at a law
enforcement picnic. Within ninety seconds, he'd spotted
someone he apparently needed to see, and he was off. See
ya, Mr. D.A.!

Digging my hands into the dough, I also vividly re-membered one particular church coffee hour, about two and a half years ago. It was summertime, and Drew had failed to be reelected district attorney the previous No-vember. Immediately after her husband's rout at the hands of the voters, Elizabeth had handed him another defeat: she'd filed for divorce. Marla had dug ceaselessly to find out the reason for the marriage's end, but had come up empty-handed, much to her dismay.

I hadn't cared, because I thought after years in the spotlight, Elizabeth deserved her privacy. I'd continued to cater the occasional fund-raising lunch, dinner, and cocktail party for her. She'd worked hard at dabbing makeup around her bloodshot eyes and keeping her up-per lip stiff. Drew had stopped coming to church, or at least coming in the company of Elizabeth, who'd always been what we Episcopalians call an "eight o'clocker," i.e., an attendee at the early service.

This particular June morning, though, Drew had re-invented himself and shown up at the later service, all smiles, with his aura of charisma still glowing. He'd looked dapper in a slim-fitting, obviously expensive gray sport coat and slacks. Instead of appearing downtrod-den and depressed, the fiftyish former district attorney had been buoyant, chatting with folks, glad-handing about, making sure everyone knew he was as gleeful as a fellow who'd just lost an election by historically wide margins could be. I never did know if he dyed his hair or if his carefully combed blond-brown mane was natural, but he seemed to enjoy pushing his bangs back from his sculptured face, a face that boasted enviably high cheekbones.

In charge of after-church snacks that day, I'd made lemonade and several batches of my newly developed recipe for Piña Colada Muffins. Also key to this particular memory was the fact that as I'd mingled among the parishioners with my tray, I was wearing an apron. I'd assessed Drew Wellington surreptitiously at first, while he was talking enthusiastically to Father Pete, who'd just returned to commission after suffering a heart attack.

As it turned out, Drew had been asking Father Pete to reintroduce him to Marla. I'd happened to be standing next to her, still wearing my apron, still holding my tray.

When Father Pete had asked if we remembered Drew Wellington, the former prosecutor, Drew had ignored me and said, "Why, Miss Marla, I do believe you need me to tell you about map collecting." With my invisible status, I'd had no trouble noticing the twinkle in Drew's eyes and his suggestively furrowed brow. *Are you interested in me, Marla?* he seemed to be asking. *Do you have money you'd like to put in my care?*

Marla had reeled back. "I don't need a map, 'cuz I know where I'm going. How about you, Drew? Do you have a destination in mind?"

"I also just apprised you of the presence of our longtime parishioner, *Goldy Schulz,* whom I believe you know," Father Pete had said, so clearly aggrieved that I'd blushed.

Drew had looked at me blankly and said, "Right. You're the one married to a sheriff's-department investigator. We've met before." And then he'd asked Marla if she wanted to impress her friends with an old map of Bermuda.

Marla had said, "How about an antique map of Antigua?" and Drew had chuckled knowingly. Had he known Marla was making fun of him? As I shuffled off, I doubted it.

I pushed and kneaded the dough. After the coffee hour, Marla had given me the scoop. According to one of the St. Luke's women, Elizabeth Wellington had agreed, somewhere along the line, to give Drew a large chunk of change, somewhere in the neighborhood of two and a half million. Drew, supposedly recognizing that two and a half mil probably wouldn't be enough to retire on, was using Elizabeth's money to invest in real estate and set himself up in the map business. He was also sucking up to women with lots and lots of money, of which Marla was definitely one.

In fact, this very evening, Marla had told me that Patricia Ingersoll—the weight-loss queen who'd talked so boringly to the Episcopal Church Women in October— and Drew Wellington had been set to marry. Marry when? And had they had a long-term affair or a short one?

There was no doubt in my mind that Marla was hot on the trail of finding out.

I tried to bring Patricia's face back into focus. Four years ago, Patricia had married Frank Ingersoll, a widower and single father of a twentyish daughter. I'd loved catering their wedding reception, and it wasn't just because Frank, who'd retired early from a Silicon Valley start-up, had paid for the party. It was also because Frank, who was wealthy, and Patricia, who was gorgeous, had seemed deliriously happy. The reception had been a grand affair, held at the couple's fabulous new house in Flicker Ridge. Then Frank, who'd only been in his midfifties, had died quite suddenly of an aggressive type of leukemia. Lovely, slender, and now—the gossip had it—heir to the bulk of Frank's forty million, Patricia could easily have been hypnotized by a prosecutor who had taken on the persona of an extremely charming map dealer.

Ah, charmers. I had been unhappily married to one for seven years. The ultrasuave Drew Wellington had neither fooled nor impressed me. In fact, both at that long-ago picnic and at the more recent coffee hour, all my dangerous-man signals had rung like the bells of St. Mary's. I'd avoided Wellington, no doubt about it—and he hadn't seemed too eager to get to know me either.

Nor had I been impressed, I reflected as the dough became supple under my fingertips, with the law-and-order message Drew Wellington had been touting during his campaign. Ah, the irony! Now that I knew the particulars of his attempt to hide his DUI, it seemed that Drew hadn't felt constrained to follow much law and order himself. There had been that article—

Wait a minute.

Somehow Drew Wellington had always managed to get publicity for himself. In a newspaper interview last month, three years after he'd been defeated in his reelection bid, Drew Wellington had first bragged about his business. He'd claimed to be running "the largest and most reputable map dealership west of the Mississippi." *Yeah, right,* I'd thought, *let's have a little hyperbole.* Unprovoked, he'd then launched into a negative critique of the Furman County Sheriff's Department. Referring to Sandee Brisbane's leap into an inferno last summer, he'd said law enforcement officials had "let a murderer get away." Once again, I'd thought: *Yeah, right!*

Alas, nobody from the paper had bothered to mention that a crowd of cops and firefighters had witnessed Sandee's leap into self-immolation. What did the former prosecutor think we should have done, vaulted in after her? As my mother used to say, "If your best friend jumps into the ravine, are you going to jump in there, too?" Since I was scared to death of the ravine near our New Jersey home, I always shook my head. No way was I, at age five, following anyone into *any* abyss.

I cut the dough into twelve pale pieces. The former prosecutor had been a charismatic charmer; my violent, cruel ex-husband, whom Marla and I had dubbed the Jerk, had been cut from the same cloth. I moved the knife with precision. Come to think of it, I liked using a very sharp instrument to slice things when I was thinking about the Jerk. I know, I know, *get over it.* But sometimes that took a while. In point of fact, I didn't think I'd ever get over being repeatedly beaten up by the Jerk, any more than I would recover from being so surprised to find his shot-up body in his Audi TT.

Shot up by Sandee Brisbane, the same Sandee Brisbane I could have sworn had been near Drew Wellington just before he turned up dead.

If I'd seen Sandee, then why, why, why was she back? Had she killed Drew Wellington? Had she come out of her hidey-hole because Drew Wellington had recently ridiculed the sheriff's department for not catching her?

It seemed to me that if a former district attorney was talking about how you needed to have been caught before you jumped into a fire, the last thing you'd do is show up and say, "Hi, I'm not dead! How about prosecuting me for murder?"

I was startled by someone impatiently ringing the doorbell, then hammering on the door itself with a hand or a fist. Surely the media could not know *already* that I'd been at the library when Roberta had made her grisly discovery? I washed my hands and quickstepped down the front hall, afraid the incessant banging would disturb Tom. But there was no way I was opening the door until I could see through our peephole who was gracing us with a dinnertime visit.

It was not a reporter. It was Marla, who was staring at me and mouthing the words *open up!* So I did.

"I'm freezing my *ass* off out there," she sputtered once she was in our foyer, "and you're making sure it's not the bogeyman." Defying the animal rights folks, she wore a full-length mink coat and mink-trimmed boots. Once she'd shrugged off the fur and hung it on our banister, she sashayed into the living room and turned her supposedly iced-up buttocks to the fire.

"Damn!" she said, shaking out her mop of curls, held in place tonight by a scattering of ruby and emerald barrettes, a salute to seasonal red and green. "Drew Wellington! I can't believe it!" Her brown eyes regarded me skeptically. "And you found him."

"Actually, Roberta was the one who—" I didn't finish my thought.

"Ladies?" Tom, who'd been around the corner in the dining room, was holding his hand over the receiver. "Could I convince you to move this conversation?"

Marla and I obligingly raced into the kitchen. I closed the door behind us.

"Who's Tom on the phone with?" Marla demanded. I shrugged. "Don't give me that you-don't-know stuff. It's the department, isn't it? What are they thinking? Who're they suspecting? Patricia, his fiancée? Or Elizabeth, his ex-wife? Maybe both of them, working together? How about that creepy little Neil Tharp, who worked with Drew?"

"Marla, please. I haven't a clue and neither does he. They just have to get everyone together to figure out where they're going to start. Plan a strategy, that type of thing."

She fluffed up her hair behind the barrettes. "You're going to thank me for this next one. I've spared you worrying about where you're going to have the library breakfast."

"What are you talking about?"

Marla's look was triumphant. "I called one of the library trustees and offered to have the staff and volunteers' holiday breakfast at my house! At eight tomorrow morning, God help us. I hate anything happening at that ungodly hour, but I just couldn't resist . . ." She hesitated and pressed her lips together. Lately, Father Pete had been giving sermons on the Seven Deadly Sins, but he'd begun by saying that there should be an Eighth Deadly Sin, and that was spreading gossip. Marla had been put out by the lessons. "I don't want to be a . . ." She furrowed her brow, looking for a euphemism for *gossip-monger*. "I just want to hear from folks who were there, you know, what happened. Since you're not going to tell me anything."

"Hey, I'll tell you whatever you want to know. Roberta found him, and the two of us lowered him to the floor. She did CPR. That's it."

"Oh, *please*." She pouted. "There's got to be more to it than that—"

We were interrupted by the doorbell's ringing again. What was going on here? Did everybody in town want to know what had happened at the library? Maybe Tom was going to have his meeting at our house. At least that was what I thought when he answered the door.

"Do you know if there's more to it?" I demanded in a whisper. "Something to do with Sandee Brisbane?"

"With Sandee *Brisbane*? What are you talking about?"

At that moment Tom ushered Patricia Ingersoll into the kitchen.

"You know Marla Korman," Tom said. "And this is my wife, Goldy the caterer. You know Goldy, right?"

"She did Frank's and my wedding reception." Patricia's voice was raspy, and her eyes were rimmed with red. "Hi, Goldy, Marla. I . . . I'm hurting."

I walked over and pulled her in for a hug. "Patricia, I'm sorry."

"Me, too," Marla added.

"Thanks," she said, pulling away. "I didn't come here to . . . to, you know, fall apart."

"Sit down," I said gently, in case she did fall apart. "Marla, could you get some tissues?"

As bidden, Marla dug into her capacious Prada bag, pulled out a packet of tissues, and placed it beside Patricia, who had slumped into a kitchen chair. Like the former prosecutor, who could have been her cousin rather than her lover, Patricia Ingersoll was slender, good-looking, and blond. But there was no way *her* hair, with its fashionably dark roots and crinkled masses of waves, was naturally platinum. Tom cocked an eyebrow at me. I shrugged helplessly, and he backed into the living room.

I didn't know why Patricia was here. Okay, her boyfriend or fiancé or whatever he was had been an arrogant so-and-so, but she still deserved comfort.

"Patricia," I said tentatively, "can I get you something? Fix you something warm to drink? It's so doggone cold outside—"

Patricia shook her head and wiped her eyes with one of Marla's tissues. She bit the inside of her cheek and scanned the counter, with its small mountain of fingerling potatoes, its bowl of brining chicken, and its jar of champagne vinaigrette. The lengthening silence was interrupted only by the ringing of Marla's cell phone. While Marla excused herself, I put a pot of water on to boil. Marla was murmuring into her phone out in the hall. After a moment she poked her head back into the kitchen.

"I need to get across town," she said. "Excuse me, Patricia, Goldy. I'm sorry, Patricia, really I am." Marla gave me a pointed look: *You'd better tell me everything she tells you.* Then she whisked away, undoubtedly called away by a gossip emergency on the other side of Aspen Meadow.

Patricia looked at me and blinked. Her thin, angular face was tight with anguish, her lips white with tension.

"A friend called," she began, without looking at me. "Her neighbor was in the library when somebody found Drew. She said"—Patricia lowered her voice to a whisper—"that you were there helping, and that he hadn't made it."

"Law enforcement wouldn't let us back in, but it didn't look good. I'm so sorry."

"Oh, Goldy," she whispered, "I loved him. I can't believe this." She began to sob into the tissue.

I hugged her again. When her weeping abated a bit, she murmured that she was doing better. I put the fingerlings into the boiling water, then sat down beside her.

"I'm so sorry, Patricia. After what you went through with Frank, this is unbelievable."

She rubbed her temples. "Don't talk about Frank, please. I can't . . . can't take this all over again." This brought a fresh onslaught of tears.

"Patricia, I'm sure Drew knew you cared—"

"Wait, you haven't heard the worst of it. While I was still on the phone with my friend, two sheriff's-department investigators pulled up. I thought maybe they'd come to tell me about Drew. But they hadn't."

"No?"

Patricia took a deep breath. "Nope. Two investigators said somebody had seen a car that looked like mine driving away from the library. I said, 'Well, yeah, I was at the library today.' I still didn't get why they were at my house. I mean, I was numb. Then one of them presented me with a search warrant. For my house. Then I got it, duh. They think I hurt Drew. I told them that I *loved* Drew."

"Patricia, if there's evidence of foul play, the first thing the department has to do is talk to people who knew Drew."

"Talk to people? Suspect them? Turn their houses upside down?" I didn't know what to say, so I just waited for her to go on. "So . . . I told them to go ahead, and I went out my back door and up my hill to my car. I was so scared, I called an attorney on my cell." Her bloodshot eyes strayed wildly around the kitchen. "Brewster Motley. He said to come to your place, Goldy, until he could get here."

"What?"

Patricia began sobbing again. "Did I do the wrong thing to call a lawyer? That's what they do on TV."

"I'm sure you didn't do the wrong thing." Even as I tried to sound comforting, I thought, *What could Brewster have been thinking? Why come here?*

"I know, I know. Maybe I should call Brewster back. Maybe I should talk to Tom. Oh God, I don't know what to do."

"Let's think for a minute." I gazed helplessly at the dozen globs of bread dough I'd left on the counter. I imagined them subdividing and growing, then subdividing again, like amoebas.

"I called my neighbor and she looked out her window. She said the sheriff's department is making a mess in my house!" Patricia cried morosely, tugging on a handful of her platinum hair. "I suppose I should go back home anyway." She sounded as if she was trying to convince herself. "But I just can't watch them tear my place apart. I didn't want to talk about the man I loved." Tears spilled out of her eyes again. "The *dead* man I loved."

I picked up the phone and handed it to her. "Why don't you call the sheriff's department right now? Ask them if you can go home. Or you could have Tom call."

When Patricia shook her head, the mass of her crinkled platinum hair shook at the same time. "I couldn't face them at home, how can I talk to them on the phone?"

How old was Patricia, thirty, thirty-five? Younger than I was, or did she just look that way? And act that way?

"Do you . . . should you go back and wait at your neighbor's?" I asked, trying to be helpful. Patricia shook her head. I could hear Tom out in the living room, still on his cell. I felt my shoulders sag as I regarded Patricia, who looked like a wrung-out rag doll. "Let me fix you something to drink, okay? What would you like?"

Her gaze raked the kitchen. "Could I just have some hot water?"

"Some hot water?" I repeated. "For what?"

"To drink," she said.

I shuddered, but poured a bottle of springwater into a pan and set it on the stove. Plain heated water? Oh-kay. I resolved to have something myself. Was it too late in the day for espresso? Yes. How about brandy? Hmm. I wasn't quite ready for that.

"I would never hurt Drew," Patricia wailed, hugging her sides. "When they handed me that warrant, I thought, *What in the hell is going on here?*"

"Okay, okay! I'm not the one you need to convince." I searched our liquor cabinet and decided I'd have a sherry in a few minutes. I also decided I needed to get the rolls into the oven. To Patricia, I said, "Do you mind if I work on my dough here?"

When she snuffled and shook her head, I preheated the oven and poured Patricia her hot water. I drained the potatoes and set them aside, then beat an egg and carefully brushed the bread-dough lumps with it. After I'd set them in the hot oven, I turned back to Patricia.

"Have you ever dealt with a criminal-defense lawyer before?"

She looked into her teacup and shook her head. "Of course not. Listen to me, Goldy, if the police showed up at my house with a warrant? Then they think someone *did* kill Drew. And although I'm not the one who did it, I'm sure Drew *was* murdered."

I pressed my lips together and thought about Sandee's face in the window. "Can you tell me more?"

"He had horrible enemies," she said fiercely, "beginning with that bitch of an ex-wife of his. Oh God, I can't believe he's gone!" She put down her cup and wiped tears from her cheeks. "Plus, he was having problems with his business, and he had other woman . . . issues—" She stopped abruptly.

"Other woman issues?" Like with Sandee Brisbane? Should I mention her to Patricia? No, I decided. If there was anything to the Sandee Brisbane situation, as I was thinking of it, then when the investigators talked to Patricia, they could ask her.

Patricia bit the inside of her cheek again. "Maybe I should just wait to talk to Mr. Motley." She buried her face in her hands again. "Oh God, I hope he didn't suffer! Drew said I was the only one who understood him and cared about him . . . and now he's gone."

When I couldn't take it anymore, I said, "Excuse me for a couple of minutes, Patricia."

I nabbed the sherry bottle, walked out to the dining room, and poured a hefty dose of the golden liquid into one of the few remaining crystal glasses that my grandmother had left me. I had only a few remaining because the Jerk had broken most of them. The occasion had been when I'd told him that some of the women he'd had affairs with had come to our house to tell me how he'd complained about *me*. *My wife doesn't understand me, but you do. I'm not in love with her anymore. You make me feel young again. I'm in love with you. You're the only one who cares about me, so please, please don't ever leave me* . . . And at that point they were hooked, until he dumped them and went on to a new conquest, complaining about how I didn't understand him. Point of fact, I'd been one of the people who really *did* understand him. Who *had* understood him until Sandee came along and stopped his complaining forever . . .

I took a deep breath and a medicinal swig of sherry, and walked back into the kitchen.

"Goldy, what is it?" Patricia held the cup I'd given her in both hands. "Do you know Elizabeth Wellington? Have you ever had to cater for her?"

"I know her from church. And yes, I've catered fund-raising parties for her."

Her blue eyes sought mine. "D'you think she's really awful?"

"Actually, I always—" I'd been on the point of saying *always felt kind of sorry for her,* but stopped myself. I may not have liked Drew, but Patricia, poor fool, had clearly adored him.

"I feel as if I'm interrupting your dinner." Patricia's tone was guilty. "I don't know why Brewster had me come here."

"Stay, please." I felt dizzy from drinking the sherry on an empty stomach. We all needed to eat. When Brewster finally got here, maybe he'd join us for dinner, too.

The buzzer went off for the rolls and I brought them out to cool. I drained the brine from the chicken, rinsed it, and placed it in a baking pan. Then I figured, what the hell, poured some sherry over it, sprinkled it with salt and pepper, and popped it into the oven. I smashed the fingerlings with butter and cream, mounded the resulting cloud of mashed potatoes into another buttered dish, and set the timer for when the potatoes would go in next to the chicken. Which reminded me. I still had to make the gingerbreads for the garden-club door prizes.

"I'm telling you," Patricia said again, her tone stubborn, "Drew was always worried about these people he said had it in for him."

I pulled my work schedule up on my computer. "Why don't you let me get Tom in here so you can tell him what you know?"

"No, no, I'm not ready for that. I need you to help me." She sat up straight in the oak kitchen chair, as if she'd found some resolve within. "I want to know what happened to Drew, and who's responsible."

I stared at my computer. Okay, first I was a mom and a wife, second I was a caterer, and third, every now and then people wanted me to figure out what had happened to their loved ones, loved ones who were victims of crimes. Unfortunately, at the moment I had to concentrate on number two, the caterer bit.

Plus, I had to think. I hit the print button for the gingerbread recipe. The luncheon and exchange would be followed by the MacArthurs' curry dinner and dessert, for which I'd already piled creamy lime filling into graham-cracker pie crusts. Once the printer had spat out my gingerbread recipe, I turned back to Patricia.

"Patricia, I would like to help you. Really I would. But right at this very minute, I need to cook. May I please try to get somebody over here to be with you? Should I call Marla to come back? She's my best—"

Patricia snorted again. "Omigod, not that Marla Korman. I'm so glad she left. Talking to her is like putting your conversation in the *Denver Post*."

"Well, I wouldn't go that far—"

Tom poked his head in the kitchen. "You gonna be here for a while, Patricia?" he asked mildly. "I've got some calls to make, and then I'll be out."

Patricia sniffled. "Yes, I'll be here. Goldy's cooking and I'm helping."

Tom retreated from the kitchen and, without missing a beat, went back to talking on his cell. I wanted to tell Patricia that she wasn't helping; she was impeding my progress. But I couldn't deny I wanted to hear what she knew about Drew Wellington and his many enemies. I also was getting very worried about Patricia's emotional state. She'd had a huge shock and seemed on the edge of breaking down. Better to keep her here and let her talk it out, maybe with Tom if she ever became willing to speak to him, or at least with Brewster. But after asking for my help, she had become quiet, sitting at my kitchen table and sipping her cup of water. Her cell phone rang, and I felt both frustrated and relieved when she answered it.

I turned my focus to my gingerbread recipe, which made enough batter to fill three castle molds. This wasn't the kind of gingerbread that you made into slabs and glued together with royal icing. That glue-into-houses was cookie dough, and it was much more troublesome, especially at high altitude. No, this was the soft, cakelike variety of gingerbread, the kind you topped with lemon sauce or vanilla ice cream or, if you were feeling *teddibly teddibly chichi*, crème fraîche.

On cardboard rounds, wrapped with crackling cellophane and festooned with metallic ribbon, they would be great prizes for the cookie exchange. Just reading the ingredients—unsalted butter, dark molasses, sour cream, dried ginger, grated gingerroot, and freshly ground black pepper—made me dizzy again. Or was I becoming dizzy because I'd once again thought of Drew Wellington's corpse?

Do not think about anything. Stop worrying about Patricia. Just cook, my mind commanded. I retrieved a pound of unsalted butter and a plastic container of sour cream from the walk-in, put them on the counter, and then ducked back inside for eggs and orange juice. When I came out, Patricia was staring at the butter and sour cream. I put the butter into a pan to melt and hid the sour cream behind bags of unbleached flour and, uh, sugar.

"Just a minute," she said into her cell phone. Then she stared at my counter. "You're putting all that into one recipe?"

"Yes." I wanted to say, *Patricia, you stick with your diets, and I'll take care of the cooking.* But I didn't. Instead, I rummaged around in my utensils drawer.

When Patricia signed off from her call, I decided to try to get her to open up again. "You know I'm really, *really* sorry about Drew, Patricia. I'll help if I can, though I doubt there's much I can do." I spooned flour into a measuring cup. I said, "You said that Drew was worried?"

"Yes." She snuffled again. "His business partner, you know, that toad of a man named Neil Tharp? Drew thought Neil was trying to force him out."

When she did not elaborate, I said, "Force him out why?"

She stared at her teacup. "I don't think they exactly trusted each other."

I wanted to ask why again but thought the echo would sound too much like Arch when he was three. We can't buy that bunch of helium balloons. *Why?* Because we don't have enough money. *Why?* Because Daddy says no. *Why?* Because Daddy is a skinflint. Only I hadn't said that last part.

"And there were other folks who had it in for him?" I said.

"Oh, he sold a map to a man who turned around and tried to sell it for the same price he bought it for. Then I heard there was some problem with a library, I don't know what it was, because Drew didn't tell me. Anyway, the guy who tried to sell the map was named MacArthur, you heard of him? I know his wife, Hermie. The husband is named . . . *prosciutto*? No, wait. *Smithfield*. Apparently no one told Smithfield MacArthur you buy something for retail, but if you want to sell it, you have to offer it at wholesale price. Sometimes I wonder how rich people earn their money, they're so damn *stupid*."

"How long ago was this?" I asked cautiously.

"Oh God, I'd have to think."

"Anybody else out there who had it in for Drew Wellington?"

She held her teacup in both hands again, although I was sure any warming strength it had once had was gone. "Well, as I said, he was having problems with his business."

"The map business? Did he have an attorney business, too?"

"He *was* an attorney. The map dealing began as his hobby, then developed into a business. Some people were jealous of him, I know that. I . . . even thought someone was following him around." She arched an eyebrow at me.

"Somebody following him around?" I echoed. "Someone who was jealous?"

"I really shouldn't say anything," she said.

"Why not?"

"I just . . . don't feel comfortable with it. In terms of people I know were jealous of him, there was Elizabeth. She was furious that he was making so much money."

I wanted to say, *She was, was she? Was she the one following him around?* But our conversation was interrupted by a gentle knock on our front door. For some reason, the knock worried me. It was too serious, too knowing. Was Arch all right?

"Do you suppose that's Brewster?" Patricia asked, her voice hopeful. She got to her feet and turned a bright face to the kitchen door, which was a mere ten yards from our front door.

But it was not Brewster Motley, criminal-defense attorney. The step was too heavy, the door was opening too quickly . . . and revealing Tom, followed by two deputies from the Furman County Sheriff's Department. The deputies marched across the wood floor, and right there in my kitchen, they whipped out a pair of handcuffs.

"Patricia Ingersoll," said one, "you are under arrest for the murder of Drew Wellington. You have the right to remain silent—"

She dropped the teacup and it shattered. "Goldy!" she cried, her voice full of despair. "Help me! What do I say?"

"Nothing!" I shrieked after her as the deputies led her down our front hall. Patricia was protesting loudly, so I wasn't sure whether she'd heard me. "Wait for Brewster!" I hollered.

Tom yelled, "Goldy! What are you doing?"

Defiantly I raised my voice a notch. "Patricia, did you hear me?"

But she was gone.

6

Tom lifted his chin, set my face in his gaze, and stepped into the kitchen. When he closed the door behind him, I thought, Uh-oh.

"Goldy, what do you think you were doing?"

"You mean, what *was* I doing? Trying to help Patricia."

"Sit down."

Hell. The buzzer went off, so I put the mashed potatoes into the oven next to the chicken, then tried to arrange a small plate of crackers for us to have while we chatted. But Tom, who was right behind me, said, "Don't."

So I didn't. I sat and studiously avoided his eyes. I knew what he was thinking: that the wife of the county's lead investigator should not be yelling at a suspect—make that a suspect *in custody*—that she should duck all the questions law enforcement would throw at her. The department people would say, *What side does that Goldy Schulz think she's on, anyway?* And Tom would look bad, and his lieutenant would call him in, and then the captain would get involved, and Tom would be reprimanded . . .

"Now, what I'm going to tell you," Tom said, "is just for your ears. Understand? No Marla. No Julian. And God knows, no Patricia Ingersoll. Got it? Will you look at me, please?"

"Okay, okay." I gazed into his green eyes that were the shade of the deep ocean. "I'm sorry, but . . ." I started over. "Look, I have information for you, from Patricia. Drew Wellington had all kinds of enemies—"

He held up his hand, and I shut my mouth. "We know. We also know that our guys got a tip to go see Patricia. Somebody saw a silver BMW X-5 racing away from the library. The kind of car Patricia drives."

"Did they get a plate?"

"Goldy, it was and is *snowing*. Which means poor visibility."

"She told me she was at the library earlier today—"

Tom shook his head. "She was his girlfriend. A vehicle resembling her car was seen racing away from the library. She was already a person of interest, so they got a judge to give them a quickie search warrant. Maybe they knew other things I'm not even aware of yet. Now listen. There was an X-Acto knife right there in the middle of some big scrapbooking mess she had on her dining-room table. And it had blood on it."

Gooseflesh pimpled my arms. "Tom, I wasn't sure I saw blood—"

"There was blood at the library. Not a whole lot. But it was there."

I frowned. A silver BMW X-5 had been racing away from the library? Somebody—who?—thought it was Patricia's, even with thick snow coming down? Half the people in Aspen Meadow had X-5s. Was someone framing Patricia? If so, why? I felt confused. After the sherry, I needed some caffeine to ignite my thinking power, no matter what it would do to that night's sleep. "Tom, may I please make myself an espresso? My brain needs to be sufficiently kindled before I explain to you why I believe that Patricia is not so surpassingly, irretrievably stupid that she would leave a murder weapon out in plain sight."

Tom's sigh behind me made me wince. "If drinking coffee will somehow open your ears and your mind, then go ahead."

As I fired up the espresso machine, I felt an onslaught of second doubts. Had I been wrong to tell Patricia not to speak to the police officers? I didn't know. She'd been distraught, and at the same time eager to talk to me. Yet verbalizing her feelings in front of law enforcement officials was the *last* thing she should do before having a criminal-defense attorney at her side. Then the cops would have her story, and once her narrative of events was recorded, they would compare every single word she said afterward to that initial account she'd been so eager to spill.

I poured the sherry down the drain and watched dark, caffeinated liquid spurt into my espresso cup. I stared at it and asked myself why Brewster had told Patricia to come here. Why hadn't Brewster told her to sit tight at her own house? Unfortunately, he wouldn't be able to enlighten me about this, I supposed, because of that doggone attorney-client privilege. Maybe Patricia would tell me . . . when I visited her. I shuddered.

I slugged the espresso, then put the cup back under the doser and pushed the button for another double shot. I wasn't ready to resume my argument with Tom, so I stared out the kitchen window. It was just after seven, and Tom would have to be leaving soon—and without dinner, unless I got my act together. Outside, the night was as black as ink. Oh my, how I preferred the Colorado summer to its winter. But here we were, in the middle of my busy holiday season, with parties chockablock into next week. I should have been drained from all the work I'd already done, or exhausted from the prospect of all the work I still had to *do*. But I wasn't. I quaffed the second espresso, and within two minutes of standing there, I was wired.

I sat down next to Tom. "Okay, first. Patricia is a former client. And sort of a friend."

"Excuse me, but Patricia is *not* your friend. You told me she drove you nuts when you did her wedding reception four years ago. Then this fall, at that luncheon you did for the Episcopal Church Women, you wanted to stuff a gag down her throat for telling folks they were all fat. She even told them to eat that fake margarine. And all of a sudden tonight she's become your friend, because she seeks you out for help?"

"Give me a chance here, will you? There's no such thing as fake margarine, there's only fake butter, and that's called margarine, which, in my opinion, no one should ever use." Tom rolled his eyes. "Second, of course she would think to come here, to talk to me, you know, because of my reputation of, sort of, helping you—"

"Of sometimes involving yourself, insinuating yourself, into official investigations, you mean? Is that why she drove over, to get you to exonerate her?"

"Tom, she said Brewster *Motley* said she should come here."

"Oh, yeah? And where is Mr. Motley now, I'd like to know?"

I groaned. "Just 'cause he isn't here doesn't mean he's not on his way."

"But why would she call Brewster unless she thought she needed him?"

"So that makes her look guilty, the fact that she called an attorney before the cops even arrived here?"

"Usually, Miss G. Remember when I had you lawyer up when you were suspected of killing your ex? It didn't look good to the guys who arrested you, but the last thing I wanted was for you to start yakking away."

"Thanks for the vote of confidence."

"You're welcome."

"Tom," I rushed on before he could take charge of the conversation, "how reliable is this source of yours who told you about the BMW?"

Tom tilted his head. "We don't know, do we? That's why they're called anonymous."

I bit my bottom lip until I thought it was going to bleed. "She's being *framed*, don't you see? Someone wants to get rid of the former D.A. He or she knows Patricia is vulnerable, maybe because Patricia loved him but wasn't married to him. So this person plants a weapon at Patricia's house. Then they call in a tip. Easy, as we say in the food biz, as apple pie, or peach cobbler, or—"

Tom held up his hand. "Tell you what. Why don't we agree to disagree? I've told you more than I should have, probably, and you *have* to keep it to yourself—"

"I will, Tom. But if you get autopsy results or other leads or evidence that tend to exonerate Patricia, will you tell me? I don't believe she would have sought me out unless she was afraid of being set up, don't you see? You're going to have to tell Brewster and his team everything, anyway."

Tom tsked. But before he could reply, the doorbell rang once more. Through the sidelight I could see Brewster Motley, criminal-defense attorney extraordinaire. First Marla, then Patricia, now Brewster. Instead of making coffee, I should be filling up a punch bowl.

"Hey, Goldy," Brewster said once he'd come inside. Relaxed as always, his tan-from-skiing boyish face broke into a scampish grin. That smile of his, always mischievous, invariably hinted at his just escaping a fourth-grade teacher's punishment. He ran his hand through his tadtoo-long hair. Then he shrugged his dark gray cashmere coat off his wide shoulders: a surfer shedding a towel. Underneath, he wore a black V-neck sweater and jeans. "I came out in a hurry." His tone was apologetic, then puzzled. "I don't know what's going on here. Um . . . a woman named Patricia Ingersoll called me. She was going to meet me at your place."

I stared at him. "She said you told her to come here and wait for you, but she didn't say why."

"So is she here?"

Tom, standing beside our couch, did not move a muscle. Nor did he offer any explanation to Brewster. My skin began to itch as the silence between the three of us lengthened. Brewster shifted his coat over to the hand holding the briefcase. He raised his eyebrows at me. "Is somebody going to tell me what's going on?"

I swallowed. "Look, Brewster . . ." I faltered. "Patricia Ingersoll has been arrested for the murder of Drew Wellington, the former district attorney. Police officers just took her down to the sheriff's department."

Brewster's wide, handsome face wrinkled. To me, this situation was beginning to resemble one of those Russian dolls that you keep opening, only to find another one inside. "She's been arrested. Anything else?"

"She was really upset," I rushed in to say. "In fact, she was a mess. She was grief-stricken over losing her . . . well, I guess he was her fiancé. And then she was stunned when the police turned up at her house with a warrant—"

"A warrant?" Brewster asked. "What kind of warrant?"

"The search kind." Tom's tone was matter-of-fact.

"I think somebody's trying to set her up," I interjected.

Brewster narrowed his eyes at this assessment and smoothed any expression from his face. Apparently we were no longer in a comic dilemma. He lowered his briefcase to the floor and quickly put his coat back on. "Guess I'm on my way to the jail." He turned to the door. "Goldy? Tom? Good night."

"But wait," I protested as Brewster slid out our front door. "How will we know what's going on? Will somebody give us a ring?"

"You'll have to ask Patricia that," Brewster called over his shoulder as he scooted nimbly down our icy walk.

Tom put on his coat and announced curtly that he had to go down to the department for his meeting.

"But our dinner's almost ready," I protested.

"Save it." And with that, he strode out the back door.

So. All of a sudden I went from worrying about rising bread dough and feeling as if I was holding an unannounced open house, to eating alone and feeling like a failure. I had failed Tom by trying to help Patricia. I had failed Patricia by trying to keep her from getting into more trouble than I presumed she was already in. And maybe I had failed Drew Wellington by not racing out as soon as I saw Sandee, or the woman I thought was Sandee, and screaming for help, before she could kill another man.

I set the chicken and potatoes aside to cool; we could have them another night. After a while my gingerbread houses came out of the oven. Those spicy, cooling mansions filled the kitchen with the scents of ginger and cinnamon. I cleaned up all the bowls, pots, and pans, then fixed myself some leftovers and cleaned up from that.

Time was marching slowly, so I called Marla. She was "working the gossip lines," she promised, but so far she had nothing to report. Maybe by the time I arrived at her house the next morning, she would have something, she said. I wasn't really calling to find out anything substantive, and I had promised Tom not to talk about the X-Acto knife, which meant I shouldn't talk about the arrest either, because then Marla would want to know all the details. But I wasn't calling about any of that. I felt suddenly cold inside and out, and I just wanted to visit with my best friend. But before I could get those words out of my mouth, her call waiting clicked, and she was gone.

Next I tried Arch, who said, "I'm fine, thanks, Mom. Is Tom working on the Drew Wellington case?"

"Yes."

"That's awful," Arch said. "He was a good guy."

"How did *you* know him?"

"He came to our American history class and showed us maps. They were really cool, with lots of colors and stuff. He didn't bore us with a lot of dates either. We asked him how he'd learned so much, and he said he was an autodidact."

"Is that Latin?"

"No, Mom, it's Greek. It means you taught yourself."

"So what made him such a . . . good guy?"

"I don't know. He said his favorite thing to study was smuggling."

"Smuggling? That's what he taught himself? As in, how folks used to smuggle rum?"

"He talked about how the countries that had the maps controlled trade. In the fifteenth, sixteenth, or even the seventeenth centuries? If the Portuguese or Spanish authorities caught a foreigner smuggling out one of their top-secret maps to the Indes, the foreigner would be executed. And in wartime, traitors have always smuggled out maps showing military encampments and defenses. They put the maps inside their underwear, their boots, you name it, to give to the enemy."

"Traitors smuggled maps, huh?"

"Yes, and some Mennonites who were emigrating to this country were afraid they wouldn't be able to bring over seeds of the winter wheat they'd raised in Ukraine."

"But we have winter wheat all over the Midwest in this country."

"We do *now*," Arch said patiently, "because the Mennonites brought the seeds over with them. Not all of them hid the seeds, but some did."

"So, where'd they put them?"

"In their clothes, Mom. Now please, I need to study."

I told him good luck on the exam and hung up. So spies had smuggled out maps to trade routes, war traitors had smuggled out maps in their undies, and some of the Mennonites had concealed seeds in their clothes, eh? I'd once caught a guest trying to steal a whole beef tenderloin from a party. He'd stuck it down his pants, but when he moved, it had slipped to the floor. I'd picked it up and firmly asked him to leave. Marla, who'd been attending, had called after him, "George, we knew that wasn't all *you* in there!"

Thinking of that party, and of Marla and her antics, made me realize again how lonely I felt. I glanced at the clock: half past eight. Well, I knew what would make me feel better, or at least warm things up: *cooking*.

There really wasn't anything left to do except prep the lettuce that would line the plates for the garden club's strawberry salads. I washed the leaves and wrapped them. Nine o'clock. Time had been passing too fast, and now it was going too slowly.

I decided to add another dish to the garden-club ladies' buffet. I mean, what was a ladies' lunch without a molded salad? A friend in the Episcopal Church Women had shared a recipe for a holiday molded salad that was made from lime Jell-O, mayonnaise, horseradish, sliced bananas, and crushed pineapple. It sounded weird but was actually luscious—and festive. I hunted up the ingredients, drained and boiled the pineapple juice, mixed in the Jell-O until it dissolved, then stirred in everything else and poured the concoction into several oiled molds. I put the molds in the walk-in, then stared at the marble counter Tom had so lovingly installed. I glanced at the clock for at least the sixth time since he'd left: 10:30. He must still be in his meeting.

But he hadn't called, as he usually did. Dammit to hell. Fighting with the Jerk for seven years had made me quail at the prospect of marital conflict. I didn't know how to handle it, because before I could get close to handling anything, the Jerk had always slapped my face and yelled at me to shut up!

I forced myself to check my computer. Was there anything else that needed doing for the luncheon? There was not. At some point, the police would have to let me into the library to retrieve the dishes, silverware, and linens I'd set up for the breakfast . . . but I imagined that wouldn't be any time in the immediate future. Luckily, I had plenty more where those had come from.

I clicked over to my calendar. The MacArthurs' dinner loomed. I'd promised Hermie a genuine twelve-boy curry. Unfortunately, I suddenly remembered, I didn't have the main dish put together, and on the condiment side, I was still a few boys short.

The previous evening, I'd prepared, strained, and chilled the chicken stock. This morning, I'd defatted the stock. The chicken I'd used to make the stock was also going to form the base for the curry . . . as soon as I could skin and bone all those thighs. I put on my plastic gloves and got to work.

There's nothing quite like skinning and boning cooked chicken thighs to concentrate the mind. The work was tedious and dull, and required none of the aesthetic sense and skill one needed to prepare a *salade composée,* nor the culinary know-how involved in making soufflés or timbales. For the fiftieth time, I mentally ran through the events I'd witnessed at the library.

I'd been setting up when Arch and a bald fellow had become embroiled in an altercation. Then I'd noticed someone stalking through the shelves at the back of the library, and right after that, I'd seen Sandee, or someone who looked just like her, at the windows. Had she been the one creeping around the stacks? I thought so. A few minutes later, the emergency exit alarm had gone off. I'd heard Roberta moaning for help. We'd lowered Drew Wellington to the floor. I hadn't been able to find a pulse.

Then Neil Tharp, Drew's assistant or business partner or whatever he was, had demanded information from me. So had Elizabeth Wellington. I hadn't given them any.

I also went over what I'd learned: that Marla said Drew had had woman problems, and that the cops still thought Sandee was dead. Plus, the cops had led me to believe that there was some kind of scandal associated with Drew Wellington's election defeat. And it wasn't just trying to get the news of his DUI hushed up. Okay, I was speculating . . . but could there have been something else? Something worse than what had come out in the news? Unfortunately, I hadn't had the presence of mind to ask Tom about it once we'd gotten home.

Also, Drew had been receiving threatening e-mails, and Patricia Ingersoll and Drew Wellington had been an item. But for some reason, Drew had complained into a cell phone that his ex-wife and his *girlfriends*, plural, were making life difficult for him. Who were the girlfriends? Or had he just been boasting?

And then Patricia had come over, sobbing and asking for help, because she was scared. She'd had lots to say about Drew's enemies, including the fact that she thought Drew was being followed. Drew and his partner, Neil, were on the outs. But before she could go into much detail, she'd been arrested.

Which you had to admit, was pretty darn quick. A bloody X-Acto knife had been found in Patricia's house? Someone was going to an awful lot of trouble to get Patricia arrested before Drew Wellington's body was even cold.

I placed all the chicken morsels into a large vat, covered it, and placed the vat into the walk-in. Then I chopped apples and onions and sautéed them in butter and curry powder. The luscious, pungent aroma perfumed the air. I added flour, cooked it into a roux, and added judicious amounts of stock until the sauce was thick. Then it was time for adding whipping cream. Patricia Ingersoll wouldn't have approved, but my mind screamed, *Yum!*

I retrieved the vat of chicken, stirred all the morsels into the sauce, and set the whole thing aside to cool. Then I opened a new file in my computer. I titled it simply *Drew,* then wrote down all the things I knew and all the things I wanted to know. At the top of the list was: Did I in fact see Sandee Brisbane? After she killed my ex-husband and confessed to the crime, had she indeed escaped through a burning forest? If so, then why in the world was she back in Aspen Meadow? Because Sandee or her look-alike wanted something from Drew Wellington, I guessed. But if so, what? I stared at the screen.

Sandee's parents were dead. Tom had told me her boyfriend was long gone back to Nashville and was living with another woman. But Sandee Brisbane had graduated from Aspen Meadow High School; I'd seen her photo in a yearbook. Not only that, but she'd worked at the Rainbow Strip Club. So I was willing to bet that *somebody* in town knew more about Sandee than law enforcement did.

I thought I heard a noise outside, and I jumped. What was the matter with me? I did a check of the security system: everything was turned on and working. Was my paranoia exploding because I was upset about Drew? No, I told myself. I'd seen dead people before. I was married to a homicide investigator; I knew the nature of his work. But this thing with Sandee was personal. She'd killed my ex-husband, in revenge for raping her when she was a hospital patient. Now I believed she was back, and I was afraid.

At midnight, my brain and body gave out, so I showered and went to bed. Much later, I registered Tom running the bathwater. The clock said it was just before two. When he rustled the sheets, I asked if he wanted to talk. He said no, and mumbled something about being wanted down at the department first thing in the morning. The county pathologist and the coroner were working overtime tonight.

"I don't want this case to come between us," I whispered once the lights were out.

Tom pulled me in for a long hug, his cool, slightly damp skin next to my already warm body. It was delicious and made me shiver with delight. He murmured, "Nothing will come between us." Then he fell asleep.

The next morning, Tom was up even before our alarm went off at five. By half past five, I was standing in our kitchen, bleary-eyed and foggy-brained, tapping my foot as I waited for the espresso machine to hurry up and heat.

"I'm afraid to ask how much of that stuff you've had in the past twenty-four hours, Miss G." Tom's voice startled me. "You should try some of the coffee from our department machine. That'd cure your addiction in a hurry."

"Thanks for the words of encouragement," I replied as the twin ropes of espresso finally began spurting into my cup. "Remember, you promised to tell me if you found out anything significant."

"So how do you define *significant,* wife? That there was so much snow outside the library emergency exit, we couldn't even tell how many people had been there?"

"I want to know if I did indeed see Sandee Brisbane at the library. She killed John Richard and she could go after Arch."

Tom's ski parka made a silky brushing sound as he put it on. "That proves my point: that you are not the person to try to search for someone you think was stalking Drew Wellington." He gave me a serious look. "Drew was a prosecutor. We're going to look at everything, Goldy, which means you don't have to."

"You're going to have your cell phone on today?"

"Are you planning on calling me while I'm meeting with my lieutenant? Or when I'm listening to the coroner give his report?"

"Okay, okay." I sipped some espresso, then allowed myself to be kissed on both cheeks.

At the door, Tom said, "Look, the temperature dropped like a bomb last night. It's two below zero out there, and I want to make sure your van starts."

"I'm just going to Marla's. Hopefully, folks will have gotten the word that the library shindig is at her place."

"You're not going anywhere if your engine doesn't turn over, Miss G. Give me your keys, okay?"

"Sure. Thanks." I rooted around in my purse until I found my key chain. Once Tom was out the door, I tossed my espresso, which had gotten cold. Then I steamed some whipping cream, pulled a second double espresso, and combined the two into a hot, foamy mass. If it was that cold outside, I could work off the extra calories trucking my stuff to and fro.

Back to business. I sipped my drink and printed out the day's menus. My walk-in revealed the wrapped grapefruits, ingredients for the cheese pies, and ham. I hustled these, along with the hotel pans of French toast, that also required an egg mixture—this one containing Grand Marnier—that I would bake at Marla's house. The trays of Christmas Carol Coffee Cake and Bleak House Bars looked passable, despite Boyd's premature decimating of same. It was good I always made plenty of food. Besides, if the weather was as cold as Tom had said it was, we might see very few folks at Marla's place. Once the temperature dropped below zero, Aspen Meadow folks tended to weave themselves inside cocoons.

Outside, I gasped as the wind bit more shrewdly than it ever had in northern Denmark. Out in the driveway, my van, which was running, exhaled plumes of exhaust. Thank goodness for Tom, who had already taken off in his Chrysler. Balancing the box with the grapefruit and pie ingredients, I moved forward too quickly, and my boots slipped on the stepping-stones. I plunked into a stone wall and barely avoided crashing into one of Tom's lovingly developed beds of *Lamium maculatum,* now blanketed with white. Once I'd righted myself, I inhaled more of the crystalline air and blinked. All around, every tree branch was perfectly coated with snow. But some of it was blowing into my mouth as I started forward, slid again, uttered an obscenity, and finally heaved the box into the rear of the van.

It was a miracle that I managed to load the food by quarter past seven and start out for Marla's place, over on the upper-crust side of town. On Main Street, even though it was early on a Saturday morning, I knew I had to be extra careful, as it was hard to see a thing, including any vehicles that might loom in front or in back of me. Snow blew in great swaths across the pavement, occasionally completely enclosing my vehicle. I couldn't see how close the car behind me was, or worse, what vehicle might suddenly heave into view. Once I had to brake when a delivery truck appeared out of nowhere. The grille of a pickup loomed in my rearview mirror, and I thought he was going to hit me. It was one of those old trucks you see all the time in Colorado, remnants of the fifties, I supposed. Anyway, I sure hoped the driver had had his brakes checked in the intervening decades.

"Thank God you made it," my best friend greeted me when I pounded up her front steps and hit the doorbell with its brass-engraved nameplate: *Chez Marla.* "Come on, I've already got my coffee machine going."

Marla's was undoubtedly the only place where I would feel entitled to show up at the front door, and where the hostess would offer me time to warm up and have a hot drink, in this case another double espresso stirred with cream and spoonfuls of designer fudge sauce. I hugged my friend, took a sip of the drink she offered, and promised to finish it in a bit. Then I backed the van up to the garage doors. Marla offered to help unload the boxes, but I begged her to stay put and field phone calls, in case folks from the library staff were confused as to whether the breakfast was still on, and where it would be held.

"I've already heard from half a dozen people who aren't coming," Marla admitted, her voice rueful.

"I don't want to know any more, it'll just depress me. Let me finish with these boxes, and I can start cooking."

Marla, who wore a red-and-green-plaid taffeta hostess gown, insisted on taking each box as I arrived at her back door. Once inside my friend's kitchen, I marveled, as usual, that it was so well equipped—two Viking stoves, a pair of ovens, and three sinks—not to mention great expanses of black granite sparkling with veins of white quartz. Marla had had all of it installed the last time she'd done a remodeling. I always found myself annoyed as well as jealous of this opulence, because Marla did not even cook. But I found this same phenomenon in other houses where I catered. The larger and more luxurious the kitchen, the less likely it was that either husband or wife did anything more in there than make coffee and mix cocktails. Still, I had learned to revel in these situations, because it meant these folks were in ever more dire need of a caterer.

I put on my apron, washed my hands, and preheated the ovens. Marla shook a finger at me.

"You didn't tell me Patricia Ingersoll had been arrested."

"You didn't ask."

"Cut the crap, Goldy. And what's that stuff you started to tell me about Sandee Brisbane?"

I worked at unwrapping the ingredients for the cheese pies. "I thought I saw Sandee Brisbane out by Regal Ridge a few weeks ago. Then I thought I saw her at the library last night." Marla's eyes widened and her mouth dropped. Silence fell in the kitchen, an unusual occurrence whenever you were with Marla. "You didn't find *that* out from the country-club set you've been calling, did you?"

"Sandee survived the fire in the wildlife preserve? How? And if she did, where's she been for the last six months? Not to mention, why would she come back here?"

"All good questions, Marla, for which I have no answers." I mixed the ingredients for the pies and placed them in one oven, then put the ham on a roasting pan and slid it into the other oven. Finally I eyed the pans of French toast. Did Grand Marnier lose its taste or alcohol content if it sat overnight in the refrigerator, suspended in an egg mixture? "Will you taste a piece of French toast if I fry it up quickly for you?" I asked Marla, interrupting her interrogation.

"Is there sand in the Sahara?"

I hunted for—and quickly found—a never-used, and undoubtedly prohibitively expensive, copper sauté pan. Once I had several pats of butter sizzling, I dropped in two egg-and-Grand-Marnier-soaked pieces of brioche. Meanwhile, Marla interrogated me on whether the sheriff's department believed Sandee was back, and by the way, what had they found out about Patricia Ingersoll that had led to her arrest?

"You never tell me anything," she complained as she snitched a corner of unsliced brioche.

"I tell you everything," I countered, "if you just give me a chance."

"By the way, Louise Munsinger called this morning to say Drew was indeed going to marry Patricia, but there was a problem. Something with Elizabeth, she thought. Did you know that?"

"No. Did you get any details?"

"Oh, Louise didn't know any," Marla said, her voice grumpy.

"If you learn something, it might help Patricia," I replied. "Also, we need to find out as much as we can about Sandee Brisbane—"

"Is that French toast about done?"

As it turns out, Grand Marnier does *not* lose its flavor or its proof value if it sits overnight. While Marla made *mm-mm* noises, I bit into the rich toast, with its crunchy exterior and warm, meltingly moist interior. There are rewards to catering, and one of them is that your delight in food can be indulged from time to time.

"You ought to mix Grand Marnier into the syrup, too," Marla mused as she finished up her piece. "And then serve some more of the liqueur neat, on the side? Once the librarians have a few bites and sips, you'll be able to find out if there's anything they aren't telling you about the demise of Drew Wellington. Maybe something they saw on the surveillance camera?"

"Whatever was recorded on the surveillance camera was turned right over to law enforcement, I can assure you." I rinsed my dish and thought of something I hadn't asked Marla. "Why was Louise Munsinger, of all people, calling you early this morning? She wasn't at the library."

"Noooo, but she does have a cell phone, and somebody who was driving by the library last night saw your van there, and then found out what had happened. So Louise was calling me, as your titular best friend, to find out if you'd still be catering the garden-club luncheon today."

"Why didn't she just call me?" I asked, irritated. "Of course I'm doing my planned events." I glanced around at the morning's offerings. French toast and cheese pies, coffee cake, ham, and chocolate bars. *Fat brings them back* was an adage quietly passed between caterers. No kidding. I didn't have a single client who would love my potatoes au gratin if I used skim milk and low-fat cheese. Just the thought made me ill.

Insomuch as my thoughts could be called a chain, Marla broke it. "I don't know Louise Munsinger well, but once I got her talking, she was a font of useful information. She'd already talked to Hermie MacArthur, who is extremely upset that Neil Tharp invited himself to her party tonight. To fill in for the missing Drew Wellington, apparently."

I sighed. So much for honoring your dead boss by doing a bit of grieving.

I looked in on the ham, which was sputtering, spitting, and filling Marla's kitchen with an inviting scent. I placed the liqueur-soaked brioche underneath it. Onward and upward, as they say.

"This is not the first time this has happened to me," I said. "Somebody dies, and all of a sudden someone jumps in to take their place at a party? That feels weird. Why not just say it's okay to be one person short?"

"Don't ask me." She was neatly folding forks, knives, and spoons into snowy-white cotton napkins. "And to talk about map collecting, ugh. The only time I need a map is when I'm driving a rental car without a navigation system." She began to arrange the wrapped silverware in a napkin-lined basket. "Still, there's going to be a lot of big money around that table. A lot of big, *unattached* money."

"Unattached to another worthy investment, you mean?"

"Yup." She did a little dance around her kitchen. "Hermie should have invited me to fill in for Drew. Then we could have had some fun at that party tonight, instead of being forced to listen to boring old Smithfield give a geography lesson and talk about his acquisitions. Double ugh." She two-stepped over to her stereo closet. "I'm going to turn on some music." Marla may not have used her kitchen, but she knew how to make Frank Sinatra sound as if he was in the next room.

I checked the ovens. The toast was golden, and the cheese pies were rising. Since none of the library folks were here yet, I turned down the temperature, as I wanted to make a dramatic entrance with the puffed pies, which had a tendency to deflate pretty quickly. Once the French toast and ham were out, I could turn that oven to broil, so I could quickly do the grapefruit topped with brown sugar. When the doorbell rang, I prayed that everyone was arriving en masse so that I could bring the hot food out all at once. This was a caterer's favorite wish, which rarely came true.

Meanwhile, Marla's phone beeped, and she trilled that she needed to go answer it.

"Do you want me to get the door?" I asked.

"No!" Marla cried over her shoulder. Then she hollered in the direction of the front door, "It's open!"

Oh, marvelous, I thought.

I retrieved the ham and placed it on Marla's elegant buffet. This particular piece of furniture was a polished antique cherrywood piece that would have made Tom chartreuse with envy. Marla had set it beautifully with white linens and Versace china, and placed an enormous basket arrangement of holly, ivy, and red-and-gold bows in the center. In fact, her entire house looked gorgeously festive, with spruce ropes laid across every available surface, and bubbling lights strung in front of each window. She had Aspen Meadow Floral come in every year to do the decorating, which she oversaw to the last detail. When the florist had finally left, she'd called to say, "The Christmas season is so exhausting!"

The doorbell rang again, with no Marla to answer it. I cursed under my breath and hustled back toward the front door. As I was racing into the foyer, Roberta Krepinski stepped into my path.

"Roberta!" I cried.

"Yes?" The reference librarian's eyes were rimmed with pink and her cheeks were puffy. Her red hair was caught up in a cotton-candy froth of ponytail, as if she hadn't had time to fix it this morning. I doubted she'd gotten much sleep. I hadn't known she wore contacts, but clearly she did, and hadn't been able to find them or get them into her eyes this morning. Instead, she wore glasses with rectangular lenses the size of dominoes. They made her look older and more authoritarian.

"I'm not doing well," she said.

"Okay. Why don't you sit down, have a cup of coffee? You look really—"

"The police have closed the library until Sunday. In spite of the snow, journalists are swarming all over the place and slipping down the hill behind the reading room." She stopped to catch her breath. "This morning I had chest pains, and I don't feel good—"

At which point she collapsed forward and passed out in my arms.

7

I cursed anorexia as I struggled to keep rail-thin, ultra-light Roberta from cracking her head on Marla's stone foyer. She was oddly unwieldy. I screamed for Marla to bring some smelling salts or a bottle of ammonia to the door. When Marla rushed into her foyer a moment later, she was holding a bottle of peroxide.

"It's all I had," she said apologetically. "What's the matter with Roberta?"

"She fainted." I clasped Roberta while staring at the peroxide bottle. Did it have a strong scent? I couldn't remember. "Look, Marla, would you please open the bottle?"

"You're going to do her hair? It'll come out looking like crap."

"Marla, for heaven's sake!" I gently turned Roberta onto her back, so that she was resting on a slender Oriental rug. Then I lifted her head. "Okay, now run the top of the bottle under her nose, all right?"

"It doesn't smell like anything," Marla protested, giving the open bottle an experimental sniff.

"Then go look for some ammonia, would you, *please?*"

"I'm not going rummaging around in my cleaning lady's supply closet!" she protested. "I wouldn't even know what to look for." She eyed me passing the bottle slowly under Roberta's nose. "You spill that stuff on my Khirman runner, I'll sue you for all you're worth." And off she dashed to hunt for ammonia.

When she returned with the ammonia and a shot glass, she did the pouring honors herself, then traded the shot glass for the peroxide bottle. This time when I ran the head-clearing liquid under the librarian's nose, she sputtered.

"Oh, golly, what happened?" Roberta asked, her voice weak. She blinked at me, then looked quizzically up at Marla. "I just had this terrible nightmare—" When we shook our heads, she said, "Oh, okay, it wasn't a dream." She groaned. "Let me get up."

I handed the ammonia to Marla, who disappeared with it. Then I stood up and helped Roberta to her feet. She wobbled slightly, lifted her chin, and pressed her lips together. She looked so young, so innocent, and so wounded, my heart went out to her. She said, "I'm sorry to be so Victorian. Fainting, for crying out loud. Well, I haven't had anything to eat. And I was just so upset . . ."

"Let's get some food in you first." I moved toward the kitchen, where I still had work to do. "Want some coffee?"

Roberta followed me and sat reluctantly at Marla's black granite breakfast island. "Two investigators came to my house. They said Drew Wellington was dead, and that he'd been, uh, murdered."

I nodded.

"Then Neil Tharp called me." Her voice went from brittle to shaky. "He said Patricia Ingersoll was arrested for killing Drew." When I again signaled the truth of this, she went on: "He wanted to know if I'd seen Patricia at the library."

"Well, I'm not sure that—"

"Do the police have evidence that Patricia did this?" Roberta asked, her voice insistent.

"I suppose they do, or she wouldn't have been arrested," I replied. "But I have a feeling she'll be cleared soon."

"Why do you have that feeling?" Roberta asked, her chin trembling. "Does that mean the police will be looking for even more evidence, and the library will be closed even longer while they pull up the carpeting?" She retrieved a crumpled tissue from a pocket of her sweater, a belted baggy gray knit that had seen not just better days, but better years. Roberta blew her nose, then raised those pained red eyes at me. "Patricia was in the library that afternoon, but it was much earlier. Neil Tharp, Drew Wellington's business partner, was there, too. I'm not sure about Elizabeth Wellington, although the police did ask me about her." She blushed with sudden guilt. She patted the frizz around her ponytail and avoided my eyes. "Oh dear, I'm not supposed to divulge when patrons come in, or even who's in the library at any time."

I carefully picked up the second pan of soaked brioche and put it into the oven. "Just tell the police what you know. And only the police," I added.

"I did, I *did*." She glanced around the kitchen, as if she'd just noticed we were alone. "Where is the rest of the library staff? The volunteers?"

"That I can't tell you, because I haven't a clue."

Roberta, sitting on one of Marla's elegant leather stools, slumped in defeat. She kneaded the corners of her ragged sweater, lifted her head to gaze around Marla's kitchen—made immaculate by the absent cleaning lady—and knitted her brow into deep lines, as if she expected the rest of the guests to jump out from the cabinets.

"Remember I told you Neil Tharp called me early this morning?" Roberta asked, her voice still sour. "Well. In addition to telling me that Patricia had been arrested and asking me if she'd been in the library, he *also* said Elizabeth Wellington wanted to know if I'd found any papers beside Drew's body. He was asking on her behalf, he said, and he demanded to know what the surveillance camera had recorded. Did he think I picked up stray documents and was even allowed to see what the police had downloaded from our video system? No, I stayed up all night worrying about the library."

Roberta began to weep quietly. What was with Neil Tharp, anyway? Why was he teaming up with Elizabeth Wellington? Had Neil's association with Elizabeth, whatever it was, been the reason Drew didn't trust him anymore, as Patricia had told me? Or was Neil just trying to protect the map business's assets in the wake of Drew's death? With Elizabeth Wellington's influential fund-raising contacts, though, surely they could have bothered someone official to find out the status of the investigation. Why hound me, or a defenseless librarian who didn't eat enough and was prone to fainting spells?

I tried to make my voice as soothing as possible. "Roberta, could I please fix you an espresso, cup of coffee, something like that?"

She sniffed and stowed her tissue. "I'd rather have tea, if you don't mind. Herbal, if it's available."

I delved into my beverage supply box for tea bags, started water heating, then sat down next to Roberta. "I hope you didn't tell Neil Tharp what you knew. In fact, you shouldn't be telling anyone a single thing about what you saw in the library yesterday. Did the sheriff's-department investigators not remind you of that?" I asked gently.

She groaned. "Yes, yes, of course they did. And no, I didn't tell Neil Tharp a thing. But he's not my real problem." Her red-rimmed eyes sought mine. "The library is my problem. Here's what will happen," Roberta went on. "People will start calling me, demanding to know what's what. They'll hit the button for the reference desk. When I answer, they'll say, 'Didja see my fourth-grade teacher at the library on Friday? Maybe she did it, and now she'll go to jail.' I wish I could make a sign that said, 'Please don't ask us about the investigation.' But I can't, because then folks who haven't heard about Drew Wellington will say, 'What investigation?' Another problem we're going to have is voyeurs, people asking us, 'Where was he killed? Where was he sitting? Is this his blood on the carpet?' " Roberta exhaled and nodded her thanks as I placed the tea in front of her.

"You saw blood?"

"Yes."

I paused. "I wasn't sure what I saw."

"You weren't right up next to his chest." She sipped her tea. "Well, I don't suppose I need to worry about all the phone calls and nosy visitors if they keep the library closed for more than a few days." When she looked at me questioningly, the red veins in her eyes were hugely magnified behind the rectangular lenses. "Goldy, people *rely* on us. If I'm going to have a life again, I need to go back to work. I want to help people order books from other libraries. I want to work on the book sale. We have CDs, DVDs, and all kinds of stuff to organize and price! I can't just stay home!"

Marla tiptoed into the kitchen behind Roberta's stool. Her eyebrows rose as far as they would go as she pointed at me and mouthed, *I need you.*

"Roberta," I said, "calm down. Everything is going to be okay." Marla stepped boldly into the kitchen as if she'd just arrived. Roberta was honking into her tissue again. I said, "You'll reopen soon and be able to do all that work. And please. My husband would emphasize how important it is that you *not talk* to anyone about what patrons you saw or didn't see at the library yesterday, afternoon or morning. If you think of anything you haven't told the investigators, you need to write it down. They'll be interested."

"I'm interested," Marla said brightly.

Roberta dug in her sweater pocket for more tissues. I patted her awkwardly on the back. She went on as if she hadn't heard me: "I feel as if everything is bearing down on me. I'm not married, no kids, not even a pet. I have nobody to talk to." She began to sob again.

Marla and I exchanged a glance. Marla shrugged. I took a deep breath.

"Okay, okay, maybe it would help you if we talk about it a little," I said. "Do you know how long Drew was at the library?"

Roberta swallowed. "He comes, came, in every Friday, to meet with clients."

"Why?" Marla asked before Roberta had even had time to answer my question.

Roberta's eyebrows climbed her forehead. "Drew told me his neighbors in Flicker Ridge didn't appreciate him having a retail business in his home. They complained about the clients' cars parked in front of their houses and informed him through their lawyers that he needed to rent an office or a store. He wasn't ready to do that, he told me, so was it okay for him to meet with clients at the library? Strictly speaking, he shouldn't have been conducting for-profit business in the library." She sighed.

"But he said he was tutoring his clients, too, at no cost to them! He was so nice and so charming, I said yes."

"So," I interjected, "when did he come in yesterday?"

"I'm not sure exactly what time he arrived, but he asked me for help with an atlas around three. I remember, because it was before school let out, and I'm always watching the clock because of the onslaught of kids we get wanting books before the weekend."

"And the video?" Marla asked eagerly.

"Marla!" I protested.

"There's not much to tell." Roberta's tone was apologetic. "The sheriff's department made a DVD from our one surveillance camera. They downloaded everything from when Drew arrived at the library to the time when the police arrived." She moaned. "People in the grocery store are going to stop me and say, 'What was Drew reading, kiddie porn?'"

People to see. An atlas. Hmm. Like Marla, I was overcome with curiosity. What people? An atlas of what territory? But that was just the sort of thing Tom did not want me to ask the librarian, dammit. I was also desperate to find out if Roberta knew Sandee, and if so, had she thought *Sandee* was at the library the previous afternoon? Was Sandee one of the people Drew was supposed to meet? Had she shown up on the surveillance recording?

I was clear on one thing. If I was going to find out what Sandee was doing at the library, and if I was going to help Patricia, I'd need to know what exactly Drew had been doing at the library. Meeting with what clients? Also, I'd have to remind Tom to find out about the atlas.

The doorbell rang again. Roberta looked into her teacup. Marla raised her eyebrows at me, more insistently this time. I still had the grapefruit to broil, and I had to watch it every second. Plus, I had to keep an eye on the second pan of French toast. What did she want me to do, answer the door, too? If not, then what in the world did she need to talk to me about?

"People are going to descend on me," Roberta moaned. "I'll never have a moment's peace."

Marla exhaled and scampered out while I preheated the broiler. At the sound of voices, I slid in the pan of Great Expectations Grapefruit. Roberta Krepinski still stared into her teacup.

"Roberta," I said finally. "Anybody asks you questions in the grocery store, at the gym, or anyplace else, you say, 'The sheriff's department has asked me not to talk about Friday afternoon.' Period. I know it was a shock, but you'll feel better soon, I promise. Why don't you go to the bathroom and splash some water on your face? Then you can come out and greet your staff and volunteers, who have traveled through the snow to come to the breakfast."

"What about the crime scene itself?" she asked, turning to me. "Who's going to clean that up?" Once again, she appeard distraught. "There was blood on Drew's chest, and it was oozing . . . Will the sheriff's department disinfect the area?"

"Blood oozing?" When Roberta didn't answer, I dug out my address book, nabbed a piece of Marla's lilac-colored stationery, and scribbled the number for Front Range Cleanup.

"All right," I said, my voice filled with more confidence than I felt. "When the cops are done, if that corner is still a mess, you place a piece of heavy-duty opaque plastic over the chair and the floor, and seal it all with duct tape. Put a big 'Do Not Touch' sign on the plastic. Then you call these guys"—I tapped the paper—"and they'll come out and fix you up."

Roberta drained her teacup and took the paper. She looked dubious. I wondered how she'd feel when she called the cleaning company and they showed up in their white truck with their motto emblazoned in black on the side: "Front Range Cleanup—You Squash It, We Wash It."

★ ★ ★

Only five of the library staff and one of the volunteers ended up at Marla's, in spite of the library trustees having faithfully called everyone to tell them about the change of venue. I wasn't surprised, because I didn't believe just the weather would keep people away. When a violent crime upsets the calm of a community, especially a small town, folks tend to withdraw. They're afraid, and I don't blame them. Compound murder with deep snow and unplowed side streets, and you had a recipe for party disaster.

Still in all, we had a nice breakfast. The food was wonderful, if I do say so myself, and the library folks tried to do a stiff-upper-lip routine. But there were long, glum silences, and in the end, folks didn't eat very much. The staff assured me they would carefully store all the serving dishes, china, and silverware I had had to leave in the reading room. I promised *them* that the sheriff's department in general, and my husband in particular, would get the library reopened with all possible haste, and we could have *another* party. We'd have it just the way this one was supposed to be. They shook their heads, not comforted. When the last staff member finally traipsed back to her car carrying pans of leftovers, I turned to Marla. I hadn't had even a minute to visit with her since Roberta had spilled her guts to us.

"After we revived Roberta, what did you need to talk to me about?"

Marla crossed her arms. "Cecie Rowley called me back. I'd asked her to find out what she could about Patricia and Drew, and she says she just heard that the two of them were going to get married on New Year's Eve, in the Bahamas."

"That's interesting. I'll call Tom and tell him."

"He'll love talking to Cecie, I promise."

While I put in a call to Tom's voice mail, Marla started to clean up. Once I was off my cell, I began to pack up the last pans of leftover food.

"Forget that," Marla said. "Just take the desserts. The pies won't keep, and I'll freeze the ham. Or maybe I'll bring ham biscuits to St. Luke's tomorrow. I'll say, 'Have some goodies from the ill-fated library scene-of-the-crime breakfast!' "

"Please don't." When she didn't answer, I said, "Marla? Come on. Don't."

"You're such a fuddy-duddy, Goldy. And after all I've done for you. 'Gee, Marla,' " she mimicked, " 'thanks for offering your house for the library breakfast! Don't know what I would have done without you!' " Her mischievous glance caught mine. "Don't you have another catering event to do? I'll see you there." And with that, she shooed me off to my conference center.

She was right. I did have the garden-club ladies coming all too soon.

Fortunately, the weather had cleared, and only a few puffs of cloud moved across an enormous expanse of blue sky. I traipsed along the path made by the fellow Marla pays to use his snowblower on her driveway, then revved up the van. Julian had promised to meet me at the center, thank goodness, and maybe he'd been lucky and found another server. He would also be helping out with tonight's dinner. And somewhere in there I needed to take a pill that would give me another eight hours' sleep.

My cell phone buzzed as I was coming up to the waterfall, where the lake empties into Lower Cotton-wood Creek. The top of the waterfall looked spec-tacular, like an enormous abstract sculpture. In actuality, it was ice that had attached itself to the dam's cement structure.

"Yes?" I barked into the phone. If somebody was asking me for information about Drew Wellington's murder, they'd get a much more frosty reception than they had from Roberta Krepinski.

SWEET REVENGE · 157

"Miss G.?" Tom's calm, reassuring voice filled my chest with warmth. "Didn't it go very well with the librarians?"

"There was hardly anybody there, but it went fine. Did you get my message?"

"Y'mean about Drew and Patricia? Apparently there were a lot of rumors about that." I told him about Cecie Rowley, and he said, "We've been hearing that they were going to get married at St. Luke's and have the reception at the Aspen Meadow Country Club, or else they were going to get married at the county courthouse and have the reception in the Bahamas. According to Drew's neighbors over in Flicker Ridge, they might have been married already, or at least they sure seemed to be on their honeymoon. One nosy lady has her kitchen window facing Drew's big house, and she said Patricia was coming out the door early in the morning, every morning. Drew would catch her there on his porch and give her a long kiss. Including yesterday morning," Tom added. "According to this neighbor, Patricia used to take his face in her hands and rub his cheeks just as she was leaving. She'd laugh and say, 'Now go shave!'"

"This neighbor managed to see and hear a lot."

Tom grunted. "And was proud of it. She spearheaded the movement to force him to meet clients at the library.

But even with his business moved elsewhere, this gal still used binoculars to spy on Drew. She even had a special device from an electronics store that amplifies sound."

I braked for a gaggle of skaters who were crossing the road from the lake's overflow parking lot. Our local rec center ran the skating at Aspen Meadow Lake, and the area where folks were allowed to don their blades was at least half a mile away. This must mean, I realized dully, that the Lake House's own parking lot was full, which would also mean that skaters would be leaving their vehicles in the lot of my conference center, which was only a few hundred yards from the Lake House. If the garden-club ladies didn't have room for their cars, I was going to have to call a tow truck to remove the intruders' vehicles. I rubbed my forehead.

"Goldy? You there? Did you pick up anything else at that breakfast?"

"Roberta Krepinski, the reference librarian who found Drew, told me some things. She's really shaken up by what happened. But I think you already know most of them from her. She said Patricia and Neil were definitely in the library yesterday afternoon—were they on the surveillance video?"

"I don't know yet. What else?"

"Well, Drew Wellington told Roberta he was at the library to meet some people."

"Some people, plural?"

"That's what he told her. Then he asked Roberta to help him with an atlas around three o'clock, she thinks."

"She didn't tell us about the atlas or that he was having a meeting. She just said that she saw him in the library that afternoon."

"I guess she didn't realize it was important, or she forgot. She's not in very good shape."

"An atlas, huh? Did she say what kind of atlas he wanted?"

"No, but if you ask her about it, maybe it will jog her memory."

"Anything else that might help us?"

"Roberta seemed pretty worried about how long you'd keep the library closed and what to do about the blood on the carpet. But the big news is that Neil Tharp called her early this morning and said he was representing both himself and Elizabeth Wellington, just the way he did with me last night. He demanded to know two things: what papers of Drew's they found at the library, and what the surveillance camera showed."

Tom paused. "So. We have an atlas and papers we don't know about, and we have folks being nosy about the surveillance video, all while inviting themselves to an upscale party. Seems folks want to divulge more to you and Marla than they're willing to tell us."

"What do you mean?"

Tom took a deep breath. "Oh, it's all premature at this point. They're doing the autopsy now. Photographing everything they have, that kind of thing."

"Photographing everything they have? What do they have?"

"Miss G."

But my curiosity, piqued before and now positively raging, would not be so easily dismissed. When the light turned green, I gunned the engine. The van shot up the hill past the ice-crusted waterfall. "Tell me what you're talking about. What have they found? And does it explain why Sandee was in the library? Does it tend to exonerate Patricia?"

"*Tend to exonerate,* listen to my wife. Ah, I don't know. The guys didn't seem to think it meant anything." He paused. "You know I collect antiques."

"Of course I do," I said impatiently.

"Well, one of the things we took out of Drew Wellington's inside coat pocket was a map."

"A map?"

"Yes. Looks to me like a very old and *valuable* map."

8

Are you sure it's an old and valuable map?"

"Could be a doodle. Maybe it's an abstract painting, one of those things that looks the same whether it's right side up or upside down."

"*Tom.*" I pulled into my event center lot. I concentrated on weaving the van between about fifteen haphazardly parked vehicles—all left, no doubt, by folks who'd gone to the lake. I shook my head. "Do you think Drew had the map in his coat to sell to these clients he was going to see?"

"Well, now that we know he was meeting someone or ones at the library, we can try to find out. We're working on tracing the map and how Drew may have ended up with it."

I took a deep breath. "Have you found out anything about Sandee? Has anyone else seen her?"

"We're working on it, but so far, we've come up empty."

"How's Patricia doing?"

"Miss G. The jail is not a hotel. The guests don't call down here to tell us how they're doing."

"Tom," I said suddenly, "do you know if there's any other scandal associated with Drew Wellington, aside from him trying to get news of his DUI suppressed?" He paused a bit too long. "Tom? Are you there?"

"There was something. I'm not sure what."

"What do you *think* it was?"

Another silence. "Let me dig around. If it had just involved him, then everyone wouldn't have become so tight-lipped. Miss G., I have to go. Nothing about the map to anyone, okay?"

"Of course."

I signed off, then stared at my event center. It was an old log hexagon, into which I'd—or I should say, *Tom* and I had—put much work, but which still demanded more. The sloping roof reminded me it needed to be replaced, and new gutters should be installed at the same time. Around the foundation, snow covered freshly graded soil.

Beneath *that,* there was new plumbing that had consumed a sizable chunk of earnings from Goldilocks' Catering. And now the parking lot was full of vehicles that would have to be towed away before I could make any money on a garden-club party.

But still. At this moment, when a feeling of pride swelled inside my chest just to see the place, a place I still had trouble thinking of as *my* catering and conference center, no worries could smash my optimism. The ringing of the cell phone jolted me.

"Miss G.?"

"I thought you had to go."

"Sorry I had to sign off so quickly. It was nothing. You all right?"

"As all right as I can be, after pulling into my lot and seeing it full of illegally parked cars."

"Want to talk later?"

"No, no, let me think. I still need to know what was going on with Drew Wellington so I can try to figure out why Sandee is here."

"We all need to know about Drew Wellington."

"Tell me about that map, would you?"

"It doesn't say 'Pirate Treasure Here,' if that's what you mean. I just got a glimpse of the thing, when our crime-lab guys were emptying Wellington's coat pockets. One of our guys said it looked valuable, and I agreed, but that's all we know until we call in an expert. The map appeared to have blood on it, too, so I'm not sure what we'll be able to find out from it, if anything."

"And what happens to the map now?"

"First our guys have to look at it. Then they'll photograph it and call in somebody who specializes in maps. Right now the team is doing their usual routine. They're investigating Wellington, backtracking his movements. They're going to see who his enemies were, that kind of thing. Don't worry, we'll try to figure out if this map is significant in some way."

"I want to see it."

Tom chuckled. "You're joking, right?"

"Look, Tom, remember I'm doing a curry dinner tonight at the home of Smithfield and Hermie MacArthur?"

"Remind me why this is important."

"The MacArthurs are map *collectors.* Serious ones. They're independently wealthy, and they live in that big place in Regal Ridge Country Club that I told you about. Drew was supposed to be at their dinner tonight, a party celebrating an acquisition Smithfield has made. They're still going to have it, I'm pretty sure, because no one has called me. Smithfield MacArthur is going to give a dog-and-pony show, with me serving the dinner and maybe helping in some undetermined way. Neil Tharp has invited himself, to replace Drew."

Tom muttered something under his breath.

"Anyway, perhaps Drew had the map in his pocket because he was going to take it to the party."

"I promise, our guys will check it out. I need to put you on hold for a sec."

I gazed at Aspen Meadow Lake, where ice fishermen sat expectantly beside their drilled holes. The lake, now covered with snow, had been the scene of a gruesome discovery six months ago: the body of Cecelia Brisbane, Sandee's mother, had been found inside her car, under the water. It was the theory of law enforcement that Sandee had killed her mother for not protecting her from her predatory father, and in particular, for not believing her story about what the Jerk had done to her.

Wait a minute. Earlier I'd wondered if Drew had been at the library trying to track down or get in contact with his stalker. What if, big *if* here, Drew hadn't been planning to met with clients yesterday, but with Sandee? He'd been critical in the press about how the cops had handled Sandee's case. Could it be that that article had somehow led Drew directly to Sandee? Perhaps they'd been in communication. Maybe Sandee or her look-alike had been trying to find

Drew at the library when I saw her. But if Tom thought my theory about the link to the MacArthurs and map collecting was *pie in the sky*, he'd think the theory about Drew attempting to meet with his stalker was *pie on Pluto*.

"Sorry, Miss G. I really need to go this time."

"Fine. You don't think Drew Wellington could have made an attempt to find Sandee by himself, do you?"

Tom snorted. "Unlikely. If our guys couldn't find her, it's very unlikely a D.A. no longer connected to law enforcement could locate her, I don't care how good a map he had."

I exhaled. "But you'll tell me what you find out about the map that was on him?"

"I'll see what I can do."

I told him I loved him and signed off. Then I called Gary's Garage and reluctantly requested a tow truck to get rid of the skaters' cars. As I hopped out of the van, another vehicle, what looked like an old Toyota, rumbled past the other cars in the lot. As the Toyota made its way toward where I was standing, I checked my watch. Nine o'clock? Could a woman in the Aspen Meadow Garden Club really be so eager to come for lunch that she'd show up three hours early? I set a discouraging frown onto my face, ready to tell this early arrival that her presence was not okay. As Tom had pointed out, I had work to do.

But it was not an early-arriving member of the garden club. It was Grace Mannheim, a woman I had met this past summer. She jumped out of her car and approached me with her springy step. All of her prematurely white hair fluffed out around her elfin face as she smiled at me and waved.

I liked Grace. Her sister had been killed in a hit-and-run accident in Aspen Meadow that had been anything but accidental. In working to solve that and a related crime, Grace and I had become sort-of friends. I'd learned that she was single, lived in Boulder, and played women's senior softball. I admired Grace. When I'd visited her in Boulder, she'd come up her street after I'd parked and carefully noted my van and its bumper stickers. She'd been able to tell me all about myself, my business, and my family. I thought of her as the *Daughter of Sherlock Holmes.*

Just after Thanksgiving, Julian had started renting an apartment over Grace's garage. He said she inspired him, with her dedication to senior softball—Grace was fifty-eight—demanding a year-round physical-fitness regimen. I knew what he meant. There was no question in my mind that Grace Mannheim was in much better physical shape than I, more than twenty years her junior.

This opinion was confirmed as Grace strode quickly toward me, arms pumping. She wore a ski vest over a simple white shirt and black pants, black tights, and black thick-soled shoes. The wind puffed out all the downy hair around her head as she approached me. *Hup-two, hup-two.* I felt tired just watching her.

"Grace!" I called. "What brings you here?"

"Julian said you needed help with your garden-club luncheon!"

I doubt even Noah had felt the flood of relief that washed over me at that moment. "Thank you, thank you, thank you." I hugged her. "Come on inside."

She followed me to the French doors leading to the dining-room section of the center. As I turned the key in the lock, I felt momentarily embarrassed. Grace's house had been immaculate and spare. Had I left everything in order here, in my space? Okay, yes, I was proud of having my own venue for events. Still, sometimes I thought I was exaggerating when I described this oddly built log building, formerly a restaurant, as an event center. When we walked inside, I noticed once again how the smell of grilled meats and thousands of wood fires still lingered in the air. This was true no matter how much air freshener I sprayed in the place. But when I turned on the twinkling lights that festooned the small forest of artificial Christmas trees, Grace gasped.

"Gorgeous!"

And, I was happy to note, the scent in the air was fresher than usual, probably because of the presence of a dozen gorgeous spruce, holly, and pine arrangements that the garden-club ladies had made up and delivered the day before.

"This is a beautiful place to work," Grace said, her voice full of admiration.

Well, then. As Grace and I headed toward the kitchen, I squared my shoulders and felt proud again. I loved this space, from its old-fashioned hearth in the center of the dining room to its uneven wood floors. The floors made carrying loaded trays a precarious enterprise, but so far, I'd avoided a disaster in that department. I glanced at the big round tables as Grace and I walked past. I'd rented gold-rimmed white china. It looked stunning next to the overflowing greenery baskets, which I'd asked the garden-club ladies to decorate with big red bows. I was *so* glad I had attended to all this before all hell had broken loose at the library the previous night.

In the kitchen, I turned on the bright, Tom-found chandelier and asked Grace if she'd like some coffee. She swept the space with her gaze, taking in the stainless espresso machine, the walk-in refrigerator, the freezer, sinks, and shelves full of glass jars and metal cans, all shimmering in the light.

She pulled out one of the ladder-back chairs Tom had found to go with an oak farm table he'd brought from his cabin. "Yes, please, two shots. And if Julian has bestowed you with any of his famous fudge, I'd love some of that, too."

I exhaled and fired up the machine, then clattered espresso cups into saucers. While the coffee machine was heating up, I placed the cream, sugar, napkins, two dishes, and the can of fudge on top of the farm table. The can actually held two fudge favorites: one was Julian's patented dark concoction dotted with sundried cherries. The other was my own holiday favorite: fudge mixed with crushed peppermint candies. Breakfast!

When I served the espresso, Grace made the appropriate *ooh* and *aah* noises, said no thanks, and drank the dark stuff without cream. After she'd taken a sip, I told her she was very welcome, and concentrated on my own dose of caffeine. When things remained quiet, I fastened my gaze on the holiday fudge, in which the peppermint candy glistened like ice. I popped a piece in my mouth and closed my eyes. The luscious, melting texture of the dark chocolate was a perfect foil for the crunch of peppermint. Why didn't more people have candy first thing in the morning? And while we were at it, how about ice cream for the first meal of the day? I'd given it to Arch when he had his tonsils out—

"I'm here first of all because Julian asked me and I wanted to help you," Grace began finally. "But," she said after a pause, "I know about Patricia Ingersoll and her accusers." Her accusers? Had I imagined it, or had Grace's voice hardened? In any event, my antennae zinged straight up.

"Okay." I concentrated on sounding nonchalant. "I guess the news is out everywhere about Drew Wellington—and Patricia's arrest. But I'm not supposed to talk about the case."

Grace's tone softened. "You don't have to talk to me about it if you don't want to, Goldy, but I need to get into Drew Wellington's house."

I burst out laughing so fast that coffee shot out my nose. Okay, I wanted to know about Sandee Brisbane. Patricia Ingersoll had been arrested. There was that map they'd found on Drew. And now Grace Mannheim wanted to get into the victim's *house*.

"Are you nuts, Grace?" I asked when I'd recovered. "The police investigators are there now. They're combing through every note, every file, every bit of correspondence they can find. They're tracking Wellington's movements, checking who called him and the folks he called, from both his home phone and his cell, and when the calls took place. They're not going to let *you* into the place. And even if they did, which is a very big *if,* I doubt you'd find anything of significance."

Grace said smoothly, "If you don't know what I'm looking for, how can you say I won't find it?"

"What are you looking for?"

"Something that belongs to a friend of mine."

"What?"

"She hasn't given me permission to say."

I took another piece of fudge and chewed it thoughtfully. "There's such a thing as impeding an investigation. Obstructing justice."

"I'm doing neither."

I gave up on that tack and said, "So do you know Patricia? Or does your friend whom you're helping?"

Grace pressed her lips together, all the while assessing me with those dark blue eyes of hers. What was she thinking? It was as hard to tell this time as it had been when I'd first visited her.

"I know Patricia." She didn't say anything more.

Why did I always feel as if Grace controlled every conversation? "Come on. Don't give me such a hard time. I'm trying to help Patricia, too, but we have to be reasonable."

"You have misgivings about talking to me," she said at length. "Why? Do you think my emotions, my fondness for Patricia, say, are coloring my thinking? As I recall, it's because of your emotions, your feelings one way or the other, love or hate, that you get involved solving crimes."

"Well, I suppose—"

"Stop, let me say my piece." She canted her head to one side. "I'm not being emotional. In fact, I've found that when I'm trying to figure something out, I need to be as bloodless as granite."

"Blood or no blood, you're not going to get into Wellington's house. And why do you think you'd find things the Furman County Sheriff's Department missed?"

"Because I see things. I do research." She pursed her lips, and once again that delicately featured face of hers made me smile. "I'm not kidding, Goldy. Yes, I offered to help Julian and you with the lunch today, and I will. But I didn't make the offer until I heard Patricia had been arrested."

How do people hear these things? I wondered. *Are the gossip lines better than police-band radios?*

Grace went on: "I found out her boyfriend, Drew Wellington, had been murdered last night at the Aspen

Meadow Library. You were there, I heard, although you didn't find the body. Patricia had been in the library earlier in the day. Neil Tharp, Drew's right-hand man in his map-collecting business, was in and out of the library. Elizabeth Wellington, Drew's ex-wife, we don't know about. But probably most significant of all, Larry *Craddock* was there."

"Who is Larry Craddock?"

She crossed her arms. "Bald? Bad-mannered? Aggressive? He's a map dealer. Drew used to do business with him, but they had a falling-out. I think Drew drove him out of the market. Drew certainly was more successful than Larry, at any rate." I blushed, thinking of the fellow who'd harassed Arch. "Ah, I see you may have encountered him."

"Maybe. There was a bald man who was very uncooperative at the library last night. They kicked him out."

"That sounds like Larry. As I understand it, the man is obsessed with maps. He also loved his map *shop,* which went under. Drew used to brag that he could always undercut Larry's prices. You want my opinion? Drew was in map collecting for the money. Larry, if you'll allow a bit of possible exaggeration, was in it for his life."

"Back up. Did you get hold of the surveillance video

from the library? I mean, how do you know all this stuff? I thought the cops were the only ones—"

"They are. But Drew's death is big news and people are talking about it. I made phone calls. I paid visits to old friends. I've been up most of the night."

"If you've been up all night, you're going to find catering awfully fatiguing."

"I took a power nap very early this morning." Grace smiled. Once again I found her impenetrable gaze disconcerting. I glanced longingly at the fudge. Would I have better powers of observation if I had another couple of pieces? "Don't worry about me," Grace said, her voice gentle. "I really will help you, and I do want to help find out what's . . . going on with Patricia."

I took a deep breath. I needed more coffee. I needed another report from Marla, and I wanted to know what Tom had found out from the surveillance camera—if he'd tell me—and if there were any other skeletons in Drew Wellington's closet. It hadn't even been twenty-four hours since Drew Wellington's body had been discovered, and Grace Mannheim knew half the people who'd been in the library. Or at least it seemed that way. Marla might have to give up her Gossip Queen crown.

"Listen, Goldy," she explained, "I came to know Patricia quite well because I knew Frank, her late husband.

After Frank died so suddenly, Patricia started running a sort of self-help group for people who wanted to lose weight. When she started a Boulder chapter, she told me they were having trouble finding a place to meet. So I offered my house. I . . . grew to like her."

"*You* needed to lose weight?" I pulled myself another espresso. "You, Ms. Senior Softball? Baloney."

"I don't have anything against people trying to improve themselves. After Frank passed away, I knew Drew Wellington became her lover because she told me. I was glad to see her getting back out into the world after being widowed so young. Drew even dropped her off and then picked her up at my house a couple of times."

I slugged down what had to be my twelfth shot of espresso that morning. "Did Drew talk much about his business? You said he bragged about how much money he was making. What sort of maps did he sell?" I asked.

"Old maps. Maps of the Old World. Maps of the New World. They're collectors' items, antiques. They go for a lot of money these days."

"Yes, don't I know. Did Drew ever mention meeting clients at the Aspen Meadow Library?"

Grace narrowed her eyes at me. "Is that what he was

doing when he was killed? Meeting a client? Did he have a map with him?"

I could feel my cheeks becoming hot again. "I don't know." Yeah, right. And there was Grace, reading me like a fat, fudge-loving foodie. "You say that Larry Craddock was in the map business, too?"

"He helped Drew out when Drew was just getting started, after Drew lost the D.A. election. I guess you could say Larry was Drew's mentor. But Larry doesn't really have the temperament to be a salesman," she said. "One time when Patricia was waiting for Drew at my house, this bald fellow marched onto my front yard. He stood there on the grass as if he owned the place, stamping from foot to foot, impatient for something. Impatient for what? I wondered, since this was my place. Had he not lost the weight he wanted to? I asked myself. Was he going to give Patricia what for? I grabbed the Mace from my cookie jar—I'm not talking mace the spice, here, I'm talking Mace the—"

"I know."

"But then Drew's Bentley pulled up, and Patricia, who'd been watching from my dining-room window, ran past me, out of my own house. Turned out, Larry hadn't been waiting for Patricia, he'd been waiting for *Drew*. Drew hollered for Patricia to go back into my house, that he would handle things. She turned on her heel and came racing back. At that point, Larry began to shout at Drew, saying he was ruining his business, and that Drew owed him and should let him in on some deal Drew had going, or Drew would end up being sorry. Drew said something to him that calmed him down, and he left. I wanted to call the police, but Drew insisted it wasn't necessary."

"Uh-huh," I said as caffeine finally sparked in my veins. "Who told you that this Larry fellow was at the library yesterday?"

"One of the calls I made was to the Furman County Jail. You leave a message for an inmate, she can call you back. Which Patricia did. And she told me she'd seen Larry Craddock at the library."

I began to get worried myself, but not about Larry Craddock and whether he was the bald man who'd fought with Arch. I needed to bring in the crates holding the garden club's chicken, the salads, and the rolls. The tables had to be set. I was not, by God, going to have a second event in two days wrecked by issues of crime and punishment.

"So are you going to let me help with the lunch or not?" Grace asked, her chin tilted up. "You could learn all kinds of things from me that would help in the investigation. Between the two of us, maybe we can figure this thing out."

"You can help me," I said at length. "But I'm not sure we can talk about what happened to Drew Wellington."

Grace turned and began that quickstep out of the kitchen. Over her shoulder, she called, "Why ever not?"

"Because my husband the investigator would go nuclear!" I called back.

Over the next two hours, Grace refrained from asking me any more questions and worked smoothly doing the setup. When the tow truck from Gary's Garage arrived at half past nine, she oversaw the removal of the errant vehicles. Julian showed up at ten, as promised. He seemed to be enjoying getting to know Grace, as he nodded to acknowledge her and said, "You can be our extra server after all? Cool." He put down his first crate of vegetables and gave her a quick smile and hug.

"Hey," I said, half teasing, as I rinsed the baby artichokes he'd brought, "what about me?"

Julian crossed the kitchen and embraced my shoulders. Then he gazed critically at the baby artichokes.

"You going to prep those?" he asked.

"Feel free to take over, Bistro Man."

"No problem, boss. Plus, I found some great asparagus, and the chocolate cupcakes look fantastic." Julian's
compact, muscled body darted in and out of the kitchen
as he brought in foodstuffs. Then he washed his hands,
chose an appropriate knife, and retrieved his favorite vegetable cutting board. He set to work trimming the vegetables. I sighed. When I was Julian's age, I'd been a young
mother up to my elbows in laundry, housecleaning, meals,
child care, and dealing with an impossible husband. As a
result, I'd tossed perfectionism out the window. Julian, on
the other hand, seemed to enjoy being fussy and deliber-
ate. More power to him, I thought as I moved on to buttering the big pans that would hold the chicken.

Grace, meanwhile, was making neat piles of forks,
knives, and spoons while cross-examining Julian on any
knowledge he might have of Drew Wellington.

Julian concentrated on his cutting board. "I know he
was seeing, you know, ah, having an affair with Patricia
Ingersoll, 'cuz Marla told me. Patricia is that woman
who heads the weight-loss—"

"I know her," Grace interrupted briskly as she gazed
at my printout for the chicken prep. She asked if it was
okay to drain the brine off the chicken, rinse it, and pat
it dry. Since it was a messy job, I was all too happy to

acquiesce. I started to show her where the plastic gloves were that she needed for poultry handling, but she said she knew where they were. How she seemed to have a second sense as to where everything was located in the kitchen, from utensils to foodstuffs, was beyond me. Had she somehow scoped the place out before I arrived? I told my paranoid brain to take a break, and began counting the rolls.

"I did a low-fat, low-cal dinner for Patricia's Losers group when they met at a Boulder church. It wasn't fun." Finished with the artichokes and asparagus, Julian turned on the water so that it gushed into my big steamer. When he moved over to the stove, he went on: "The prep took forever, because Patricia wanted fifty different types of chopped vegetables, a frittata for an appetizer, grilled halibut with stir-fried vegetables for a main course, fudge soufflés for dessert. Technically, it was all low-calorie. But if you had seconds and thirds, which some of the members wanted, you wouldn't be losing any weight." Julian looked up from the stove and scowled at us. "Those women came out to the kitchen and began snacking on all the prepped veggies! They were starving, they said. They cut corners off the halibut while I was grilling it. They kept ordering me to hurry up with the appetizer, and then, while the eggs were setting up, one of them lifted the pan lid and dug her fork into the center of my frittata." Julian shook his head and turned back to the printout. "Since we were in a church, I kept praying she'd get salmonella before the dinner ended. And people wonder why chefs become crazed. It's a defense, I'm telling you. You start screaming at folks to get out of your kitchen, you holler that they're wrecking your food, you shriek that they're idiots and you're going to double-charge them or walk out, and pretty soon you've got some street cred in the bitch-slap department."

"Julian!" I exclaimed, but Grace was laughing. Then she frowned.

"Julian," she asked, "did you ever cater for Drew Wellington?"

"Now *there* was a narcissist," Julian observed as his tennis shoes squeaked across the kitchen floor. He peered into the walk-in, then reemerged with unsalted butter. "Drew Wellington. What a jerk."

"He's dead, Julian," I said in what I hoped was a low, respectful tone.

"Well, that figures," Julian replied, without missing a beat.

"Julian!"

But Grace held up a hand to keep me from talking. "I need to know why you said that."

"Because he stiffed me, that's why!" Julian said vociferously. "The only reason I came all the way over to Flicker Ridge to cater for him was 'cuz Goldy and Tom were on a fishing trip, and 'cuz Drew was old pals with the owner of the bistro where I work. Drew seemed to have *lots* of old pals. Guess his being a former district attorney let him still play the *very* big shot role. But he lost his last election, right?"

"Sounds as if you hated him, too," I said.

"He gave me no tip. Not a nickel. Even Patricia Ingersoll's women dug into their purses when I was cleaning up. I guess they felt guilty that they'd done so much food snitching. But not Drew Wellington. I doubt he knew the concept of guilt."

Grace said quietly, "And you say that because?"

Julian shook his head. " 'When's the event starting, Mr. Wellington?' I asked him when I catered his dinner party. Six o'clock, he told me. So I got there at four to set up. The door was open, but there was nobody home. Then his guests started showing up at six. Pretty soon it was six-thirty, seven, seven-thirty. The food got cold, people said they needed to leave, but Mr. Inconsiderate was nowhere to be found. When he finally breezed in at eight o'clock, he didn't even apologize. When I asked him why he wasn't at his own damn party when it started at six o'clock, he said, 'Because I knew you would be here. Didn't you take care of the guests?' I wish I would have punched him out. But I was still hoping for a tip."

"I'm sorry, Julian," I said.

"It's not your fault, Goldy." Julian went on, still speaking heatedly: "I'll tell you what, I couldn't *stand* how everyone made nice to him, you know, to his face. I didn't do it. When Neil Tharp—you know, his assistant?—called and asked me to do another dinner party for old Drew, I told him, 'You get everyone there, your boss included, sit them all down at the table, and I'll come over and cook.' He hung up on me, and that was my spectacular finale of catering for Drew Wellington."

I shook my head and thought that I might have been tempted to bitch-slap Drew Wellington myself . . . if I only knew what bitch-slapping was. "What did the bistro owner say?"

"Aw," Julian replied, "he said most folks who had to deal with Drew eventually gave up. I said, 'Thanks a lot!' He felt so bad he gave me a big gratuity himself, and that was that."

Grace set her chin firmly. "Did the bistro owner say who else hated him, or couldn't get along with him?"

"Well, I don't think old Neil liked him very much, in spite of his holier-than-thou attitude, and 'Don't we all just love Drew, and isn't he marvelous, we have to cut him a little slack.' *Go ahead, guy,* I finally thought, *cut him all the slack you want, and while you're at it, slit his throat, will ya?*"

"Julian!" I protested. "He's dead!"

"I care!"

"Neil Tharp didn't like him very much," Grace echoed. "What specifically makes you say that?"

I noticed all three of us had stopped working, so I got busy patting the drained chicken with paper towels. *Somebody* had to feed the garden-club ladies.

"Oh," Julian said, "it felt to me as if Neil was frustrated with Drew."

"Frustrated because?" Grace pressed.

"I couldn't put my finger on it, 'cuz I only catered for Drew that one time." Julian shook his head. "When Drew finally showed up at his party, Neil seemed to be watching him real carefully, as if he was waiting for the Mighty One to make a mistake, so he, Neil, could go in and clean it up. I'm telling you, Neil Tharp reminded me of Uriah Heep, all squirmy and watchful and waiting for his chance to take over somebody else's business."

"Somebody's going to have to take over *this* business," I interjected, "if the three of us don't get hot with the prep." Julian raised his eyebrows and started pulling out his sheets of frozen gnocchi. Grace peered at the prep sheets and began crumbling dried tarragon over the chicken. I hauled out the ganache-topped chocolate cupcakes and began arranging them on chilled dessert plates.

As it turned out, it was *not* one of the garden-club ladies who showed up early. Julian, Grace, and I had bent so assiduously to our tasks that we did not hear the kitchen door open. When a male voice shouted, "Hey, Goldy Schulz!" the first thing I thought was that Tom was going to bawl me out for leaving the back door to the kitchen unlocked. Well, maybe it was the second thing. The first thing I actually thought when my head shot up and I saw Larry Craddock striding in my direction was, *Will I be able to get rid of this guy before the garden-club ladies show up?*

"I didn't know who you were at the library," Craddock sputtered. "I wouldn't have gotten so upset with you if you hadn't been rude to me first!"

"My son," I answered with some heat, "simply asked you to stop using your cell phone. There are lots of signs saying cell calls aren't allowed in the library. And you attacked him for it!"

"I barely touched the kid," Larry protested. "*You* broke my phone. And you didn't have to set the police on me!"

"The police are talking to everyone who was in the library when Drew Wellington was there, Mr. Craddock, especially people who knew him. And in the meantime, we aren't supposed to be discussing the matter with anyone else."

Larry looked around the kitchen, his eyes wild. His voice became belligerent again. "I need to talk to you. It's very important."

Clearly Larry could not take a hint. The kitchen offered numerous weapons, but was entirely too cramped a space in which to argue with someone as boorish and oblivious as this guy. Plus, he was blocking the way to the back door.

"I'm afraid we have work to do. You'll have to excuse us." I leaned toward Julian and Grace, and whispered, "Out, out, out." They followed me with some reluctance into the dining room, where there were big double French doors, if we needed to make a quick exit.

"Hey, wait, I really have to talk to you. Hey, Three Stooges, come back here!"

Yeah, sure. What I wanted to do right then was run and hide. But I was determined to do no such thing. Instead, I turned around and faced Craddock.

"I am not going to talk with you," I said in a loud, measured voice, "when you are screaming at me."

Larry's shoulders sagged a bit and his resemblance to a newly picked red beet subsided. His bald head became pale and gleamed in the dining room's overhead lights.

"I just want to know if the cops found anything on Drew Wellington." He stamped one of the beautiful rented gold-and-white dishes with his thumb as he talked.

"I don't know what you're talking about," I said. "And could you please take your hand off the china?"

But he didn't. "Listen, map collecting runs in my veins. My father collected and so did my grandfather. But for them, it was a hobby. I know about maps and love them, but hey, I'm a businessman. I always want to make a deal."

"Larry—" I began.

"Just listen, will you? Yesterday afternoon, before he turned up dead, Drew Wellington showed me two"—he cleared his throat—"rare maps. He offered to sell them to me. I wasn't sure of the maps' provenance, which means where they came from—"

"We all know what *provenance* means," Grace said crisply.

Larry raised his voice a notch, but not back up to the yelling level. "Drew couldn't give me a good explanation! So I went to that back reading room, where they have a wi-fi connection. I didn't have any luck online, so I called this map-collecting attorney I know. He's another hobby guy." When Julian took a breath to speak, Larry rushed on: "Never mind, don't interrupt me. The attorney's secretary gave me the bum's rush, said he was in a meeting.

I said it was an emergency and she said he'd call me back. I went over to where I'd first met with Drew, over in that corner, and he wasn't there. I waited and waited for him."

"When was this?" I asked. "And how long did you wait?"

"Jesus, lady, you're as bad as the cops. It was before you got there. After I waited about twenty minutes, I was sure Drew was double-crossing me, that he was selling the maps to someone else. But his briefcase was on the floor. Okay, I looked inside. I mean, it wasn't locked! And only one of the two maps was in there."

"Larry," I began again, "you should tell all this to the police."

"I did! But they don't care about the maps. They only care about whether I was an enemy of Drew's, and I said, 'It's more complicated than that!'"

It sure is, I thought. Complicated in that I had the garden club showing up in less than an hour. Did I dare to glance at my watch? *Wait,* I thought, *I have an idea.* "More complicated?" I asked. Larry Craddock's face turned furious as he nodded. "Is the issue complicated by a woman named Sandee Brisbane? Did Drew ever mention to you that he knew her?"

When Larry Craddock drew his face into a puzzled expression, his wrinkled forehead extended up into his bald head. "Sandy who? He knew a lot of girls, but I don't think she was one of them."

"A lot of girls? What do you mean, a lot of girls?"

"Well," Larry Craddock said, his tone sarcastic, "if I said he knew a lot of *boys* you'd know what I meant, wouldn't ya?" He paused. "Look, I'm just trying to find out what happened to those maps he had on him. I'm not going to let Neil Tharp cheat me out of them. Drew offered them to *me first.* So, you're married to an inspector, right? Did he tell you they found those maps?"

"Buddy," Julian interjected in a low voice, "we're trying to run an event here. You need to leave."

"Shut up!" he snarled at Julian. "I'm not talking to you."

"Please," I said in the most conciliatory voice I could muster, "don't lose your temper again. Listen to me. I don't know about any maps. Why don't you ask the sheriff's department what they found?"

Larry looked at the floor, pulled his mouth into a frown, and shook his head, as if he were trying to converse with an unusually stupid child. My throat constricted. What if the garden-club ladies moseyed in, expecting to see us setting out strawberry salads, and instead found us caught in one of Dante's circles of hell: trying to talk to a crazy bald guy?

SWEET REVENGE • 191

Larry addressed me with exaggerated patience: "I don't want to talk to the sheriff's department because they don't care about maps. I'm asking you if they found anything, because supposedly you're the one who knows these things."

"What?"

"Don't b.s. me, lady. I heard you help the cops with their investigations. So you know! Why won't you tell me?"

"Larry, you heard wrong. I don't know anything. I don't even know if you're telling the truth about Drew offering to sell you some maps."

Larry Craddock raised his voice several notches. *"Are you calling me a liar?"*

"No," I replied evenly, "I'm calling you a trespasser who needs to leave. Please go, or I'm going to call the police."

"Jesus, lady! What the hell did the cops find on Drew Wellington? All you have to do is answer my one question, and I'll go! They *must* have found those maps, or the *killer* stole them, and they're going to go back out on the black market!"

I shook my head. Larry finally took his hand off the china and used it to grab my arm. Behind me, Grace gasped.

"Let her loose," Julian announced as he moved forward, his swimmer's body balanced on the balls of his feet, "or I'll find something to whack you with, and it won't be a map!"

"You stay out of this, asshole!" Larry dropped his hold on me and swung wildly at Julian, who ducked out of the way and shot out with his own fast fist. It connected with the underside of Larry Craddock's chin. Julian's other hand then popped Craddock's Adam's apple. Larry Craddock stumbled backward, emitting croaking noises as he grabbed for purchase on the chairs, tables, the dining-room columns . . .

His hand snagged a tablecloth, unfortunately, and as he headed down toward the floor, he took fistfuls of linen with him. I couldn't believe how quickly a cloth loaded with plates, silverware, crystal, salt and pepper shakers, a filled butter dish, and a magnificent green-and-red centerpiece could crash, break, tinkle, and roll all over the surrounding area. The only thing not crashing around was Larry Craddock, who lay unmoving under an upside-down pinecone-and-spruce-branch floral arrangement.

"Oh God!" Julian exclaimed. "Goldy, I'm sorry!"

"We'll clean it up," Grace said smoothly. Where did that woman get her calm? I wondered.

We gingerly called Craddock's name. When there was no reply, we removed the centerpiece. I didn't know if it was the hit to the Adam's apple or the conk against the table or the floor, but Craddock was only half conscious, and he was mumbling unintelligibly. Grace and Julian hauled him out the French doors and left him there, then locked the doors and called the cops. Alas, the centerpiece had landed on Craddock's pants before bouncing onto his face. So when Sergeant Boyd himself arrived with a patrolman to haul a moaning Craddock away for trespassing, creating a nuisance, "and anything else I can think of," Larry had a big wet spot right in the area where a man wouldn't want it.

"I'm going to get you, Goldy Schulz!" Craddock shouted as he was loaded into the black-and-white. He'd regained his temper apparently.

Boyd said, "Don't make me add menacing to your list of accomplishments here, pal."

9

Goldy, God, I'm so sorry," Julian kept saying as he wiped up flowers, pinecones, spruce boughs, and bits of floral clay. "When are the women due?"

I checked my watch: quarter to eleven. The women weren't due for an hour, so we would probably be okay. Thank God Grace had come. She was very swift and sure of herself, I noticed as she first swept, then swabbed the floors with my new mop. She had managed to find a long black apron that she'd tied around her slender waist. My own waist, I thought as I washed my hands in the kitchen sink, could use some, well, *narrowing*. But I quickly banished the thought from my head as I carried out the plastic bags of cookies. New Year's with its resolutions would come soon enough, I reflected as I set out the shiny green miniature shopping bags that each guest would take home.

"Gosh, boss, did you pack all of these cookies we made?" Julian, also recovered from the Craddock interlude, had cleaned himself up and was back in catering mode.

"I did."

"You're very competent," Grace said, her voice admiring. "Now just tell me what you need me to do."

This I did. Soon the chicken was roasting, the gnocchi were cooking, and a big pot of butter, to go over the gnocchi, was bubbling merrily on the stove. We put out the platters of salad, warmed the rolls, and decorated each cupcake dish with a fresh flower from several bunches left by the same ladies who'd made the arrangements. Julian carefully stirred the sweet-sour dressing for the strawberry salad, then expertly unmolded the holiday molded salads. Finally he began to prep the avocados.

When I was out in the kitchen, I heard my cell phone making the buzzing noise it does when I've left it on vibrate. Cursing, I raced over to the coatrack and dug the phone out of my jacket pocket. Immediately there was Arch's impatient voice saying, "Mom! Jeez! I about gave up on you!"

"I'm here, hon, getting ready for the garden-club luncheon." I kept my voice calm, a sure antidote to Arch getting overexcited or upset. "How was the Latin exam?"

"*Bonus.*"

"You got extra credit?"

Arch groaned. "No, Mom, it was good, it was *all right.* I was trying to find out if I could go snowboarding with Todd and Gus, but they might have left without me."

"I very much doubt that your best friend and your half brother would leave the school without you. Where are you now?"

"I'm at home. Mrs. Vikarios brought me back here because I need to know where my ski stuff is. Hall closet? There's like a ton of stuff in there."

"It's all your stuff," I replied, still composed. "If you can't find your mittens and whatnot, you might want to think of organizing the space you're looking into, and giving away things you don't use anymore."

"Not now, Mom, they're waiting outside. Do you think my equipment might be in my closet upstairs?"

"It's a good possibility. Why don't you pull everything out and look? Don't hang up, though, because I want to know what your plan is."

"Oh, Mom." From the background came the tromping noise of him banging up the stairs. This was followed by much crashing and cursing. In my mind's eye, I saw tumbling books, notebooks, toys, and everything else Arch had accumulated in his fifteen and a half years. Why was he so surprised he could never find anything? "Okay, here we go," he said. "Mittens, hat." More thrashing and grunting was followed by, "All right, I have my snow pants. Gotta go, Mom."

"Where are you going snowboarding?"

"Over at Regal Ridge. You already signed the release, remember? Oh, yeah, and may I drive the Vikarioses' van?"

Since I'd taken the interstate down to the Regal Ridge exit in November, then negotiated the winding road up the mountain, all when there was no snow on the ground, I knew the answer to that one. "No, sorry." I also recalled the ski and snowboard area itself, which abutted the interstate. At one time, the place had been a bona fide, if tiny, ski area, with a single lift. After the operators had been unable to afford the liability insurance, the area had gone up for sale. Although the ski run was supposedly standing unused, renegade boarders had cut a path up the side of the mountain and strung an ad hoc, entirely unsafe rope along the trail. After several kids had ended up breaking their legs and being airlifted out, pressure from parents had induced Furman County

Open Space to purchase the hill and make it into a ski and snowboard area—with the old path chained off.

The Regal Ridge Snow Sports Area, as it had been renamed, had proven to be immensely popular. When I'd seen the place, with its thick crowd of local skiers and snowboarders, my stomach had clenched. I'd hardly been able to look at the rope along the west side of the run, the only barrier between all those snow-sports enthusiasts, the crummy old path between the trees, and a drop of three hundred feet onto jagged rocks. I'd swallowed hard as Arch explained that nobody had been hurt since the new rope had gone in. At that point, he'd started in with "Everyone gets to go, am I going to be the only one whose mommy won't let him?" Finally, reluctantly, I'd given Arch permission to snowboard there with his pals.

"Mom, hello? You there?"

"Yes, yes, go ahead. Will you call me on my cell when you're ready to come home?"

Arch groaned again and said he would. I disconnected and wondered how old Arch would have to be before parenting him came easily. Forty, maybe?

"He's having trouble finding his stuff?" Julian asked. I hadn't even heard him come up to my side.

"Arch used to be neat, almost obsessively so. But now he hangs on to everything. He's become a bona fide packrat."

"Know what? I used to be one, too. Grace cured me. She helped me sort through my stuff when I moved into her garage apartment, and I ended up donating half of everything. Now I have all kinds of room, and less-fortunate-type folks are benefiting. Plus, the whole exercise gave me a huge amount of energy."

"D'you have any energy left over to help Arch?" The two of us circled the table Larry had wrecked. Julian had spread a clean tablecloth. All we needed to do was arrange new place settings. Grace had also laid her hands on a trio of tiny green candles, which she'd positioned in the table's center to replace the busted floral arrangement. No question, the woman had the knack for minimalism.

"I think our first guests are arriving," Grace called from the French doors. "Didn't you want to set out the door prizes?"

The gingerbread houses! Julian and I bolted for the kitchen. We nabbed the cellophane-wrapped cakes and walked carefully to the Roundhouse entrance. Grace had pulled a table over to the door, and even managed to round up a basket for the tickets.

Just in the nick of time, as it happened. Plodding up the steps was Louise Munsinger, the new president of the Aspen Meadow Garden Club. Louise, in her early seventies, had lost none of her vitality. Her wrinkled, rectangular face was topped with hair dyed jet-black. She wore it pulled back severely from her forehead and tied in a bun at the nape of her neck. Her bulldog frown and blocklike body encased in a long sable coat put me in mind of Stalin. But a dictator was what the AMGC had needed, after a native-trees-only group had splintered off—their term, not mine—the previous year. Threatening them with the horticultural equivalent of disbarment, Louise had brought the rebels into line and reunified the club.

"Will one of you be taking the tickets?" she demanded now as she shed her fur coat and tossed it at Julian. Julian, ever athletic, snagged it. "The tickets are numbered and perforated," she went on, "so each one needs to be carefully torn, in order for each member to check her number for a door prize." Louise lifted a thin black eyebrow at me, and I nodded.

"We'll be careful, Mrs. Munsinger," I promised.

She assessed the dining room with her icy gaze, and my stomach did backflips. She sniffed and said, "The dining room looks very presentable."

Well, thank God for that, I thought. And then a fur hit *me* in the face. I gasped, then grabbed it, the way I'd once caught Scout the cat when he'd jumped out of a tree. "Excuse me!" I couldn't help crying, once I'd righted myself and pulled the pelt off my puckered mouth.

"Aren't you hanging up the wraps?" Elizabeth Wellington asked me. Her dark eyes were red-lined, as if she hadn't slept much last night. Her bristly hair stuck up all over her head. I was surprised that she had come to the luncheon, given what had happened to Drew.

"Uh." I coughed and spat out a few animal hairs that clung to my lips.

"Here, boss," Julian said, "let me have it." He relieved me of the stole and disappeared with both furs.

"I want to talk with you later, Goldy," Elizabeth said.

Terrific. I so enjoyed these conversations with people who demanded to speak with me. Watching her retreating back, I noted Elizabeth was wearing a scarlet suit in that shade favored by older women. Marla and I had dubbed it "Menopause Red."

With Grace at my side, I put Elizabeth out of my mind and hustled to the kitchen. We checked on the chicken and gnocchi, brought out extra plates just in case, and looked for Julian. He'd hung up the furs on a makeshift rack and was taking—and gently tearing—the tickets for the first arrivals. He looked at me and gave a tiny shrug. *Guess I'm manning the door.* I nodded my gratitude.

Once the women were seated, Grace, Julian, and I ferried out the chicken, vegetables, and gnocchi and placed them next to the salad platters on each table. Louise had insisted that the food be served family style, in order to avoid "those ridiculously long buffet lines." We followed quickly with the hot rolls. Louise dinged a knife against her water glass, to indicate that everyone should be quiet. She gave a short welcome, pursed her mouth into a tiny O, and announced that she would be speaking briefly during the lunch, then drawing the door-prize tickets at the conclusion. With the tables now filled with garden-club members, dishes clanked as they were passed. When the conversation level grew to a low roar, we three worker bees retired to the kitchen for a brief respite.

"Don't *tell* me we're not having wine," Marla said over my shoulder. I jumped—she always managed to startle me—and said no, Louise hadn't wanted any booze. In the fashion incarnation of Christmas, Marla was wearing a flowing, bright red silk dress with a holly-green cummerbund. "Louise is *cruel*," she pronounced. "And just look at all these Christmas decorations. *Cruel Yule*."

Julian said, "Now there's the holiday spirit."

"You bet." Marla pulled a wine bottle out of her capacious Louis Vuitton purse—which purse she'd decorated with a red-and-white corsage all its own. "Open this for me, will you, Julian? It's a Riesling spätlese, very rare, perfect with chicken and gnocchi."

I smiled in spite of myself. While Julian rustled around for a wine opener Grace shuffled and clinked wineglasses until she'd set out four of them on the oak farm table.

"Who's going to be using four glasses?" I asked mildly. "The staff here"—I indicated Grace, Julian, and me—"isn't allowed to imbibe during working hours, sorry."

"Speak for yourself," Grace said gaily as she clinked glasses with Marla. "I don't want any pay. I just want some of this gorgeous wine."

Marla, happy to have drinking company, took a large swig from her glass. "I cannot bear to listen to Louise say one more word about the success of our—make that *her*—tree-planting campaign," she began. "You'd think we were greening up Antarctica. And the trees we planted ended up being native pines and spruce anyway, so we didn't need to have all that controversy, after all."

"Still," Julian put in, "the fire in the wildlife preserve did destroy thousands of trees. It's a good program, and the garden club is doing a super job, even if you don't like to listen to her talk about it."

"Well, I *don't*," Marla replied. She took in the three of us with a devilish twinkle in her eye. "When I saw Elizabeth Wellington whack Goldy with her mink stole, I decided I had to sit next to the old battle-ax. All that anger had to be coming from somewhere, right?" She sipped her wine. "Poor thing, she was really, really in love with that ex-husband of hers. Talk about deluded, oh my God. There he was, this great-looking guy, he was her age but looked ten years younger. I mean, she used to love him *so* much. But not after what he did to her, she just told me."

"What did he do to her?" Grace asked. Something about Grace's tone made me assess her. It was not an innocent question. Why would Grace care what Drew had done to his ex-wife?

Marla refilled her glass. "You know Drew tried to have the DUI hushed up." When we nodded, she said, "He'd had too much to drink at a funeral, is what he claimed. So sad about some fellow lawyer pal who died, and so on. But nobody bought it, and trying to keep the arrest quiet cost him the election. Case closed on the scandal? That's what most folks in Furman County thought. Turns out, wait for it." She drank from her glass, then went on: "Drew had a fifteen-year-old girl in the car with him when he was stopped. I *knew* there was some story about him with much younger women, I just didn't know the particulars. Anyway, Drew insisted to the cops and Elizabeth that he was taking this girl home, but they'd already passed her house and his car was weaving back and forth on its way down a dead-end lane when the cops pulled him out for a Breathalyzer test. Which he failed."

"Who was the girl?" I asked.

Marla shrugged. "Elizabeth clammed up at that point. But when she left for the restroom, the gals at my table jumped in saying that nobody knew who the girl was because there was some privacy thing that her parents had insisted on. So it's unclear exactly what he was up to with that girl. But Elizabeth must have had a pretty good idea, because she filed for divorce after the election." Marla and Grace clinked glasses again, and sipped.

"Which table is this?" I asked. "And are they still talking about Drew?"

"Table eight," Marla said obligingly. "And yes, they are still dissecting old Drew Wellington. One last thing that earned him Elizabeth's hatred? You've heard about the two and a half mil?"

I said that I had.

"Well, I always thought it was a divorce settlement, but it wasn't. In the course of the marriage, Elizabeth inherited some money. Now she's sort of hinting that he got some of it before they were even divorced. I don't know the details yet, and Elizabeth might not share those, 'cuz they could make her look stupid."

"And who inherits Drew's money now?" Grace asked; too quickly, it seemed to me.

"Don't know," Marla countered. "They didn't have any children, so Drew could have left it to anybody. I haven't found out *everything*."

"How'd you find out as much as you did?" Julian asked.

Marla's eyes twinkled again. "You don't think I just brought one bottle of wine, do you? Though if you ask me, Elizabeth has been indulging since before the lunch even started. By the way, Goldy, Hermie MacArthur is at the table. Tonight's your curry party at her house, and she's still bemoaning the fact that Neil Tharp has invited himself in Drew's place. Better get over there!"

She swept out of the kitchen. Grace and I raised eyebrows at each other. I nabbed the ice-water pitcher while she grabbed a spare basket of rolls.

"Ah, the Gossip Patrol," Julian said as Grace and I made for the kitchen doors. "I'll take care of the rest of the dining room's refills. Just let me know what you find out at table eight."

Marla had reseated herself by the time Grace and I arrived, trying to look unobtrusive, at her table. Elizabeth Wellington was just outside the French doors, alas, speaking into her cell phone. There must be a fund-raising emergency somewhere.

"I know what Elizabeth regrets," Cecie Rowley said, her voice low. Cecie and I had served on several church committees and she nodded at me. "Or what she must regret," Cecie went on. "That Drew made so much money after he lost the election, selling his real-estate investments and setting up as a map dealer. Rumor is that he was good for several mil."

The women murmured and cooed. Several mil! How many maps did you have to sell to make that much? Marla looked at me and raised her eyebrows. Clearly, neither one of us believed you could make that much in cartographic commerce.

"Map dealer, schmap dealer," said Rosie Barton, another woman I knew from St. Luke's. Her voice was more bitter than cider vinegar. "Drew told my husband that if we bought a particular map of the East Coast, from Massachusetts down to New York Harbor, then in a year it would be worth fifteen thousand bucks. Well, a year later, we had a knock at our door from a private investigator. He said he represented what he called 'Special Collections' at Stanford University. He wanted to see the map . . . and said it was theirs!"

There was silence at the table. I checked out Hermie MacArthur's face. Under the heavy coating of powder, it had turned redder than Marla's dress.

Cecie said, "My land! Did you try to get a refund?"

Rosie laughed. "Absolutely. Drew said he didn't make refunds. He also refused to reimburse us for it. He said the investigator was full of it. Now we've had to hire a lawyer, and the whole thing is devolving into an expensive mess. I hate to speak ill of the dead"— Marla again raised her eyebrows at me; ever notice how folks spoke ill of the dead as soon as they said that?—"but Drew Wellington was a bastard." Rosie looked up to make sure Elizabeth was still outside on her cell phone. "No wonder poor Elizabeth divorced him."

As if on cue, Elizabeth barged through the French doors and went hunting for her fur stole. Once she'd found it, she banged back out without saying farewell to anyone. Hmm. So much for our having a chat.

There was an uncomfortable silence at the table. Finally Marla said, "Well, Rosie, you'll just have to find something else to hang on your living-room wall."

Rosie snorted. "I'm putting up a map of Colorado. A contemporary one."

The conversation turned to other ways to make money, or to lose it, both sure bets for energetic conversation in Aspen Meadow. Grace and I finished refilling the water glasses and breadbasket, and hightailed it out to the kitchen.

"Remember Larry Craddock said Drew was a crook?" I asked Grace. "I didn't really believe him. I mean, Drew may have been an unsavory hypocrite, but this seems to be on a whole different level."

Grace tilted her head. Her white hair shone around her. "Perhaps not a crook. But certainly someone you wouldn't trust when it came to investing in maps."

"They're ready for dessert," Julian announced from the kitchen doors. The three of us bustled about, ridding the dining room of serving platters, bowls, and entrée plates, and scooting back out with dishes of the ganache-topped chocolate cupcakes. As far as the dessert went, there was a general rule of catering: *Serve women chicken or fish for a main course, and you must serve chocolate afterward. They'll feel as if they've earned it.*

When the women had cleaned their plates, Louise Munsinger announced the door-prize winners, who joyfully accepted their gingerbread houses. Then Julian, Grace, and I passed around the bags of Christmas cookies for the "exchange." The garden-club members oohed and aahed. They seemed happy, even thrilled, not to have to do any baking. As Marla had said, the Christmas season was so exhausting.

When it was all over and most of the garden-club members had departed, Louise Munsinger approached me. My heart descended to the nether regions. What fault would she have found? But again she lifted her eyebrows, and I told myself she was smiling.

"That was lovely. We can't equitably divide up the extra cookies, so I hope you will keep them."

"Thank you, Louise. We'll find a use for them."

She handed me the final check, then lifted an eyebrow in the direction of Grace. "Should you really have an older woman doing so much work?"

"Not to worry," I said hurriedly. "Grace is in better physical shape than I am. And she's so impressed with what you all have done with the replanting of the Aspen Meadow Wildlife Preserve," I lied, "she just wanted to be a part of it, somehow."

Louise straightened her shoulders, a gesture of pride. "We *have* done a lovely job, a very impressive job, Goldy, as a matter of fact. Even the Furman County sheriff, on behalf of his entire department, thanked us for our thoroughness."

"The sheriff thanked you?" I was bewildered. Tom had not told me about *this.*

"Of course," Louise replied brusquely. "You know, they thought that woman, that stripper who was poor

Cecelia Brisbane's errant daughter, might have died in the fire."

"Sandee, you mean."

Louise sniffed. "I never knew her name. I'm only aware that after the sheriff and his men couldn't find her, he asked us to divide up the entire area of the fire into quarter-acre parcels. We paid for a surveyor to come help us. The sheriff said that they couldn't risk young kids, you know, the Cub Scouts and whatnot, to go hiking in the summertime and find the skeleton of some woman who had run away from the police after she murdered . . . well, she murdered *your* ex-husband, didn't she?"

I nodded. "Yes. She confessed and then she ran into the fire."

"We were very thorough," Louise said, her chin lifted. "We raked and replanted every quarter acre affected by the fire. And there was no skeleton of a missing stripper."

"Uh-huh."

"She must have gotten away," Louise said with another sniff before she marched out the French doors.

Grace, Julian, and I set to work cleaning up and putting the conference-center dining room to rights. It took almost two hours to wash and replace all the silverware and glasses, water the centerpieces, pack up the rented china, and sweep the floors. When we were done, I turned off the holiday lights and joined my two-person staff in the kitchen.

"You two were incredible," I said. I handed them each a wad of cash. "I don't want to hear a word, Grace, you're taking it."

"I'll just give it to charity," Grace said. "But it's certainly clear to me that the pair of you do earn your money. I'm exhausted." I thought of what Louise had said as Grace ran her thin, spidery hands through her cloud of white hair. "And you said you had another event to cater tonight?"

"We sure do," Julian replied, smiling.

"And are you going to get a nap between now and then?" Grace asked, her voice suddenly worried and nurturing. Julian couldn't help it; he laughed.

"We'll have about ten more shots of espresso and be good to go, right, Goldy? And I'll be putting sugar in mine, get even more of a buzz."

"Sounds great to me," I agreed. "Let's lock up."

I looked at the six extra bags of cookies Louise said we should keep. I had plenty more at home, so I gave Julian and Grace one each, then on impulse decided to take the last four dozen down to the Furman County Jail. Patricia's desperate pleas from the night before still vibrated in my ears. In fact, just the thought of her sobbing voice, and the memory of her trying to wrench herself away from the policeman, filled me with guilt. She had begged me to help her, and what had I done? Asked a few questions at catered events, and tried to get Tom to tell me more than he should have.

"I'm taking these down to the jail," I announced as I dropped the extra cookie bags into my big carryall.

"The *jail*?" Grace asked. "Whatever for?"

"I'm going to see if they'll let me give them to Patricia." On second thought, the sergeant in charge of whatever floor Patricia was on would probably veto that idea, although how I'd be able to smuggle drugs or other contraband into frosted Santa bars was beyond me.

"I thought Patricia was in some weight-loss group," Julian reminded me as the three of us walked through the kitchen exit.

We trod gingerly down the snow-and-ice-covered path to the parking lot. I said, "I have no doubt that somebody at the sheriff's department will eat them." In fact, if I left them in the department snack room, they'd disappear faster than Sandee Brisbane had.

Julian, who had keys to our house, said he was going back for a shower and to change clothes. While we offered Grace the same opportunity, she declined and said Marla had invited her to bathe at her house and take a nap, maybe spend the night if she was too tired to drive back to Boulder. Apparently Louise Munsinger wasn't the only one worried about whether Grace should be catering.

"Did *you* find out anything to help Patricia?" I asked. "Something I can report to her when I see her?"

Grace's dark blue eyes looked momentarily startled. "Something to help Patricia?" she echoed. "No. But if I do, I'll call you." She made no more mention of going into Drew's place, for which I was grateful. With a quick wave, she guided her old Toyota out of the parking lot and was gone.

The van's engine revved, and by the time I'd reached the interstate, the vehicle's interior was actually warming up. How cold was it, anyway? High teens, low twenties? And the sky had again clouded up and looked ominously dark, which was depressing, as it was only two in the afternoon.

Arch had left a message on my cell saying he needed to be picked up at four at Regal Ridge, and could Gus and Todd come over for dinner and to spend the night? I groaned, then put in a call to Tom, to ask if, once I brought the boys home, he could fix them dinner and oversee them, whether it was in making popcorn or setting up a DVD. What I didn't say, but hoped was understood, was that I wanted Tom to keep the kiddos from doing what fifteen-year-olds are tempted to do, and that was to dip into Ma and Pa's liquor cabinet.

"Schulz," he said when I'd finished my message.

"Can you take care of the boys?"

"I heard what you said, Miss G. And yes, I'd love to take care of them and fix them dinner. What's more, I'll offer them white wine as an aperitif, red wine with dinner, and cognac for dessert."

I sighed. "You're hilarious."

"Aw, you won't even let me tease you anymore. I gotta hop, but tonight I want to hear about the garden-club ladies."

I disconnected and thought of what I'd learned, that Drew might have been a crook. I pulled into the parking lot that abutted the entrance to the jail and wondered if Tom had found out the same thing.

In winter, the Furman County Sheriff's Department looks like an imposing outpost in the middle of the Siberian hinterland. Its concrete walls soar five stories, but because there is no demarcation between the floors, it appears much taller. Even the bank of wavy-glassed windows, which allows sunlight to flood the interior, resembled a tall block of ice.

Snow had begun to fall again. I looked at my cell, and decided to try Aspen Meadow High, just to see if they could give me any information about Sandee Brisbane. Would they know about relatives Sandee might have had, besides her parents? Would they tell me who her friends were? Probably not, but I had to start somewhere. I had no idea whether the Furman County public schools were still in session, or if anybody would be there on Saturday.

The information operator connected me with what she said was the main number of Aspen Meadow High. What I got was the high screech of a fax machine. I tried information again, and my new helper said there was only one other number for Aspen Meadow High. It was another fax machine. When my hearing had recovered, I called information again. This time I asked the operator to stay on with me. I didn't necessarily want a person at the high school, I said, but I was hoping for voice mail. The operator tried what she said were the two numbers listed for the high school, then said there was nothing more that she could do for me after that. Both numbers were connected to fax machines.

Your tax dollars at work!

As the snow thickened, I slowed the van and tried Calhoun, the last name of Bobby, Sandee's ex-boyfriend. This was an even longer shot; there was no Robert or Bobby or Bob Calhoun anywhere in the Denver metropolitan area. Finally I phoned the Rainbow Club, where Sandee had been a stripper. This time I got a real person, a woman, to whom I politely explained what I was looking for: anyone who had known Sandee Brisbane, who might have been working under the stage name Sandee Blue or Sandee Calhoun.

"I'm sorry, we don't have anybody by that name," the woman replied.

"Well, how about Lana della Robbia or Dannyboy?" I asked desperately. "They both knew her, and they might know who her friends were—"

"Lana and Danny are both behind bars for money-laundering!" the woman cried. "So if you're looking for them, you're either a cop or a criminal." And with this, she hung up.

Clearly I would have to find another way to dig into Sandee's life.

By the time I got off the phone, a solid curtain of snow was falling in front of the sheriff's department. Where was Tom? I wondered. No, no, I wasn't going to bother him again. He might not approve of my visiting Patricia, and I didn't want to get into an argument about it. I took a deep breath, snagged two bags of cookies, and traipsed through the slushy muck to the imposing entrance to the jail.

When I told the desk sergeant I wanted to see Patricia Ingersoll, he said, "You're her attorney?" He sounded dubious. Undoubtedly my caterer's shirt and pants, printed with pictures of flying pots and sauté pans, and now spotted with salad dressing and who knew what else, did not make me look very lawyerly.

"Just a friend."

The desk sergeant rang up someone and talked in a low voice. After that he handled two incoming calls, disappeared for what felt like an age, and finally came back. His switchboard buzzed, at which point he told me I was free to go up to the fourth floor, the women's wing, where the desk sergeant would let me through to a bank of telephones, and I'd be able to talk to Patricia while looking through a glass wall. Would I be able to give her anything? I asked. Absolutely not, he said. I handed the fellow the bags of cookies, which surprised him, and told him I was Investigator Schulz's wife, and to distribute the goodies as he saw fit.

"Schulz's wife?" His Adam's apple bobbed up and down. Was I imagining it, or was that a note of fear in his voice?

I nodded and started up the staircase. Caterers get little exercise beyond racing around the kitchen and serving folks heaping platters of roast beef, potatoes, and chocolate cake. We think this is enough to keep us in shape, but it really isn't, especially if you have to taste the beef gravy, see if the potatoes need more cream, and swallow a teensy corner of chocolate cake, just to make sure they're all, as my motto promises, *just right*. Of course, climbing four flights of stairs probably didn't qualify as enough exercise either, and by the time I got to the fourth floor, I thought I was going to have a coronary.

The sergeant on four directed me to a booth with a phone, and soon I was face-to-face with Patricia. No question about it, orange wasn't her color.

"Oh God, Goldy," she said, "I'm sorry you're not . . . well, sorry, thank you for coming. I thought you were my lawyer." She wiped tears away. "These *stupid* cops! I didn't *do* anything. They will not *listen* when I tell them I loved Drew."

"I'm listening."

"Thanks." Her eyes spilled more tears. Her normally perfectly waved platinum hair fell around her face in greasy strands, and her face was blotched from crying. "I just don't know what to do next."

I kept a soothing tone in my voice. "What did they tell you about why you were arrested?"

Her eyes got wide, but her eyebrows did not climb her forehead. *Hmm,* I thought. *Botox.* Like the previous night, her voice was pleading. "I'm a scrap-booker, okay? I keep before and after pictures of all the folks in *Losers,* and everybody loves it. Somebody told the police they should investigate me for Drew's murder. I told you last night how the cops showed up at my house with a warrant. I managed to get out of there, but my neighbor said she could see them up-ending tables, dumping out papers, and tossing my scrapbooking stuff all over the floor. I called Brew-ster, he said to go to your house. Apparently, in the cops' thrashing around, they did snag one of the X-Acto knives I use for scrapbooking. The cops insist this knife has blood on it. If it did, I told Brewster, it had to be *my* blood. I always knick myself when I'm doing a scrapbook. Any blood on that knife had to be old. And dry. Plus, I'm AB negative. I don't know what type blood Drew had, but mine's very rare. But did the cops believe me? Hell no." She choked back a sob. "This sheriff's department is so screwed up. Your husband is working for an incompetent organiza-tion."

I ignored this. "So now they're testing the blood on your knife?"

"Yes, Goldy, that's what I've been trying to tell you!" Patricia was practically shouting, and I held the phone receiver an inch from my ear. "As soon as they get the test results, I'll be out of here and able"—she whacked the Plexiglas window between us with her free hand—"to sue this department for false arrest. That'll serve them right."

"If it's your blood," I said confidently, "then they'll release you. Listen, you told me last night how Drew was having problems with several people—Elizabeth, Neil Tharp, and Smithfield MacArthur. Do you know more about what was going on with them? Or do you know anyone else who had a beef with Drew and a motive to kill him? If you and Brewster can offer the police a plausible theory, then it would help clear your name."

I was hoping she'd bring up Drew's stalker, who I still believed was Sandee Brisbane. But instead she said, "Neil Tharp. He was trying to take over Drew's business. Drew hired him last year because the business had gotten too big and he couldn't keep it afloat on his own. He needed help keeping in touch with investors, getting back to them quickly, finding the exact maps they were looking for. You know how rich folks are. You don't coddle them, they get pissed. Some collectors were beginning to have temper tantrums, and it was Neil's job to calm them down."

"Was Smithfield MacArthur one of those temperamental clients?"

"He's a baby like the rest of them. You have to take their calls, sweet-talk them, reassure them that they're going to *make* money, not lose it. Do you know if the library surveillance camera recorded any of Drew's investors?"

"I don't know what the investigators are seeing on the surveillance stuff. They're probably reviewing it now." I thought of bald, angry Larry Craddock . . . and of Sandee. "Roberta Krepinski, the librarian, told the police you were there yesterday afternoon."

"Oh, jeez, why can't that woman mind her business? Her *own* business?" Patricia shrugged. "I was meeting someone from Losers. Ralph Shelton, the cops can check." I nodded; I knew Ralph. He'd never looked overweight to me, but sometimes people have an unusual idea of what it means to look healthy and fit.

"Did you talk to Drew when you were at the library?" I asked. "The cops thought he might have been meeting a client there. Did he mention if he was?"

"I didn't know Drew was there and I didn't talk to him. I didn't see anybody who would have been meeting Drew at the library, either, except for maybe that damn Larry Craddock. I avoid him more than I would a carrier of bubonic plague."

Having had two unpleasant encounters with the man, I shared her feelings, but still I asked, "Why?"

She rolled her eyes. "Larry Craddock was always whining about how he taught Drew everything about map collecting, but Drew was way more successful than he was, and should take Larry on as a partner, and stuff like that. He had a store with the most ridiculous name—Larry's Map Lair. Would you buy something in a store with that name? Well, anyway, he had to close it. He sort of blamed Drew for that, too."

"Why did he think it was Drew's fault?"

"Larry claimed that Drew kept undercutting him with clients. But mostly I think he was just jealous." She waved her free hand. "Larry says he loves maps more than anyone in the world, and he's a great dealer, and people should come to *him* because he has such a great appreciation for what he's doing, blah, blah, blah. We sometimes ended up at the same cocktail parties, given by the big map collectors? Larry would bug Drew to do business with him, and I had to listen to Larry rant and rave about how much he loved maps, he had adored them his whole life, et cetera, et cetera. You could be bored to death listening to him. I'll take the plague any day. It's quicker and less painful."

"Oh, dear."

"I also told the cops all about seeing Larry at the library yesterday, and my meeting with Ralph. I dropped off some old cookbooks for their book sale. Last time I looked, that wasn't illegal." She paused. "Goldy."

My shoulders sagged. "What?"

Patricia leaned forward, so that her small, perfect nose was almost touching the Plexiglas. "You have to help me find out who killed Drew."

"Look, Patricia, I was asking questions about Drew *because* I was trying to help you. But as soon as they have the blood test from your knife back, you'll be cleared. The police are good at their job, Patricia, we should let them handle it."

"Excuse me, but the police are not good at their job. If they were, I wouldn't be here!"

"I know you're upset about what happened. But the department has to follow every lead."

She took a deep breath. "Listen, Goldy, I'm really scared. I told you Drew had lots of enemies . . . and I started to tell you the rest of it last night." I waited. Patricia went on: "There was something worse going on. Somebody was stalking Drew. A woman. She was sending him threatening e-mails, and she left a dead mouse on his doorstep." She screwed her mouth to one side. "Well, actually, Drew said it was a vole."

My skin prickled. "A woman was stalking him, and left a rodent on his doorstep?"

Patricia nodded. "Young-looking, maybe late twenties. Brunette." Patricia lifted her chin. "Okay, well, I didn't want to bring this up, but it's somebody you know."

I tried to make my face passive, but Patricia, probably used to reading the lies in the faces of cheating dieters, caught it right away.

"You know who it is, don't you?" she said quickly, her face angry, triumphant. "You know who I'm talking about. I saw her once parked at the end of Drew's road. I thought, *Hmm. That face looks familiar.*" Patricia's manicured index fingernail tapped hard on the glass. "I'm not a dumb blonde, you know, Goldy. I can read the newspaper just like anyone else."

The desk sergeant entered from Patricia's side. "Miss Ingersoll?" his muffled voice announced. "The blood test just came back."

"That was quick," I muttered.

"You're free to leave the jail now, Miss Ingersoll," the sergeant said.

Patricia said, "Yeah, no surprise, eh, Sergeant? You gonna give me an apology?" But he had gone. Patricia turned back toward me. "Goldy, I know you talked to the cops. They must have told you about Drew's stalker. *I* told you about it last night."

"You hinted at it. And how did you get a blood test done so quickly?"

"Brewster insisted on it. Anyway, you and I both know who this stalker might be, and how dangerous she is. What if she decides to come after me, too? Or what if it was one of the others—you know, Elizabeth or Larry or Neil or even Smithfield, in a disguise?"

"Well, I—"

"I can't keep looking over my shoulder, waiting for this killer to strike. Look, I'll pay you to find out who killed Drew."

"I'm not going to take money for looking into this, Patricia," I protested. "Maybe you should hire a private investigator to help you, someone who does this for a living."

"I'll hire you to cater our big Losers New Year's banquet," Patricia went on, undeterred. "At New Year's, everybody goes on a diet, so we have a low-cal banquet to celebrate. I charge a hundred bucks a pop, and the profit is almost forty percent for whatever caterer does it. Plus, I pay cash."

"Patricia, come *on.* Did you tell the cops what you've told me? Did you tell the cops what you know about Drew's stalker? About who you think it is, and the vole, and everything?"

"Of course I told them. But I don't really think they believed me. After all, Sandee Brisbane's supposed to be dead, isn't she? So to them, I just looked like someone who was trying to pin the blame on a ghost."

I pressed my fingers between my eyebrows. I was getting a colossal headache. "Drew reported the e-mails and the police were taking it seriously. And maybe this stalker isn't who you think it is. Maybe you're just imagining you saw her."

"Sandee Brisbane killed your ex-husband. I didn't imagine that. Now she may have killed my fiancé." Tears again spilled out of her eyes. "Drew and I were going to get married at Christmas. Our gift to each other." She bit her lower lip. "I'm sure the woman I saw was Sandee. She didn't die in that fire, and now she's come back here, and she went after Drew just the way she did your ex. What if she comes after me now? Maybe she'll stalk you or your son. You have to help me, Goldy. We both have a stake in this! Please think about it."

With that, Patricia hung up the phone. She moved quickly out of her chair and toward the door that led back to the women's section of the jail. I sat there, pondering the implications of what she'd said. Sandee might have come back to hurt me. Sandee might have come back to hurt *Arch*.

Of course, I'd been having nightmares about both possibilities since the twenty-fifth of November.

But I was still stuck with the overwhelming question, Why *had* Sandee come back to Aspen Meadow, anyway?

10

I sat, stunned, for a few minutes as I tried to think of what to do. Finally the sergeant told me it was time to go.

"Criminals do that, don't they?" he remarked as he walked me to the staircase. "Make ya feel awful whenever ya see 'em."

I wanted to retort that Patricia was no criminal. I'd catered her wedding reception, for God's sake. I'd seen her put a forkful of low-cal angel food cake into Frank Ingersoll's waiting mouth. She'd burst out laughing when he'd swallowed it, and she'd winked at me. Even if she'd figured out Sandee was following Drew, and had been less than pleasant to deal with, it wasn't all her fault. The sergeant had told her she was free to leave. So . . . she'd been let go. But I supposed sergeants became jaded and saw most of their charges as guilty. So instead I merely thanked him and walked haltingly back down the stairs. I tried to think. By the time I arrived at the ground floor, I had gathered my wits enough to realize I wanted to talk to Patricia some more.

I asked the desk sergeant if I could give Patricia Ingersoll a ride home. A smile cracked his doughy face as he said he would make a call and find out the prisoner's status. After a few moments of bureaucratic squabbling interspersed with being put on hold, the sergeant informed me that my friend was all set and didn't need transport, as he called it. When I asked if I could meet my friend at the door where she was being discharged, he replied that she'd already left.

"That was quick."

"Yeah, they're usually real eager to get out of here." I got another big smile, which I returned. The sergeant was much friendlier since I'd given him the cookies, and he offered the information that a couple of folks from Brewster Motley's office had dropped off Patricia's car in the jail parking lot. I shook my head, trying to imagine how much Brewster's office would bill Patricia for *that* particular favor. On the other hand, it probably wouldn't have worked to fold Patricia into my van alongside Arch, Gus, Todd, and a truckload of snowboarding equipment. The three boys would call and holler to one another and command me to *turn up the music!*, all while Patricia tried to tell me her theories about Drew's murder.

Perhaps it was good Patricia had her own transport.

I plodded toward the van through the whispering fall of snow. I realized that my visit with Patricia had not made me feel like a kind, moral person who had visited her catering client and friend in need. Instead, after the library breakfast and the garden-club lunch, my interchange with Patricia had made me painfully weary. I wasn't talking run-of-the-mill weary, but bone-weary, ready to spend a day or two in bed. Maybe that was because now, given what Patricia had said about Drew's stalker, I was convinced that Sandee Brisbane was really alive and somehow involved in what had happened to the former D.A.

Were we next, as Patricia feared? Remembering John Richard's shot-up, bloodied body, I simply could not face the thought. Plus, I was scheduled to cater tonight, and for that I needed to be alert. Instead, I leaned against the van for a few moments, drinking in the cold, snowy air.

What was called for, I decided once I'd pulled myself together and started the van chugging out of the department lot, was some more caffeine. Or chocolate. Or both. In any event, the boys would *definitely* want steaming cocoa with marshmallows melting on top, so I rationalized stopping at an expensive coffee shop to do some indulging.

Fifteen minutes later, after laying out enough money for the down payment on a car, I concentrated on not allowing my hands to wobble as I carried a heavily laden cardboard tray out to my van. I'd splurged on new thermally lined covered mugs, which the coffee-shop employees had happily washed. They'd filled three of them with extra-hot cocoa mounded with fluffy marshmallows, and one with extra-hot mocha—for yours truly. I put the tray on the passenger seat, started the van, and pulled out my mocha.

The first sip was too hot. I replaced the drink in its carrier as unexpected tears rose in my eyes. Back on the road, I stomped on the accelerator and kept myself warm hoping Sandee was somewhere extremely cold. Incredibly, this worked for the entire twenty minutes it took my straining van's engine to make it back up the hill, to the Regal Ridge Snow Sports Area.

Even at four o'clock, darkness was descending like a velvet cloak. Enormous overhead lights at the RRSSA illuminated the thick veil of swirling flakes, behind which skiers and snowboarders merrily squirted down the mountain. I could not make out Arch and his pals, so I parked in the lot facing the ski slope, alongside a line of cars with their motors running. I had no doubt that those vehicles held mothers as worried and protective as yours truly. Why did we think anxiously watching for our children would keep them from harm? I had no idea.

I put in another call to Tom, reached his voice mail again, and told him where I was. I left a brief summary of my visit with Patricia Ingersoll, which had brought up more questions than it had provided answers. And speaking of questions, had Tom discovered anything about Sandee? I asked. Oh, and I'd had a bit of an encounter with Larry Craddock. Sergeant Boyd could fill him in on the details. Also, Larry had claimed that Drew had had *two* valuable maps, and had offered them for sale. Meanwhile, Drew had only had *one* map on him, which the department had discovered inside his clothes. So either somebody had stolen the additional map, leaving the one inside the coat, or somebody had stolen both, and Drew had had another map in his inside pocket when he'd offered the first two to Larry.

What did Tom think? I wondered.

And while I was asking questions, I went on, had the department figured out by what means Drew Wellington had died?

While speaking into my cell, I furrowed my brow as I noticed a particularly fast-moving skier. It was a woman, judging from her slender shoulders and long hair. She wasn't wearing a hat, and her curly hair flew out above her goggles and around her head. As I watched in horror, she began to ski even faster as she approached a group of kids waiting in the lift line near the bottom of the hill. The kids yelped and jumped out of her way, but the woman kept on going. What was the matter with her? Was she in some kind of race? If so, with whom? I thought I heard her scream for help as she approached a crowd of skiers who'd already reached the bottom and were making their way over to the lift line. The woman was still skiing madly, out of control.

She crashed into the moving snake of skiers like a grenade. Bodies, skis, and poles went flying. There were shouts for help. I leaped from the van at the same time that a dozen mothers with the same idea jumped from their vehicles. We all were intent on hurrying over to see who was hurt and how badly. Unfortunately, it was slow going. A cold wind bit through my jacket. My sneaker-clad feet slipped and slid on the snowpacked pavement. By the time I got to the scene of what Arch and his pals would have called a *major yard sale*, I was cursing snow sports. Really, though, I was once again ripped up with worry: this time over whether my son was at the bottom of the pile of bodies.

But Arch was not there. Other mothers fretted over offspring, brushing off snow, checking for sore spots, and casting murderous glances at the woman who'd been skiing so wildly. Still flopped on her backside in the snow, she was sobbing uncontrollably. Perhaps she hadn't injured anyone but herself.

Beside the prone figure, a mother was clutching her son to her. He looked about ten, and seemed more curious about what had happened than he was hurt. Still, the mother hollered at the woman, "The ski patrol should yank your ticket for the rest of the season! You don't belong on the slopes."

"That's enough," I told the angry mother. I leaned over the crying woman. "It was an accident." Oh God. The skier was Roberta Krepinski.

I looked around. The angry mother was stomping back to her car. Farther away, there were mothers tending to their kids and members of couples assuring one another that they were okay. Alas, there were never more than two members of the ski patrol on duty at RRSSA, and neither one of them was anywhere in sight. I slipped through the white stuff until I got to a snowboarder, and asked him to see if there was an extra person manning the lift who could come over and help us. Then I knelt down next to Roberta.

"It's Goldy." I kept my voice low. "Tell me if you think anything's broken. Only don't move."

"Oh God, Goldy, I'm so sorry." Roberta grunted and tried to right herself.

"Stop! You're only going to make yourself feel worse."

"I'm okay, really. It was so stupid." She began blubbering again. In spite of my warnings, she rolled over on her right side and cursed her skis as she released them from her boots. With a terrific moan, she heaved herself into a sitting position. "Did I hurt anybody? Oh God, please say no."

I glanced around for any lingering mothers or injured skiers. "I don't think so. Not seriously, anyway." She moaned again and tried to get onto her hands and knees. "Please don't try to get up, Roberta, you're just going to—"

"I'm fine!" She collapsed clumsily onto her backside, then put her head in her hands. She'd lost one of her gloves in the collision, and her hair was hanging in wet clumps.

"Roberta, come on. How about some aspirin? I've got some in my car. Come to think of it, I've got some hot—"

"I don't want aspirin . . . Please don't go to any trouble. I just felt dizzy again, the way I did this morning when I fainted. I . . . lost control of my skis. I've never been a good skier. I shouldn't have come here. I was trying to get my mind off everything that's happened."

"Okay, lady, calm down." The stocky, red-suited ski patrolman had schussed up so quickly, I hadn't even heard him. He released his skis and bent down. "Be quiet for a minute while I check you out, okay?"

"No!" she yelped. "I don't want—"

"Does this hurt?" the man asked, grasping Roberta's ankles.

"Please, I'm okay. Just let me go home. Okay, my toes are frozen. But if you'll just get me to my car, I'm sure they'll thaw and—"

"How about this?" The patrolman, undaunted by Roberta's protests, continued his probing until he had thoroughly checked her for injuries. Once he'd determined nothing was broken or sprained, he helped Roberta to a standing position and requested that I take her skis and poles. "Can you get her warmed up before she tries to drive her own car?" he asked me. For the first time I saw his deeply lined, tanned face. "I don't want her to drive when she's shaken up like this."

"Yes, yes, of course."

The patrolman's expression was one of relief. When he'd skied away, I picked up Roberta's skis and poles and helped her to my van, which I'd left running, thank

God. Once I'd moved the drinks tray and situated a shivering Roberta in the passenger seat, I handed her the mocha, now just warm instead of boiling hot, and ordered her to drink it. She took a big swallow and put the mug back in the holder.

"I'm really much better now. I think maybe I'm coming down with something, a cold or the flu. I should just go home and go to bed."

"This has been difficult on everybody," I commiserated. "I was just at the jail, where I saw Patricia Ingersoll—"

"Do you think she killed Drew?"

"No, and the police don't either. She's been released. The evidence they had against her proved to be a nonstarter."

Roberta reached for the mocha and drank some more. Her face looked troubled. "I know she's kind of a friend of yours, but . . . she may not be as nice a person as you think she is."

"Oh? What do you mean?"

"She's at the library an awful lot. She's even held some Losers meetings there. And I would see her talking with her hairdresser nearly every week or so, and I don't think it was about her coiffure."

"Really? How do you know the person is her hairdresser?"

"I know because she's my hairdresser, too. Although you could never tell it now," she muttered as her fingers attempted to untangle the masses of curls. "There are a lot of rumors that my hairdresser may also sell prescription drugs, like Ritalin, on the side. People take Ritalin illegally, as an energy booster or to help them concentrate, or to lose weight. Exercise and diet sometimes aren't seen as enough, if you want to be really thin."

"You're saying Patricia buys Ritalin from her hairdresser in the library?" I asked, incredulous.

"I don't know that that's the case for sure, or I'd call the police. But it does seem rather strange that they're always meeting there, isn't it? I mean, especially since they aren't checking out any books."

So there was drug dealing in the library, in addition to murder. The world was going to hell in a handbasket.

I checked my watch as Roberta continued to drink my mocha. I didn't mind. Arch and the boys were due at the van in ten minutes. Roberta seemed to have calmed down, and a question was gnawing my brain. Had Roberta ever seen *Sandee* at the library? In any context? Sandee was a former stripper, and I wouldn't have put it past her to deal drugs—or anything else, for that matter.

"Roberta, were you in town when my ex-husband was found murdered last summer?"

She sipped the mocha. "Yes. Why?"

"Do you know," I said slowly, "or *did* you know Sandee Brisbane? She was Cecelia Brisbane's daughter." When Roberta didn't say anything, I swallowed. "Sandee confessed to murdering my ex. Then she disappeared into that big forest fire we had last summer, up in the Aspen Meadow Wildlife Preserve."

Roberta shook her head. "I knew Cecelia. Not Sandee, or Alexandra, as Cecelia called her. I read that Alexandra—Sandee, that is—had been burned to death in that fire. If she's dead, why are you worrying about her?"

I bit my lip. "There's a possibility she's still alive. Patricia thinks Sandee was following Drew and her. You know the young woman who was sending hostile e-mails to Drew Wellington from libraries, whom the police were looking for? It might be Sandee."

Roberta gave me a dubious look.

"Listen, Roberta," I plowed on. "I'm convinced I saw Sandee at the library yesterday afternoon, right before you found Drew. She . . . it looked as if she might be watching him. Or maybe she was meeting with him, or planning to, I don't know. Sandee scares me, Roberta. She killed John Richard. She could be after Arch. Or me. Maybe you saw her and didn't know it, or noticed something relevant. Some little thing that you wouldn't think was important at the time? It could help me figure out why Sandee was at the library and what her interest in Drew Wellington might have been. She's a young woman, slender build, with long brunette hair. Please tell me if you think you might have seen her."

Roberta exhaled a long stream of air and looked out the windshield. "No, I haven't seen her, Goldy. One of those threatening e-mails did come from our library, though. Unfortunately, our surveillance system is digital, and doesn't keep more than the previous two days of images. So we don't have a face to go with the use of the computer that day." She bit the insides of her cheeks. "There *was* something else strange that happened yesterday afternoon. Around half past three, Drew Wellington apparently staggered up to the checkout desk. The librarian who was manning the desk thought he might have been . . . hurting in some way. But Drew didn't check anything out, and the librarian got distracted, and next thing you know, he was gone."

"You're sure he didn't check out a book? Did he return one? Did he talk to anyone?"

"No, nothing. That's all I know. Look, I should go. Thanks for being so nice and helping me out. And for the mocha. I'll find a way to pay you back, Goldy, I promise."

"You don't have to pay me back, and you don't really have to go," I assured her. "You're not bothering me in the slightest." I felt as if I was clinging to her, my source of information, my reference librarian. Maybe, in spite of what she said, she'd seen Sandee eyeing Arch. Maybe she was the one person who could help. "Roberta, please don't *leave*!" But she had already slid her lithe body out the door, which she slammed behind her. She took a moment to retrieve her skis and poles, mumbled her thanks again, then took off. In the distance, a muffled gong sounded for the ski lift to close, which meant no more up trips, just down ones. I watched Roberta's red hair, the ringlets now hanging like seaweed, bob through the crowd of skiers. I hit the dashboard with my fist.

"Hey, Mom, chill!" Arch opened the passenger door, but his voice sounded far away. I glanced over at him. Arch, with his goggles on top of his head, had drawn his sweaty, impatient face into a mass of wrinkles. "We need you to push the button for the side door, okay?" I whacked the dashboard again. "Mom? What's the matter, anyway?"

"Nothing!" I cried as I banged the steering wheel with both hands.

"Do you have a lot of stored-up anger?"

Dear God, I thought, *deliver me from a tenth grader taking an elective in psychology.* "I'm fine." I hit the button to release the side door. "Just put your snowboards in the back and hop in."

"Right, Mom. You just smacked that dashboard and the steering wheel 'cuz they were pissing you off."

I took a deep breath. Arch worried about me endlessly, and occasionally covered up his concern with brattiness. "Sweetheart, I'm fine. Look. I've got cocoa for you, Todd, and Gus, and it's getting colder every second you leave that door open."

Arch muttered, "Oh, *Mom.*" Still, he quietly acquiesced, and within five minutes the snowboards were loaded and the boys had stowed the rest of their gear in the back of the van. I handed the boys their drinks, and there was a chorus of thank-yous. My tires crunched over the packed snow of the parking lot as we joined the long line of cars. Ahead of us, clouds of exhaust crystallized in the freezing air. As we headed home, the boys sipped their hot chocolate and talked in excited tones about shredding, cruising, and having yard sales, which had nothing to do with domestic decluttering and everything to do with what my generation called *wiping out.* Well, at least they were happy.

I joined another string of cars on the interstate, their bright brake lights already illuminating the tarry dusk. When my cell rang, I slowed and tentatively answered. I didn't like the idea of trying to talk while I was on a snowpacked interstate, with white stuff still coming down and three boisterous teenagers in the backseat.

But it was Tom. Every muscle in my body relaxed, and suddenly I didn't mind giving my mocha to Roberta, because Tom's voice was like cocoa, and it did, in fact, warm me up. "Hey, Miss G. Heard you visited the jail and didn't even stop in to say hello."

"Sorry. I was there seeing Patricia, and then I had to come pick up Arch and his pals. Patricia was pretty upset—"

"Yeah, yeah, Miss AB Negative. Too bad she didn't confess to you, we coulda wrapped this thing up, gone home early."

I lowered my voice. "What do you think about all the stuff she told you? That Sandee was following Drew. That Sandee left a dead vole on Drew's doorstep. I don't know why she didn't tell me all this when she came over to our house last night, do you?"

"No, I sure don't. But you're bent on helping with this case, huh? You're worried about Patricia, and you're worried about Sandee Brisbane?"

"Well, yes."

"Oh-kay. Well, if Patricia had a videotape of Sandee Brisbane following Drew, or if we could get a good shot of someone leaving the vole, we'd be more inclined to believe her. All we know is that both you and Patricia claim to have seen someone who looks like Sandee Brisbane, but with long brunette hair instead of the short blond variety."

I added, feeling less confident, "And the vole?"

"Oh, for God's sake, Goldy. If it had been a real threat, don't you think Drew would have called it in? He was already paranoid about those three very vague e-mails. He would have told us about a dead rodent. For all we know, that vole just up and died of old age on Drew Wellington's stoop."

"All right, all right." I was conscious of the traffic slowing. "You know I've got the curry party to do tonight for the MacArthurs. I'm so sorry I won't see you until late." I waited to make sure the boys were talking and wouldn't hear me, then I lowered my voice to a whisper. "I miss you."

The boys erupted in gales of laughter. Had they been listening? Hmm. Maybe Drew Wellington wasn't the only one who was paranoid.

"I miss you, too, Miss G. By the way, thanks for sending Larry Craddock our way in a patrol car. He doesn't like you and Julian and whoever was helping you today very much. But he did tell us about the two maps Drew showed him, including the one left in his briefcase."

"Did he provide a description of it?"

"You bet he did. And it's not the one we found on Drew."

"Well, aren't you glad I helped you with that?"

"I'm ecstatic."

"Here's something else. Roberta thinks Patricia might have been purchasing Ritalin from her hairdresser at the library."

Tom actually laughed. "We didn't find any Ritalin in Drew's system. But I swore I'd give you an update on Wellington once we knew what did in fact kill him. He was poisoned. We found heavy doses of cyanide and Rohypnol in his blood. Rohypnol is a date-rape drug, illegal of course, but available all over. The Rohypnol was in his flask, along with his sour mash. The cyanide was mixed into the coffee in his thermos. He also was stabbed with an X-Acto knife, as it turns out, but it didn't kill him."

"For God's sake."

"Half past three, we've got Drew Wellington on the surveillance camera, walking as if he's real drunk, up to the library's front desk. He disappears for a few minutes, then he limps back out. He didn't ask for help of any kind, that's the weird thing. Did he know he'd been drugged? Did he think he'd just had too much to drink? Because he was over the legal limit for DUI."

That jibed with what Roberta had told me. "Drugged, drunk, poisoned, and stabbed. I still don't get it."

"He had a drinking problem. He'd always had a drinking problem. And the flask of sour-mash whiskey in his briefcase didn't help."

"Yeah, I saw the flask."

"Our theory is that he was drugged with the booze, then thought he might feel better if he had some caffeine. And that's what killed him."

"Let me get this straight. He came into the library just before three, maybe already having started drinking. He asked Roberta for help with an atlas, said he was there to meet clients, and then offered two maps for sale to Larry Craddock. Drew might have been planning to meet with someone else as well. He also sat in the corner to sip some more whiskey. At half past three, he stumbled up to the checkout desk to do nothing. Larry Craddock says that he went *back* to Drew's corner and waited for him for twenty minutes, apparently while Drew was, uh, still doing nothing."

"Maybe he was in the bathroom," Tom offered.

"That's an awful long bathroom break. Anyway, Larry says he gave up and went back to the reading room. Then, apparently, Drew returned to his chair in the corner without asking for help, drank the cyanide-laced coffee, got stabbed, and died. This just makes less and less sense."

"All right, here are two more things for you to chew on while you're serving your curry dishes."

"Shoot."

"This was a couple of months ago. Neil Tharp gave Rohypnol to his girlfriend. Well, she wasn't really his girlfriend. She was a girl he picked up in a bar and brought back to his house. The drug can make you feel relaxed and like you want to have sex with someone. But this gal didn't, and she had enough sense to lurch out Neil's door and call 911. We booked him, don't worry, but he said to check his blood, which we did, and he also had it in *his* system, and he said they both took it to get high and have an orgy. Although who would want to have an orgy with that guy is beyond me. As you would say, yuck."

"Okay. So Neil can get bad stuff and has used it before. What's the second thing?"

"Drew Wellington had been accused of cutting maps out of valuable atlases. Like in the rare-book rooms of university libraries. A library aide at Stanford found an X-Acto knife blade right near where Drew was sitting one time. They hired investigators and even found one missing map. But Drew beat the rap because of the way the arrest was handled."

"Had Drew *sold* stolen maps?" But I knew the answer to this already, because of what I'd heard from Rosie Barton, though Drew had claimed that map wasn't hot.

"We don't know if he sold squat. It's not as easy to get a search warrant in California as it is here. He walked off before they could rummage around in his briefcase and on his person. The library's rare-books librarian and a volunteer staff did a painstaking inventory, and yes, they're missing some valuable maps, cut right out of atlases, some of them checked out by Wellington. But they don't know *when* those maps were stolen."

"Tom, I heard Rosie Barton, a garden-club member, talking today about Drew selling stolen maps." I told Tom what I'd overheard from Rosie.

"Okay, thanks, we'll talk to her."

"Don't go yourself, okay? I don't want the garden club to think their caterer is eavesdropping on their conversations."

"But that's what you're doing." When I didn't say anything, Tom chuckled. "All right, Miss G., we'll say we put it together from other sources and records. Only, there are very few records, even fewer receipts for bills of sale, at Wellington's place. In the last five years, it looks as if he paid taxes on—get this—only about fifty thousand dollars' worth of annual income."

"Fifty thousand dollars? But he supposedly took the money he got from Elizabeth and increased it exponentially!" I thought for a moment. "Did Neil Tharp have any records?"

"Nope. Or so he claims."

"Well, did Tharp have knowledge of Drew pilfering maps? I mean, that he's admitted to you."

"You bet he did. He's our other source, if Rosie Barton clams up on us. Tharp thinks Drew was killed by someone who'd been sold a valuable map he'd stolen from a big collection. You go to sell that kind of thing, it's been reported stolen, you're going to be in a whole lot of hell from the FBI."

"Okay, so maybe someone was anticipating trouble from the FBI. But tell me why a person who'd *bought* a stolen map wouldn't just tell the *FBI* who had sold him the map. Then the Bureau could go out and arrest that guy—"

"Good question. But sometimes people don't want to own up to law enforcement that they've been duped by someone smarter than they are. Look, I gotta go. I've got a whole list of people here who dealt with Drew Wellington, and I've got to start calling them."

"Wait. People don't want to own up to law enforcement that they've been taken for a ride? So then what?"

"So, Miss G., sometimes they'll go out and deal with the person who made them feel like a dummy. Sometimes they'll kill him."

11

Tom disconnected, and suddenly I missed him terribly, his wisdom, his loving glance, his body enclosing mine. Wait a minute . . . I didn't have to suffer, right? I mean, we were married, weren't we? So I called him right back.

He picked up on the first ring. "Did I forget something?"

Ah, caller ID. I whispered into the phone, "You didn't tell me you, you know"—I lowered my voice another notch—"that you loved me." Embarrassed, I turned my head to see if the boys were listening, but they were all intent on a handheld video game that Arch was vigorously punching and groaning over.

"You need me to do that?"

I thought of Patricia, her grief and her loneliness. "Uh, I guess so."

"I've got some guys here right now," Tom warned, his voice businesslike. In the background, male voices made noises about leaving him alone. They would come back later or call, they offered.

I could hear the desperation in my voice, but didn't care. Put it down to visiting an enraged woman in jail. "Just, can you come home early? I'd love to see you before I have to head out for the curry party."

"You got it." This time when we hung up, I didn't feel quite as emotionally disconnected.

I sighed and tried to mull over all Tom had told me about Drew. Yesterday afternoon, the former D.A. had come into the library, ostensibly to meet clients. Larry Craddock claimed Drew had been there to show him some valuable maps, but I wasn't sure I trusted Larry's version of events. Roberta said Drew had told her he was meeting people there, so who else besides Larry—if Drew actually met with Larry—might Drew have been planning to see? Had he already been drunk when he arrived at the library? Or had he just curled up in a cor-ner to surreptitiously sip whiskey from the flask in his briefcase? Had the Rohypnol been in there already, or had someone poured it in while Drew was, say, asking

Roberta about an atlas? What about the cyanide? I had the same questions regarding when Drew's coffee had been spiked with that particular poison.

In any event, he'd drunk at least whiskey before lurching to the library's front desk. Had he had any coffee at that point? I doubted it, as cyanide was notoriously fast acting. Nor, I was willing to bet, had he been stabbed by half past three. Someone who'd been knifed with an X-Acto blade would know he'd been attacked.

So he'd been drunk, and possibly drugged, when he staggered to the checkout desk. He hadn't taken out any books. He might have been in pain, but he hadn't asked for help. Why not? Had machismo reared its head, or had he been afraid that once again, someone would discover that he had a drinking problem? Maybe he had been so drunk, he just assumed anything he was feeling was a result of the alcohol.

Sandee had been watching him, I knew that for sure, now that I had confirmation from Patricia that Sandee was indeed alive and had been stalking Drew. Patricia and Neil had also been at the library yesterday. Our local book cache was a popular place, apparently. But with only one surveillance camera at the front of the library, nobody had been recorded doing anything nefarious. Sandee, in sending threatening e-mails to Drew from public libraries, had certainly proven adept at avoiding surveillance cameras.

And then there was the map that Drew had in his coat when Roberta and I found him. Had he been trying to make a sale? Had he just completed one? Larry had told the police that Drew was trying to sell him two maps. If the one in his coat pocket was one of them, what might have happened to the other one? Had he sold it to somebody else? Why have one map hidden on his person? He'd asked to see an atlas "to check on something." With his propensity for stealing maps, could he have stolen a map from the library and tried to keep the theft hidden? I doubted very much that there were maps of any value in the Aspen Meadow Library, and made a mental note to ask Roberta or Tom about it.

Sandee Brisbane, who'd been stalking Drew, had been a member of the Aspen Meadow Explorers. That was one of the reasons she'd known her way around the wildlife preserve so well. So if Sandee took an interest in exploring, could that mean she was also interested in *maps*? Could she be involved in the valuable map business as well?

But that didn't really make sense. If it was true that Sandee had escaped the big forest fire in the preserve, and I believed that she had, then she would have to have known *current* maps of the preserve, wouldn't she? Not antique or rare ones. In any event, just as I doubted that there were valuable maps in our town library, I also found it hard to believe that there were anything beside topo surveys and such of Aspen Meadow and Furman County on those shelves.

I turned off the interstate and immediately slowed down, as the snow was already packed on the byway leading into town. The plowing folks were concentrating their efforts on the major highways, as usual. *Okay, where was I?* I thought. Talk about being lost. Oh yes, maps of our region . . . folks were always claiming that they'd found an old map that pointed the way to a chest of gold that Jesse James's gang had supposedly buried in our area. They were willing to sell the map . . . for a price. Uh-huh. So the logical question in all this was, if you had a map that showed the way to untold riches, why didn't you go and dig the treasure up and become wealthy? Why did you just want to sell the map to that spot?

I didn't know, and trying to think of the answers, plus maneuver the van, was giving me a headache.

"Want me to drive, Mom?" Arch piped up.

Oh, right, hand the wheel over to an inexperienced teenager when the white stuff was accumulating and we had two other kids in the car. "I'm fine, thanks," I called back. "We're almost there."

"But you slowed down, as if you were having trouble."

I gingerly piloted the van around a police car with its lights flashing . . . the officer was giving someone a ticket. Who would speed in these conditions? Somebody, apparently.

When we pulled onto our street, we had a good six inches of new white stuff, and of course we were unplowed. After two attempts, my van refused to make the climb from Main Street to our house. And I had an event that night. How was I supposed to get to the MacArthurs' place?

I allowed the van to drift backward until it was almost next to the curb and almost parallel.

"Nice parking job, Mom," Arch observed, and I was too preoccupied with my own problems to wonder whether he was being admiring or sarcastic.

"Could you boys please unload your stuff here?"

"Wow! Let's snowboard down Arch's street!" Gus exclaimed, and Arch and Todd busied themselves with getting ready to do just that. I tried to think back to my childhood in New Jersey. Had I ever been an adrenaline junkie? No, I told myself firmly as I plodded to our driveway. I was convinced that particular addiction was strictly a boy thing.

My shoulders dropped in relief when I saw Julian's trusty Range Rover parked in our driveway. We could load up his vehicle and then drive in tandem to the Mac-Arthurs' place, if necessary. Thank God for Julian. There was one thing caterers needed in their assistants more than skill with food; we needed dependability.

In the kitchen, Julian was bent over his job, which at that moment was filling a dozen porcelain bowls with curry condiments: chopped chutney, hard-cooked egg yolks and whites, raisins, coconut, and all the rest. Since curry is infinitely better done ahead and allowed to rest, I was glad I'd already made the sauce, even if I'd had to do it late last night, when I was exhausted.

"Hey, boss," Julian greeted me as he lifted his chin and smiled. "Glad you're okay. Where are the guys?"

I explained about having to leave the van at the foot of our road, and how Arch and Company had decided to snowboard down the unplowed street. Although I thought this was not at all appealing in the way of snow sports, Julian's only comment was "Cool."

I washed my hands and removed the hotel pans filled with chicken curry from the walk-in. I pulled off the plastic wrap and used a teaspoon to taste a tiny bite. The sauce tasted like heaven, even cold. Although I occasionally ground my own spices, I left the grinding of the fresh curry I used to a Thai shopkeeper in Boulder named Orasa. Orasa, whose age I had guessed to be between forty and sixty, had had a difficult time selling only spices the first couple of years her shop near the University of Colorado was opened. And then she had decided to make her own incense, soap, and candles. Now the tiny shop was always mobbed with a mélange of students, tourists, and potheads, who allegedly boiled the curry in water to cover up the drifting scent of marijuana.

"Yesterday I picked up beer from a couple of Boulder microbreweries," Julian said as he vigorously chopped salted peanuts for one of the condiment bowls. "I know it's the thing to serve with curry, but are you sure the MacArthurs are going to go for it? Aren't they the snobby wine type?"

"They are indeed." I snapped the tops onto the hotel pans and zipped back into the walk-in for the rice. "But I also picked up some expensive Dutch, German, and Canadian beers. Everybody will get a choice." I hauled out the pan of rice, then went back in for the brews. "And anyway, with the appetizers, they can have the fanciest wines they want." I placed the three six-packs on the counter and looked at Julian with concern. "The hors d'oeuvres!"

"Don't worry, I remembered." Julian's smile brightened his handsome face, and I saw why his cell phone often buzzed with calls from young women. He ducked into the walk-in and brought out two trays covered with plastic wrap. Each tray was dotted with perfect rows of triangles. "Wild mushroom risotto in phyllo, my latest creation for the bistro. Three dozen, all yours. They're served hot, and are good with fancy white or red wine." He put the trays on the counter and reached back into the walk-in for two more trays. Under the wrap I discerned small lettuce wraps with an asparagus spear and slice of avocado peeking out from each one. "Shrimp-salad rolls," he explained. "Served cold, and also great with wine."

"You're a god. I'll square with you later."

Julian snorted. "Don't worry about it." He cocked an eyebrow as he looked out the window over the sinks. "Still snowing out there. The roads are going to be snowpacked and icy. You sure they're going to go ahead with this?"

I said, "Oh, hell," as I realized I hadn't even checked my messages, and the machine light was blinking. I pressed the button, and Julian and I only had to hear Hermie MacArthur's voice say, "We're going ahead with the party," before we were once again bustling around the kitchen. "Everyone lives nearby, and they all want to try out their four-wheel-drive vehicles in the snow." Her voice crackled over the bad connection. "Oh, and we've added one person to the dinner, I hope that's all right." Julian groaned, and I broke out in a sweat. "Actually he invited himself to replace Drew Wellington and . . . there was nothing I could do about it. Also, could you bring something vegetarian? Our daughter is grounded to her room and, well"—Hermie cleared her throat, and it came through my machine as a crack of thunder—"anyway, she'll have a friend with her, too, and I think she's also a vegetarian. Don't worry, I'll pay you." Hermie's voice had turned huffy. "Although I don't know why I should have to—" At that point my machine cut her off. Thank God.

"You'd better believe you're going to pay us," Julian muttered as he retrieved a Gruyère quiche from the freezer side of the walk-in. "Oops, there's somebody banging on your front door."

It was Tom, arriving home later than I'd hoped. Still, I smiled. He looked like a young, handsome Santa, his nose red and shiny, his hair and dark parka dusted with snow, his arms full of packages.

"Ho, ho, ho," he said merrily when he saw me. Could this man always read my mind? Apparently so, and there was nothing I wanted more at that moment than to be swept up the stairs by Santa and shown some lovin'.

I walked toward him, relieved him of half of the packages, and gave him a big hug and a long smooch. I shivered, and not just because he was cold.

"How are the roads, Santa Claus?"

"Terrible, Mrs. Claus. You're still doing the MacArthurs' shindig?"

"Yes, I'm afraid so."

"Better take your sleeping bags, then, because the snow's really coming down." He picked up the packages, then walked past me into the kitchen, where he heaved his bags onto the marble counter. "I, meanwhile, have been given my marching orders by the boys, who are still outside on their snowboards."

"Please tell me they're okay on the road. Could they accidentally slide into Main Street?" That helicopter-hovering-mom tone that Arch hated so much still crept into my voice from time to time.

"They're fine." Tom returned to hang up his coat. "There are cars that have slid in the mess at the bottom of our hill. Nobody's coming up this way until a tow truck pulls those vehicles out. You all will have to go up our hill to get out." He winked at me. "Regarding the boys? I did have to take a flask of tequila away from them."

"Tom!"

He laughed all the way up the stairs. Julian reminded me that we were supposed to be at the MacArthurs' place by seven at the latest, so we could get all our preparations ready for an eight o'clock party. And, he added, we should forget my van and just take his Rover. I reluctantly agreed.

I called a good-bye to Tom, slipped into my parka and new boots that had a thicker tread on them than any of Goodyear's snow tires, and heaved up the first of our boxes. When Arch, Gus, and Todd saw Julian and me schlepping out boxes, they offered to assist us, and we had Julian's Range Rover packed up in less than a quarter of an hour. Bless the boys for helping. I doubted they actually felt altruistic motives. Anything to be thought of as "cool" by Julian was good enough for them.

And Julian was pretty cool himself, I thought as I swallowed and gripped the Rover's leather passenger seat while Julian maneuvered up our hill. Unfortunately, to get to the road leading to the interstate, we had to go down an icy hill that was steeper than our own street. Somebody in a Jeep came up too fast and began to slide wildly on the ice. *Note to SUV drivers,* I wished someone would say to Colorado newcomers, *four-wheel drive helps you on snow, not ice.* Julian, muttering obscenities, careened onto a ridge, whipped wildly past a "No Parking" sign and a juniper hedge, then galumphed down onto the snowpacked road out of town. The rest of our trip was slow going but steady, and my heart didn't climb into my throat again until we were making our final ascent to the MacArthurs' house.

The road to Regal Ridge was unplowed but not un-traveled, and Julian kept the Rover going steadily up-hill. Once we entered the Regal Ridge Country Club area, instead of a guardrail, which the home owners' association would have deemed unaesthetic, bulky boulders had been placed between the road and the chasm that separated the Ridge from the interstate. The rocks, now blanketed with snow, took on the un-real cast of frozen animals. I shivered. When we finally pulled around into the dead end where the MacAr-thurs' sprawling stucco house was located, I exhaled in relief.

"Well, darlin', you made it. How 'bout that?" Hermie MacArthur raised her almost colorless eyebrows and feigned surprise as she pushed open her side door. What did she think, we were going to ditch her? But I said nothing, only smiled up at her. She'd had her gray-blond hair styled in a curly mass that framed her broad face, and her light blue eyes missed nothing as she looked us up and down. I hadn't been able to tell, in our previous meeting, whether her Southern accent was real or af-fected, but now I decided it was real.

"I was just telling Smithfield I didn't know who I was s'pposed to call if y'all didn't show up, with these people coming . . ." On and on she chattered, and I nodded and smiled politely. Eventually I managed to zone out her talking as I brought in boxes. Julian, who moved much faster than I did whether he was wearing boots or sneakers, was doing the same thing. "I hope y'all brought some canapés," she went on as she surveyed our trays, "because Smithfield has some things to say t' the guests, I think that's the Barclays comin' now—"

Mercifully she disappeared.

"Hermie?" Smithfield MacArthur's ham face was redder than usual. "Now where did my wife go?" he demanded.

"She didn't say," Julian replied confidently as he leaned into the Viking stove to preheat it. "Are you going to serve the cocktails to the guests?" he asked. "We just need to know when to bring in the food—"

"I need help with my map!" Smithfield cried. "That's what I need."

"I'll help you," I offered. I ignored Julian groaning beside me, wiped my hands on my apron, and scooted after Smithfield. The needs of the host are foremost. Oops, that reminded me. I raced back to the kitchen door and stuck my head in. "Don't forget to heat up the quiche for our vegetarian teens—"

"I'm working on it. Just go see what the big guy's problem is."

Smithfield's problem, as it turned out, was how he was going to display his map of Colorado Springs.

Strictly speaking, it was a panorama, showing a snow-capped Pikes Peak, the aptly named Garden of the Gods nearby, and the town nestled at the base of the hills. Smithfield pointed impatiently to one side of the map, which was mounted on an indeterminate sort of board.

"Lift it carefully, then place it on the buffet and lean it against the wall."

I swallowed and looked around. The buffet was where we were supposed to lay out our bains-marie for hotel pans of curry and rice. No more. Smithfield had summarily shoveled the bains bases—already set out by Hermie, as promised—onto one of the four beige couches that had been spaced between massive walnut furniture in the cavernous living room. Great.

"Lord, girl, will you pay attention?" Smithfield snapped. "Place it exactly in the middle of the buffet."

I did as directed, thinking it had been a very long time since I'd been called a girl. With the panorama in place, Smithfield ordered me to hold it still as he fiddled with the overhead lights, which he brought from dim to bright. I blinked, thinking this was hardly the light one would want at dinner.

"Ah," he said finally. "Much better." He beamed at me. "What do you think? Isn't it magnificent?"

I squinted so I could see him. "It's fantast—"

Smithfield held up a meaty palm to stop me and quirked one of his bushy eyebrows. "Did you know William J. Palmer wanted to make the Springs an exemplary town in the bad old West? One of high moral character with no booze allowed?" Smithfield barked a laugh as my eyes widened. I was thinking of the curry that needed heating, the side dishes that had to be set out, and my need to find a new place for the buffet offerings. Yet here I was getting a lecture on high moral values in Colorado Springs.

"No, sir, I didn't know, but—"

"And the Barclays, our special guests tonight, are from Colorado Springs," he crowed, rubbing his hands together. "They are going to love—"

"Oh, Smithfield, what in holy hell have you done here?" Hermie shrieked as she appeared at the entry to the dining room, a pair of guests in tow, the presumptive Barclays. "What a mess!"

"Hermie! This is a panorama worth ten thousand dollars! It's not a mess. It's a thing of beauty—"

"Oh, you and your maps," Hermie grumbled as she bustled forward. "If it's worth ten thousand dollars, then why don't you *sell* it for that? Or is that too much to ask? Oh Lord, these doggone maps." She shot me a furious look, as if her husband's collecting folly were somehow my fault. Then she impatiently lifted one corner of the panorama. "Goldy, help me move this thing off the buf-fet."

"Stop!" Smithfield ordered. "*I* will help you. Mother of God, Hermie, why do you always have to jump in and try to take charge of things you know nothing about?" He quickstepped forward and raised the other corner of the panorama. "All right, put it on the mantel."

"Smithfield!" Hermie shouted. "I don't want it on the mantel!"

"Then it goes on the buffet."

Gripping the sides of the panorama, they seemed to be at an impasse. Mr. Barclay, a tall, slender man with hair the gray tint of pine bark, shifted from foot to foot as his short, chunky wife licked her lips. They both looked to me for a clue as to what they were supposed to do.

"Let me fix you a cocktail while we set up the buf-fet," I said pleasantly as my two hosts grunted and fret-ted and argued as they crab-walked to their hearth, which was topped with a long wooden mantel full of Native American knickknacks.

"I'm Dr. Zach Barclay," the tall man said as he held out his hand. I managed not to ask if "Doctor" was his first name while he turned to the woman at his side. They were both dressed in the style I thought of as Colorado Casual, dark slacks and bright silk shirts.

"This is my wife, Catherine. I'll open some wine for us. You look as if you're wanting to get back to something."

"Or someplace," Catherine Barclay said with a knowing smile. "Like the kitchen. Don't worry, I'll set up your bains-marie. I like to cook myself," she said apologetically, "and Zach is always complaining about the amount of equipment I have. If it's got a French name, he complains, it costs twice as much. Go ahead, I can do this."

Ecstatic to be dismissed, I scampered back to the kitchen. The luscious scents filling the space eased my stress. Caterers were often asked to do all kinds of odd jobs at the party destination, but moving an expensive panorama around was a first for me. And, I hoped, a last.

"The hors d'oeuvres are almost done," Julian announced, "plus, the daughter of the house just called down to say she and her girlfriend want their vegetarian dinner in about forty-five minutes. We can do the canapés and soup together, if you like. Then either you or I can take the girls some canapés, their quiche, some dessert, and maybe a salad, if we can find something in the MacArthurs' refrigerator—"

"And the other one can serve the curry with all its condiments?"

Julian nodded. "Which duty would you like? Uh, the young lady upstairs says she has her girlfriend visiting," he added. "I made up a tray with two place settings."

"Oh Lord, give me the kids. Although I feel guilty handing over the main course to you." In the background, the doorbell bonged. Great—more guests arriving, and I had no idea whether Hermie and Smithfield had settled their differences. "First, let's make sure the bains are set up, too. Our host moved them to the couch, and one of the guests, Catherine Barclay, promised to move them back. I have no idea whether she knows what's what."

"I can handle that," Julian assured me, and I felt no doubt that he could. He walked confidently out of the kitchen while I rummaged in the MacArthurs' refrigerator for more dishes to offer the teenagers. Eventually, I found, washed, and spun spinach for a salad, made them a plate of wild mushroom risotto in phyllo that would only need a brief heating, gathered up half a dozen rolls and a stick of butter, and placed all these goodies on the large tray Julian had meticulously set. Last I popped the quiche into the oven.

By that time, Julian had returned, and he said all the guests but one had arrived. Unlike the folks coming to the library breakfast, *these* people didn't want to cocoon when there was crime or bad weather in town. In fact,

Hermie had warned that the cold weather and snow had piqued the guests' thirst, and they were already passing on the fancy wines and slugging down bourbon, scotch, vodka, and gin.

I whispered, "Uh-oh," and nabbed the nearest platter of cold hors d'oeuvres. Julian hurriedly pushed the first sheet of phyllo-wrapped risotto into the oven, grabbed another platter of the cold shrimp rolls, and together we dashed out to the living room. Guests hitting the liquor hard on empty stomachs was like aiming a rocket-propelled grenade into your party. Luckily, the deep freeze outside had piqued folks' appetites as well as their thirst, and as we made our rounds, I thanked heaven that Julian's bistro boss had bestowed appetizer blessings on us.

Neil Tharp squeezed between the Barclays and nabbed three shrimp rolls in one hand.

"Help yourself, Mr. Tharp," I said pleasantly.

He lifted his pudgy chin and said, "I will." But he didn't sound pleasant.

When I was making my second round with hot hors d'oeuvre, Hermie pulled me aside. "We can't wait for Larry. Could you serve the soup now?"

"Absolutely." Maybe Larry Craddock had driven over a cliff. I mused over whether this was good news or bad news as I ladled steaming dumpling soup into heated bowls. The curry, meanwhile, had begun to bubble, and with any luck, we were going to pull this party off, whether or not Larry showed his bald head and angry face.

After we'd served the soup, the timer went off for the quiche.

"Boss, go serve the girls." Julian used hot pads to remove the quiche from the oven. "I've got the curry and condiments covered."

"You're the best." Without hesitating, I heaved up the teenagers' tray, checked that there was a back staircase, and finally, imitating unset gelatin, slithered out.

Upstairs, I walked down a long, plushly carpeted hallway until I found the only room with a rock-star poster on the door. Sometimes teenagers, in their attempt to be avant-garde, end up being remarkably conformist. I'm sure I had been exactly the same way, only with a different star on the door, and no caterer to bring me dinner when I'd been banished to my room.

"Yeah, come on!" a voice from inside called. Not an auspicious welcome, I decided as I tried to balance the tray and simultaneously open the door. But it opened suddenly, and I fell forward. It was only with an enormous effort of balance that I kept the quiche from going airborne.

"Hi there," I said politely. "I'm Goldy."

The two girls, who couldn't have been more than fourteen, regarded me awkwardly. They'd slathered their faces with a bright turquoise, puttylike concoction that I assumed was some kind of skin treatment. The only part of their faces not pasted with blue was their eyes, which peered out from masklike white Os. They'd wrapped their heads with towels, and each had pinned a brooch just above their widow's peaks, to keep the turbans in place. The one who had opened the door was taller than her friend, although I couldn't really tell, because the other sat on a bed covered with a plush pink quilt. Her thin mouth was pulled into a disapproving pucker. I noted that she was so thin, her legs and arms resembled twigs.

"I'm Vix Barclay," said the one who'd opened the door, motioning me forward to a white built-in desk. "And that's Chantal. I'll just move all this stuff over." Vix shoved a pile of papers onto the floor. "Chantal, you're a slob."

"I am *not,*" said Chantal. To me, she said, "Thanks for the food. Did you bring any booze?"

"Why, hello to you, too," I said pleasantly. "I'm your parents' caterer tonight. Your mother asked me to bring you your dinner."

"I said," Chantal went on in an imperious tone, " 'Did. You. Bring. Any. Booze?' "

"Chantal!" Vix squealed. "How the hell did you get grounded in the first place? Jeez!"

"No, I didn't pick up any alcoholic beverages on my way to your room," I said lightly, placing the tray onto the cleared spot on the desk. "But I brought all kinds of good food—"

"Have my parents stopped fighting?" Chantal demanded. "I could hear them all the way up here."

"They're working on it," I replied, my tone still light. "Shall I set you two places?"

"They're both *really* pissed," Chantal said, her voice conspiratorial. Since she hadn't answered my question, Vix, who seemed more tractable than her friend, kindly began removing items from the tray to the desk. "My *mom* is pissed because, like, one extra guy is coming to this party you're cooking for."

"Extra guy?" I asked dully. Someone besides Neil Tharp? Had I made enough curry?

Chantal went on: "I'm like, 'Mom, call the cops if you don't want people to crash your party.' She's all, 'He's not technically crashing, since he's taking someone else's place, and you know your father would have a fit if I got the cops up here, with their sirens and all.' Maybe *I* should have called them. That would have been fun."

"You were going to call the cops?" Vix echoed in a

worried tone. "And get them all the way up here *again*? I don't think either one of them would want that." She turned to me and smiled, which must have been difficult with all that blue plaster stiffening her facial muscles. "Maybe this guy won't make it because of the snow. My parents have a Hummer—"

"The replacement guest is here," I told them. "His name is Neil Tharp."

"Oh, *him*," said Vix.

"Vix, will you stop?" Chantal said. Clearly she wanted to be in charge of the conversation. Vix, who seemed unhurt by Chantal's reprimanding her, went about arranging their place settings. I, however, was both annoyed and curious.

"Who called the cops before?" I asked.

"The neighbors," Chantal and Vix said in unison.

"Anyway," Chantal hurried in to say, "so that's why my mom's pissed, and don't be surprised if she takes it out on *you* tonight."

"Don't worry," I replied. "I'm used to it."

"Better you than me," Chantal said ruefully.

"Your father's angry, too?" I asked. "Do I need to worry about him taking anything out on me?"

Chantal and Vix exchanged a look. A few clicks of a cat clock on the wall passed before either one of them answered.

Vix finally said, "Mr. MacArthur is angry about a map he bought from a guy. The guy was killed yesterday, so he's dead and can't be bawled out by Mr. MacArthur. His name was—"

"Drew Wellington," I supplied. I looked at Chantal with curiosity. "But your father's down there showing a map right now. A panorama, actually. He seems proud of it, not angry. Is that the one he bought from—"

"Drew?" Chantal supplied. She moved over to a mirror and checked the consistency of the turquoise cement. "*I* don't know. But whatever one he did buy from Drew, it was, like, ninety thousand dollars. And then something went wrong with the deal."

"What went wrong?" Did these girls know more than the police did in this investigation? "One map was worth ninety thousand dollars?"

"Not anymore!" Chantal squealed, and both girls broke out in gales of laughter. "Poor old cheap dad won't buy me a mountain bike, and then good old Drew rips him off for ninety K. It's so ironic."

"Good old Drew?" I repeated. "Did you know him?"

The girls looked at each other, unsure of how much to divulge, it seemed to me. Oh, how I wished that they didn't have that blue stuff obscuring their facial expressions. Guilt, shame, anger? I couldn't tell.

"Yeah, we knew him," Vix finally said. She pressed her lips together, since they didn't have blue stuff on them.

"He was cool," Chantal agreed. She nodded and dislodged her turban. When a few stray curls of black-and-pink hair tumbled out, she poked them back under the towel. Then she lifted her chin at me, and her tone became defiant. "And guess what? *He* didn't have any problem giving us booze."

"*What?*"

"Wow, is there an echo in here?" she asked me. "I mean, come *on*."

"So," I said calmly, trying to make sure I had this story straight, "Drew Wellington gave you alcoholic drinks?"

"He gave us a *lot* of booze," Chantal replied, her tone proud. "Too much, actually. Anyway, Vix and I and some girlfriends got into our, you know, lingerie? And we turned on the stereo and outside speakers, so the music was blasting, like, really loud. We went outside and started hooting and hollering and dancing around? Oh, man, we were just having a good old time."

"And that," said Vix, "is why the neighbors called the cops."

12

Goldy!" The male voice and knock at the door startled all three of us, and when the door opened slightly, the girls shrieked. "There's something here you should see." Julian's tone was urgent, and he was careful to keep the door only slightly ajar.

"I have to go," I said to the girls. "You know what to do with your tray when you're done?" When the girls groaned and rolled their eyes, I took this to mean that they did. "And there's lime pie in the kitchen, if you want some," I added quickly before scooting out. I certainly hoped they didn't wear their . . . lingerie when they came downstairs.

Julian had already started for the back stairway. He was walking quickly and shaking his head. "Everything was going really well, and everybody was digging the curry, and Mr. MacArthur was giving a little talk . . . and all the guests were paying attention to him, and he was loving it—"

"A little talk about what?"

Julian was descending the staircase. "Where Dutch thieves used to hide maps when they were trying to smuggle them out of Portugal in the sixteenth century. It was cool; he said he wanted me to stay and listen, so I could learn something—"

"Oh, Julian, I'm sorry." Julian had graduated from Elk Park Prep with high honors; he had been at Cornell before transferring to the University of Colorado. But clients inevitably treated us as if we were uneducated dunces.

"It was interesting," Julian insisted as he reached the bottom of the steps. "If you controlled the trade, you could make lots of doubloons, or whatever they called them. Stealing maps was punishable by death!"

"Yeah, I know. Arch told me."

"Mr. MacArthur was saying how over the centuries, thieves have tucked maps into the jackets of other books, they've sewn maps inside their hats, and everybody was listening really well, and then Neil Tharp, you know, Drew Wellington's creepy assistant? He got into a fight with another guy."

"Neil fought with somebody?" By this time we were both in the kitchen. I strained to hear arguing voices, or worse, the crash of people falling over furniture. "Here at the party?"

"You bet. Old Neil got into it with that bald dude I had to slug at the conference center. What's his name, Craddock? He finally showed up after the guests had already gone through the buffet line." Julian began to lay out the dishes and dessert forks for the lime pies.

"Larry Craddock." My spirits sank at the same time that I heard Craddock's familiar shout.

"Why don't you go ask the girl?" he howled. Where was he? Downstairs? Or in the garage? It was hard to tell. "Maybe she knows something!" he shouted. "Should I ask her, Neil?"

"Turn on the light, you dummy!" Neil Tharp's high voice replied. "I can't see a thing!"

Their voices were indeed coming from the nether regions of the house. Had the party broken up already? I looked nervously back at the center island, where Julian was loading dishes and silverware onto a tray. Would my first time catering for the MacArthurs also be my last? What about the big luncheon Hermie wanted me to do on Monday?

"Don't worry," Julian said as he came out of the refrigerator holding the pies. "I think the MacArthurs were glad to be rid of them." He frowned as the men bellowed at each other. "Sounds like they're trying to find their way to their cars. Maybe they're in the garage."

"Hey! Tharp!" Larry's booming voice traveled upward, and was followed by the scraping and groaning of an automated garage door being opened. Larry said something else, to which there was a muffled reply and question. Then Larry's voice was suddenly much clearer. "So, what are you saying, Tharp? That I should ask the *cook*?"

Excuse me? I scurried over to the bank of windows that overlooked the driveway. I strained to listen and worked even harder to see something, anything. Outside, all was dark. Right next to the windows, the still-falling snowflakes reflected the lights of the kitchen. More hollering came from outside. I frowned. Small wires traveled downward from each of the windows. On the left side of the casement was an array of switches, one of which was bound to illuminate the driveway . . . but one of which might *also* set off the burglar alarm. Hearing the squeal of the alarm would be the final blow in finishing up this party.

But wait—the side door, the one we'd come through to bring in our supplies, was still partly open, because Hermie had said we should leave it cracked, to help dispel the scent of curry. She'd pressed the panel of buttons to reset the alarm, she told me, because Smithfield was "unbelievably paranoid" about someone stealing his maps. I raced over to the door and looked back at Julian, whose face was frozen in incredulity.

"What the hell are you doing?" he asked. "I wanted to tell you about the fight so you could witness it from the kitchen!" I put my finger to my lips and gently pried the door farther open. Julian tsked and backed through the kitchen door, holding the tray with the pies and plates. "That's fine!" he said merrily. "I'll do the desserts, you do the conflict. Great idea."

"Maybe you'll have more luck than I did, Tharp." Larry Craddock's voice rose through the snow. He must have been standing outside, I figured. Looking for his car? Or just wanting to keep arguing? "She's a *bitch* and her kid's a *brat*. First chance I get, I'm going to teach them both a lesson, I swear!"

Oh, I thought, *really?* I pulled the kitchen door all the way open. The stairs down to the path that led to the driveway were loaded with at least four inches of new snow. I looked for the men, but couldn't see them. They must still have been standing near the garage.

Breathing deeply, I tiptoed through the white stuff till I was at the bottom of the steps. Nobody was going to teach me a lesson, or Arch either, for that matter, without my having something to say about it, thank you very much.

"Goldy, Judas priest, I swear." Julian's stage-whispered voice from above caused me to jump, and I almost lost my footing. "Where do you think you're going?" When I didn't respond, he began creeping down the stairs behind me. "Skulking around at a client's house," he mumbled. "This is sure to bring us all *kinds* of new bookings. For *sure*. By the way, they insisted on cutting the pies by themselves."

"Thanks, Julian," I whispered. "Now hush, will you?"

He groaned with exasperation. Once he was beside me, he handed me a sweatshirt. "Here, put this on. I don't want to do the rest of the Christmas catering with you sick in bed. Where are those guys, anyway?"

As if in answer, Neil Tharp screeched from around the corner. Unfortunately, his words were muffled, since I was pulling on one of Julian's well-worn "Elk Park Prep Swimming" sweatshirts. My head emerged long enough to hear Neil say something like, "You have it! You son of a bitch! Don't deny it. You've got it!"

"You're so sure of that," Larry shouted back, "why don't you call the sheriff's department, have them come search my place?"

Neil cried, "Don't deny it! Don't tell me he didn't give it to you!"

"That asshole wouldn't even give me the time of *day!*" Larry yelled. "Why don't you go ask his girlfriend? That's what *I'd* do. She's the one who . . ." Neil's whining reply was too low for me to make out.

Larry was shouting again. Honestly, the guy was going to blow out his vocal cords one of these days. Whatever it was he said, it hadn't satisfied Neil, because the next thing we heard was a loud *"Gah!"* followed by "Get your hands off me, you dumb *bastard!*"

One of them threw the other into the wall of the garage, and the whole house shook. Shouts and sounds of choking followed. I looked desperately at Julian. "Shouldn't we do something?"

"Yeah! We should go inside. Come on, Miss Nobel Peace Prize." He yanked at my sweatshirt. "Let's get out of here." More *you bastards* and *you stupid son of a bitches* echoed around the corner. Then suddenly it seemed as if they were getting closer. One of them slammed into the gutter system, making it whine and reverberate. Julian tugged hard on my sleeve and bared his teeth. I decided that the better part of valor might indeed be to scurry up the stairs behind him. We had just scampered into the kitchen when we heard Larry Craddock's voice coming from much closer.

"Dammit, Neil, maybe you need to ask the girl. D'you think there might be something you didn't know about your boss? Or something the girl's *parents* didn't know about your boss?"

When Julian and I peered out the windows, we could see the two of them, both covered with snow. Larry was at least half a foot taller than Neil, but Neil was wider. And, apparently, he'd had a bit of martial-arts training, because when he squawked, "Shut *up!*" he was able to lunge effectively. Larry went reeling back down the driveway, from where he'd come.

"Your boss was a criminal!" Larry's voice, now hoarse, faded back around the corner. There was the sound of a car door being opened.

Neil yelled, "Hey, you thief! Get back here so I can pin you down and call the cops—"

"Try the cook, dummy! Her husband's a cop, so maybe she can help ya out."

"Larry!" Neil again. I caught a brief glimpse of him charging down the driveway. He slipped sideways on the snow but kept barking at Larry. "Give me what belongs to our business!"

"I keep telling you, *I* don't have it!" Both of these guys were determined to get the last word in, apparently. Julian went back to doing dishes. When I tried to shush him again, he just shrugged. Outside, Larry hollered,

"How long d'ya think it'll be before the entire map world finds out what your boss was up to? I keep tellin' ya, ya need to ask his girlfriend."

Standing safely back in the kitchen, I pushed the door open a bit more, in time to hear Neil respond sourly, "Oh, like she's going to tell me anything—or give me anything."

"Then go ask the girl!" Larry yelled. There was a thumping noise, as if someone had been thrown against a car, followed by more grunting and hacking. "You stupid dumb bastard! Force her to give it to you before I kick your butt over this cliff!"

At that moment something the size of a tennis ball sailed up, up, through the snow. Terrified, I realized it was coming right at me. I ducked out of the way, just in time to see one of the windows shatter with a terrific crash. Glass exploded into the kitchen. The burglar alarm shrieked, which caused yelling and consternation from the distant dining room. More stamping and hollering and revving of engines boiled up from the driveway.

Outside, car headlights blinked. From two cars? First one, then another vehicle roared away. I hurried in the direction of the dining room, toward Hermie and Smithfield. I needed to find out what we were supposed to do. Call the cops? Call whatever security company they used?

Smithfield was hurtling toward me, and I stepped out of his way. I didn't know where Julian had gone—maybe he was still standing by the sink working on the dishes, trying to make everything appear normal.

"Will you tell me what the hell is going on?" Smithfield demanded. "First those two dealers start fighting, and now somebody's broken into our house!"

"Not exactly," I replied, but he ignored me. Hermie followed him back into the kitchen, and I brought up the rear. Julian was already patiently pulling off half a roll of paper towels, one by one, as if eruptions of glass happened all the time at our catered events.

There on the floor lay a snowball that had broken into pieces, revealing a—wait a minute—a paring knife. I moved around our hosts to help Julian. Several curious guests peered around and over Hermie and Smithfield. Our hosts, hands on hips, still demanded to know from anyone who would listen how this could have happened. Matter of fact, this was downright inhospitable, and what was the matter with this neighborhood anyway, etc., etc.

After I'd wiped up melting snow and glass bits for a few minutes, I stared at the knife. When I was growing up back in New Jersey, mischief-making boys would crouch by the side of the road and throw these kinds of weapons at passing cars. One time, a rock-inside-snow missile hit our old Buick as we were coming home from church. The rear-seat passenger window had shattered, and I was showered with glass. At ten years of age, I'd been traumatized.

I kicked myself out of my reverie and scrambled over to a wall of tall cabinets, where a moment of rummaging yielded a broom and dustpan. The guests were edging toward the mess, and I had to sweep up the window glass before someone got cut on it. Hermie and Smithfield were now arguing with each over whether they should call the sheriff's department. Some of the guests were pulling out their cells, just in case.

Meanwhile, the house phone rang, and Hermie and Smithfield scrambled over each other to get it. Smithfield won, and announced that the security company wanted to know if this was a false alarm. The guests murmured that maybe people should start checking all of the house's doors and windows. I wondered why the alarm hadn't gone off when Craddock and Tharp opened the garage door, but maybe that didn't happen if you opened it from the inside. Smithfield was barking into the phone that no, it wasn't a false alarm, and they should get over here, by God! And then he decided to call the sheriff's department; he gave them the same command.

The guests who'd been standing by to see if anything else exciting was going to happen filtered back into the living and dining rooms. Time to go, they were saying,

Thank you so much, need to get back before the snow gets too deep. Finally it was only the Barclays who stood by, trying to soothe a hysterical Hermie. By the time all the other guests had left, I had most of the glass and snow swept up. Julian appeared beside me with a garbage bag and more paper towels.

"I thought you had tossed something at the window," Hermie called to me. "A pot or dish that had somehow frustrated you. Ah mean, Goldy darlin'? How did this happen at our party?"

"Mrs. MacArthur, I don't know." I tore a paper towel from the roll and carefully picked up the knife before someone kicked it or fell over it. The way things were going tonight, either could easily happen. I went on: "This is what took place. Somebody threw the snowball at your window. I think the knife inside the snowball must have made it heavy enough to crash through the glass and set off the alarm."

"But what were they aiming for?" Smithfield had returned from seeing off the other guests and now wanted to be in charge again. "Were Neil and Larry actually hitting each other? Were they using knives? Were they throwing *snowballs* at each other?"

"They were fighting," I replied slowly. "I don't know about knives or snowballs. But it was just . . . an argument that sounded as if it got physical. Please try to relax until your security people arrive. They'll know the best thing to do."

"I don't know about that, Goldy," Hermie said impatiently as Catherine Barclay handed her a moistened, folded dish towel. Hermie immediately applied the compress to her forehead. "Thank you, Catherine darlin'."

She turned toward us and explained, "I'm afraid that in times of stress I need . . . something to bring down my temperature."

We all paused in awkward silence, waiting for Hermie's anxiety-induced body heat to abate.

"Oh, Hermie," Smithfield began, "for God's sake—"

Hermie removed the compress, cleared her throat, and shot Smithfield a withering glance. To me, she said, "Did you see one of those men throw this . . . thing through the window? Because then he should replace it! Those secured windows are so doggoned expensive. I want to throw that knife away—it scares me. I don't want the sheriff's department messing up my kitchen any more than those men already have."

Smithfield shook a finger at his wife. "Don't you dare do that, Hermie! I *want* the police here. Our home has been threatened!"

"But then our neighbors will be wondering why the police are coming here *again*," Hermie said, moaning.

"Our neighbors the Barclays are right here, and the Upshaws are in Florida," Smithfield replied dismissively.

"Which is where I wish we were." Hermie stood up and ran more cold water onto her compress, wrung it out, and then reapplied it to her forehead. "My dear Smitty, don't you see that people will see and hear the police cars with their lights and sirens, and think we're just a haven for criminals?"

Smithfield lifted his chin and arched his pale eyebrows in my direction. "Can you get your husband to hush up the policemen's cars?"

"I can call him on my cell and ask him to have them turn off their sirens," I said, with more confidence than I felt. But I desperately wanted to reassure the MacArthurs, because I wanted to keep them as catering clients. I punched the numbers for our home phone and gave Tom an extremely abbreviated version of what had happened. "The MacArthurs want to know if the sheriff's deputies can turn off their sirens."

"No way," Tom replied. "If the MacArthurs want help there quickly, then our cars have to run their sirens so drivers on the road will get out of the way. They don't run their sirens, folks won't know to move, and it'll take the department twice as long to get there."

"Thanks."

"You going to tell me what's going on there, Miss G.?"

"When I get home," I warned him, to let him know I wasn't in a private place to talk to him.

He sighed and hung up.

"Mr. MacArthur," I said humbly, "the police can't turn off their sirens." I explained the reasoning behind what Tom had said, but Smithfield MacArthur was having none of it.

"Why can't I get what I want from the police?" he shouted. "It's my home that was threatened!" When I blinked in astonishment at his rage, Smithfield took a moment to try to pull himself together. Then he turned to the Barclays. "Shall we call the girls?" he asked, forcing joviality. "Think they've finished with their beauty session by now? Come on, Hermie, let's see our guests out."

"Oh, Smitty," Hermie replied with a groan. She reluctantly lifted the compress from her forehead, then looked around at the kitchen with its still-unwashed dishes. She gave me a look: *This better be cleaned up, and soon.*

Sure, Hermie, I thought. *Whatever you want.* I might not have influence over the sheriff's department vehicle-sirens-and-lights policy, but when it came to dishes, Julian and I were the whiz kids. At the moment, we were still booked to do Hermie's luncheon on Monday, and I

SWEET REVENGE • 293

wanted to stay in her good graces. She was my first client in Regal Ridge Country Club, and the place was full of wealthy, potentially party-giving folks—even if the appearance of a police car was anathema.

Julian peered through the gaping, jagged hole that the projectile had made. "Y'know, I don't remember a *whole* lot from high school physics, even though I liked it. Still, those guys were around the corner, not right below us. And anyway, you'd have to be farther back"—he indicated with his chin—"like, over in the neighbor's yard or something, to get an arc on that sucker so it would go through this window." He pulled back and hugged his sides. "Damn! It's getting to be like a big walk-in refrigerator in here! Let's finish up, bug out of here, scoot back to your place, and let the MacArthurs deal with the cops, the security guys, and the window."

"We can't leave before law enforcement gets here." I held up a folded oversize garbage bag and a roll of duct tape I'd found in a drawer. "In the meantime, we need to do something about that window."

Together we covered the jagged hole, which looked even worse with a garbage bag over it, but at least the frigid wind wasn't turning the faucet water to ice cubes. Soon we were back into our normal rhythm of washing, drying, and packing up. A wave of fatigue swept over me.

"So," Julian said at length, "who do you think threw the snowball?"

"A neighbor." I picked up our first box and headed toward the kitchen door. "Tired of all the noise."

"The neighbors are basking in the sunshine of Southern climes, remember?"

"There are folks all up and down this street, not just next door."

"The neighbor could have thrown the snowball at the two guys fighting, Goldy," Julian said, his tone stubborn. "The neighbor could have called the *cops*. And I still don't think either Larry or Neil could have been aiming at the other one. I mean, you'd have to be really plastered to have aim that was that *bad*."

"Julian, I don't know."

"And you don't want to talk about it, even though you were the one who insisted we go down there and spy on them. What's up with that?"

"What's up with what?" It took me a moment to realize it was Chantal who had shuffled into the kitchen. She had washed the blue stuff off her face, and actually looked younger and more innocent. She had curly black hair with dyed pink stripes, bright eyes, and shiny cheeks that were accentuated by the thick collar of a full-length hot-pink terrycloth robe. "What's been going on down here? Vix and I heard the alarm go off, and we thought, *Omigod, we're being robbed!* We locked my door, but then no bad guy came knocking. Holy crap, what happened to the window?"

"Somebody pitched a snowball through it," I said, omitting the bit about the knife. "Did you two see anything?"

She shook her head. "No. A snowball? That's it? I'm telling you, nothing exciting ever happens around here. And then something exciting does happen, and I'm not even here." But then she realized Julian, who was twenty-two, muscled, trim, and extraordinarily good-looking, was in the room. She gave him a demure, flirtatious smile. "Well, every now and then, something exciting happens. Or it could happen."

Julian, bless his sweet heart, returned her smile. But he didn't say anything, so Chantal reluctantly floated out of the kitchen.

"Julian, I want to go look at something, okay?" I asked.

"Sure, crime fighter. And anyway, I can wash dishes faster when you're not here."

Wonderful, I thought as I made my way back down the steps to where Larry and Neil had been arguing. I looked at their footsteps in the snow, and where the snow was tramped down. It was as I thought.

What I hadn't said to Julian, and what I hadn't di-
vulged to Hermie or Smithfield, was that I really did *not*
think the knife-snowball had been thrown by Larry or
Neil, aiming it for the other one. Julian had been right.
Judging from where Larry's and Neil's voices had come
from, down the driveway, and where the snowball had
come from—about fifty feet away, some distance from
the driveway, if not the neighbor's yard—the knife had
not been thrown by them. Nor, I guessed, had it been
meant for them.

At the base of the steps, I looked over at that side of
the driveway, then back up to where I'd been standing
by the lit kitchen window. What had I been doing, exactly? Listening. Okay, eavesdropping. And anyone
who'd been looking that way would have seen Julian and
me standing there, with the light shining behind us.

No, the knife hadn't been aimed at Larry or Neil or
even Julian. It seemed to me—in fact, I thought it was a
virtual certainty—that someone actually had been aiming that crude weapon at me.

13

I didn't have a whole lot of time to ponder these questions because a sheriff's department deputy showed up. Despite Hermie's worries, he had arrived so quietly that neither of us had heard him. First he interviewed Hermie and Smithfield. When it was clear they knew little, the officer asked to take statements from us. He was an older fellow, large and beefy, with a nameplate that said "Yerba." He asked about Larry and Neil, then took the knife away in a bag. He said there was no way to look for footprints in the dark, when so much new snow had fallen, and with more coming down so rapidly. But the department would try to send out a team the next day.

Julian and I, meanwhile, had to pack up and leave. I turned on the floodlights so Julian could back the Rover right up to the side steps without hitting them. The snow was still coming down thick and fast, and neither of us could have faced another mishap that evening. He opened the tailgate, and together we began loading up our boxes. But before we were halfway through, a security car with a yellow light flashing on its roof reversed, beeping loudly, down the driveway, effectively blocking our route out. It was almost eleven at this point, and if the skirmish between the rival map dealers or the policeman's lights hadn't awoken the rest of the folks on the street, the rhythmic horn tooting surely would.

"Look, could you question us first?" Julian asked as a young man wearing a dark uniform and a billed cap stepped out of the car with its painted sign: ROCKY MOUNTAIN SECURITY SYSTEMS. "We're the caterers," Julian was saying, "and we're gonna pass out from fatigue if we don't get out of here."

The security fellow's shirt was emblazoned with the name "Alan," but he said, "Please call me Al." I thought he was joking, but I only nodded, and back up the staircase the three of us trooped.

"Do the home owners know I'm here?" he asked, once he'd taken off his hat and revealed a thin, pale face. I immediately wanted to give him something to eat, but I knew Julian would have a meltdown if I started haul-

ing food out of the MacArthurs' refrigerator. Julian really *did* look exhausted, and since he'd done the lion's
share of the work at the party, I just pulled out three
stools surrounding the breakfast island and invited the
two of them to sit down. Al refused, so Julian and I sat
and waited to be interrogated.

"I don't know where the home owners are," I told Al,
"but it's a huge house, so they may not have heard you
come in."

"I'll find them," Al assured us. He pulled a small
notebook from his pocket and began methodically questioning us. When had the altercation begun, he wanted
to know, had we seen the men carrying out anything that
belonged to the home owners, when had the window
been broken, and who did we think had broken it? By
the time Julian and I had given our replies, I was so tired
I was ready to be cooked for Christmas pudding myself.
Which made me realize something I hadn't thought of
when we were talking to Officer Yerba: Did I need to
check with Hermie regarding the Monday party, or
should I just try to get out of there without further
crises?

It was the latter, as it turned out, because Smithfield
MacArthur shouted to us—didn't these people believe
in an intercom?—wanting to know if the security people
had arrived. When I traipsed out to the museumlike liv

ing room, where Hermie and Smithfield were drinking liqueurs by their twinkling Christmas tree, and told them Al was indeed here, Smithfield stormed back to the kitchen ahead of me, grumbling about my not telling him sooner. First I hadn't moved the panorama properly, now I was failing as a butler. But I'd decided that unless the client asks you to have sex on the kitchen floor between courses, you have to do what they ask—and figure out a way to add your extra services to their bill.

Smithfield's face turned from pink to red as he summarily bawled Al out for not getting to their house before the sheriff's department. What was Smithfield paying Al's company for? he wanted to know. Not having sirens? I wondered. When Smithfield stopped for breath, Julian asked if we could skedaddle, and Al nodded, apparently used to this kind of abuse. Julian walked quickly back to the kitchen. But I was not going to go until we were paid.

I stood quietly beside a chair while Al apologized to the MacArthurs for the delay. He didn't point out that snow had made driving difficult, that the snowpacked byways had probably been clogged with abandoned cars, or that he'd been with us in the kitchen doing his job for the last ten minutes. Instead, he began to ask questions in low tones.

After a few minutes, during which I said nothing but only stood beside a chair, Smithfield looked up at me. "What do you want now?"

"To be paid," I said quietly.

"Oh yes, of course." Hermie levered herself out of her chair, squared her shoulders, and walked ahead of me to the kitchen. And lo and behold, she did have a check already written out to us in her kitchen desk. She handed it to me and I thanked her and said I'd see her Monday.

"All right, then," she said sadly. Her tone implied her hope that the next catered event would go better. But she said no more before returning to the living room.

I whipped out my checkbook and wrote Julian a more-than-generous check for his participation in this train wreck of a party.

"Boss, you don't have to do this now."

"Yes, I do. And as soon as you take this money, we'll finally be able to get out of here."

He pocketed his check, thanked me, and together we packed up. I could not wait to get out of that house. In fact, I was tempted to grab my last box, race down the snowy steps to the Rover, and yell *Woo-hoo!* But I didn't.

The way home was slow going. The roads through Regal Ridge had not been plowed, and no cars had been down the MacArthurs' road since the sheriff's-department and security-company vehicles. To make matters worse, an additional six inches of snow had fallen since the end of the party. But Julian was a painstaking driver, and I knew I was in good hands.

"Had any thoughts on who could have thrown the knife-ball?" I asked once he reached the interstate.

"I still think it was someone on that street. I mean, who else? Somebody was mad that those two guys were arguing, and he thought the fastest way to stop the fight was to set off the MacArthurs' alarm."

I shook my head. "I don't believe it."

"You're paranoid."

"Hey, Miss G., Julian," Tom greeted us when we finally traipsed through the back door. "I was getting worried about you. Successful evening?"

"Eventful," Julian replied, "but I'm going to let Goldy tell you about it. I promised the boys one of us would get them over to the RRSSA tomorrow to snowboard. We can do the logistics later, if you want. But I've got to get some sleep or I'm going to be toast."

"I've already set up your sleeping bag in the boys' room," Tom assured him. "Arch wouldn't have it any other way."

Julian nodded and bade us good night. As he was plodding up the stairs, I watched his face, and sure enough, he
broke into a huge smile. Julian's parents were dead, and
he had no siblings. He didn't actually want to tell us how
much he enjoyed being embraced as part of our family—
I'd learned the hard way that young men didn't like to
show their emotions. But he secretly reveled in being reminded of how much we all cherished him.

"So, Miss G." We'd moved into our living room, where
we sat beside the Christmas tree. Loaded with lights that
Tom and I had both accumulated during our unmarried
years, it could have lit up the neighborhood. "I gather
the party at the MacArthurs didn't go particularly
well?"

"It was hell," I said, then stood up to warm my hands
by the fire Tom had built. "Don't get me wrong, the
food was fine. But two of the guests—Larry Craddock
and Neil Tharp, to be specific—started arguing, then
ended up taking their fight outside, where they were
pushing and shoving each other around. Then somebody, maybe one of them, threw a knife inside a snowball that broke one of the kitchen windows."

"A *what*?" Before I could answer, he said, "I hope
you called the department."

"The MacArthurs did. Fellow named Yerba came
out?"

Tom nodded. "Good man. Any idea who threw it?"

"Not yet. But wait, there's more. While the MacArthurs and their guests were stuffing themselves with curry, I took a vegetarian dinner up to their teenage daughter and her friend. They're about fourteen, I'd say. And they claimed that Drew Wellington used to give them booze. At least one time, they told me, somebody called the cops to break up the party."

Tom got up and headed for the kitchen. "I think I'm going to need coffee to hear this one. You up for an espresso?"

"If you're fixing. Have to tell you, though, I don't think it'll keep me awake. I'm too tired."

But I was wrong. Tom took out his trusty notebook to jot down all the details of what the girls had said about Drew Wellington. He said he didn't remember a sheriff's call to that address, but he would check. Had I asked the girls when Wellington had given them alcohol, and how many times? I shook my head and sipped my coffee, which Tom had doused with whipping cream. As I was telling him about the tussle between Craddock and Tharp, about how Tharp claimed Craddock had stolen his property, and how vehemently Craddock had denied it, I felt a surge of energy, what a caterer friend of mine had dubbed *the dreaded second wind*. At the same time that the newfound vigor was coursing through Ye Olde

Veins, I remembered that Neil Tharp frequently attended the earlier, eight o'clock service at St. Luke's, as well as the later service with his boss. That way he and Drew managed to chat up as many congregants as possible. Or maybe he was just hoping to get some clients of his own. Neil had been as dedicated as Drew in the practice of drumming up business. Somehow I doubted that Neil had been as successful as Drew. That, I reflected, was just what Neil probably hoped to change.

"I have to cook," I announced, and stood up.

Tom looked ruefully at our espresso cups. "Caffeine at midnight. I've created a monster."

"How does cherry pie sound?"

"Messy." But he picked up his notebook and our empty cups and followed me into the kitchen.

I stared into the dark depths of the freezer side of our walk-in and tried to think. Where had I been in the story of that night's events? Oh yes, the missing item. Mislaid? Misplaced? Or just plain gone? "Craddock insisted that somebody else had to know about the missing thing, whatever it was. Wellington's girlfriend—which one, we don't know—or 'the girl,' whoever that was. I have to say, I thought he meant Chantal, the MacArthurs' daughter. Craddock kept saying, 'Go ask the girl.' " I pulled out a pie crust I had made and frozen before baking, in case of a rainy day. Or a snowy night, for that matter.

Tom preheated the oven for me, then sat at our kitchen table. "So, did Neil Tharp come back up to start questioning Chantal about his missing property?"

"No, that's when all hell broke loose with the snowball. The noise it made was huge, and both Craddock and Tharp hightailed it out of there." I stared at the crust: July had been the last time Colorado had had any fresh sour cherries—the best kind for pies—but the canned variety would be just dandy. I banged around in our pantry looking for some while Tom washed our espresso cups. When I came back out clutching a pair of cans, I found Tom scrounging in the freezer side of our walk-in.

"Tom? You're going to cook, too?"

"Nope. I'm just getting out a couple of coffee cakes I made during one of your catering events." He emerged holding two zipped freezer bags, each of which held one of his sour-cream Bundt cakes. "You're going to the early service tomorrow, aren't you? I suppose you're going to try to have a chat with Neil Tharp?"

"You suppose correctly." I was annoyed that Tom was able to interpret my intentions so easily. But Larry had told Neil he should talk to the cook, and Neil had wanted to chat with me Friday night outside the library, so I might as well facilitate things. I put cooking parchment inside the crust, then placed a load of ceramic pie weights on top, to help the pastry keep its shape.

"Be careful, Miss G. Tharp has already shown a willingness to get physical, and we could do without any more flying snowballs. I'm going to go check on the boys," Tom announced. "I want to make sure everyone has a piece of floor to sleep on."

While Tom was gone I popped the crust into the oven, then stirred the cherry juice, cornstarch, and sugar mixture together in a large saucepan. How had I gotten mixed up in this whole mess with Drew Wellington in the first place? I mean, the guy was appearing more and more like a slimeball. It had only begun yesterday afternoon, when Larry Craddock had blown up at my son and then at me . . . then Drew had been killed in the library, while I was working there . . . and of course, I'd seen Sandee, or thought I'd seen Sandee, the woman who had killed my ex-husband. She had appeared to have been stalking Drew. Hadn't she? I felt less and less sure of everything I'd seen, but maybe it was because I was tired.

And then Drew's girlfriend, Patricia Ingersoll, a former client and sort-of friend—even if she was obsessed with tasteless diet foods—had asked me to help her. She said she and Drew had planned to get married at Christmas. She'd also said she had seen the woman who might be stalking Drew, and that she recognized this woman from the newspapers as Sandee Brisbane. Meanwhile, Drew had continued to take an interest in nubile teenage girls—girls to whom he gave alcohol.

Make that an *incredibly disgusting* slimeball.

By the time Tom returned to the kitchen, the luscious-looking cherry mixture was bubbling merrily. While I took the crust out of the oven, Tom looked into the saucepan, sniffed, then cocked an eyebrow at me. "I don't suppose the family is going to get any of this, right?"

"You can get some if you come to the eight o'clock service with me." I poured the cherries into the pan, stirred them through the thickened juice, then tipped the whole thing into the waiting crust. I'm not much for lattices—they're way, way too time-consuming for the garden-variety caterer to mess with—so I just carefully placed the top crust over the mountain of cherries, sealed it, slit it, and brushed on a bit of beaten egg white. I placed two sugar cubes inside a plastic bag, crushed them with a cooking mallet, and spilled the resulting crystals onto the top. I positioned the pie on a baking sheet and slid the whole thing into the waiting oven. Then I fixed myself another espresso—I figured, what the hell—and sat down next to Tom.

"So, are you going to come with me and talk to Neil Tharp?"

Tom cocked that eyebrow at me. "We already *have* interviewed Mr. Tharp. That's how we heard his explanation of the Rohypnol. Want to hear what else he had to say?"

"You know I do."

"First of all, even though I do value your input on these investigations?" I rolled my eyes and thought, *Here it comes.* "Miss G., please. Neil Tharp has already gotten into one fistfight with Larry Craddock, who hasn't been reluctant to come after you either. Remember, Tharp remains a suspect, and whoever murdered Wellington has a number of ways to attack people. Got it?" When I nodded, Tom held up a finger and disappeared. When he returned, he was holding one of his antique silver trays, on top of which were poised a bottle and two small crystal glasses. I couldn't help it; I burst out laughing.

"What, I can't hear about Tharp as a suspect without a wee nip of something?"

"Please don't knock this expensive port I bought just for us."

"Thanks." I watched him go through the ceremony of opening the bottle, and adored him all over again for remembering that I love port, but only the good stuff. Once I kicked out the Jerk, I was too poor to do anything but have a tiny *sip* of the good stuff, which I did when I was working with André, my mentor. André had insisted that I taste the port before he used it to sauce pork loin. "Ne-*vair*, ne-*vair* use cheap vine," he would say with a frown and bunched gray eyebrows, as if he knew I used it all the time, which of course I did. Following his dictum, I had never used inexpensive varieties when cooking for clients—but I'd kept them on a high shelf in case the Jerk, who had still driven me nuts after we were divorced, was up to his old antics and I was tempted to have a glass. When I'd wanted to sip a quality vintage, I'd had to either a) wait for Marla to invite me over, or b) wait for Marla to bring a bottle when she came to visit. This she did once she had tasted some of my screw-on-cap vermouth and immediately had run to the bathroom making gagging noises. After I married Tom, he enjoyed indulging me, or *us*, as he put it, by purchasing choice wines and foodstuffs whenever his own wallet was fat. But I didn't remember news of a bonus or raise, so now I was suddenly wary. "Are you buttering me up before lowering the boom about something I did?"

Tom tsked and poured. "Always so suspicious. No, after the espresso, I want us to sleep tonight." He glanced at the clock. "Or what's left of tonight." He handed me a glass, then sat back down. We clinked and sipped. The wine was smooth, fiery, and lingered on the tongue. When I smiled my thanks, Tom gave me a satisfied, loving look. "Back to my story. According to Neil Tharp, and Craddock confirms it, on Friday, Drew Wellington wanted to offer Larry Craddock two different maps at great prices, or at least at what Tharp considered great prices. Drew Wellington was presenting his old rival with the peace pipe, as they say in these parts. Are you following me so far?"

I nodded and inhaled deeply. The heady scent of baking cherry pie mingled with the rich aroma of the port. "Craddock sure didn't seem as if he was in any mood to do business, much less make peace, when Arch and I had our run-in with him."

"I'm getting to that."

"Plus, I thought you *did* find a valuable map on Wellington."

"That was a map from, let's see"—here, Tom flipped back a few pages in his notebook—"1869, showing the surveyed part of Nebraska. The transcontinental railroad is on there, as are three Indian reservations— Omaha, Otoe, and Pawnee. It's worth about three or four thousand bucks, give or take."

"That was the low price?"

"That's retail, Tharp says. Wellington was offering it to Craddock for fifteen hundred."

"But Craddock didn't bite, or Wellington wouldn't have still had it when somebody killed him."

"Right. Our man Tharp also claims Wellington had gotten his hands on a map of "—Tom perused his notes again—"Texas, from 1844."

"I thought Texas didn't come into the Union until later—"

"It didn't. That's why map dealers and collectors were so interested in this one." Tom sipped his port and checked his notes. "Wait a minute, I want to get this exactly right . . . this second map had been commissioned by the Senate to look at the issue of whether Texas should become a state. What was then called the Bureau of Topographical Engineers went out and did the survey, under the purview of the State Department. According to Tharp, it was a fantastic map, and shouldn't have been sold for a penny under ten thousand."

"Uh-huh." I looked in at the pie. It was not yet oozing juices, which would be the sign it was about done. "Where had Wellington himself obtained these maps?"

"Tharp was fuzzy on that, and for good reason. He didn't know, he claimed, where Drew got, as he called it, 'most of his stock.'"

"And they were business partners?"

Tom shrugged. "Tharp said Wellington was going to offer the Texas map to Craddock for four thousand."

"So if Craddock sold it to a client, he'd make a good profit. Six thousand or so, right?"

"Yeah, but the worst is ahead." The worst is ahead? I took another swig of port, although my head was already reeling. Texas? Nebraska? If Drew Wellington had had one of Kansas, he could have been the expert on all the states that eventually sent skiers to Colorado.

"According to Tharp, there might have been a *third* map. It was of what they call the New World. North America, from 1682. Worth a couple hundred K, but possibly to be offered to another client for a mere one hundred K."

"What? Are you joking? What other client?"

"I am not joking. I don't know the other client, and Tharp didn't know the particulars, because, he says, Drew didn't tell him." Tom pulled out his notebook and read me the details Neil Tharp had given him of the New World map that Drew might or might not have had on him. Unfortunately, I felt my head get woozy, as if the sudden effect of the night's work, the blowup at the MacArthurs' house, my sudden urge to bake, and the wine were hitting all at one time. "Miss G., are you interested in this?"

"I just need to sleep. Can you give me the executive summary, before I pretend to Neil Tharp that I'm interested in buying some of his collection?"

"He says we have one lost or stolen map, that of Texas. We also have a missing map of North America, from the late seventeenth century. Tharp claims Craddock must have made some kind of deal for the Texas map with his boss. Either that, or he stole both of them, Tharp says, the Texas map and the North America map, because we didn't find either one on Wellington's body, in his suit, or in his effects. Also, there was no money on Mr. Wellington either, no check, no promissory note, nada."

"What did Larry Craddock tell you? He was certainly anxious to get his hands on what he just called 'missing maps' when he came to the Roundhouse."

"Craddock claims that he did want the two maps Wellington showed him, but he told Wellington he didn't immediately have the money available, even with Wellington's reasonable prices. He explained to Drew that he'd have to make some calls and rearrange his finances, and get back to him. But that's not what he did."

"At the conference center, he told us he went to check the maps' provenance."

Tom cocked an eyebrow. "Yup. Craddock says he went into the reading room to use the wi-fi connection and get online to see if the maps had been reported stolen. He didn't have any luck, because the Web site that map dealers and libraries wanted to set up to report thefts isn't running yet. He claims he then made a call to an attorney who's a mad map collector. You ask me, they're all mad." Tom paused. "Anyhoo, the lawyer was too busy to talk to him, no surprise there. Larry left a message for the lawyer to return the call, then went back to the corner where he'd first met with Drew. But guess what? No Drew."

"Right."

"Timingwise," Tom went on, "this coincides with what we have on the surveillance video, that Drew was stumbling around up at the checkout desk, only he didn't check anything out. After twenty minutes of waiting, Larry thought Drew was double-crossing him, selling the maps to someone else. So he looked in Drew's briefcase. And there was the map of Texas."

"Drew must have been pretty drunk to leave it like that. What about the maps of Nebraska and North America?"

Tom shook his head. "The Nebraska map is the one we found on Drew, but we have to assume the Texas and North America maps are either missing or stolen. Maybe stolen by Larry, although he insists he would never do such a thing. And if you believe that, I've got a nice mountain to sell you on the Colorado plains."

My thoughts went straight to Sandee, as they had ever since I'd seen her the previous month. What was she up to here in Colorado? And then there was Roberta, who'd found Drew's body, and any number of library clients who might have thought it would be cool to rifle through the papers of a guy who looked as if he were asleep. And there were the paramedics, and—

"Don't worry, we're interviewing everybody we can find who even might have come in contact with Drew. Everyone swears there were no maps."

"And so what's your theory?"

"Neil Tharp thinks Larry Craddock stole the Texas and North America maps after he dumped the drug into Wellington's coffee. Oh, that's another thing. Wellington always brought a thermos of coffee into the library with him, to keep himself awake while he did business. He also brought a flask of sour-mash whiskey, to keep himself mellow."

"Both of which were drugged."

"Yup again. But the important thing, from Mr. Tharp's viewpoint, is that we did not find any money, nor did we find those two more valuable maps."

The timer buzzed for the pie. I took it out and placed it carefully on a rack. The golden crust sparkled under its crown of sugar crystals; thick, dark cherry juices bubbled out of the cracks.

"Gorgeous," Tom said.

"It's not bad," I said with a smile.

"I meant you, dear wife." And with that, he put his arm around my waist and helped me up the stairs—to bed, finally.

When the strains of Mozart's *Eine kleine Nachtmusik* drifted out of our alarm, I didn't get up right away, because I was dreaming that I was in Vienna, and I was sleeping on a soft feather bed. When Tom rolled over and said, "That's you, Miss G., if you're still going to the early service."

With my eyes closed, I murmured, "That's wrong. I'm listening to a little night music."

"Not anymore," Tom said as he whacked the radio button.

I couldn't face reality, not with snow drifting onto my eyelids, the memory of music still playing softly in my ears, and the promise of coffee and Sacher torte nearby— no, wait, not Sacher torte, cherry pie . . .

"I took the liberty," Tom announced from above me. I took a deep breath and was about to protest again when I realized Tom had brought me a steaming latte.

"You spoil me, husband." When I sat up, all my muscles, bones, and tendons creaked at once. It had been a long night. Did any caterers still do parties after they turned forty? I doubted it, and I was still in my early thirties. "How's the weather?"

Tom had shifted off the bed and was looking outside. "Hard to tell, it's still so dark." He ducked and squinted to look through the pines at the one streetlight that illuminated a patch of our sidewalk. "Looks as if we got a total of about ten inches of new snow." He squinted again. "And the plow came through during the night. Did you hear it?"

I sipped the luscious, hot drink. "I don't think I would have heard an air-raid warning during the night. I don't even remember going to bed."

Tom shook his head and chuckled. "Yeah, I had to undress you. Believe me, that was no fun at all."

"Very funny." I took a last slug of the coffee and checked the clock: half past six. That meant I had an hour to shower, dress, pack up the pie and Tom's coffee cakes, and get my van over to the church. Which reminded me. "Well, since you had so much fun stripping me, would you be willing to strip my van of snow? It's down on Main Street."

Tom took a deep breath. "What are husbands for in the morning, except to bring their wives coffee and get their vehicles ready to do battle with the world?"

I thanked him and walked toward the bathroom. "Wait. Stripping. Strippers. Did you all find out anything new about Sandee Brisbane?"

"We did. We found Bobby Calhoun in Nashville, actually. He says he hasn't seen Sandee since the fire. But here's the weird thing. When we questioned him, he said he wasn't that much into computers, and he never noticed when Sandee was 'doing the computer,' as he called it. But after the fire, when he was on a singing gig one time, he came into the house he and Sandee had been renting and noticed her laptop was gone. He said he immediately thought he'd been burgled and checked his gun collection. Sure enough, his Sig Sauer was missing."

I stood, paralyzed, by the bathroom door. "She stole my gun and used it to kill the Jerk. Are you saying she stole another gun?"

Tom looked rueful. "She did indeed. And Bobby did report the stolen gun to us, six months ago. But he forgot to mention the laptop."

"Anything else before I shower?"

"Actually, yes. You knew Drew Wellington, as did we down at the department. But you and Julian saw him in party situations—"

"Julian only saw him once, and that was when Drew showed up really late at a dinner—"

Tom held up his hand. In it he held a DVD. "Just let me finish. You saw Drew in party situations when he'd been drinking, right?"

"Yes," I said tentatively. "I saw him a couple of times."

"Did he take drugs, too?"

"That I didn't notice."

Tom said, "Could you look at something with me?"

"Sure."

We walked quietly down the stairs. I made myself a fresh latte while Tom fiddled with the DVD player. Finally we settled in the living room.

"Miss G., thanks. This is a copy of the library's surveillance video, from the time Drew Wellington came in just before three o'clock to when Roberta found him in the back corner by the emergency exit."

"It's okay with your guys down at the department that I see this?"

Tom was messing with the TV. "They *want* you to look at it, see if Wellington looks the way he did when he'd had too much to drink, or maybe when he'd been indulging in drugs, or both. We're trying to establish when he drank his booze with the Rohypnol in it, when he drank the poisoned coffee, and what the *hell* he was doing stumbling around the library, instead of asking for help."

"Are you sure the library only has the one surveillance camera?" I asked as the grainy video popped up on the screen.

"Yes. Facing the main entrance and exit doors." Tom pointed. "Those are the electronic gates that sense if you're filching a book without checking it out. You also can see the edge of the circulation desk."

I watched carefully as Drew Wellington, hale, hearty, and handsome, strode confidently through the electronic gates. He smiled broadly, knowingly, at the staff at the circulation desk, and even lifted his briefcase in greeting.

"Isn't there audio on this thing?" I asked.

"We're not talking the security cameras at the Denver Mint, here, Miss G. There's no sound."

Tom began to fast-forward past people going in and out. "Stop it," I said almost immediately. The camera was focusing on a young woman with brown hair, clad entirely in black. "That's the woman I think is Sandee."

Tom peered at the screen. "Could be, I guess. You saw more of her than I did. A lot more."

"Okay, okay, I went to one of her strip shows last summer, but it was to *talk* to her."

Tom sighed and fast-forwarded through more folks coming in and out. Larry Craddock was distinguishable by his bald head and charging gait. He strode into the library at about a quarter past three, checking his watch, as if he had an appointment. I watched the parade of the rest of the library patrons. If Patricia Ingersoll or Neil Tharp or Elizabeth Wellington was among those coming in, she or he was wearing lots of obscuring winter clothing, or a disguise. I shook my head.

"Wait, here we go," Tom said.

At half past three, Drew appeared on the video, stumbling up to the desk. He stopped, looked around, and seeing no librarian, lurched off to his left.

"Where was he going?" I asked.

"No idea. He didn't ask for a book, didn't ask anybody who works at the library to help him out. I checked, and if he thought he was going to puke, the men's restroom is in the other direction. Ditto with the pay phones, in case he didn't have his cell with him and wanted to call for help."

I stared at the screen. The self-assured attorney-turned-map-dealer who'd waved his briefcase at the library staff when he first came in was no longer there. Instead, I saw a man who looked as if he were physically ill. I said, "He's not carrying his briefcase. Is there any evidence he was going toward the newspapers, or to dump change into the copying machine? Those are the only things I can think of that are over on that side of the library."

Tom shook his head. "Nope. There's that hallway you were using when you unloaded your van, and there actually is another security camera outside that exit, pointed at the Dumpster. Reason for that is that the staff thought somebody was playing pranks on them, tossing their trash all over the parking lot. But it was a bear. That camera didn't pick up your van or the vehicle that was blocking you, unfortunately, since it's aimed at the Dumpster and not at the parking spaces there."

I asked, "Is there anything else down that hallway besides the exit, that might have been Drew's destination?"

"Not much. There's the circulation workroom, the lunchroom, and the storage area, where they keep volumes for the used-book sale. That's it. And there's no evidence Drew either went into or came out of any of those rooms. The librarians swore to our guys who secured the library that all three rooms were closed and dark."

"Maybe he got lost," I said.

"And him the map guy." He stopped the video. "So, how does he look to you, Miss G.? Drunk? Strung out?"

"He appears very drunk. I certainly never saw him that plastered at any party I catered. But if he had a drinking problem—"

"Oh, he definitely did," Tom observed. "A well-known drinking problem. The question is, Did he come to the library drunk and drugged with a very small amount of Rohypnol? Or did he come just feeling a bit tipsy, then somebody put Rohypnol in his flask and cyanide in his thermos once he got to the library? We don't know."

"Sorry I couldn't be more helpful."

"It's okay." He started the video again, speeding up the frames. At just past four, yours truly, carrying the box I used for dishes, marched across the screen. Tom whistled.

Then I spotted someone coming in just after I did— someone I recognized. "Stop the video. Is that Smithfield MacArthur?"

"Yes. He told us that Drew asked to meet him at the library, although he didn't specify why. But MacArthur was late getting there because, he says, he had trouble driving on the unplowed streets. He says he couldn't find Drew and assumed he'd missed him. You'll see he leaves the library about ten minutes later."

Tom started the video again. The two of us watched as Drew staggered back into view, then out again, presumably going back to his corner. Smithfield MacArthur then reappeared, his red face looking furious as he raced out.

People checked out books and left; a few hurried in to do copies or look for things to borrow. A short man who might have been Neil Tharp turned away from the cameras and exited through the doors. Hank ushered out a protesting Larry Craddock. Finally, the woman appeared with her little boy. The mom was carrying a sack that presumably held the Disney videos, while the little tyke raced out ahead of her, into the snow.

"That's it," Tom said as he ejected the DVD. "Thanks."

"You're certainly welcome."

"You know that used-book sale I just mentioned? While you and Julian were catering tonight Arch had his pals help him clean some of the stuff he doesn't want any more out of his room. He said you and Julian both told him to get his act together organizing, so he figured he'd enlist his own private army. He promised them some of Julian's fudge, plus any of his castoffs they wanted." I shook my head, thinking of Tom Sawyer conning his buddies into whitewashing Aunt Polly's fence. Tom went on: "They've packed the outgrown clothes into bags. They're about halfway through sorting the books. Those will be going into boxes, and they promise they're going to put all of it into the back of your van, once we retrieve it from Main Street. You don't have to deliver the books for the library sale or the clothes for Aspen Meadow Christian Outreach today if you don't want to or don't feel up to it. But I just wanted you to know what was going on if you saw a lot of stuff in the back of your vehicle. I can shuttle it around later, if you want."

"I'll see how I feel. One of us is going to have to do it, before Julian and I cater the luncheon at the MacArthurs' house on Monday. What's the last thing you wanted to tell me?"

"You'd asked us to do background on Sandee, so I did. We couldn't find anything. Remember, neither her mother, Cecelia, nor Sandee herself tried to turn in her lascivious father. You still think she's the one you saw over by Regal Ridge and in the library?" I nodded. "Remember, when you saw her last summer, she'd had plastic surgery and changed her hair color from when she lived here, so even her own mother didn't recognize her."

"Yes, yes, I know. And her mother wore specs as thick as wavy glass blocks."

Tom pulled out his trusty notebook and flipped to a page. "Sandee went to Aspen Meadow High School and graduated without distinction, except for her membership in the Explorers Club."

"She was lost," I said in a low voice. "A lost soul. She wanted to figure out where she was going, if even in a literal sense."

Tom shrugged. "Her father was murdered, which is still an unsolved case—"

I snorted. "Not in my book it isn't. I'm sure Sandee killed him, too. Sandee had no alibi."

"We didn't consider her a suspect back then, because we didn't have her motive. Well, you asked me to do the background check, and I did. Goldy, look at me." When I turned to him, I knew my face gave away my despair. Tom dealt with lawbreakers all the time, and I knew, as did he, that he could handle the details of sex crimes better than I could. "Miss G., I'll go pack that pie and the coffee cakes into your van now, if you want. Get the snow off it, warm it up for you."

"Thanks so much." I turned to take a shower, but was stopped by Tom, who came over to give me a hug. When he'd gone downstairs, I turned the shower on extra hot. I didn't care if the water scalded me. The memory of Sandee Brisbane, who'd taken vengeance into her own hands eight years after the Jerk had raped her, made my skin feel dirty and cold.

I wanted to wash off that sensation in the worst way.

14

Half an hour later, I was showered, dressed, and in our kitchen, where I was sautéing chicken thighs—for Jake, our beloved bloodhound. Our veterinarian had told me I could cook up poultry, rice, and carrots, all without spice, and the dog would love it. He'd been right.

"I know you're not taking fried chicken to the coffee hour," Tom said over my shoulder. "That's sort of a summer dish, isn't it?"

"Very funny. This is for Jake." I poured in raw rice and carrots, added water, and covered the pan. "Please keep it on very low heat until everything's done. Should take about half an hour. Cool and bone the chicken before you give it to him."

"Aye-aye, madam. That bloodhound is going to love you, or rather me, forever. Should I wake the boys up for church?"

"Up to you."

"Maybe I could bribe them, remind them of Julian's promise that one of us will take them over to Regal Ridge to snowboard, after they'd done their duty to God."

"I don't know, Tom," I teased him. "Do you think God would approve of you offering enticements in exchange for holy behavior?"

"Trust me, I'm a deal maker from way back. And the folks I offer deals to have been conducting themselves in much worse ways than Arch and his buddies."

I kissed Tom's cheek and pulled on a jacket. I was just about to take off for St. Luke's when my business line rang. I closed my eyes and tried *not* to visualize Hermie MacArthur ringing me up to cancel the next day's luncheon. Tom checked the caller ID.

"It's Marla. Are you sure you want to talk to her? You've only got forty minutes before the service begins."

I sighed and took the phone. "I know this must be important," I said into the receiver, "or you wouldn't be calling at ten after seven."

"And good morning to you, too, best friend." She sounded distracted, or tired, or troubled in some way.

"Are you all right?"

"I'm fine," she said breathlessly. "Listen, this afternoon the Broncos are playing their last game of the regular season. Can you do a party for me? I've got this new big-screen TV, and everybody wants to . . . nothing fancy," she went on, "just enough for eight people—"

"Marla, are you out of your *mind*? You don't even *like* football. And anyway, today's my one day to catch up on—"

"Oops, there's my call waiting. I'll give you the menu at church. Come to the early service, okay?"

"I'm already going to the early service!" I screeched.

"You don't need to yell," she said and hung up. I slammed down the phone and uttered a string of creative curses under my breath. Talk about unholy behavior.

"Problem?" Tom asked.

"Oh, Marla wants me to make food for eight people for today's Bronco game. I still have to prep Mrs. MacArthur's lunch, and there's Arch to look after, and anyway, I wanted to have time to talk to Neil Tharp at church today, not go over some new menu Marla's dreamed up." I slumped into one of the kitchen chairs. "Maybe I just shouldn't go at all."

Tom walked over and held out his arms. I stood reluctantly and allowed myself to be embraced. He said,

"Just think of it. Not only do I now get the great culinary challenge of cooking for the dog, I also can experiment on eight of Marla's well-heeled pals. D'you think they'd go for something made with hamburger?" When I groaned, Tom said, "Miss G., go to church. You'll feel better."

I trudged out the back door toward the garage. A grainy midwinter snow fell steadily. The billions of crystals hitting the neighborhood looked and sounded like a celestial sugar bowl being dumped from above. The weather was bitterly cold, and every now and then a sharp wind snapped through the pines. The temperature had dropped at least ten degrees from the previous day. I couldn't imagine Arch and his buddies wanting to snowboard in this.

Tom had not only cleared off and warmed up the van, but moved it back to our driveway from Main Street. I shivered anyway and thought I should have worn a sweater under my jacket. The frigid breeze seemed to be blowing right through my vehicle's closed windows. I made my way slowly down our road, then turned left toward St. Luke's. Crusted levees of snow and ice lined Main Street. To my right, clouds of steam billowed up the banks of Cottonwood Creek. The winter had been mild up to this point, and the creek was still much warmer than the surrounding air.

When my tires crunched into the church parking lot, the first thing I saw was Marla's new Lexus LC, a metallic inky-blue sporty model. Honestly, that woman bought cars the way I purchased mixers. Marla, clad head to toe in her politically incorrect mink, had her arms crossed and was tapping the toe of one of her mink-trimmed boots, as if she'd been waiting for me for several hours. I swallowed my dismay and tried to figure out what was going on with her, because if she'd bought a big-screen TV, it was to see what new fashions were being worn by celebrities.

"Listen, Marla—" I began as I walked up.

"You listen," she said, her expression dark. "Something's going on with that Sherlock Holmes–type woman from Boulder. You know, Julian's landlady, who helped you with the garden-club lunch yesterday? Grace Mannheim?"

I squinted through the falling snow. "What are you talking about?"

Marla looked around quickly, as if white-haired Grace were about to pop out from behind a spruce tree, wielding an ax. "Let's go inside, to a room where we can close a door."

"I've brought cherry pie and coffee cakes for after the service. Can you help me bring them in?"

"Oh God, the things I do for you," Marla grumbled as she followed me to the van.

"Don't start. You want me to do a party for you this afternoon—for eight people, no less?" I pulled open the sliding door and hauled out a basket of paper plates, napkins, and plastic forks.

"Oh, I didn't mean it. That was just my excuse for getting you here early." As she hooked the basket over her right arm, she glanced up at the sky. It had only just begun to brighten. "What the hell time is it, anyway? It looks and feels like four in the morning."

"Half past seven." I handed her the cherry pie. "Be careful with this. And by the way, Tom is at home making a luncheon dish with ground beef for eight people, for you and your celebration of a new big-screen TV."

"Oh, good!" she called over her shoulder as she sashayed toward the church entrance. "I'll invite some folks over."

How would cherry pie look splashed over mink? I wondered. I immediately brushed away such sinful thoughts, balanced Tom's two sour-cream coffee cakes on a tray he'd helpfully put next to them, and followed Marla through St. Luke's heavy wooden doors.

When we were safely ensconced in the church kitchen, with our baked goods on the center island, the door closed, and the bamboo curtain pulled tightly across the serving window, Marla dramatically shed her fur coat and faced me.

"I invited Grace to shower and stay at my house, Goldy. She looked tired at the garden-club lunch, and I wanted to help out."

"She told me she was doing that. You're great."

"Right. But listen. Remember Grace said she wanted to help get Patricia Ingersoll out from under the sheriff's department's cloud of suspicion?" When I nodded, Marla went on: "She showed up yesterday and wanted to be involved with the catering, right?"

I couldn't imagine where this was going. "Speaking of catering, could you wash your hands and help me get these goodies ready?"

Marla growled. She hated to have her elaborate tales interrupted. As she was drying her hands, she said, "You know I don't get good cell service at my house?"

"Welcome to the mountains."

"Yes. Well. That means Grace had to use my phone. And that's no bother, either, of course."

"Don't tell me you listened in on one of her calls."

"Stop interrupting me, and I'll tell what I *did* do." She raised her eyebrows and took a deep breath. "I was checking my calls-received thingy, the way Arch taught me. And as I was beeping through them, up popped this number from 'Ingersoll.'"

"Patricia called you? Or she called Grace at your place?" I started rummaging through the cupboards, looking for china plates on which to put the coffee cakes.

"Are you going to let me finish this story?"

I slapped the dishes down on the island and shot her a look. "Please let me get ready for the coffee hour. I really, really need to talk to somebody this morning. That's why I came early, in case he did."

"In case who did?"

"Marla!"

"Okay, pay attention. This Ingersoll number on my phone wasn't an Aspen Meadow exchange. I thought that was weird, because as far as I know, Patricia still lives over in that house she and Frank built in Flicker Ridge, before he got so sick. Did they have another house I didn't know about? I wondered. To find out, I pressed the button to redial. A woman answered. I said, 'Patricia?' And this woman replied, all hostile, 'This is *not* Patricia.' And so I said, 'Oh, sorry, my telephone indicates you called my number. I live in Aspen Meadow, and Patricia Ingersoll is my friend.' And this woman came back with, 'Too bad for you, then.'"

"*What?*" I stopped searching for a pie server in the jumble of the silverware drawer.

Marla leaned over the island and made *mm-mm* noises as she unwrapped one of Tom's coffee cakes. "Yes, that was my reaction, exactly. Just give me a piece of this, would you? I'm ravenous. I didn't have time to eat this morning, I was in such a rush to get over here and talk to you."

I finally nabbed a dull butter knife, cut the cake, and levered a large slab of it onto a paper plate. Marla didn't wait for a fork.

"You'll be proud of me, Goldy, I managed not to lose my temper talking to this woman." She chewed a bite of cake. "Yum-*my*! Did you make this?"

"Tom did. Did this lady you called say who she was?"

"No, so I asked her. She said she was *Whitney* Ingersoll, and that Frank Ingersoll had been her father before her mother died and *that bitch*, as she called Patricia, married her father. So why did she call me? I asked. She said she wasn't calling me, she was calling Grace Mannheim, to see if she'd made any progress. And that's where I screwed up, because I said, 'Made any progress on what?' At that point, Whitney Ingersoll sort of pretend-gasped and said, 'Oops, oops, I have to go.' Before I could protest, she hung up on me."

"That's it?"

"Isn't that enough?"

I glanced at my watch. It was twenty to eight, and I had no idea if Neil Tharp was here, or even if he was going to show up at all. "Listen, I remember Whitney Ingersoll. She came to Frank and Patricia's wedding. Now please, I have to check on whether my guy's arrived."

Marla shoveled in more cake. "*What* guy?"

"All right, all right, it's Neil Tharp. He was at a party at the MacArthurs' party last night, and said some things that made me want to talk to him some more."

"Oooh! The MacArthurs' party! Is that the one where somebody shot a hole through their French doors?"

I sighed. Honestly, this town could take a cap-gun incident and make it into a nuclear showdown. "It was a snowball, and it broke a kitchen window."

"Some snowball."

"There was a knife inside."

Marla cut herself another piece of cake. "Oh, dear, how inhospitable. Do you want me to talk to Grace about Whitney Ingersoll? Or do you want me to snoop surreptitiously?"

Since *surreptitious* was not a word that could effectively be applied to anything Marla did, I said, "You could just ask her and see what she decides to say. Actually, Grace did seem awfully curious about the whole Drew Wellington situation yesterday." When Marla nodded, I glanced ruefully at the center island. "Would you be willing to root around for a sharp knife to cut the pie? And then put the pieces on these paper plates along with slices of coffee cake? I need to go look for Neil Tharp."

Marla twirled and reached deftly for the butcher block containing the kitchen's cutting utensils. *Now why hadn't I thought of that?* It took her less than five seconds to pry out the first piece of pie. When she cried, "Oh, goody, cherry! My favorite!" I skedaddled out of there.

The snow was still falling relentlessly, and after three seconds out in the cold, I raced back inside and asked Marla if I could borrow her mink. Since I caught her red-handed and red-mouthed as she forked in mouthfuls of pie, she merely nodded. I slipped into the luxuriant fur and was immediately amazed at how heavy the doggone thing was. No wonder it took ermine-sporting royals forever to march up to their altars to be crowned.

Maybe it was the mink that made Neil Tharp pause as he made his slow way across the parking lot. I must have looked like a wealthy mark, because he immediately began limping straight toward me. Had he been limping at the library? I had only seen him for a few moments at the MacArthurs' party, while I'd been making the rounds with the dumpling soup. But as he came closer, I noticed that he also had a black eye and a very puffy left cheek. He hadn't had *those* the previous night. His thin black hair looked wet, as if he'd just showered. But he hadn't shaved, probably because it would have been too painful to run a blade over his swollen face. If I hadn't known he'd been in a fight, I would have thought he'd been in a bar brawl.

"Excuse me," he said, trying to sound bright and cheerful. He blinked at me through the snow. "Are we acquainted? I'm Neil Tharp." And then he reached into his pocket and pulled out a card. "Neil Tharp, Independent Dealer in Rare and Antique Maps," it said, with a phone number and local post office box.

I hated to disappoint him, or myself, for that matter, because wearing a full-length mink was giving me all kinds of power. I took the card and nodded at him. "We are acquainted, Neil."

"Goldy?" he inquired, his tone still bright and optimistic. He shuffled a bit closer. "Why are you wearing a mink?"

"Because I'm cold. But not as cold as I was last night, when I saw you getting into it with Larry Craddock outside the MacArthurs' house."

"Oh, Christ," he muttered.

I wagged my finger at him. "Sorry that fight last night makes you limp today, Neil. But that doesn't mean you can take the Lord's name in vain outside His house."

"I need to get inside. There might be people I should talk to in there."

"Neil, I am someone you should talk to. Last night, did you throw a snowball with a knife inside it at the MacArthurs' kitchen windows?"

His chin sagged. "No, of course not."

"Did you see who did?"

He shuffled from foot to foot. "I'm . . . I'm not sure."

"What did you see, then? That you're sure of?"

He looked at the snow-covered ground, then back up at me. The muscles along his jaw bunched. "Maybe there was someone over in the neighbor's yard. I couldn't be certain. It was dark."

"And maybe the person who threw the snowball was Larry Craddock?"

Neil's expression darkened further. "It could have been, I don't know. That son of a bitch was moving all over the place, going in and out of dark places, then jumping out to hit me and shout some new . . . thing."

"Neil, what is going on? On Friday I was trying to cater a party at the library, and your boss was murdered, maybe while he was doing a map deal. Then last night you and Larry Craddock had a meltdown. I thought you fellows in the map world were distinguished, pipe-smoking types."

Neil's shoulders sagged. "We used to be."

"Before what?"

He shrugged and avoided my eyes. "I don't know. Listen, could we go inside? I'm freezing out here."

I replied that of course we could, but I asked if we could go into the kitchen so we wouldn't be interrupted. Once there, Marla drew her eyebrows into a tent of worry when she saw Neil's beat-up face and watched his slow, painful limp. She showed remarkable restraint, I thought, by not giving him the third degree. She did, however, shoot me a meaningful look before silently exiting the kitchen. *I want every detail of this conversation.* I handed her her mink, and she sashayed out.

Neil leaned against the island. "Why are you so interested in Drew Wellington?"

I took a deep breath. "Well, there's the fact that Larry Craddock attacked me over those maps of yours, and your insistence that I tell you what papers were with Drew Friday night, because you were looking for those maps. But the main reason is that when I was at the library, I saw a woman who used to live in Aspen Meadow. She looked as if she were lurking in the stacks . . . and then I saw her at the windows, near where Drew was." I paused while Neil gave me a look indicating he didn't know what I was talking about. I inhaled again. "Well, this is going to sound silly. She seemed to be watching Drew, who was sitting in the corner of the library, beside the emergency exit. I have reason to believe that this woman was the person who had sent Drew threatening e-mails for the last month. Did he tell you about that? And I know who she is."

Neil's mouth opened in awe. "What? Some strange woman? Watching Drew? Do you know who she was? Do you have a picture of her or something?"

"No, sorry, I don't have a picture of her." I pressed my lips together, then plunged ahead. "I might be wrong, but think I do know who it was. Her name is Sandee Brisbane. Six months ago, she confessed to killing my ex-husband."

"Jesus H. Christ."

"Neil, not again." I watched his face carefully, but he didn't register any familiarity with Sandee's name. "Sandee . . . knew the Aspen Meadow Wildlife Preserve really well. She disappeared in there during the big forest fire last summer. The sheriff's department assumed she'd died. But they never found her corpse or her skeleton. So, I was wondering." I felt silly, as if I were grasping at a microscopic straw. "Could it be possible she was one of your customers? She belonged to the Aspen Meadow Explorers when she was in high school here. Could she have purchased one of your maps? Have known Drew?"

When Neil shook his head, his face suddenly looked like a marshmallow that had fallen into the fire. "How old is she?"

I thought back. "She'd be about twenty-two or twenty-three. She's a former stripper, and very pretty."

"A stripper? Named Sandee? Her name's not setting off a carillon in my head. And anyway, we don't—didn't sell maps that would help you get from point A to point B. No modern maps, in other words. Now, if we had a map of the wildlife-preserve area that Lewis and Clark had used, that would be another story."

I sighed. Then very casually I asked, "So . . . what was the big fight between you and Larry about last night? I mean, I'm catering another party for the Mac-Arthurs tomorrow, and I'd rather not have it wrecked, if you don't mind."

Neil gave me the kind of look you might see from someone who'd just swallowed a tablespoon of vinegar. "Nobody's going to disrupt your party. Simply put, Drew Wellington had some maps with him when he died. They were very valuable. I know that Drew was going to offer them to Larry at a good price Friday afternoon at the library. But then Drew was killed, and I had to move heaven and earth to get the sheriff's department to tell me what they found on Drew. That's why I tried to ask you about it first, the night of the murder. Elizabeth—Mrs. Wellington, Drew's ex-wife—happened to be with me then—we ran into each other in the parking lot. I had been at the library, as I told the police, although I hadn't spoken to Drew there. I was about to get into my car when the commotion broke out." He looked dejected. "All the sheriff's department found was the less expensive of the two maps Drew had hoped to sell to Larry. And so I strongly suspect that that bald-headed bowling-ball brain, Larry Craddock, killed Drew, and stole the other two maps he had with him, one worth a few thousand, the other worth a fortune."

"You know the cops initially arrested Patricia Ingersoll for the murder?"

"Oh, yeah?" Neil's eyebrows climbed his wide, pale forehead. "Why didn't they keep her?" When I shrugged, he said, "Do you know, last year she pretended to be interested in maps? She said she needed one of the trans–Mississippi West for her living room. I should have said, 'Yeah? What, you read about it in a catalog?' But I didn't. Instead, when she wanted to be introduced to Drew, I did it. And then pretty soon they were an item, and she wasn't interested in buying *squat*. Look, don't talk to me about that *bitch*."

"So, you don't like Patricia either?"

Muffled organ music began to thread through the closed kitchen door. Neil gathered up his briefcase and headed toward the exit. "I have potential clients to meet after church."

"Father Pete won't like you trying to do commerce during the coffee hour."

"I don't care," Neil called over his shoulder, and limped slowly out of the kitchen. The next time I saw him, he was pulling a price sheet out of his briefcase and handing it to the Merediths, an elderly couple who lived in Flicker Ridge. Neil then shuffled up to Mildred Stubblefield, a sixtyish woman whose husband had cancer. The Stubblefields were childless, so each week someone from the ten-fifteen service sat with John Stubblefield so that Mildred could attend the eight o'clock. Everyone—including Neil Tharp, I had no doubt—was also aware that Mildred Stubblefield would inherit five million dollars when John passed away. But everyone—except Neil, I now guessed—had managed to keep from talking about the money situation to Mildred. I raced over to try to intercept him, but was too late.

"Mrs. Stubblefield," he was saying, "a map of New England from the eighteenth century would be just the thing your husband would want for his sickroom, I am quite sure—"

"Mr. Tharp!" I cried once I was at his side. "There's something of great import that I need to talk to you about!"

His face dropped when he saw it was only the caterer. Mildred Stubblefield graced me with a thankful smile and walked toward the table holding the bulletins.

"I know you haven't suddenly remembered that you want a rare map," Neil said sourly.

"You're right." I put my finger on my chin, as if in deliberation. "But I was wondering if you had a book for the civility-challenged. Civility is not so rare, as it happens."

"What are you talking about?"

But I was saved from elucidating by the opening strains of the organist playing Bach's Prelude. I nabbed a bulletin and scooted into a pew. A moment later, Marla slid in beside me.

"What was *that* about?" she asked under her breath.

"Neil has no manners," I whispered.

"Tell me something I don't know."

"He doesn't like Patricia Ingersoll any more than her stepdaughter, Whitney, seems to."

Marla grunted. Across the nave, the slithery sound of ski jackets was suddenly distracting. I nearly fainted as Tom marshaled Arch and his slumber-party pals into a pew. The boys all looked as if they were still half asleep. Much eye rubbing and yawning accompanied our progress through the Scripture lessons. But the boys were there, so I had to hand it to Tom. He was not above shooting me a look of triumph.

"Today," Father Pete intoned at the beginning of the sermon, "I want to continue acting as your somewhat unorthodox shepherd, by carrying on with our discussion of the Seven Deadly Sins." Beside me, Marla perked up. "On this, the next to last Sunday of Advent, we come to Greed," Father Pete went on. Marla groaned.

"For God's sake!" she whispered. "This is the sixth week of this! Are we going to get to Lust by Christmas?"

"We are all lost souls," Father Pete went on while cocking his head and casting a half grin in Marla's direction.

Beside me, Marla tugged her mink around her shoulders and closed her eyes. She was a generous woman, and I had no doubt that she'd donated an amount equivalent to the cost of the Lexus to the rector's discretionary fund. But I also was aware that she wouldn't enjoy being lectured to—not this early in the morning. And of course, a bellyful of carbohydrates would now be having a soporific effect.

Father Pete talked for a while about materialism. Then he asked, "Now, why do you all think Jesus overturned the tables of the money changers inside the temple? Because he was angry? Because he was having a bad day?"

Everyone waited. Sometimes Father Pete's questions weren't merely rhetorical, and he expected an answer. As the silence lengthened, there was a rustling and heaving behind Marla and me.

"Or do you think, perhaps, that he thought folks should just be foresighted enough to bring the right kind of coins for the collection box? Or do you think he was distressed that people were motivated by greed?"

The bumping noise in the pew in back of us was accompanied by someone crashing about. Marla awoke with a start. A woman cleared her throat, as in, *Stop it!*

"Brauggghhh!" a male voice cried from behind us. A nimbus of musk floated forward. I turned around in time to see Neil Tharp struggling to push his briefcase past the plump knees of the matron beside him. She cast an angry glance up at him as Father Pete stopped midsentence to allow the interruption to finish. Neil Tharp ignored both the matron and Father Pete as he crashed out of the pew.

Apparently he'd had enough.

15

He looked awfully peeved," Marla whispered under her breath. "Didn't somebody famous say 'greed is good'?"

"I thought you were asleep."

"I was concentrating."

A loud "Ssh!" erupted from behind us. We turned to frown at the matron, but she had slid down the pew to make room for Tom, who now held his finger to his lips. Marla and I both burst into giggles, which in turn *did* make the matron glower.

"Mom!" Arch whispered loudly from across the nave. "Grow up!"

Sensing he was losing his audience, Father Pete launched into what he promised was a concluding thought about greed being the opposite of generosity.

"Acting in self-interest is diametrically opposed to acting for others," he said slowly, "and I hope you will all bear that uppermost in your minds . . ." He paused. The congregation waited in anxious silence. Another question? As the silence lengthened, everyone seemed to be wondering, *Where is he going with this? Didn't he just say "in conclusion"?*

Father Pete raised his thick, tentlike black eyebrows and boomed, ". . . when you remember to renew your pledges for next year! If you don't, Santa Claus will be extremely ticked off!" As relieved laughter swept through the small congregation, Father Pete smiled. "I just wanted to impress upon all of you that it is better to *give* than to receive."

"Marla," Tom announced, leaning forward and tapping her on the shoulder, "before the game this afternoon, you need to know that sometimes it's better to *kick* than to receive."

All things considered, the coffee hour went well. I needed to talk to Tom about my visit with Neil Tharp, so I asked Marla if she could serve the treats. She obliged by twittering about with a tray, from which she handed folks plates of pie and cake slices. She announced merrily to anyone who would listen that she had baked them using old family recipes. Which wasn't entirely a lie; she and I were family. Was lying one of the Seven Deadly Sins? I couldn't remember.

"Tharp said he hated Patricia Ingersoll?" Tom asked after I first informed him he wouldn't have to cater a football party for Marla. "Well, that figures, doesn't it? Neil had conflicts with Drew, right? And according to Patricia, Drew's girlfriend, Drew didn't trust Neil anymore. So it makes sense that they didn't like each other. These people, I swear." We were interrupted by his cell phone ringing. He whacked the wooden doors to take the call outside. I followed, not to be nosy, but because I truly did want to resume our conversation. Well, maybe I was a little nosy.

The cold hit me like a slap. Tom, impervious, was holding his cell flat against his ear. His face was a sudden mask of seriousness. "Where?" he asked. A moment later, he closed the phone, shook his head, and strode off toward his Chrysler.

"Tom!" I called after him. "What's going on?"

"Take the boys home!" was all he said. He gunned his car out of the parking lot and headed up Cottonwood Creek, toward town.

I shivered and held my sides. "That was weird," I said, although I was alone outside the church. Behind me, the wooden door creaked open.

"What are you doing out here in the cold?" Marla demanded. "I've got a lady in here wanting to know how to make this pie. When I told her it was an old family recipe, she said, 'Oh, yeah? How old is Goldy—' "

"Wait," I cried. My gaze had caught on a green station wagon going too fast down the canyon, away from the direction in which Tom had gone. I recognized the vehicle, but more importantly, I thought I recognized the *driver*. Still, this time I wanted to be completely sure. I whirled on Marla. "Lend me your car! Please! Quickly!"

"What?" Marla stood immobilized. One hand held the big wooden door open, the other grasped the tray that now held only a solitary piece of coffee cake. "What are you talking about? What did you see?"

"Sandee, Sandee, I saw Sandee," I blubbered as I pushed past her and hightailed it into the kitchen, where I was pretty sure Marla and I had left our purses. I looked around wildly for my coat, but the Sunday-school kids had dumped all their snowpants and coats and boots in a pile . . . on top of the plastic milk-carton container where I'd tossed my coat. I looked around for our purses.

Marla, meanwhile, must have handed the tray to an unsuspecting parishioner because she stayed right behind me. She snagged her Louis Vuitton purse just as I was about to pounce on it.

"Do tell me," Marla said as she rooted through the bag, "how am I supposed to get home?"

"Can you go faster? And look, could you take Arch and his pals over to the Regal Ridge Ski Area in my van? I'll give you my keys, 'cuz I need my purse with my driver's license. Hurry!" I knew I was talking too fast, that I was moving too quickly. But I had to know if that had been Sandee, and if so, where she was going. The way I saw it, I now finally had a chance to find out what was going on, and why she was here.

Marla handed me her key chain. "First my fur, now my car. You want my house? It's only a few blocks away—"

"And you'll remember the boys?" I cried as I raced toward the kitchen exit.

"Of course." Marla shook her head. "Here, take this, you'll need it." She heaved her mink at me.

It was only after I'd started the Lexus that I wondered if my generous friend would be able to find my coat in the chaotic pile in the kitchen, so she could keep herself warm in my slow-to-heat-itself van. But Marla was nothing if not resourceful. As the Lexus zoomed out of the parking lot, I fixed my mind firmly on catching up to Sandee Brisbane.

I wasn't used to driving a car that had anything like the pickup of Marla's sporty LC. Whenever I touched the accelerator, the Lexus shot forward with a roar. More than worrying about catching up with Sandee, I became more nervous about the packed snow and ice that still lined the road. Once I went too fast around a curve that followed Cottonwood Creek, and the rear wheels spun out, stalling the Lexus in the lane that should have held oncoming traffic. Heart in throat, I thanked God that the two-lane highway was empty at that point. I started up again and accelerated more soberly. Pointing the car eastbound, I continued cautiously in the direction the green station wagon had taken.

A mile down Cottonwood Creek, traffic came to a halt. I could guess the reason: starting at nine, the Troublesome Gulch Roadhouse served the most popular Sunday brunch in Furman County. Finding a spot in their too-small parking lot was always dicey.

I pressed the button to bring down the window. I hadn't had time to do anything with Marla's mink except throw it over my knees and lap, and the cold air made my eyes sting. Still, I craned my neck out the window, and thought I saw, four cars up, Sandee's green station wagon, also stopped.

There was no oncoming traffic, but I couldn't take a chance in the left lane. I took a deep breath, leaned on the horn, and accelerated onto the gritty, narrow shoulder. Bewildered faces took me in as I quickly passed their cars on the right, totally illegally of course. One, two, three, and then . . . there was Sandee. I had to stop so I could keep one hand on the horn while the other pressed the driver-side window button.

"Sandee!" I called. "Pull over! I need to talk to you!"

Perhaps it's instinctive, the way we respond to our names. In any event, she turned her head to glance at me, but only for a moment. Her position in the station wagon was above me, since I was in the low-slung driver's seat of Marla's sports car. Still, I knew it was Sandee Brisbane. Her hair, now brunette and long, was pulled into a ponytail, and she wore no makeup at all. When she saw me, her mouth tightened into a frown.

Sandee was not afraid to pull the station wagon into the left lane. But at that very moment, the screech of oncoming sirens split the cold air. I could even hear Sandee shriek a cussword as she maneuvered the wagon back into her lane. Meanwhile, behind us, the line of folks wanting parking places had closed up.

"Dammit to hell," I yelled, but it was no use. First one, then another police car squealed by, heading west up the canyon, toward Aspen Meadow. There was no way to flag one of them down. I desperately scanned the interior of the Lexus. If Marla had a cell phone in there, it sure didn't jump out at me.

When there was a break in the police cars streaming past, Sandee again wrenched the station wagon into the left lane. Daring death, she accelerated. Cursing, I leaned on Marla's horn, yanked the steering wheel to the left, and followed her. If a car hit Sandee head-on, I reasoned, I could duck onto the left shoulder and avoid an accident.

But truth to tell, I wasn't really doing much reasoning. Again the sound of sirens split the air. Sandee slowed, and I thought she was going to steer her car into the right, that is, the legal, lane. But she did not. Instead, she zoomed past a line of stores that included a gas station, a café, and a store boasting "Western Antiques." Just after Don's Detail Shop, she wrenched the station wagon to the left, onto a side road that I was not aware even existed. Unfortunately, when I tried to make the same left turn, I miscalculated the pitch, the angle, and the way I needed to steer. The result was that I slammed Marla's brand-new Lexus into the outside wall of Don's Detail Shop.

The problem with an air bag deploying, I realized, is that it's not done in slow motion. One moment you're driving along, the next you've been punched in the chest with excruciating force. If I'd had anything in my stomach, I'm sure I would have puked.

"What the hell are you trying to do to me?" Sandee Brisbane towered over me, her body shaking with rage.

As I sat in Marla's smoking, ruined Lexus, my body aching from the punch of the air bag, with glass all over the dashboard and the front seat, I thought of several smart-ass suggestions of what I'd like to do to Sandee Brisbane. The side window was broken, and I could have said something if I'd been able to. But I was having trouble getting my mouth to work. Also, my mind went to Bobby Calhoun's stolen Sig Sauer. Did Sandee have that gun with her?

"Stay out of my way, Goldy, do you understand?" The muscles in Sandee's jaw bunched. When I didn't reply, she grabbed my hair and yanked my head to the side, away from the headrest. The pain made my eyes sting with tears.

"Stop!" I cried, my voice feeble.

"Are you listening?" Her grip on my hair tightened. "Leave me alone!"

I said, "Could you please let go of my hair? Please? Let go?"

She pushed my head forward, still clutching my hair. I turned my face as far away from her as I could, for a reason.

"Goldy!" she cried. "Look at me when I'm talking to you."

"If you could just . . . slowly rotate my head toward you. I think I've got a torn muscle in my neck."

She did as I asked, so I got a good look, finally, at her car, an old, olive-green Volvo station wagon. I blinked, trying to get the numbers of the license plate, but they were covered with dust, probably by design. There was a blue parking sticker, though, on the rear bumper. Hmm. Again Sandee twisted my head to meet hers. I gasped with pain.

"Sandee." My voice sounded parched. "Did you kill Drew Wellington?"

She guffawed. "That's a laugh."

"But you know who he is. Or was."

Sandee raised one eyebrow and did not answer.

"Sandee," I tried again, "why are you here?"

She leaned down into my face. Her smile was cruel, it seemed to me. Or knowing. "I'm protecting my assets."

"They'll find you." I wheezed, then coughed.

"No, they won't." Then she said, her face still caught in that stiff smile, "They can't find me if I'm not lost."

All I could think of was Father Pete's words: "You're a lost *soul*." And then I stupidly repeated, "Did you kill Drew Wellington? Why are you here?"

Suddenly Sandee held up a long knife in her left hand. "Don't *you* try to find me." She brought the knife— what was it, one of those kinds you use for hunting?—up to my face.

"I have a child," I pleaded as fear scurried across my skin.

Sandee raised her eyebrows. *"I have a child,"* she mocked, her voice a high singsong. Then she tipped my head back until I shrieked for her to stop. With her left hand still holding the knife, she sliced clean through my hair. Then she held up the strands and sprinkled them over the ground. Before I could react, she turned on her heel and took off.

I couldn't help it; I sobbed. Things had happened too fast. I'd seen Sandee hauling butt down the canyon. Thinking I was doing the right thing, I'd borrowed Marla's car and followed her. Now I'd wrecked the Lexus, and Sandee had issued a very personal threat— and damn near scalped me.

I didn't think things could get any worse until police vehicles again began streaming relentlessly up the canyon. When one signaled and pulled over, I wondered what the penalties were for wrecking a friend's expensive sports car. Should I tell them about Sandee? I wasn't sure.

As it happened, the patrolmen who stopped said

they couldn't raise Tom, but yes, they would try to flag down Sergeants Boyd and Armstrong, who were on their way. *On their way to what?* I wanted to ask, but didn't. Less than five minutes later, I was so happy to see the two investigators get out of their black-and-white, I started crying again. When they rushed over, were they shaking their heads, or was it my imagination?

"Mrs. Schulz, are you all right?"

My words came out in gasps. "Never. Been. Better."

Boyd wrinkled his brow as he leaned over the window. "What happened?"

"What the hell . . . do you think . . . happened? I wrecked . . . my car."

Armstrong's chin dropped. "This is your car? I don't *think* so."

"Whose car is this, Mrs. Schulz?" Boyd again.

Armstrong suddenly sounded perplexed. "And what in the world did you do to your *hair*?"

"Could you . . . please get me out?"

It took them more time than I would have thought to free me from the Lexus. Meanwhile, they continued to pepper me with questions and comments.

"Marla's car, eh? Bet she won't let you borrow one of her vehicles again soon."

"Following Sandee Brisbane? Again? When was the last time you saw an eye doctor?"

Finally, finally, when I was out of Marla's car, wrapped in her torn mink, they got serious. "All right, Mrs. Schulz, we're going to call an ambulance."

"An ambulance? I'm fine! All that joking around, what was that about?"

"That was to keep you from losing it. We have to get you looked at." Boyd eyed the back of my head. "So are you going to tell us what happened to your hair?"

"Sandee Brisbane cut it."

"Why?"

"Why don't you ask her? I don't know. And can we get into your car? I'm freezing." When they continued to look at me dubiously, I said, "I know my spine, okay? I'm a caterer and know all about back pain. I'm fine. My neck's not broken, and because of the headrest I don't have whiplash. I'm not bleeding and I don't have any broken bones."

"Uh," said Boyd. "And where'd you go to med school again?"

I lifted my chin. "Med Wives 101, since you ask."

"What is that?" Armstrong asked. But I knew it was a rhetorical question, and to prove it, I stamped through the snow to their steaming patrol car and waited for them to open the door.

"Uh, just for the record," Boyd called to me, "could you show us your license and registration?"

I pivoted, marched back to Marla's car, and wrenched out my purse. Thanks to my daily yoga practice, I was able to stretch and reach through to snap open Marla's glove compartment. A bunch of papers spewed out and I caught a handful. When I reemerged from the Lexus, I ignored my aching neck and chest, sifted through the papers, and handed them the registration. Then I located my driver's license and handed that to them, too.

Once I was in the back of Boyd and Armstrong's patrol car, they asked me a few more questions. I answered them while they took notes. When they stopped talking, I pressed my lips together and wondered if I could take a turn asking questions.

"What's with all the police cars? Tom raced out of church after he got a cell call. Where's everybody going?"

Sergeants Boyd and Armstrong exchanged a look. Finally Boyd said, "Someone saw a body lying on a rock, right in the middle of Cottonwood Creek. Just below the waterfall. The body was submerged and not moving."

"Who was it?"

Armstrong hooked his left arm over the seat. "You had a run-in with him? Map dealer? Bald guy name of Larry Craddock?"

Boyd said, "He's dead."

16

Sergeant Boyd, was he murdered?"

"Well, I don't think he was going for a swim."

"Suicide?" I asked.

Armstrong shook his head. "We're not there yet, okay?"

Oh Lord, I thought, *Sandee killed Larry Craddock, too. But no one will believe me,* I reflected just as quickly. "Guys?" I said. "Is Tom there?"

"One of the first ones," Armstrong replied.

"Could you take me to the scene? Please? I want to see Tom." I was also thinking, *I may be able to see something you all might not catch,* but Sandee had already laughed in my face half an hour ago, and it hadn't been a pleasant experience. I didn't want to risk it again.

"Hello?" I repeated. "Could you take me up to the waterfall?"

They both laughed. "You're so lucky that it's still snowing," Boyd said.

"Why am I lucky?"

"Because there's an accident alert in effect. That means you don't have to report crashing into Don's Detail Shop until tomorrow. 'Less you want to go call Don now, wait until he shows up—"

"Never mind." Ahead, prowler lights pulsed through the snowflakes. All traffic along Main Street had slowed. I thought of Sandee's strong, dry hands pulling my hair, of the horrible scratching sound the knife had made as it sliced through my hair. "Can you just tell me *how* Larry Craddock died? Was he shot, did he drown, what?"

"Nope." Boyd again. "Nope, as in we can't tell you, because we don't know, okay?"

I almost let out with a sarcastic, *Thanks a lot,* but actually, I did owe them gratitude for picking me up. Without warning, their prowler stopped behind a row of cars exhaling plumes of exhaust. We weren't quite up to the turnoff for our street. I craned my neck to see, but could only surmise that law enforcement had the road blocked off at the traffic light.

"You can't just let me out here," I protested. "Isn't it possible to get me closer to Tom?" I was trying to sound innocent, but I wasn't sure it was working.

"They're not going to allow you near the falls," Armstrong warned. "They will not permit you to go near that body. So don't try to get through, okay?"

"I will not try to get through," I promised. "As a matter of fact, now that I think about it, I can walk to our house from here," I assured them. "It's only a block and a half." I got out of the car. "Thanks for the ride, fellas. And for helping me."

They said I was welcome, turned on their lights and siren as they pulled into the empty left lane, and passed the line of stopped cars.

I actually sort of did intend to go home. What did I care about Larry Craddock? I mean, the guy had attacked me, and he'd threatened Arch. And of course there was nothing I could do for him now. But something was bothering me and preventing me from slogging up to the house. What was it?

Before turning up our street, I climbed the snowy set of steps to the Grizzly Saloon, until I reached their covered porch. I sat gingerly on a bench that was flanked by Christmas trees adorned with blinking colored lights. Country music throbbed from inside the saloon. This didn't help my thinking any, nor did my newly

shorn scalp, which was freezing. Plus, I suddenly realized, I was hungry. So I had no coffee, no food, no
warmth . . . and no insight into what it was that was
giving my accident-addled brain trouble.

Sandee. That was what was causing my mind to mal-
function. Sandee, Sandee, Sandee.

So she was here after all. I hadn't been wrong about
that, despite all the joking from Tom and his cohorts.
And she was *protecting her assets*? What in the world
did that mean? And even though trouble and violence
had enveloped local map collectors in the last week—
everything from glass-breaking snowballs to sudden
death—somehow, Sandee didn't impress me as being the
map-collecting type.

I pulled the torn fur around my shoulders in a
wretched attempt to warm myself up. What did I
really know about Sandee Brisbane, in the final an-
alysis?

She'd drowned her mother for not protecting her
from a predatory father, whom she'd probably also murdered. She'd shot and killed the Jerk for raping her when
she was a young teenager. She'd threatened me and my
son. And of course she'd just come racing away from a
crime scene. That was the second time in three days
she'd been near a murder. Had she killed Drew Wellington and Larry Craddock, too? If so, why?

I heard law enforcement officials calling to one another. From my vantage point perched above Main Street, I could see them unrolling yellow crime-scene tape. Up ahead, the road was indeed blocked off. In the right lane, frustrated motorists were making U-turns and heading back down the canyon.

I couldn't see a trace of Larry Craddock.

But if I could have, what good would that have done? What was it that was making me feel I *needed* to see the crime scene, if indeed it was a crime scene?

Because I wanted reassurance. I wanted, I suddenly realized, to believe that Sandee had *not* killed Larry Craddock. In spite of everything, I felt sorry for the former stripper. Yes, six months ago she had murdered two people. Not that I approved of vigilante justice. But you could at least make the case that both of those acts of violence had been well-thought-out acts of revenge.

So would somebody please tell me what kind of vengeance she could possibly be seeking on a couple of *map dealers*?

I had no idea. I looked again across Main Street and the parking lot that abutted Cottonwood Creek. Steam was rising from the creek and mixing with the falling snow. *Think, think, think,* I told myself.

Sometimes, Tom had told me, you could determine motive just by looking at a crime scene. If a single woman is killed and her tires are slashed, you look for a jealous wife whose husband had been having a fling with the victim. Ditto with a jealous husband. Signs of torture usually indicate a sicko. If indeed Larry Craddock had been murdered, could the scene up the street inform me on the subject of motive?

Okay, I told myself as I rapidly crossed Main Street, I was going to keep my promise to Boyd and Armstrong. Technically, I was not trying to *get through to* the crime scene. But I had traipsed with Arch and the Cub Scouts along lots of paths abutting Cottonwood Creek. I knew how to get around the boulders, and I was aware that I might be able to get *above* wherever Larry Craddock lay. In fact, I was relatively sure I could manage to get a pretty good gander at the creek, and maybe the body, without screwing things up.

The snow was still falling fast. I traversed the parking lot, which only held a few cars, each of which sported a thick hat of white stuff. When I reached the creek, I blinked and tried to make out where the stepping-stones were that Arch and I had shown the Cubs when we'd gone across. Unfortunately, every single boulder in the creek was completely covered with snow, and the icy water flowing around them looked as if it was going awfully fast. Finally I spotted the place below the parking lot where Arch and I had used a meandering path of small boulders whenever we fished as a way to get over to the other side.

The water looked awfully cold.

Go, just go, I told myself. So I did. I tried to think of myself as nimble as I hopped across, and I worked to dispel the word *slippery* from entering my thoughts. When I made it, I thanked God in heaven and all the saints I could think of. Episcopalians weren't very big on saints. *Maybe we should be,* I mused as I trod carefully along the path that was actually fairly easy to make out, as it was the only smooth area of snow leading up the creek toward the falls.

Ahead, I could again hear sheriff's-department officers calling to one another, something about video. Okay, so the fellow from the crime-scene unit had his video camera pointed at the scene. With any luck, the sheriff's department hadn't yet moved anything. Now I just had to get about twenty yards or so above where they were.

Right.

To my left, the ground rose steeply. There was no beach to speak of, just those big boulders—in the stream and along the bank. That's what made the fishing good. The trout liked to hide away from the open water, and people couldn't get through easily to catch them. The problem was, it was a lot easier to walk along the path undetected when there was full foliage from deciduous bushes and cottonwood trees. Now I felt exposed. I knew I had to start climbing up the hill pretty quickly and take cover behind evergreens or risk being spotted by the police on the scene.

I took a deep breath, tried to pick out where I was going to head through the pines, and began to ascend through a soft, slippery blanket of snow covering pine needles. Branches slapped my face, and I tried not to gasp. Snowflakes chilled my scalp. I cursed Sandee. Here I was trying to help her . . . and she sure hadn't been very nice to me.

Finally I stomped through to a slight clearing. I was about twenty yards above the cops swarming around the creek. As far as I knew, nobody had seen me. I looked down and tried to make out Larry Craddock.

It didn't take long. His egg-shaped head and stocky body lay almost exactly at midstream. Blood darkened the snow on the rocks near his corpse. Somebody had hit or attacked him with a gun or knife, then dragged his body to midstream. Which seemed very odd.

But Sandee's hands had been completely dry. Even if she'd had gloves on, if she'd dumped Larry midstream, her sleeves would have been wet. When she'd held my head back with one hand, her forearm had not even been moist.

So she couldn't have killed him. At least not in my unscientific estimation.

I blinked as I looked down at the creek again, and turned my head to the right. Downstream from Larry Craddock's body, beyond the place where the cops had strung yellow crime-scene tape, wrapped against a rock, there was a square of paper with red stains on it, probably blood. It was the wrong shape for a newspaper. I craned my head around to get a better look.

Was it a map?

I was so excited I reached for my cell phone, and that was my mistake. I lost my balance and began tumbling, hard, through evergreens and cottonwoods. I slid, grabbed for branches, yelped, and tried in vain to get a purchase on the hill. But the slick, soft surfaces made that impossible.

Down at the creek, I could hear cops hollering at me. "Halt!" they cried. "Stop moving!"

Great idea, if only I could do it. I let loose with a long, loud string of curses as I continued to hit rocks and trees, and to bounce along a thick blanket of snow-covered pine needles.

"She's trying to get away!" a cop shouted. "Head down the creek!" This was followed by splashing noises.

My body thudded onto a spit of gravel, then rolled into the creek before I could get any traction with my feet. I tasted blood and prayed I hadn't lost any teeth. My purse strap was wrapped tightly around my body, which lay half in and half out of water. My neck was in agony. I spat, cursed, and awkwardly put my hands up. Three policemen surrounded me, their weapons drawn.

"Oh, for God's sake," one of them said. I couldn't see who it was because I was blinking creek water out of my eyes, which I was desperate to rub. "Stand down," the cop ordered the others. They grumbled, but holstered their weapons.

Finally I got my eyes open. I was staring into Armstrong's disgusted face. He spoke into a radio.

"Somebody go tell Schulz his wife is here, will ya?" This was followed by crackling noises. "Where? Right here with me." Armstrong looked at me and raised an eyebrow. "In the water." He shook his head. "How? I don't know." Another pause. "No, I don't know why either. Just tell him she fell in the creek."

Armstrong asked if I needed a stretcher. I spat out more creek water and told him no, I just needed him to help me get up. The frigid water stank and I seemed to be lying in a pool of muck. Marla's beautiful fur coat was streaked with dirt and half soaked, and now felt like a suit of lead weights. My back hurt and I had scratched up one side of my face where it had dragged across some gravel. Otherwise, I assured him, I was okay, just embarrassed. His look said, *Which you should be.*

Tom appeared almost immediately and lifted me to my feet. Once he had me on firm ground, he brushed off some of the debris I'd accumulated in my roll down the hill. Then he held me at arm's length for an assessment. His eyes were filled with a grimness and fear that scared even me.

"Goldy, I'm taking you home."

"No, I'm okay, really." Icy water streamed down my legs and I began to shake. Tom took a blanket another officer handed him and wrapped me inside it. "Just have somebody take me home," I begged. "You stay here and do your job."

"I know you mean well," he said right into my ear. "But you are making my job very, very difficult."

"I'm sorry. I'm sorry. I'm sorry. But I do have to tell you something." He started to interrupt, but I said, "I saw something downstream. I'm afraid it's going to float away. Your guys haven't gotten that far. I mean, their tape isn't around it. Anyway, I think it might be a map."

I pointed. "About twenty, thirty yards. It looked as if it had blood on it."

"All right, let's go."

At first I thought he meant "Let's go search for the map," but of course he didn't. We half walked, half stumbled up to the walkway on the other side of the creek. The cops had put up an orange tarp that completely surrounded the area where Larry's body lay. But I didn't even try to get another look.

On the way home, I told Tom about seeing a woman, the same lady whom I'd suspected was Sandee, racing down the canyon, away from Aspen Meadow. I'd followed her and wrecked Marla's Lexus. The woman had come back and confronted me. Actually we'd had a not-too-pleasant interchange. And she was, in fact, Sandee Brisbane, whom I'd suspected all along had been in town for at least a month.

"She told you she was Sandee Brisbane." We were sitting in Tom's warm Chrysler at the base of our street. Outside, sheets of snowflakes washed over the neighborhood. "Did now-we-know-you're-Sandee happen to tell you where she was staying? 'Cuz we could use that address."

"No, but she gave me this haircut."

"Yeah, I noticed that. So you had a conversation that wasn't friendly. What did she have to say?"

"That I should stay out of her way."

"Yeah, a lot of people think that."

"Please don't joke. I asked her if she killed Drew Wellington."

"What'd she say to that one?"

"Oh, well, she didn't answer. I also asked her why she was here, I mean, here in Aspen Meadow."

"She reply to that one?"

"She said she was protecting her assets."

"What assets?" He wrinkled his brow at me. "No, she didn't tell you that either."

I shook my head. "I told her that you all would find her. She said she wasn't lost and I shouldn't come looking for her."

"You get a make and model on her car? Or a license plate?"

"A dark green Volvo station wagon. Sorry, it was snowing, so I couldn't make out the license plate, which was covered with dirt anyway."

"Okay, Goldy, but after trashing the Lexus, and seeing Sandee, why didn't you just go home? Boyd and Armstrong told me they saw you, and that you were in bad shape. They didn't take you home because of the traffic, and because you *promised* them you'd just walk up to our place."

"I swore to them that I wouldn't try to come through the taped-off area. And I didn't. What I did was cross the street, the parking lot, and then the creek—"

"What are you, a lawyer now? You didn't come through the crime-scene tape, you just went around it?"

"Wait. I went higher up to see Larry's . . . remains . . . because I wanted to believe that Sandee hadn't done it."

Tom gazed out the windshield at the rapidly falling flakes. "Uh-huh. This must be what they call women's intuition, which isn't logical and doesn't make any sense. What were you going to do, check out Larry's body for Sandee's skin under his nails? Look for fingerprints on a murder weapon we haven't found yet?"

"I saw the blood," I said firmly. "I saw him in the middle of the stream. Sandee had rough, dry hands. Her sleeves weren't wet. And," I added feebly, "the knife she used to cut my hair didn't have any blood on it." Tom gave me such a skeptical look that I added plaintively, "I feel sorry for her."

"She killed her mother and maybe her father and definitely your ex-husband, she makes threats and cuts off your hair, but you just can't wait to clear her of being a suspect in the killing of Larry Craddock. This is making more and more sense."

"Tom, please. How was he killed?"

He exhaled and looked up at our house. "I'll tell you if you'll go right up and shower, and promise me you won't leave our place until I call here."

"Okay. But please. I told you about the map, or what I think is a map. Just give me some information, okay?"

"He was bludgeoned with something, and then, looks like, he drowned. Held underwater. He probably was barely conscious at the time from the blow to his head, and his hands fell in the water, so there's no way we're going to get skin samples from underneath his fingernails, if there was any there in the first place. We haven't figured out what was used to hit him yet. Now go."

I thanked him, trudged up our sidewalk, and rang our bell.

"I know you're checking up on me," Marla trilled as she opened the door, "but I took good care of your son. I didn't take him snowboarding yet because he's not done—" She looked me up and down. "Good God, what happened to you? What happened to my coat?"

"I wrecked your coat, and I wrecked your car." Marla looked at me and blinked, then blinked again. "I am really, really sorry."

"Arch?" she called up the stairs. "C'mere so I can bash your head in, do a little quid pro quo for your mom here. You just took your Latin exam, you know what *quid pro quo* means, don't you?" Arch yelled back something unintelligible. "She wrecked my mink and she totaled my Lexus, that's what!" Marla hollered.

"Come on, guys," I said wearily, "please. I've had a really hard time this morning, okay? I am sorry about your car. I'll pay the fur repair and cleaning bill, and the deductible for your car, all right? I promise."

"Deductible, hell. I'm getting a new coat and a new car." Marla took hold of my shoulders and turned me around. "Ah, now I see. You wrecked my mink and my Lexus in a desperate attempt to get away from a crazy hairdresser."

"Let me take a shower and I'll explain everything." I dropped my purse on the floor and shrugged off the fur coat.

"This should be good," Marla grumbled as I traipsed up the stairs. "Can you just tell me where my car is so I can call a tow truck?"

I called down the location of Don's Detail Shop, apologized again, and headed to the bathroom, where I peeled off my clothes and turned the water on as hot as it would go. And it felt good, even on my shorn head and scrapes. My neck pain was down to a dull throb.

Marla rapped on the door when I was through with the first lathering of shampoo. "Don't blow-dry your hair!" she called. "Just towel yourself off, throw on some clothes, and come downstairs."

I'd just wrecked her five-thousand-dollar mink coat and her sixty-thousand-dollar sports car, so I was not in a position to argue.

Down in the kitchen, Marla had spread a sheet on the floor, and she'd put a chair in the middle of it. On the table, she'd laid out three things that didn't seem to go together: a pile of towels, a pair of scissors, and a wine-glass filled with a dark, steaming drink.

"Sit," she commanded.

"What are you doing?"

Marla put her hands on her hips. "First, making you drink a glass of glüwein, my own concoction, which will ward off the cold that you would otherwise be sure to get. Second, I'm going to cut your hair so that it's even."

"The hell you are! You get your hair cut for two hundred bucks a pop. What makes you think—"

"Goldy," she reassured me, "cutting hair is a little-known talent of mine. Now sit the hell down, or I'll call the cops about you wrecking my car."

Of course I knew she wouldn't. But she would threaten, cajole, wheedle, and threaten some more until I did what she wanted. I sighed and sat down.

Marla began to comb and snip. "So what have you been doing since you stole my car and wrecked it?"

"I didn't steal anything—" I began. But the scissors stopped moving, and I gave up. I told Marla about the knife-wielding Sandee warning me to stop chasing her. I also told her that Sandee didn't seem too worried about the cops catching her, and how she wouldn't tell me if she killed Drew. All she *would* tell me was that she was protecting her assets.

"Her assets, huh? What assets?"

"Good question."

"All that would only have taken half an hour." Her tone was matter-of-fact as she combed and snipped. "But you've been gone almost two hours. And why did Tom bring you home? He couldn't have just happened to run into you down at Don's Detail Shop."

"No, he didn't. Did you hear a bunch of sirens a while ago?"

She stopped cutting. "Don't tell me *that* was you, too."

"No, it wasn't." I told her about Larry Craddock. "They don't know for certain whether it's murder or an accident, but I very much doubt that he stove in his own head, then jumped into Lower Cottonwood Creek."

"And you know this because?"

I sighed. "Because I wanted to see his body. As awful as that sounds, I wanted to check if there was any way Sandee *couldn't* have done it."

"What? Sandee the one whose wild left turn made you crash my car. Sandee the hairstylist. You're losing me here, girlfriend."

"I know Sandee killed the Jerk, but she did it because he raped her. And her mother, that was because she did nothing to protect her, when Sandee was a kid." I stopped talking. From the corner of my eye, I could see blond wisps of what used to be my nice head of Shirley Temple hair tumbling to the floor. "She's only killed when she had a reason, when she's been seeking revenge. And there's no reason for her to kill Drew or Larry, at least nothing definite. I don't think that's why she's here."

"Maybe Sandee's a map collector, too," said Marla. "Maybe Drew and Larry cut her out of a good deal, and she's coming back for vengeance." I shrugged and shook my head. "Oh God, Goldy, don't shake your head!"

Half an hour later, I was looking at a passable layered cut, sort of a cross between Tinker Bell and Peter Pan, that hid the worst of the damage at the back. Marla peered over my shoulder into the bathroom mirror, anxious for coiffure approval. "You did a great job," I said sincerely. "Thanks, really."

"Uh-huh," Marla said. "Well, you never would have found a haircutting place open on Sunday in Aspen Meadow."

"No place could have done better."

She winked at me as she called Grace Mannheim and asked her to come get her. "This way, we can ask Grace what she's up to over here, anyway, digging around for Frank's daughter."

"Okay," I said. "Oh, one more thing. What do I call the cut, anyway, if Tom asks?"

Marla smiled. "I know what you *don't* call it. I spent a semester at Oxford fifteen years ago. When my hair was getting unmanageably long, I asked some girls at a party if they knew of a good beauty salon where I could get a cut. I said I wanted a *shag*. Six guys at the party immediately offered to give me a shag."

"I know what a shag is," Arch said as he bounded through the kitchen door. "It's a f—"

"Arch," I interrupted, "how're you doing on the room cleanup?"

"Julian said we could take a break. Gosh, Mom, what happened to your hair?" When I warned him with a look, he opened the walk-in and gazed inside. "Yeah, when the lacrosse guys gave me a Bic, I didn't want to talk about it either. There's nothing like a shaved head to get people to start asking questions." He slammed the refrigerator door. "I can't find anything to eat."

"I will find you something," I promised. "Can you tell me what kind of progress you've made with all your piles?"

"Lots of progress. We've got five bags that can go out to the trash, three bags for the thrift store, and I finished sorting through my books for the ones that will go to the library book sale." His smile was full of mischief. "There are books in there from England, so the people at the library's used-book sale can learn what a shag—"

"Arch!" I cried. "Would you guys like a snack, or more than a snack?"

"We'd like lunch," Arch replied. "Please. We're starving. Do you have any enchiladas frozen?"

"I'm sure I can dig some up." To Marla I said, "Thanks for not hollering at me about your coat and your car. I'm really, really sorry. My insurance will—"

"Forget it, will you—"

The doorbell rang: Grace Mannheim.

"That was quick," Marla said. "She's never been over here, has she? Most people can't find their way around Aspen Meadow, even if they do have a map."

I shook my head. "Grace is just a remarkable person. Let's get her in here and grill her about this Ingersoll person."

Grace breezed in and pulled off her knit cap. Her cheeks were rosy, her white hair fluffy with static. She took in my haircut, but was too polite to say anything. When I offered her something to drink or eat, she declined. I told her please to have a seat in our living room. Then I rummaged through the freezer side of the walk-in until I put my hands on a glass pan of enchiladas. I pulled them out, removed the foil, and stared at the contents. Twelve, thank God. I was ravenous. I covered the pan with waxed paper, set the enchiladas to defrost in the microwave, and quickstepped into the living room.

"Your car is wrecked?" Grace was asking Marla. "How did that happen, or shouldn't I ask?"

"It's a long story that I'll tell you," Marla replied. "But only after we get home and I get a large glass of scotch in front of me."

Grace shifted her gaze to me and again looked inquiringly at my hair. "I know there's a story here," she said finally.

"Marla gave me a new coiffure after church," I explained. "And by the way, the two of us have some things to ask you."

"I have to answer questions, but you don't?" Grace asked.

I clenched my teeth and gave her a stern look. "We're way past the time when it's okay for you to be glib."

"Oh no," said Grace, resigned. "I think I know what's coming."

I said, "Go ahead, then."

Grace frowned. "I knew when I didn't get cell-phone reception at your house, Marla, that caller ID might give me away."

"Okay," I said smoothly, "it has. Now tell us what you have to do with someone else named Ingersoll, someone who isn't Patricia."

Grace exhaled. "Her name is Whitney Ingersoll, and she's Frank Ingersoll's only daughter. It's sort of complicated."

Marla and I waited and said nothing. For us, this showed extraordinary restraint.

"Sort of complicated," I finally echoed.

Grace rubbed her hands together. "Frank Ingersoll, God rest his soul, was worth a lot of money."

"A lot of money?" Marla asked, ever the competitive one when it came to bucks. "How do you define a lot of money?"

Grace said, "Not all of it is actual cash, stock, or bonds. It's real estate, art, plus some stock and whatnot. In all, it's worth between forty and fifty million."

Well, I thought, *what was an extra ten million here or there?* Marla merely nodded.

When Grace seemed reluctant to go on, I said, "I do remember Whitney. She was Patricia's maid of honor. In her toast at the reception, she said she was glad her father had found a soul mate. They all seemed so happy."

"Yes, everybody was in a good mood at the beginning," Grace echoed. "I know for sure that Frank was over the moon, at least until he got cancer, of course. That's when everything went to hell, and not just for Frank." Grace, reflecting, stopped talking.

I was becoming weary of prompting her. "Grace! My hair's going to grow as long as Lady Godiva's while I'm waiting for you to tell me what's going on."

Grace said, "Okay, okay. This is very difficult, so please be patient with me. Frank had a prenuptial agreement with Patricia. He wanted forty million to go to Whitney, who was twenty-eight when he made the will. But Frank didn't want Patricia to be destitute if he should die suddenly, which is just about what he did. So he made provision for Patricia to receive five hundred thousand a year for every year they were married. He also made her the beneficiary of a million-dollar life-insurance policy. Patricia agreed to the whole thing. But then he got cancer when they'd only been married for a little over two years."

"Two million," Marla mused. "Good, but not great."

Grace said, "Maybe that's what was going through Patricia's mind when she went into the hospital with a new will and a new lawyer. She convinced Frank, almost sick to death on chemo, to nullify the prenup. Patricia also convinced Frank to sign the new will. In it, Patricia received thirty million in cash and whatnot. She also received the house and its contents, worth about ten million. The final ten million or so would go to Whitney. Patricia mailed the new will to Whitney, and by the time Whitney received it, her father was dead. She was furious, ready to scratch out Patricia's eyes."

These people and their money, I thought.

"Whitney confronted Patricia after the service," Grace went on. "I was there, and it wasn't pretty. Whitney got in Patricia's face and shrieked, 'You bitch! You shrew! I will litigate you to *death!*' "

"I always say," Marla put in, "there's no *fun in funeral.*"

"No kidding," Grace supplied. "Whitney's been contesting the will, of course, but the case had been dragging through court. Which brings me to why I'm in Aspen Meadow."

Finally, I thought.

"Whitney keeps close tabs on what goes on in Aspen Meadow so she can learn all she can about Patricia.

When a friend called her to tell her Drew Wellington had died at the library, she called me. One of the most valuable items in the estate was a Rodin drawing."

"Rodin?" I repeated, unbelieving. "*The* Rodin?"

Grace nodded ruefully. "When Whitney pursued her lawsuit against the probate of the second will, she and her lawyers demanded that Patricia show them the Rodin. But Patricia hemmed and hawed and said it had been stolen. Frank had just been so sick, she said. She said she hadn't gotten around to filing an insurance claim. But Frank had more security devices put on that house of theirs than Fort Knox. It would have been extremely difficult for anyone to steal the Rodin from there."

"So Whitney doesn't believe the Rodin was taken," I put in, finally seeing the light. "She thinks Patricia hid it somewhere . . . and then maybe moved it to her boyfriend's house? Her boyfriend, Drew Wellington?"

"Exactly," Grace said. "And when Whitney heard Drew had been killed, she asked me to come over and see if you, my pal, whose husband is an investigator, if you, Goldy, could get me into Wellington's house."

I snorted. "She's dreaming, and so are you."

"When Patricia heard Drew had been killed," Marla asked, "why wouldn't she try to get into Drew's house and get the drawing back, if that's where she hid it?"

"Because," Grace said patiently, "thanks to an anonymous source, Patricia was arrested within an hour of Drew's body being found. While Drew's house was being secured by the police, Patricia was on her way to the Furman County Jail."

"Did Whitney call in the anonymous tip about Patricia?" I asked. "To get her out of the way for a while?"

Grace said, "Well, actually . . . yes."

17

I tried at first not to take sides," Grace explained. "I did like Patricia and I did let her have Losers meetings at my house on occasion. I saw Drew and Larry Craddock fighting. I didn't lie to you about any of that, Goldy. But Patricia's behavior troubled me. When she started seeing Drew, I hoped that would mean that she and Whitney could finally come to some sort of reasonable settlement that would be fair to both of them, so they could make a new start. Then Whitney told me Patricia's cockamamie story about the Rodin. That drawing meant a lot to Frank. So I told Whitney I would help her, and she made me promise not to tell anyone. I'm not proud I deceived you, Goldy, or you, Marla, but I was trying to do the right thing."

Exhausted by her long story, Grace exhaled and swore that was all she knew. She was giving Whitney daily updates on the Wellington case, which basically came down to whatever she could glean from me. The reason for Whitney's curiosity, Grace explained, was that Whitney wanted to be able to get her lawyers into Drew Wellington's house, to search for the Rodin.

"And because she hates Patricia," Grace added.

"Gee," I said, "d'ya think?"

I felt Grace had betrayed and taken advantage of both Marla and me. Maybe that made my body begin to ache again, I didn't know. Grace seemed to read the pain in my eyes and offered to clean up the hair mess. She hadn't asked why I'd needed a cut or why I had scratches on my face and arms. I knew she'd winkle the latest crises out of Marla, anyway, so I didn't volunteer anything. Instead, while she was sweeping I retrieved the pan of thawed enchiladas and placed them in the oven on convect. Grace and Marla said they would get their lunch elsewhere and hoped I felt better. Marla picked up her mangled fur coat.

"But wait, Marla," I said. "Aren't you supposed to go to Hermie MacArthur's brunch tomorrow? What are you going to drive?"

Marla arched an eyebrow at me. "As you said when the subject was enchiladas, I'm sure I'll be able to dig something up."

When they'd left, I put in a call to the church. Since it was Sunday and there was nobody in the office, I was automatically connected to the answering machine, where I pressed the number 2 to leave an emergency message. I said I was in dire need of a pastoral call from Father Pete. I'd just been attacked and fallen into the creek, I added, and I was traumatized. So could he please come over as soon as possible? I was desperate. I thanked him and left my number.

Since the microwave was free, I dug into the walk-in and pulled out a leftover piece of quiche. I heated it up, scarfed it down, then walked upstairs to get dressed. I knew Father Pete was a diligent pastor . . . he hated cell phones, but he checked those emergency messages quite often. Which was a good thing, because I had a very important question to ask him.

From the excited voices emanating from Arch's room, I could tell the boys were happily occupied. If I knew anything about my son, he'd found a stash of chips, candy, or both, in his room, and handed it around to his pals while they waited for the enchiladas to heat.

While I was finished getting dressed, Arch startled me by banging on the bedroom door. Had he already run out of snacks?

"Mom! Father Pete's on the phone."

"Could you ask him how soon he can come over?"

Arch clomped away, then returned almost immediately. "He's on his way. He said you were attacked and got pushed into the creek. He's worried about you." Arch paused. "Why didn't you tell me you fell in the creek?"

I finished changing and opened the door a crack. "I didn't. I rolled down a hill. And I wasn't exactly attacked. It's not as bad as it sounds, hon."

"Do you want me to call him back, say you weren't attacked, you didn't fall in the creek, and he doesn't need to come over, then?"

"No, I need to talk to him."

"Good. 'Cuz I told him you were fixing our lunch, and that he could join us if he wanted."

I groaned.

"What? I figured that was what you would want me to do. Next time, Mom, I'll let people who call know they need to call back and talk to you personally, okay? That way I won't get bawled out for doing what you tell me to do."

"I'm sorry, hon, I wasn't bawling you out—"

"Yeah, well, he'll be here in an hour."

"That's fine—" I began, but Arch had already left.

I would make this work. Twelve enchiladas divided by three hungry teenage boys, plus me . . . hmm. Not to mention that the enchiladas were made with pork, and

Julian was a vegetarian. And Father Pete, he of the big Greek appetite, was on his way. I didn't have any souvlaki or stuffed grape leaves or gyros lying around, so I was going to have to think up something new for him, too. And then maybe Tom would come home at some point . . .

Back in the kitchen, I stared into the walk-in. On the shelf where Tom put food that he labeled "*Ours,*" there were several pounds of lean ground beef and a bunch of celery. The pantry yielded olive oil, herbs, onions, and a bag of potatoes. Back in the freezer, I found smallish containers of homemade chicken stock and bags of baby peas and corn.

"Hmm," I said as I pulled everything onto the counter and stared at it. Too bad all the lamb chops in the house had already been designated for the MacArthurs' lunch. But wait. What had Father Pete called himself? An *unorthodox shepherd.* Well, then, he would get Unorthodox Shepherd's Pie. Made with ground beef instead of ground lamb, which technically made it a cottage pie, but who was I to quibble? Besides, I liked the ring of the new dish's name; I'd tell Father Pete I'd named it after him.

I filled a pot with springwater. The latest caterer's trick I'd learned was to use bottled springwater for everything, even boiling vegetables. I added kosher salt and turned the burner to high.

Busy, busy, keep yourself busy, I told myself, *or you're going to feel Sandee pulling your hair again . . .*

I peeled the potatoes, dropped them into the water, and checked on the enchiladas, which had begun to bubble. Next I nuked the chicken stock. After slicing a mountain of celery, I began chopping the onions. And that was when I again saw the blood on the rock, the map floating downstream.

"Dammit to hell," I muttered. Larry Craddock had been angry and he'd been violent. Had he gotten into a brawl with someone who'd given him a lethal push into Cottonwood Creek? And had their conflict been over the map that I'd seen in the water? Drew was no longer with us, so who did that leave? Neil Tharp? Smithfield Mac-Arthur? Were there other willing-to-kill map collectors out there whom I didn't even know about?

I began sautéing the ground beef with the onions and celery. I thought again about Sandee. She, too, had a propensity for violence. And of course there was the fact that she'd been speeding away from town when I'd started following her. But her sleeves had been dry, and if she had killed Larry, what was her motive?

I still thought this possibility was less likely. Sandee had been stalking Drew, threatening him with hostile e-mails, and I had seen her near Drew not long before

Roberta came upon him. But if Sandee had killed *Drew,* I was still missing a motive.

I spooned flour into the beef, onions, and celery, then heated and stirred the concoction until it began to bubble. This was one of the first things I'd learned from watching reruns of Julia Child's cooking shows: stir the flour into the melted butter or, in this case, melted beef fat, and allow the resulting roux to cook until it bubbles. This is how you avoid a sauce that tastes chalky with uncooked flour. I'd never been much of a patient person, until I'd learned to cook. You have to wait for the transformation of the roux to take place, or you have to start over.

Once I'd added a judicious amount of stock along with some crushed thyme and rosemary, I set the pan to simmer and went back to the beginning of my thinking.

How exactly did Larry Craddock fit into this puzzle with Drew Wellington, and perhaps Sandee Brisbane? Maybe it was the bump on the head that my roll through the pine needles had engendered, but I couldn't imagine any way the three of them could be involved. I felt so frustrated, I almost picked up a glass and threw it through the kitchen window . . .

Which reminded me. That was yet another unanswered question. Who'd thrown the snowball with the knife inside? And had I been its intended target, as I suspected, or was it thrown for another reason?

I watched the beef bubble in the sauce, and searched my brain for what I knew about Drew Wellington's circle. Patricia had been Drew's girlfriend. They were getting married, according to her. Drew also had an ex-wife, Elizabeth, who had really loved him, until she hated him. And Drew had a penchant for underage girls, something that had cost him his marriage and caused him to ply a client's daughter and her friend with booze. Drew also had been accused of stealing maps and selling them to clients, though as far as I knew, nothing had been definitively proven.

Neil Tharp, Drew's business associate, was a question mark . . . Had he been loyal to Drew? Or not? If not, why not? Larry Craddock had been Drew's mentor until they'd had a falling-out. Then they'd patched things up. Supposedly.

All this was making my head hurt. Time to put worries about Drew Wellington on the back burner, so to speak.

The timer went off, indicating the potatoes were done. I set them to drain, then added cupfuls of baby corn and peas to the beef mixture. I mashed the potatoes, then grated some Gruyère and Parmigiano Reggiano, and mixed them in. This was going to be a *very* unorthodox shepherd's pie.

I removed the enchiladas from the oven and covered them with foil. Then I put the pie into the hot oven. For Julian, I decided to retrieve a casserole of homemade pasta with cheese sauce from the walk-in. When Father Pete rang the doorbell, Arch clomped out of his room and called down, asking if lunch was ready. I replied that it would be in twenty minutes, or earlier if he could get his pals to help him finish organizing the piles of unwanted stuff in his room. Arch groaned, but began asking the troops to help him finish cleaning up.

"Father Pete," I greeted him. "Thanks for coming." I looked out at our snowy street and furrowed my brow in mock worry. "Oh, dear, you might have to move your car. The residents have a fit when they can't park on the street during a snowstorm. Could you pull your Jeep into our driveway? I'll make sure you're all the way in, and not blocking the sidewalk."

Father Pete said, "Why, of course I'll move into your driveway." He turned his rotund body and walked carefully back down our sidewalk. I donned boots and a jacket and followed him, then watched as he navigated his four-wheel drive into our snow-covered driveway.

"Little bit farther!" I called from behind him. Father Pete chugged forward obediently, and I got a good look at his rear bumper.

"Goldy, I came as soon as I got your message," Father Pete said, once he was outside his car and wading through the deep snow. "Then another parishioner called and said you'd found a corpse in the creek."

I sighed. "I didn't find him."

"Oh, dear. Who was the dead person?"

"A man named Larry Craddock," I replied.

Once we were inside, Father Pete removed a thick, knitted gray scarf that was full of holes. No question about it, the man did not care about clothes. He ran his big hands through his dark curly hair, then regarded me, his wide, olive-skinned face full of concern. "Larry Craddock, the map dealer? I met him before, but didn't really know him. He wasn't a parishioner and didn't have any family that I knew of . . . but I'm more worried about you. You said you were attacked and fell in the creek? Were you trying to help Larry Craddock?"

"No." I wasn't quite ready to spring my trap. First, I wanted to ask if he knew anything about those questions I'd posed in my Drew file.

"But I can see you've been hurt." His deep voice was filled with concern, and I almost, almost felt guilty about getting him over here on false pretenses. "Your face is covered with scratches."

"I'm okay, thanks. So, you met Larry Craddock before, when he was with Drew Wellington?"

"No, Larry Craddock came to the church about a year ago." Father Pete chuckled. "He wanted me to excommunicate Drew Wellington."

"Excommunicate him? For what?"

Father Pete's face darkened. "Goodness, I'm always telling people not to gossip, and there I go doing it. What smells so good?"

"Something I made just for you." I told him about the Unorthodox Shepherd's Pie while wishing he would gossip, just a little bit. Excommunication was a pretty serious punishment, but only if you cared that you were being kicked out of the church. My guess was that Drew had been successfully mining St. Luke's for wealthy clients. If Larry had gotten wind of this, it might have angered him so much that he'd asked the parish priest to get rid of Drew.

I poured Father Pete and myself large glasses of sherry, and hoped this would loosen him up a little bit. Noting the unset table, the priest washed his hands and, unasked, began rooting around for plates and silverware. I checked on the enchiladas, the pasta, and the pie, threw together a large salad, and tried to think what to ask next.

"What's that truism?" Father Pete asked benignly as he seated himself at the kitchen table. "That food always tastes better when it's been cooked by someone else? Or maybe it's that food tastes better when it's something you shouldn't be having because it's full of superb ingredients? No matter what I said in church today, I am a greedy so-and-so."

"You can say *son of a bitch* and I won't mind," I said.

"You wouldn't, but my mother would."

"Father Pete," I said as I refilled his sherry glass, "does your personal prohibition against gossiping mean you won't tell me anything negative about Patricia Ingersoll, Elizabeth Wellington, or Neil Tharp?"

He sipped his drink and smiled. "That is exactly what it means. But I will importune you for something to nibble on, if that's all right. Please don't think I'm the first priest a curious parishioner tried to squeeze secrets out of by getting him to drink too much, and on an empty stomach, no less."

"I'm that transparent, huh?" I rummaged in one of our cupboards, pulled out a can of salted nuts, and poured them into a glass bowl.

"Alas. You are."

He took a handful of nuts, then ducked to the side. "While you were turned around I saw that . . . did something happen to your hair?"

"Yes. It was sliced off by Sandee Brisbane, who threatened me."

Father Pete's face became drawn and still. "Sandee who?"

"Sandee Brisbane. Are you telling me you don't know her?"

The olive skin flushed dark. "Of *course* I know *of* her, because of what she did to your ex-husband. Still . . . I thought she was dead. The Brisbanes were parishioners, but it was slightly before my time at the church—"

"Father Pete, don't mess with my head. You know full well that Sandee Brisbane is alive and well. And she's a *double* murderer. Are you harboring her?"

He was indignant. "Goldy, how can you ask such a thing? Absolutely not."

"Then do you want to tell me why she's driving a car with a clergy parking sticker?"

Father Pete gave a large sigh and rubbed his eyes.

I said, "Hiding a fugitive from justice is a crime, you know."

"Goldy?"

"Father Pete?"

"Look, I'm not hiding anyone. But I *am* beginning to regret coming over here for what was supposed to be a pastoral visit."

"Where is she, Father Pete?"

"I have no idea. And I'm happy to tell your husband the same."

"But you've seen her. You loaned her a car, right? And you gave her money. Didn't you?"

"No, Goldy, I didn't. And it distresses me to hear that you were attacked by this woman. But I did what I thought was best at the time. She has had a very hard life, as you know."

"And that excuses her of murder?"

"Of course not. Look, Sandee Brisbane approached me about a month ago. I was surprised to learn that she was alive. She wanted information about several parishioners. I refused to give it to her, and she wouldn't tell me why she wanted it. I encouraged her to turn herself in to the police, to face the consequences of her actions. It didn't seem to be something she wanted to hear. She left, and I've seen nothing of her since."

I shook my head. "So how is it that she's running around Aspen Meadow in a car with a clergy parking sticker on it?"

"Well, that was a bit of a shock for me as well. About two weeks ago, I realized that a car that was given to us by a parishioner, and that we keep—used to keep—in a shed by our house, was missing. We don't use it very often, and we keep the keys under the seat. We usually just lend it to folks in the church who need a vehicle for church business. When I didn't see it, I thought perhaps we'd lent it to a current parishioner and I'd simply forgotten, or the church secretary simply hadn't noted it down. Then later on, I guessed that Sandee might have taken it after she and I had our conversation."

"She stole the church's car? Why didn't you report the theft, and her, to the police?"

The buzzer went off, and Father Pete gave me a quizzical look. I turned the heat down and crossed my arms.

"I'm truly, truly sorry, Goldy. In retrospect, reporting the theft is just what I should have done. If I had guessed that she might have threatened you, I certainly would have. But I've always believed that everyone should have the chance to make amends. I hoped that Sandee would return the car, and perhaps heed my advice and turn herself in. I didn't know that she was even still in Aspen Meadow, actually, so the probability was slim, but I could hope. I made a mistake. Though like you trying to ply me with sherry, I did so with good intentions."

I rolled my eyes. "Yeah, and you know what they say the path to hell is paved with."

Father Pete shifted the nuts around in the bowl. "Yes, they do say that. I suppose you'll want me to talk with the police, about the station wagon, and everything?"

"I'll call Tom and have him send an investigator over to the church to interview you." I smiled. "But not until you've had some lunch. Can you answer one question for me? Was one of the people Sandee was asking about Drew Wellington?"

"Yes, it was. You don't really think . . . ? She wouldn't have any reason—"

"She's a killer, Father Pete. And she may have had her reasons. We know now that she was stalking Drew Wellington and sending him threatening e-mails."

"I see." His face had grown very grave.

"But we don't know anything else for sure. Not yet."

He sat back in the chair. "When I talked to Sandee, she had very kind things to say about her time here—I mean, her time at St. Luke's. When she was twelve, her aunt, her mother's sister, was very sick, she said, and she had taken care of her four-year-old cousin and volunteered to babysit other children in the nursery. She was very protective of them. I remember Father Biesbrouck telling me a story about Sandee, actually, from that time. He knew the family well. A child called Stevie at the nursery had a red mark on his arm. He told Sandee that his mother had burned him with a cigarette. Problem was, his mother didn't even smoke. Stevie had fallen off a swing and scraped his arm on some gravel. But that didn't sound very scary, so Stevie made up the bit about the cigarette. The twelve-year-old Sandee believed him and called social services."

"I'll bet Stevie's parents didn't appreciate being hauled down to the sheriff's department."

Father Pete shook his head. "No, indeed. Plus, Stevie's father had to miss watching the Bronco game, so there was hell to pay."

"I'll bet. Was that the worst thing that happened when Sandee was manning the nursery?"

"You mean, apart from the fact that Stevie's wealthy family became Presbyterians?"

The voices of Arch, Julian, Todd, and Gus tumbled through the kitchen door at the same time their bodies did.

"We're hungry!"

"We're starving!"

"Can we have some of those nuts?"

Frustrated that my conversation with Father Pete was going to be interrupted, I sighed and pulled the pie, the pasta, and the enchiladas out of the oven. Within moments we were all digging into steaming heaps of food and salad, and I told myself to let it go. Father Pete seemed to recover some of his equilibrium, and heaped praise on me for the Unorthodox Shepherd's Pie. I felt it was the least I could do, given the rather difficult interview he'd be getting from Tom and the sheriff's department.

When we finished eating, Julian insisted on doing the dishes. To my great astonishment, Arch and his pals said they wouldn't hear of it; they were going to help, because Julian was "so cool."

I escorted Father Pete out to the front hall, where he thanked me for lunch and donned his ratty coat and scarf. As he was walking out the door, I remembered something he'd said earlier.

"Father Pete, you mentioned that Sandee had an aunt in the church, and a little cousin?"

"Yes, but I wasn't with the church then. I believe, though, that the aunt recovered and the family moved to Colorado Springs."

"Do you know what their name was? Did Sandee mention it, or Father Biesbrouck?"

"I think the aunt's first name was Caroline or Catherine, something like that. But I don't recall hearing their last name."

"Can you think of anything else about them? If Sandee had relatives in the area, it might be a clue to finding her."

Father Pete gave me a very sad look. "I wish I could help you, Goldy. I just don't—oh, wait, maybe I do know something about them."

I hugged my sides as frigid air poured through the front door. "You know something?" I prompted.

Father Pete's wide brow furrowed. "I think the aunt's husband worked for a bank."

18

As soon as Father Pete left, I grabbed the kitchen phone. The boys ignored me. While merrily washing the dishes, they were singing along to a rock version of "Good King Wenceslas." I should have had a video camera, complete with sound. Instead I took the phone to the living room.

"Tom," I said into his voice mail, "Father Pete was just here." I told him about the clergy parking sticker. I added that I hadn't been *sure* about the sticker on Sandee's borrowed car, and had had to check Father Pete's Jeep and confront him before giving voice to my suspicions. "So please don't be angry with me," I said. "He'll be able to give you the make, model, and license plate, and you can put out an APB." I related what else I'd learned, and concluded by saying that the sheriff's department could probably interview Father Pete right now, as he'd had so much to eat and drink I doubted he'd be able to do anything for the next few hours besides nap.

"Mom!" Arch called into the living room. "We want to offer you a deal."

Here we go, I thought. But I replied that I was prepared to do negotiations.

Arch's hopeful face, alongside Todd's and Gus's expectant, buoyant ones, made me want to just give them whatever they wanted, rather than bargain for it. But I'd learned the hard way that boys should *earn* whatever goodies they received or they didn't value them. Besides, whatever the three of them desired was probably either expensive, time-consuming, or both, so I needed to prepare my chip.

"It's supposed to stop snowing by one," Arch began. "And we really, *really* want to go snowboarding. Julian said the two of you had to work before your party tomorrow, but is there any way one of you could take us over to the RRSSA?"

"What's the other part of the deal, kiddo?"

Arch brightened. "That the three of us *finish* packing up all the books that are going to go to the library's used-book sale, and lug them out to your van."

"That's an awful lot of books, Arch."

"Oh, Mrs. Schulz," Todd cried, "we're going to help him. And we're going to leave room in your van for our boards, too."

"We'll make it work, we promise," Gus piped up.

"Oh, yeah," Arch said, "and we'll tape the Broncos for you. I mean, if you're going to miss it."

I reflected for a moment. "You're on. I'll listen to the game on the radio, if I have to."

"Thanks, Mom!"

"Thanks, Mrs. Schulz!"

The three of them hustled up the stairs. After the months and months I'd been begging Arch to go through his closet, desk, and bookshelves, I did not see how in the world the three of them would be able to organize the remainder of Arch's many piles of volumes in the next hour. But apparently the incentive of boarding on fresh snow was enough to motivate them. Wake up, Mom.

Before I could start prepping with Julian, my business line rang. When I checked the caller ID, my heart catapulted downward. I prayed that Hermie MacArthur wasn't going to cancel because of the new snow, which, if Arch's prediction was right, was going to stop soon anyway. But no, it was just the opposite.

"Goldy, darlin'," she began. "I'm so glad I caught you. We just would *love* to be able to add one more couple to our little lunch tomorrow. Neil Tharp called this afternoon and has something he wants to show Smithfield. Ol' Smitty was real glad, because even though Neil invited himself over here, he did show Smitty somethin' interesting. But then Neil and the other map dealer got into their little set-to, and Neil and Smithfield didn't get to finish their business. You know that other map dealer I'm talkin' about?"

"Larry Craddock." Did Hermie know what had happened to Craddock? I doubted it.

"Smithfield wants to invite him, if that's all right. I told him I couldn't have an uneven number, because of the chairs. So I called Neil, and asked him to bring a lady friend, but he said he didn't have one."

"They're probably all recovering from Rohypnol poisoning."

"What, darlin'?"

"Nothing."

"So, ol' Neil Tharp said he would just love to invite Elizabeth Wellington, because she was feeling sad on account of her husband dying—"

"Her ex-husband, you mean?"

"Yes, yes, her ex-husband, I mean. I was worried, because I'd invited Patricia Ingersoll, since she lives over in Flicker Ridge, and I've been wanting to get to know her. Also, I want to pay her back, because she brought over some cookies when we first moved in, and I thought that was nice, even though they were low-fat cookies, and Smitty made me throw them out. I *did* hear that Patricia and Drew Wellington were involved, and I didn't want to upset Elizabeth, you know—"

"Hermie," I interrupted again. "How many people are you going to have, then?"

"Well, sixteen, darlin', I was getting to that. I'm sorry, am I not going fast enough for you?"

I forced myself to be solicitous, even though my body was beginning to hurt again from my roll through the pines that had ended in Cottonwood Creek. "Of course not. It's just that today I had a bad fall—"

"Oh, darlin', doin' what?"

"Nothing. I just fell . . . on the ice."

"Fell on the ice where, darlin'?"

Agh! I said, "It doesn't matter, Hermie. So, what did you want to tell me, besides the fact that you're adding two people?"

"Well, I wanted to know what *you* thought of my inviting both women? I can't have another conflict the way we did the other night."

"I'm sure it will be fine," I lied. If Patricia and Elizabeth got into an argument, maybe I could stop it by breaking another window in the kitchen.

"No, no, I'm not sure it'll be fine at all," Hermie said.

"Why not?"

"Well, you know, first of all, Smithfield has been so upset about his whole map collection ever since Neil and Larry were here. I thought I would try to sort of make it up to Larry, too, if I was going to invite Neil, I mean. You don't happen to know Larry Craddock's number, do you, darlin'? I'd ask Smithfield, but he's been gone all mornin' . . ."

"Gone all morning?" I said, too sharply. What had he been doing? I wondered. Having an unsuccessful meeting with Larry Craddock? Maybe Smithfield was physically stronger than I'd thought, and maybe he'd done in Craddock.

"Yes, and I can't imagine where in the world—"

"I don't know Larry Craddock's number," I interrupted.

"Well, anyway, I thought maybe the two of them could try to get along, you know, for Smithfield's sake? I've always said that getting along is more important than anything you can do with money—"

"Hermie—"

"Some people just have to have things their way, you know? I was saying to Smithfield that there shouldn't be *any* reason why Patricia and *Elizabeth* couldn't get along, I mean, not with Drew gone and all . . ."

I plunked myself down in one of our living-room chairs and closed my eyes. As Hermie chatted on, I thought of that old story about the difference between a Southerner and a Yankee. You ask a Yankee how much a dime is worth. She gives you a frosty look and says, "Ten cents." You ask a Southerner, and she says, "Well, I s'pose it's not worth what it used to be, I mean, I could buy a whole pocket full of Red Hots and Charleston Chews and Sugar Daddys when I was just a little girl, and my momma would see me coming with all that sweet stuff, and she'd say—"

I must have drifted off, because the phone fell out of my hands. Hermie didn't even notice. I picked up the receiver, zipped back into the kitchen, and turned down the volume on the radio. Then I wrote a note to Julian in capital letters: *CALL ME. LOUDLY.*

Which he did.

"Who's that yelling?" Hermie wanted to know.

"That's actually my assistant—"

"Tell him to quit it, will you please? There's something important here I want to tell you, and that is that I called Patricia Ingersoll and told her I'd invited Elizabeth, 'cuz Neil wanted her, and she started yelling and screaming about how could I do such a thing, how could I hurt her in that way, and maybe she wouldn't come after all, and she was going to tell people how cruel and unfeeling I was, and I mean, I couldn't have *that*, so I said *you* would take care of it."

"You said *what*?"

"Now, darlin', all you have to do is go over to Patricia's house and talk to her a little bit, and everything will be just hunky-dory."

"Fine," I said through clenched teeth. It would probably take me less time to visit with Patricia than it would listening to any more of this story. I begged off from talking any more with Hermie by telling her I would go to Patricia's after I'd dropped off the boys at the Regal Ridge Snow Sports Area. School was out, I moaned, and the kids wanted to take advantage of that fact. Hermie said she understood, Chantal was always wanting to be driven over to that slope, which meant she had to find her skis, and her gloves, and . . . I jumped into the conversation by saying I'd see her the next morning, and so long till then. Then, I hoped not too rudely, I hung up.

"You're taking them to snowboard?" Julian asked, with a glance outside. "When?"

"In about an hour, which is when Arch says he will have finished with packing up his books, and the snow will have stopped. Plus, Hermie's added a couple of folks, and I need to buy another rack of lamb chops at the grocery store. I also have to go see Patricia to try to iron out the guest list for tomorrow's luncheon." I gave Julian an arch look. "Hermie's invited both Patricia, Drew's fiancée, and Elizabeth, Drew's ex-wife. She doesn't want a scene like at last night's party, so I'm supposed to smooth things out in advance."

"You're kidding . . . no, wait, I know you're not."

"Let's try to get this prep finished, then I'll bundle up the boys and take them."

"What about the books? Do you want to take them while I take the guys to the RRSSA?"

"Sure, that would be great, thanks. I need something else at the library, anyway." Neil Tharp had asked me if I had a photo of Sandee Brisbane, and I'd had to say no. But the library had computer archives of all the major newspapers, and I knew there would be news photos of Sandee from this past summer, run after she confessed and disappeared in the fire. I could get a copy of one and show it to Neil. If I had to go to Patricia's house anyway, I'd offer her the photo, too, and just have her confirm that it was Sandee she'd seen following Drew around. Maybe it would jog her memory of any other details that might help track Sandee down.

"I'll pack up some cookies for the boys," Julian offered. "Do you want some for Patricia, too?" When I nodded, he busied himself with these culinary peace offerings, and I again thanked my lucky stars to have such a great assistant.

I still had kitchen work to do. For the MacArthurs' lunch, we were offering a homemade tomato soup that had a bit of a spicy kick to it, to be followed by luxurious lamb chops persillade, creamy potatoes au gratin, and steamed winter vegetables. The persillade, basically a mixture of lemon zest, fresh parsley, soft bread crumbs, pressed garlic, and melted butter, had to be made at the last minute. But Julian and I had had so much practice using our handy-dandy portable food processor that we'd be able to make short work of the topping that we would press onto the eight racks of lamb chops. While Julian retrieved the bags of winter vegetables to be washed and prepped, I put my efforts toward making the first batch of potatoes au gratin.

The essence of this dish, in my view, was not the luscious layers of sliced potatoes, Gruyère and Parmesan, and heavy whipping cream, although those were all very nice. No—it was the layer of slow-cooked, caramelized onions that I'd learned to place between the potatoes. When people tasted the dish, they always said, "What's in this that makes it taste so yummy?" I would tell them, but their look of disbelief told me that no one believed that onions could truly be a "secret ingredient." Which was fine by me, because then when people wanted me to cater their elegant meals, they invariably asked for "that cheesy potato dish you make."

As Arch would say, "Q.E.D., Mom." *Quod erat demonstrandum,* indeed.

When the mounds of onions were bubbling in their pools of butter, I lowered the heat underneath the two sauté pans and started peeling the potatoes. I was halfway through slicing that most comforting of root vegetables when Tom surprised us by banging through the back door. His sheepskin coat hung loosely from his tall frame, and he hadn't bothered to brush the snow out of his hair. His face was haggard. When Julian and I asked if we could fix him something to eat, he said he wanted to spend some time with Jake first. This sometimes happened when Tom was working a particularly grisly murder: he needed to get the unconditional love of a canine before he could come back into the real world. Then, Tom announced wearily, he would have a shower and come back down for whatever food we could rustle up for him.

I sighed, and Julian shook his head. When Tom had disappeared into the living room and was rolling around on the floor with our bloodhound, Julian finally said, "Should I go make sure he's okay?"

"He'll be all right. Sometimes he needs to do this."

Fifteen minutes later, I'd finished the first pan of potatoes au gratin, and Tom was back in the kitchen. There was one enchilada left, and a third of the Unorthodox

Shepherd's Pie. Tom scarfed both down. He wiped his mouth and gave me a wide smile. "Thanks, Miss G. You always seem to know what I need." He assessed me. "Now, how 'bout you? That was a nasty roll you took."

"I'm fine."

Julian, putting together something behind me, said, "Bull. You're in pain and Tom and I both know it. You should let me do the MacArthurs' lunch tomorrow. As you would say, it'll be a piece of cake."

"Let me see how I feel tomorrow, okay, guys?" I sat down beside Tom. "Did you get my message?"

Tom nodded. "We went to the strip club where Sandee worked. It was closed on account of it being Sunday, but the staff and strippers were there having a meeting. Anyway, we asked a lot of questions. None of the current strippers knew Sandee, and the staff who do remember her don't seem to have liked her very much. So it's doubtful any of them are hiding her. Our guys are on their way to Father Pete's place right now to talk to him about the car and what Sandee might have said to him. Now that you've flushed her out, I imagine that she'll be lying low. But we're going to try to find her. We don't want her cutting hair without a barber's license."

"Tom!" I took a deep breath. "Now tell me about Larry Craddock."

"It looks as if he was hit on the head with a rock, or else he fell on a rock, and then was held underwater. There's a lot of blood. You know, on account of the head wound."

"Any idea how it happened?"

Tom shook his head. "It doesn't look like an accident. Or suicide."

"And the paper thing downstream?" I asked. "Was it a map?"

"Good for you, Miss G. It was. 'Course now, it's soaked with creek water. But one of our guys who was working on the first map? He'd made a bunch of calls to map dealers, and a library in Baltimore is missing a map just like our Nebraska map. They also say they're missing one of Texas. So our guy says he thinks this might be the second map missing from that library." Tom's green eyes regarded me. "The Baltimore librarian says both maps appear to have been cut out of the same volume . . . with an X-Acto knife."

"Good God. I guess you don't know about fingerprints," I said.

"Not yet. Sometimes fingerprints last in water, if they haven't been touched. But usually they don't. Did the church folks leave any cherry pie?"

Julian said he would check, then he hastened out to the van to search for our leftovers.

I asked, "Do you think you can find Sandee's aunt?"

Tom shrugged. "We're checking it out. But if all the good rector knew was that they had a daughter, the husband worked for a bank, and they lived in the Springs, that's not much to go on. Sorry."

"Well, I want to photocopy a picture of Sandee while I'm dropping Arch's boxes at the library. Then I want to take it over to Neil Tharp's place, and to Patricia's, to see if it jogs their memories."

Tom emphatically shook his head. "Forget it. I know you started in this thing to help Patricia, but with Larry murdered, and Sandee Brisbane running around with her knife, you're going to have to take fewer chances. Patricia and Neil are both suspects in the murder of Drew Wellington, and you are not going to their places of residence without protection."

"Are you going to protect me at the MacArthurs' lunch tomorrow, too? Because both Neil and Patricia are supposed to be attending, not to mention Elizabeth Wellington, who's coming as Neil Tharp's date."

Julian had returned with the remains of the pie, and as I took it from him, he said, "The boys are just about done with loading up the books. They're really thankful I'm taking them to the RRSSA."

"Gratitude is always welcome."

When Julian had left the kitchen, I sliced a large piece of pie for Tom. While it was heating in the microwave, I pulled out some superrich French vanilla ice cream and levered out an enormous scoop. The piece of warm cherry pie à la mode that I placed in front of Tom a moment later was worthy of a magazine cover shoot.

Tom took the fork I offered and cocked a cider-colored eyebrow at me. "You're up to something."

"You know me too well." While Tom groaned I went on: "I have to go to Patricia's anyway, because she and Hermie MacArthur skirmished over the guest list for tomorrow's luncheon."

Tom took a large bite of pie. When he'd finished chewing, he said, "That was good. But you're going to have to enlighten me on why you have to deal with a fight between two tiresome, wealthy women."

I told him that Patricia was also feuding with her ex-daughter-in-law over about forty or fifty million dollars and a missing drawing by Rodin, "a very famous nineteenth-century artist, whose drawings are probably worth quite a bit," I added.

Tom scraped a last bit of crust and cherry juice from his plate. "Thanks. I know who Rodin is."

"If I dropped in on Patricia to show her Sandee's picture and try to iron out this problem with Hermie, then maybe I could look around for the Rodin."

Tom actually laughed. "You think she would have hung it right in her living room? A drawing worth lots of moolah?"

"Tom, will you come with me to visit Patricia Ingersoll and Neil Tharp? Please? You can wear your gun."

He exhaled. "Can I listen to the Broncos on the radio?"

Half an hour later, the first pan of potatoes au gratin was cooling, and Julian and the boys had loaded their boards and gear into Julian's Range Rover. The snow had indeed stopped, although low-hanging gray clouds threatened more of the white stuff. Arch, exuberant, made me promise to come see him "catch some air," once I'd finished running around trying to talk to people.

After they left, Tom and I climbed into my van, which was loaded with eleven boxes of books. While Tom drove I called the one caterer I knew in the Springs. She said she was doing a big party for the football game but would check her files as soon as she could to see if she had ever had a wealthy banker with a wife and a daughter who might or might not be about fifteen. "It doesn't sound familiar," she said, sounding unhopeful. I just asked her to do her best. As an afterthought, I asked her to see if these people might have moved to Furman County.

Tom, meanwhile, got a call from one of his deputies, informing him that Father Pete had given him a statement and the license plate and model year of the green Volvo station wagon. The sheriff's department had issued an APB. But they weren't very hopeful either.

"Does this mean the case against Sandee will be reopened?" I asked Tom.

He was backing the van up the driveway by the rear entrance to the library. "We have to find her first. Could you see if some of your librarians could open that door for us? It'd make life easier."

When I dashed into the just-reopened library, the first person I ran into was Roberta Krepinski. She seemed in better shape physically, but she did not look happy.

"Have you seen the number of cars in our parking lot? It's full! And everyone wants to see where Drew Wellington was killed. It's all covered and taped off by the sheriff's department, but that doesn't seem to matter to the pathologically curious." She paused. "I never thought I'd say this, but I'm beginning to regret that the county got the budget to have us open on Sundays."

"I'm sorry, Roberta." I tried to sound sympathetic. But what I actually felt was uneasiness at being back in the library. "Listen, we have some books for the sale. Could you open the rear exit for us?"

"And now I heard there was another body, out in the creek below the falls. That other map dealer, Larry Craddock?" Roberta muttered as I followed her down the hallway to the rear exit. "What is this town coming to?"

"I have no idea."

Tom insisted on unloading all the boxes, because he said he didn't want me to hurt myself. "At least, not any more than you've already managed to inflict damage on your own person," he added.

"Thanks a lot."

He hefted up the first of the boxes. "Just go get your picture."

Roberta was very happy to help me locate a news photo of Sandee from the archives of the *Mountain Journal*. She gladly photocopied it for me.

"Roberta, the sheriff's department will get this figured out."

"Uh-huh. That I doubt very much." But she did manage to give me a small smile. "Thanks for asking me to do real librarian-type work, instead of answering questions on what kind of blade was used to stab Drew Wellington."

When Neil Tharp answered the door at his small frame house, he was wearing a beige sweatsuit that just about matched his skin color. He carried a heavy weight, maybe twenty pounds, in his left hand. We appeared to have interrupted his workout.

"Oh, the caterer in mink," he said flatly. He lifted his chin and regarded Tom. "Your officers just left. Why are the two of you here?"

"May we come in, Neil?" I asked. I was carrying one of the bags of cookies Julian had packed up, as well as the photocopy of Sandee's news photo. "I have something for you, and I need to show you a photograph of the woman I was talking to you about in church."

"I suppose." He was still limping, although it was less noticeable than it had been a couple of hours earlier. He racked his weight and invited us to sit down on one of two couches in his mostly bare living room. Both couches were covered with sheets. Clearly, Neil followed the decorating theme of Closed English Summerhouse.

"You heard about Larry Craddock," I asked once we were seated. It was less of a question than a statement of fact.

"Of course I heard about Larry Craddock," Neil said, exasperated. "The police questioned me about our altercation last night." He shook his head. "Larry had a propensity for violence, but that doesn't mean he needed to die."

"We don't think he should have died either," Tom said, his first words since we'd arrived.

"Do you have any suspects?" Neil asked, arching an eyebrow. "Besides me, I mean?"

"If we did," Tom replied evenly, "do you think I'd tell you?"

Neil groaned. "First Drew, now Larry. When is this going to end?"

I placed the cookies on a sheet-covered table, then handed the copied picture of Sandee to our not-very-hospitable host.

"Never seen her before," he commented flatly as he handed the photo back. I had the clear feeling he was lying. "What did she do?"

"I told you," I replied. "She may have been following Drew and sending him threatening e-mails. I also saw her right after Larry was killed."

"Well, Officer Schulz," Neil commented sarcastically, "why don't you just go pick her up?"

"You know where she's staying?" Tom asked.

When Neil didn't answer, Tom gestured to me to ask more questions . . . if I had them. I groped around in my mind for anything I might want to ask Neil about Drew Wellington or Larry Craddock.

"Do you know any more about those missing maps you mentioned to me?" I asked.

"No, as a matter of fact. But why don't you ask your husband here to let me into Drew Wellington's house, to let me look for them? No one else will recognize them but me, anyway." He gave Tom a fig-tree-withering gaze. "Will you allow me into Wellington's house? I have a key, anyway, so I could go in whenever I wanted."

"You go in," Tom said, his voice still level, "and we'll arrest you faster than you can say 'world atlas.' "

"I figured as much." Neil exhaled.

"We have a researcher working with the department," Tom said at length. "He's verified that the map of Nebraska you described is the one we found on Drew when he died—"

"Yes!" Neil interrupted, brightening. "Did you find anything else?"

Tom lifted his chin. "We found the antiquarian map of Texas, downstream of Larry's body."

"Anything else?" Neil asked, his eyes bugging out. He was practically panting.

"Yeah." Tom looked up at the ceiling. It seemed to me he was enjoying making Neil sweat even more than he already was. "Our researcher says both maps have been reported stolen from a library in Baltimore. One of their cleaners found an X-Acto blade near the atlas section one night, and they had to go through all their atlases to see if anything was missing."

"Oh God," Neil said, defeated.

"So was your boss stealing maps and selling them?"

It took Neil a long time to answer. "Will I be arrested if I didn't actually participate in a crime, but knew about it?"

"Depends on what you have to tell me. I could put a good word in for you with the D.A."

"The D.A., my ass," Neil spat. "The former D.A., Drew Wellington, was cutting maps out of atlases since before I knew him. Larry knew, I think, or at least suspected it." He shook his head. "Drew used an X-Acto knife. I pleaded with him to stop, but he kept saying, 'I just want to make one more big score,' like it was a bank robbery, or a woman he wanted to"—here, Neil gave me an apologetic look—"to, uh, make love to. Although he wouldn't have called it that."

"Did he make one last big score?" Tom asked. "In the cartographic, not the female, department?"

"He did," Neil admitted, dejected. Tom pulled out his notebook and waited for Neil to go on. "Drew stole," he said, his voice heavy, "the New World map I told you about, the one from 1682." Neil rubbed his forehead. "He stole it from what's called Special Collections at Stanford. About six months ago. That's all I know about it, except that Drew was the most calculating, narcissistic man I ever met." Exhausted by his revelation, Neil slumped back on his couch while Tom wrote.

When no one seemed willing to pick up the conversation again, I had an idea. "Do you know Chantal Mac-Arthur? Daughter to your hosts last night?" As I suspected, Neil colored deeply and began to fidget. Tom lifted his eyebrows, suddenly alert.

"Not really," Neil said hesitantly.

"What does that mean?" Tom asked. "Not really?"

Neil, suddenly confused and deflated, looked from Tom to me and then back again. "Do I need a lawyer?"

"Do you?" Tom asked. "Because if you're going to be arrested for something, then I need to tell you that a lawyer will be provided for you if you can't afford one." He glanced around the living room. "And from the looks of things, you can't afford one. You also have the right to remain silent. Has my wife asked you a question that will lead to your arrest?"

Neil exhaled nervously and rubbed his hands together. "If I confess to something, will you arrest me?"

"Oh God, Neil," I said impatiently. "Did you kill Drew Wellington? Or Larry Craddock?"

He recoiled. "No, no, of course I didn't!" An unsavory smell of workout perspiration odor was suddenly noticeable. Or was it fear that was making Neil sweat?

"What then?" I asked. This man was really beginning to annoy me, even more than he had already.

"Drew . . . well, actually, Drew and Larry and I . . . we gave Chantal MacArthur and a couple of her friends some bourbon." He gave Tom a worried look. "They mixed it with ginger ale and got really giggly."

"Where and when did all this happen?" Tom asked.

Neil squirmed in his chair, unwilling to give more details. Blood rushed to his face, which made him look even more piglike than usual.

"Don't worry," Tom said. "I'm not going to arrest you for giving spirits to a minor. But if something else went down, I need to know."

Neil pressed his lips together. At length he said bitterly, "It was Smithfield's fault. Well, actually, it was *Drew's* fault, because once Smithfield was late, Drew started acting a little nuts. I mean, the whole thing with the negligees *was* his idea."

God help us. I had the presence of mind to say, "Start at the beginning, will you?"

Neil tucked his hands under his armpits. "Smithfield MacArthur was coming back from a map show in Las Vegas. He wanted to see all three of us, he said—Drew,

Larry, me. Smithfield had said he was eager to give us news of the show. At least that was what he said into Drew's voice mail. Hermie was out shopping, but she'd left word that her daughter would let us in. I think Smithfield wanted Drew there especially, because, well, you know, Drew was always late, and Smithfield had gotten tired of waiting for him—"

"Get to the booze-and-nightie part," Tom said sharply.

"Chantal let us in and then she and her friends asked us a lot of questions, chatted about school, you know. They were cute, and, well, nubile." Tears erupted from Neil's eyes. He untucked his hands and wiped his cheeks. "I'm so ashamed. I'd already screwed up once giving a . . . drug to a woman. Well, you know about that. Drew began flirting with Chantal, asking did she have a boyfriend, that kind of thing. When she said she didn't, Drew asked if Smithfield had a liquor cabinet. Chantal was embarrassed at first, but Drew said it was okay, we were old friends of her father, and would she bring the bourbon out so he could fix us all drinks? So she did, and then her girlfriends wanted some, too. Bourbon and ginger ale, can you imagine a more girlie drink than that? When Chantal and her friends began to get giggly, Drew said, why didn't they change into something more comfortable? He was really coming on to them, acting his usual way, Mr. Seductive. He always wanted something from people, you know? They thought he was good-looking, they thought he was articulate, they thought he was smart. He was thinking, meanwhile, *What can I get out of these stupid folks?*"

Tom cleared his throat. "So, Neil. You were telling us about the girls, and when Drew told them to go put on something else."

"Well, let's see." Neil's tone had become reluctant. "I think some of the girls were scared, but some of them wanted to play along."

Tom reopened his notebook. "You know what? I'd really like to know the names of everyone who was there."

"I don't know their names," Neil wailed. "I never did. I just know they changed into little filmy nightgowns and such." He colored deeply again. "Drew loved it and asked if they could put on some music and dance. Larry realized things were getting out of hand, thank God. He said we should all probably leave. Chantal cried, 'Don't go! I'll find us some good CDs!' So she put on the stereo, real loud, and I guess she didn't know that it was on outside, too. The MacArthurs have one of those fancy systems—" He stopped when he saw Tom's warning look. "Well, I thought my eardrums were going to pop. I guess a neighbor heard it and saw our cars. She called the cops. At least that's what I heard later, because when that damn music started blaring, I thought, *I am out of here.* I raced to my car—"

"When did all this happen?" Tom interrupted.

"There should be a police report," Neil said miserably. "It was the first part of November, I think. Anyway, when I skedaddled, I passed a sheriff's-department car as I was going by the Regal Ridge Snow Sports Area."

"Did Larry Craddock get out, too, before the police arrived?"

"Yes, I think so. We . . . weren't on the best of terms, and we didn't talk much, even when we were all there drinking." He gulped. "With the girls. Drew laughed later, telling me how *he'd* gotten out before law enforcement arrived. You know, I'm just sure he *knew* the whole situation was getting out of hand. But good old Drew, he must have figured that Smithfield had made him wait and wait and *wait,* so he was going to pay him back by getting his daughter into, you know, a compromising position." Neil swallowed again. "I mean, so to speak. But why would Drew take the risk? He'd already had that incident when he was stopped for a DUI."

"With a teenage girl in the car," Tom supplied. "Did he feel entitled to do that, too?"

"I don't know. That was long before I worked for him. But Drew told me about it. He said the girl was the daughter of a rich couple who hadn't given as much to his campaign as he thought they should have." Neil paused and licked his lips. "So, the giving alcohol to a minor, even in her own home . . . is that illegal?"

"You bet it is." Tom narrowed his eyes. "You'd better *believe* it is. Do not *ever*, and I do mean *ever*, try to pull that kind of thing again, or I'll arrest you so fast on contributing to the delinquency of a minor, you won't be thinking you've been hit by a *snowball*, you'll think you've been hit by a *meteor*. Got it?"

"I won't, I won't," Neil cried. "I was only a part of it because my *boss* was a part of it, you know?"

I couldn't help interjecting, "You were only following orders. Right, Neil?"

Neil groaned and put his face into his fleshy hands. "This is going to kill me." He began to cry.

"You'll survive." Tom's tone was not reassuring.

Neil and I flinched when my cell phone buzzed. Tom didn't move. I said, "I'd better take this outside."

"I'm going to talk some more to Mr. Tharp. Give him a few warnings."

Neil started blubbering again. Somehow I didn't care.

19

Once I was outside Neil Tharp's door, I pressed Talk on my cell.

"Goldy!" Our connection was crackly, so I didn't immediately respond. "Your friend, Yvonne? Yvonne's Yummies? You called me for information about some people who had moved from Colorado Springs to Aspen Meadow?"

"Sorry." I felt dazed after seeing Neil. "What's up?"

"I think I have something for you."

"Great. Thanks."

"This fall," my friend went on, "I did a huge farewell dinner for some people who were moving back to Aspen Meadow. The group the man worked for wanted him right away, for their Denver office. Before they left, the family didn't even have time to put their place on the market. I thought somebody was living there, like maybe they were renting it or something? But I just drove by the other day, and it's still for sale. Anyway, the guy was some hotshot doctor, not a banker. But his wife's name was Catherine, and they had a fifteen-year-old daughter. The girl was named after a flower, but I can't for the life of me think of what it was. Daisy or something. She was a cute little thing, eager to help in the kitchen. Anyway, even though the guy wasn't a banker, he had a bank-type name. Barclay, you know? Like Barclay's bank."

"Was the girl's name Violet?" I asked.

"That's it! Violet. Only the mom called her something else."

"Vix?"

There was a perplexed silence. "So, you know these people? Have you done a party for them?"

"No, but you've answered all my questions. Thanks." I told her I would see her soon and hung up. So . . . Sandee's cousin, the one she had taken care of when she was twelve, the little girl whom she'd been so protective of, as she was with all young children, given the nightmare of her own family life, was now a fifteen-year-old girl. She was Violet, aka Vix, Barclay. I was quite sure that Vix was the teenage girl I'd seen in the car with Sandee back in November, when I'd passed them on the road to Regal Ridge. She was also Chantal

MacArthur's best buddy, but I hadn't recognized her the last time I'd seen her, because her face had been covered with blue glop.

She was also one of the girls who'd been present when Drew encouraged them to try cocktails.

Either the cold weather was penetrating my jacket, or I was feeling chilled from what I'd just heard. Tom, who had the keys to the van, was still inside reading Neil Tharp the riot act. I hugged myself and reflected on what my Colorado Springs friend had told me.

Sandee herself had been sexually molested when she was a teenager. She'd also been raped by my ex-husband, whom she had murdered.

Years ago, Drew Wellington had been caught driving drunk, with a teenage girl in his car. He'd lost the next election. Last month Drew Wellington and his cohorts had given little Vix Barclay booze, and invited her to put on something more comfortable.

So apparently Drew Wellington hadn't learned his lesson.

In "protecting her assets," had Sandee Brisbane decided to teach Drew Wellington his lesson, once and for all?

Had she given Larry Craddock the same lesson?

Was she planning on giving some instruction to Neil Tharp, too?

When Tom finally came out and we climbed into my van, Tom said, "Did you believe Tharp's story?"

"Absolutely." I glanced at him inquiringly, but he was staring out the windshield. "Why? Didn't you?"

"Not sure. He certainly had motive to be rid of Wellington. And he was just telling me he wants to go into Drew Wellington's house for something he won't specify. 'Just files,' he says."

"Huh. Do you think the Rodin drawing or New World map might be in there?"

"We did a thorough search and inventory. We would have noticed either of those."

I frowned. "Hermie MacArthur told me Neil had called her. Said he wanted to come to tomorrow's lunch. Apparently, Neil wanted to show something to her husband."

Tom finally gave me the benefit of his sea-green eyes. "Maybe that something was a map he was going to get out of his boss's house . . . a map that's *hidden* in there somewhere. God only knows where." Tom turned the key in the ignition. "Neil Tharp did not convince me of his innocence. You find someone who feels he's owed, someone who's already ethically mushy, and you've got a suspect." He backed out of the bumpy driveway. "Neil Tharp's boss was stealing," he went on. "His boss was also fooling around with much younger women. And hey!

Maybe Neil thought if he got rid of the boss and the boss's main competitor, he'd have the local map clientele all to himself."

Once we were out in the street, Tom lifted his chin toward Neil's modest dwelling. "At least then he'd be able to buy himself a bigger place, something on the order of Drew Wellington's rented mansion."

"But . . . if that's true, why would Neil leave one rare map inside Drew's clothing and toss another one into Cottonwood Creek?"

"Distraction, maybe. Make it look like someone else is our perp."

"Well," I said forcefully, "I disagree. And now I think I know why Sandee is back." I told Tom about the call I'd gotten and my theory about Vix Barclay, the little cousin who was the asset Sandee had come to protect.

"Could be." His tone was dubious.

"It makes perfect sense, Tom. Sandee finds out from Catherine Barclay that Drew, Larry, and Neil got Vix liquored up. So Sandee risks coming back to Aspen Meadow, to protect her cousin from sexual predators. She digs for information about Drew, stalks him, sends him those threatening e-mails, and just in general tries to intimidate him so he'll move out of town. When none of those maneuvers seemed to have any effect, she may have followed him into the library, drugged his booze so he wouldn't fight back, then dumped cyanide into his coffee, and just for good measure, stabbed him with an X-Acto knife, maybe his own. And then perhaps she went after Larry, too."

"We don't know any of this for certain, Miss G. Especially as we haven't located the handle to the X-Acto knife, the blade of which sliced into Drew Wellington. We also have to hope that handle has some of Drew's blood on it."

"I'm starting to get a headache."

"Goldy, you're getting tired. Burned out."

"I'm fine. I'm just frustrated."

"I'll run your theories by our team, okay? Thanks for bringing the whole Vix angle up with Neil."

"Just as long as your guys follow up, okay?"

"Of course. You still want to go see Patricia Ingersoll?"

"I have to. I promised Hermie I'd convince Patricia to come to the party, even though Elizabeth is going to be there. And maybe she has other information about Sandee and how she stalked Drew."

"Hold on while I call the department." Tom accelerated out of Neil Tharp's small housing development, then used his cell to call a member of his team and give the executive summary of my theory regarding Sandee. Maybe it was far-fetched, but knowing Sandee, nothing was far-fetched.

The van's tires crunched over newly plowed snow as we headed toward Flicker Ridge, where Patricia Ingersoll and Elizabeth Wellington lived, and where Drew Wellington's enormous rented house now stood empty.

"Tom," I said suddenly, "can you tell me any more about why you arrested Patricia?"

"We got a tip. It came from a pay phone in Boulder."

"Whitney Ingersoll," I supplied. "She keeps up with the Aspen Meadow gossip."

"So does Frank Ingersoll's daughter by his first wife have a grudge against Patricia? Wait, that's a rhetorical question. They hate each other. Only, we're not allowed to go talk to whoever-it-was, just because we think she left a tip on our line. Her identity is protected."

"I'm telling you, it was Whitney Ingersoll. Grace Mannheim informed me—"

"Wait. Our guys can't just drop in on Whitney Ingersoll and say, 'By the way, we heard you hated your stepmother and tried to implicate her in a murder.'"

"Okay, okay." We were passing a stand of blue spruce, now freshly frosted with snow. Just past the tall trees,

Aspen Meadow Library came into view. "Did your informant say anything about the X-Acto knife?"

"She did not. We're guessing she knew nothing about the X-Acto. Our informant did say that she'd seen a silver BMW X-5 speeding away from the library. Yes, Patricia drives an X-5, but there's no way anyone could have seen that car leaving the library, then driven the hour plus it would have taken to get to Boulder, in the snow, and call us from a pay phone. So our informant was guessing. Whitney hates Patricia, knew Patricia was Drew Wellington's flame—"

"Tom. Nobody says 'flame' anymore."

"All right. Drew Wellington's girlfriend. His bedmate. His whatever." Traffic slowed as we approached the lake. "Looks as if our guys are still processing the scene."

I studied the view to my right. Waves of ice crusted the falls where Aspen Meadow Lake spilled into Cottonwood Creek. A large curtain still kept the crime scene from prying eyes. As the cars inched forward, toward the road that would take us east to Flicker Ridge, I could just make out the wildlife preserve. The way the newly planted trees had been placed on the fire-ravaged slopes resembled a whitened cross-stitch.

Once we'd passed the lake, the late afternoon sun emerged. The meadow flanking the highway spread out like a sparkling sheet. Farther off, a sudden wind brought a fresh shower of flakes off the hills and whipped it into a snow devil. The van windshield dazzled under its new curtain of ice bits.

"You know where we're going?" Tom asked as he piloted the van through the stone walls that marked the entrance to Flicker Ridge.

"Let's drive past Drew Wellington's rented house first, okay? I just want to make sure your guys are still there."

Tom wasn't happy, but he acquiesced. The roads inside the Ridge had been plowed. This action had backfired, as the sunshine had melted the snow on the pavement and sheeted it with black ice. Tom slowed as we passed snow-hatted mansions and made the long loop through Flicker Ridge. At the far end of the Ridge, he turned right onto the short road that led to Drew Wellington's former dwelling. Two sheriff's-department vehicles were parked in front of the imposingly large one-story house, whose exterior was dramatically trimmed with silvery-gray river rocks and thick dark wood planking. No one had shoveled the driveway or the walk.

"Nice place," Tom commented. "Too big to live in alone."

"Elizabeth's house isn't far from here." I gazed up at Drew Wellington's imposing residence. Too bad it was all for show, a rented house in which he couldn't even do business. "Elizabeth's house is smaller than this."

"Oh, don't I know. We went to talk to her. I'm not going again."

Tom stopped the van, lowered the driver-side window, and waved to the first car. The officer flashed his lights.

I returned my gaze to Drew Wellington's house. "It's unfathomable to me that he could have made enough money to support such an extravagant lifestyle."

"Oh, he didn't. But that's another key to the case that you simply cannot share with anyone." Tom took a deep breath. "When we went to see Elizabeth, we asked her about the money situation with her ex-husband. She said he manipulated her into deeding him half her inheritance."

"Half her *what*?"

"Elizabeth's father died soon after she and Drew were married, and her mother followed a few months later. Elizabeth, with no siblings, was the recipient of her parents' entire estate, valued at somewhere upward of five million dollars. Elizabeth told us she was the will's executrix, which meant she had to spend months and months in Seattle completing all the paperwork. By the end of it, she was exhausted. Then, instead of welcoming her home with open arms and expressions of affection, Drew said, 'If you cared about me, you'd give me half that money.'"

I rubbed the bridge of my nose. "I'd heard something about this, but I didn't know the details. How could he possibly justify taking half of *her* money?"

"Whatever I have is yours, that kind of thing." Tom shook his head. "And he wouldn't shut up about it, Elizabeth said. So finally she gave him half of her inheritance. He used it to buy himself a little house in Aspen. Not Aspen Meadow, *Aspen*. He kept the deed in his name and held on to it. Eight years later, when they got divorced, he sold it. Multiplied his money—her money—several times over, according to Elizabeth. I'm telling you, that woman is bitter."

"I guess she would be. But if someone, *anyone*, wanted to murder Drew Wellington, why not do it here, at the far end of Flicker Ridge? The killer somehow gains entrance to that great big house, then kills him. I don't understand why someone would risk being registered by the library surveillance camera, being seen by other people, or having something go wrong."

Tom waved to his fellow officers, pulled back onto the main road, and headed toward Patricia's place. "We don't know any of those things either . . . except remember the nosy lady across the street from Drew. She might have been keeping track of *everyone* who went in and out. Plus, now we know Wellington regularly saw clients at the library, back in that far corner by the exit. Maybe whoever was planning all this out knew his routine, and for some reason didn't think he or she would be able to get into that big house. Although I have to say, the security system is very low grade. Far as we can make out, Drew Wellington kept all of his valuables in a safe that's bolted down to the floor of his basement."

"Omigosh, did your people find anything significant in there?"

Tom shook his head. "We found a couple of things, his financial statements, his will—"

"To whom did he leave his stuff?"

Tom turned down the short road that led to Patricia Ingersoll's house. Both sides of this particular byway were piled high with snow, as if the plow driver had become tired and decided only to clear one lane. Tom proceeded carefully, then said, "Get this. I'd laugh, but I'm not that much of a cynic. I did think of it, though, when Neil told us his story."

"Drew left his money to Neil?"

"Nope. Drew left his estate to Stanford University."

"*What?*"

"So according to Neil, Drew steals one or maybe more maps from them, then says, 'I'll pay ya back when I'm dead.'"

"How much did he have?"

"We're still working on that. Maybe about half a million, maybe up to five million. It's going to take our guys a while to figure out where he might have stashed cash, maps, you name it." Tom reached for the radio dial. "You mind if I turn on the game?"

"Tom! Look out!"

Tom steered my van hard to the right and narrowly missed hitting a gold Mercedes with the logo for one of the local real-estate agencies. Once past us, the woman driving the car honked angrily, as if we had been the cause of her dozing off at the wheel. Tom carefully backed out of the drift where we'd impacted.

"What was that lady thinking?" he fumed. "We've got a single lane open here, and she's driving right down the middle of it, as if she's just landed on Mars and owns the planet."

We had arrived at the end of the cul-de-sac, where Patricia Ingersoll lived in yet another dauntingly grand stone-and-wood domicile—by herself.

"Okay, listen." Tom pulled the car into the area meant for a turnaround and killed the engine. "Remember, Patricia doesn't know exactly who gave us the tip about her car leaving the library."

"She can guess, Tom."

"Let her. But it was the X-Acto knife in her house with blood on it that caused us to arrest her."

"Precipitously," I said as I opened the passenger door, "and without knowing if she had a motive." I hesitated. "Should I look around for the Rodin?"

"I don't have a warrant, if that's what you're talking about."

"Tom, please. Give me some credit. What I want to do is check what's on the walls. Ask questions, that kind of thing."

I felt a bit strange as I picked up my purse with the picture of Sandee and my bribe bag of cookies. I carefully stepped onto the driveway that sloped down to Patricia's house. Patricia had asked me to help her look into Drew's murder and clear her name, and I'd been willing to do just that. But here I was, going into my former client's house to check for stolen artwork. It didn't feel great.

Patricia opened her massive front door before we were even on her porch. Like Neil, she was wearing workout clothes. What was this, National Fitness Sunday? Unlike Neil, Patricia had a tall, trim figure. Her eyes were red, and when she said, "Hello?" her nasal passages sounded stuffed up. I wondered how long she'd been crying.

"I brought you something." I handed her the bag of cookies. "I know it's probably not on the Losers diet, but the holidays are for indulging, right?"

She looked past me to give Tom a sour look. "So, am I under arrest again?"

"No." Tom held back, not sure if he would be invited in.

"All right. Why don't you both come in, then?"

She disappeared into the cavernous house. I followed her, as did Tom. The foyer held no artwork. Silver-framed photos of Patricia with Frank Ingersoll were set in a row on a small end table. On our left, a red-painted dining room boasted a long, pale wood dining table, covered with photos and scrapbooks. That was probably where she kept her X-Acto knives. Oh Lord, I didn't want to think about her being arrested and spending the night in jail, where she'd been so miserable. Ahead of us, I thought I heard her blowing her nose.

The living room, where Patricia had preceded us, soared three stories, all of which were covered with windows. The view down into a valley that led to the invisible interstate was spectacular. Thousands of pines balanced precarious loads of snow, and fat Steller's jays were already flitting between the trees that bordered Patricia's huge deck.

Patricia sank into a leather-upholstered chair next to her cold stone hearth. Tom and I, unsure of ourselves, perched on a brown leather sofa facing her. Immediately I realized I was facing the deck, and not the soaring three-story wall, where pictures, maybe even a Rodin drawing claimed by Frank's daughter, might be hung. And where did she hide her Ritalin? I wondered. Had the cops found any of that?

"Patricia, I want to ask you a question," I said. I pulled the copied news photo from my purse and handed it across to her. "This is a picture of Sandee Brisbane. You said that you thought you recognized a young woman, who was following Drew and might be his stalker, as Sandee. I was wondering if you could look at this photo and confirm that she was the woman you saw . . . I'm also trying to find out if you've seen her anywhere recently. Or maybe you remember some other details, anything Drew told you about the person who was stalking him."

Patricia frowned at the paper. "Yes, this is the woman I saw. I thought she was . . . stalking Drew. I told you about the vole on his doorstep. And sometimes, when Drew and I were together, out somewhere having lunch or dinner, she'd be there. I always thought she wanted to say something to Drew, but each time she would slink away as if she'd changed her mind."

"Did you ever see a weapon on her? A knife or gun?"

Patricia shook her head and handed me back the photocopy. "She never got that close, or at least, not when I was there. But her face. Her face I won't forget. She stared at Drew with a sort of mixture of hatred and . . . fear. Should I be worried about this woman coming after me?"

"We don't think so," Tom commented. "But it would be good if you could take a normal amount of precaution."

"This is getting heavy," I commented, glancing into the kitchen, an open space on our left. "May I get a drink of water?"

Patricia's look was puzzled. "Of course. You want some herb tea or something? Sparkling water?"

"I'm fine," I replied. Once I'd located a glass and filled it with tap water, I turned and faced the living room, then twisted some more—as nonchalantly as possible, of course—to my right, where indeed, some artwork was hanging. I frowned. This stuff was all of the Mexican hand-embroidered variety. I wasn't exactly an art expert, but unless Rodin worked in purple and orange fabrics, I'd say his work hanging here was a no-go. Did I dare to go in the bathroom and nose around for ADHD drugs? No, I didn't.

"What are you looking for, Goldy?" Patricia trilled.

I took a long swig of water. "I was just admiring your hangings. They're beautiful."

"No maps," she said placidly.

Time to come clean. "Actually, I have two other things to talk to you about. Your stepdaughter, or whatever you would call her—"

"I'd call her a little bitch," she retorted. "What would you call her?"

Tom said, "Now, Mrs. Ingersoll, there's no need to—"

Patricia snapped, "Please, you don't know her."

I said, "Maybe we should just go."

"No, no!" Patricia protested. "Tell me what little Whitney did now. Ever since her daddy died, she's become a lot more interested in his *stuff* than she ever was in *him*. Who visited Frank every day in the hospital? I did. Who took care of him once they sent him home, and hospice took over? Me again. So if little Whit sent you over here on a fruitless journey to find her precious Rodin drawing, let me tell you something: I have no idea where that thing is. Whitney should just claim it on her insurance, and move on." She gave us a morose look. "*Moving on* is probably what I should do, too, since I've now lost both my husband and my lover. But I can't move on until I have something to *wear*. Officer Schulz," she said, "do you suppose your employees would allow me to go in and retrieve my clothes from Drew's house? Some of my best dresses are in the closet I used over there, and I'd rather they didn't disappear mysteriously, into some police wife's closet."

Tom replied, "Our officers will be pulled off Mr. Wellington's house when we have collected all the evidence we need from in there. But I can tell you with some certainty that there isn't a police wife in the county who could fit into a size two."

Patricia smiled at him for the first time. "A two. Very good. Can't get my clothes and makeup back. Very bad."

I jumped in with "Listen, there's something else I need to talk to you about. Um, as you know from Hermie, Elizabeth Wellington ended up getting invited to tomorrow's lunch at Hermie's house. Neil Tharp wanted her to come."

Patricia groaned. "The gruesome twosome."

I went on: "Hermie doesn't want you to become upset with her, so she sent *me* to smooth things out. She still wants you to come to her party."

"I don't like the idea of the difficult duo taking shots at me. And anyway," she said, "as I explained, I don't have anything to wear, since my best stuff is sitting over at Drew's place."

"Could you let her in to get her clothes?" I asked Tom. I didn't want Hermie to have a meltdown if Patricia boycotted her party.

Tom said, "Nobody can go into that house until our team is done."

"Say once the team is pulled off the house," I said to him, "then it would be all right, wouldn't it?" Tom gave me an acidic look that I ignored. I turned to Patricia. "If you could get your clothes, would you come?"

Patricia brightened. "Yes, there's a green dress I particularly like that would be perfect. I wore it to one of Elizabeth's fund-raising lunches, for the Heart Association."

"Fund-raising luncheon for the Heart Association?" I asked faintly, feeling my heart squeeze with resentment. "Who catered?"

Patricia flicked her hand impatiently. "I don't remember. It was at the Lake House." She frowned. "Wait, I think it was Two Pettigrew, from down in Denver. Anyway, Elizabeth made a big point of ignoring me." She drew her mouth into a tart expression. "But it was a huge party. I don't know what she would do at a lunch."

"I'll do everything I can to help you," I promised . . . although I hadn't had much luck delivering on my promises to her.

"Thanks, Goldy. I'd really love to have that green dress."

"Okeydoke," said Tom, heaving himself up from the sofa. "Thanks for looking at Goldy's picture."

"You're leaving?" Patricia asked. Her bottom lip began to tremble. "You're leaving me alone?"

"I'm sorry," I said, and meant it. "I'm really going to try to help you."

Once she closed the door behind us, I could hear her muffled sobs.

20

That did not make me feel great," I said, once we were settled back in the van and heading away from Patricia's house.

"Yeah, well, she'll find a new boyfriend." Once we were again out on the main road that circled through Flicker Ridge, Tom had to swerve to avoid the same real-estate agent's Mercedes. My tires caught a patch of bad ice, and we landed in yet another snowbank. "I should give that woman a ticket," he mused once the Mercedes had passed. He peered into the rearview mirror. "But I doubt your van could catch up with her. Plus, you don't have a siren."

"Oh, Tom."

He cautiously backed up the van until we were no longer perpendicular to the road. Then he did an eight-point turn to get us headed the correct way. But at the stone entry to Flicker Ridge, Tom turned right instead of turning left toward home.

"Remind me why we're going this way, Tom."

"You don't remember your son asking you to come watch him snowboard? I told him we'd pick him up, by the way."

"No, I don't remember any of that." I pressed the buttons on my cell to call Julian. Patricia or no Patricia, we needed an extra rack of lamb chops to make sure there was enough food for everyone at Hermie's luncheon. Patricia wouldn't eat much, anyway, but adding Neil and Elizabeth meant we might come up short. When my cell beeped at me, indicating I didn't have a signal, I waited until we got on the interstate. No signal. When we were finally on the road to Regal Ridge, I tried again. Nothing. I threw the cell phone on the car floor.

"Take it easy, Miss G. You have *got* to get some distance. This case is filling up your head, and you can't think clearly if your mind is stuffed with worries."

"Stuffing is what you make for a turkey." I eyed the curvy road ahead. "Could you find an open place so I can try to reach Julian?" When Tom grunted his assent, I said, "Speaking of worries, I'm still anxious about the fact that Sandee is floating around out there somewhere. Did your people go see the Barclays?"

"Goldy, I just told them about those folks a couple of hours ago. They've got to get a pair of investigators over there, then take the time to question them thoroughly—"

"And meanwhile, a killer is on the loose. Plus, I've got a luncheon to cater tomorrow. But don't fret, we're going to go be snowboarding spectators."

When we'd been on the road for half an hour, Tom turned into the parking lot of the Regal Ridge Snow Sports Area. "I swear to God, working with you is exhausting. Go ahead, try your cell. I mean, if you didn't break it chucking it onto the floor. That was actually a really good hurl; I'm going to call the Rockies pitching staff, see if they need help come spring training—"

I ignored him and again punched in the numbers for Julian.

"Goldy, God, I've been trying to reach you!" Julian's voice boomed. "Elizabeth Wellington has called about six times. She is *not* a happy camper."

I closed my eyes and held the phone out from my ear. Was Julian's voice really coming through the cell extra loudly, or did I just not want to hear what he had to say?

Did ex-wives always have to hate their ex-husband's girlfriends? Or was it just rich ex-wives who hated richer, younger, prettier girlfriends and made you listen to their complaints? Majoring in psychology hadn't prepared me one whit for dealing with boorish behavior. But, man! I was a *whiz* when it came to rats in mazes.

"Goldy, are you there?" Julian shouted. "I told her you were going over to the Regal Ridge Snow Sports Area to watch Arch and then bring him home. She said she'd meet you there. By the way, when I left Arch and his pals, he said he couldn't wait for you and Tom to come see him catch some air."

"Oh, joy. Did Elizabeth tell you whether she was coming to Hermie MacArthur's tomorrow?"

"I sort of got the feeling she was. But she wanted you to disinvite Patricia Ingersoll."

"I figured as much. Look, could you go out and buy us another rack of lamb chops?"

Julian agreed and signed off. I turned to Tom. "Julian says Elizabeth Wellington—"

"I heard. I also picked up on that extra rack of chops. Reminds me of that old variation on a nursery rhyme:

"Mary had a little lamb, a lobster and some
    prunes,

A piece of pie, a piece of cake, and then some
    macaroons!
It made the naughty waiters laugh, to see her
    order so,
And when they carried Mary out, her face was
    white as snow."

I shook my head. Okay, I realized as we got out of the van, he was trying to cheer me up. So far it wasn't working. And when Elizabeth Wellington's voice cracked the air with "Goldy Schulz! I want to talk to you!" . . . and sixteen people in the parking lot turned their heads to see this Goldy Schulz she was screaming at, my mood nose-dived even further.

I walked as quickly as I could across the snowpacked parking lot. Near the entrance to the resort, Elizabeth, swathed in a scarlet cape with mink trim, was tapping the toe of what looked like a very expensive leather boot. No question about it, she wasn't going to wear *that* outfit on the slopes.

"Mom!" Arch called out of nowhere. "Did you see me?"

I looked around wildly, trying to avoid seeing Elizabeth and her tapping foot. Finally I made out Arch, who was propelling himself across the parking lot the way snowboarders did, scooting his free foot along the snow-pack, and gliding with his other foot, which was still buckled into the board.

"So, did you see me or not?" Arch asked when he was beside me. Underneath his knitted ski hat, his face was shiny with sweat and redder than Elizabeth's cape.

"Goldy Schulz!" Elizabeth screamed again. Out of the corner of my eye, I saw Tom ambling over to her. Good, that would shut her up for a couple of minutes.

"I didn't see you," I confessed to Arch. "Where were you?"

"Mom! On the slope!" His mitten indicated the right side of the mountain. "That's where the best jumps are. Watch for me on the far side this time, will you?"

"Okay, okay," I promised. Then I looked back up at the steeply angled part of the hill he'd indicated. "That looks awful dangerous," I said. "Maybe you should—"

"Mom, *don't*." As he turned and pushed his board away, I tried to memorize what he had on: a bright blue ski jacket, dark ski pants, and that gray woolen hat. You couldn't hear anyone calling from the ski slopes. And when Arch was taking skiing lessons at Killdeer, I'd learned the hard way that when you tried to watch for your kid from the bottom of the hill, everyone looked alike.

"I've been waiting to talk to you," Elizabeth announced when she arrived at my side. "First I had to drive all the way over here from Flicker Ridge, and then—"

"I've got to go take these two calls coming in," Tom said, holding up his cell. "Might be some answers to your questions," he added, which made Elizabeth give him a stare that was unabashedly nosy. He ignored her and walked back to the van.

"Elizabeth," I said, "before we visit, can we walk over to the bottom of the slope? I promised my son I'd watch for him."

Elizabeth tsked, but marched her short, stocky body beside me all the way to the base of the RRSSA slope. Around us, crowds of nervous parents stamped their feet as they watched their children whiz down the mountain. I plodded through the snow to the right side of what I thought of as the landing area. Elizabeth, who'd become slightly unwieldy in the high-heeled boots, trudged resolutely beside me.

"Hermie MacArthur called me," Elizabeth began when we'd taken up our posts at the edge of the base. "She wanted to say she'd invited Patricia Ingersoll to this to-do at her house, and she wanted to make sure it was all right with me. I said of course it was *not* all right with me. So she said I needed to talk to you, because you were the one doing all the arrangements with the guests. Is Hermie not in charge of her own party?" She narrowed her eyes at me. "Did you, or did you not, invite my deceased ex-husband's girlfriend to this luncheon?"

I scanned the slopes, but saw no sign of Arch. "Elizabeth," I said, "I didn't. Hermie did."

"The last thing I need," Elizabeth fumed, as if she hadn't heard me, "is to be reminded of the girlfriend my s.o.b. ex-husband kept trying to flaunt in my face! Do you understand?"

"I do." I faced her and smiled. "And I have a possible piece of good news for you. Patricia may not be coming, because she says she doesn't have anything to wear."

Elizabeth's dark eyes were filled with anger. "I don't know why I should believe anything you tell me. You and Patricia are friends, for heaven's sake. You did her first wedding reception, and for all I know, you were going to do her reception when she married Drew. You've been helping her, everybody says, even though she probably killed Drew."

"Is that why you didn't ask me to do your Heart Association lunch? Because you knew Patricia was coming to it and you didn't want a caterer you perceived as her ally?"

Elizabeth's cheeks turned as crimson as her cape. "I don't know what you're talking about," she said huffily.

"Forget it. But listen. Elizabeth, you need to let go of your rage and move on. Trust me, I know something about these things—"

"What, you're in the advice business now? Because I don't need it," she snarled. Then she twirled and stomped away.

Goodness me, another visit with a wealthy woman had gone incredibly well. Not.

I turned back to the slope. I shuffled sideways to the far end Arch had indicated, away from the crowd at the base and near the ridge. All alone on that side, I figured I'd be able to wave madly at Arch, and he'd actually be able to tell his mother was admiring his boarding skill.

But there was still no sign of a bright blue jacket and dark pants. I wasn't worried, I told myself, because I'd made no calculation of the length of the lift lines. As I stamped from foot to foot to keep myself warm, I wondered why there were so few kids skiing or boarding down the right side of the hill. The reason for this, I eventually realized, was that whenever a kid did hurtle down that way, he would hit first one jump, then another, and kid and board would hang in the air for what seemed like an eternity.

Perhaps it was because I was concentrating so hard that I was unaware of someone coming up behind me. Suddenly I was hit very hard in the back. The impact of the blow took my breath away.

"Wait!" I managed to cry. "Stop!"

But whoever it was paid no heed. My attacker grabbed my shoulder and shoved, sending me flying farther to the right, into the trees, and down a slope. We were out of sight of the skiers and boarders now. Below us, I could just make out the chasm that separated the ski area from the next mountain over. If I went over that cliff, I wouldn't live to tell the tale. I dug in my feet, purposely dropped to my knees, and fell headfirst into the snow. My attacker growled something unintelligible, then quickly jammed a knee into the center of my back, forcing me down into the snow so that I couldn't breathe.

I struggled furiously, pushing with all my strength to get that knee off my spine so I could roll over. I tried to grab behind me with my arms. But the knee only came down harder, and a gloved hand seized the back of my head. Dizziness assaulted me, and I tried to keep my eyes closed against the snow. Pain exploded in my chest from the lack of air. Then a hot breath and a hoarse voice were next to my ear.

"Stick to your catering, bitch!"

With a final shove, my enemy whacked me even farther into the snow. I saw stars and breathed in ice.

Somehow, and without my realizing how much time had gone by, I regained consciousness. I was inhaling oxygen; I was alive. I'd managed to turn my head to the side, but could not remember doing so. I was still lying in the snow. I tried to move, but my muscles were not responding very well. I was aware that I was very cold. Already it was darker, but I couldn't have been out that long, I realized. Still, where was Arch? Tom? Did anyone know where I was?

"Mom!" Arch's voice seemed to be coming from far away. "Are you okay? What are you doing way over here?" When I could only groan, my son's voice, nearer this time, said, "Wait. Let me call Tom on my cell. Is he here? Should I call 911? Hey, *guys!*" he cried. "Todd! Gus! Come help my mom!"

"Mrs. Schulz," said Todd, "what are you doing in the snow? Should we turn you over?"

"Wait, Todd. Aunt Goldy?" This was Gus, using the moniker we'd devised for him. "I'm going to check for broken bones, all right?"

I said, "Mmf."

As Gus gently, methodically, squeezed all my limbs, I heard Arch talking rapidly into his cell. "Yes, yes, she's over here. Can't you see us? Look, Todd will wave to you!" I caught a glimpse of Todd running up the slope, swinging his arms. My chest and throat were burning, and my muscles felt horribly weak.

Gus soon finished with his medical examination. The Jerk *was* his biological father, after all, and even though John Richard had never known, and wouldn't have cared, that he'd fathered a child out of wedlock, it looked as if Gus might have inherited some of my ex-husband's analytical and academic skills. Whoopee.

"I'm going to turn you over now, Aunt Goldy," Gus's voice reassured me. "Then Arch and I will take off our jackets and spread them over you. Quickly now, Arch, turn her on three. One, two, three."

Arch did as directed, and soon I saw my son's bare hand in front of my eyes. Snow flicked to the side; he was brushing it off my face. "I'm putting my mittens onto your hands, Mom," he said.

I could barely feel my son's hands on my cheeks. Most of me felt numb. It was as if my body couldn't remember how to take commands.

"Jesus H. Christ," Tom cried in the distance. And soon I was aware of his body, too, close to mine. "I'm going to pick you up in a sec," he said gently. I blinked and made out his face above mine. "Gus, can you keep those jackets over her as we walk back to the van? Arch, here, take my keys and start it up. Todd, can you bring all of your guys' boards?"

By the time Tom had me back to the van, I'd begun to feel my face again, and my limbs had begun to work, though my lungs still hurt.

"We're going to the emergency room at Lutheran," Tom announced as he slid me into the backseat and buckled me in.

"The hell you are," I said in a voice so raspy it could have grated cheese.

"Todd, you get in front with Arch and make sure he's going the right way. Gus, get in on Goldy's other side and hold her hands. I'm going to take her face."

I griped again that I was fine, that Arch only had a learner's permit, and that he, Tom, should stay in front. I was just a little cold and weak, I protested, and I certainly didn't need to be stuck in an emergency room for the next four hours while people with blood oozing from every pore—

"What happened?" Tom interrupted as he gently rubbed my face. "Did you fall? I tried to reach you on your cell, but you weren't answering, and I couldn't find you anywhere."

"I must have gone right past you, Mom," Arch piped up from the front seat. "I didn't see you way over there in the trees—"

"Just pay attention to your driving, will you?" I said.

"Ex-*cuse* me, Mom." Arch shook his head, which looked abysmally short up there in the front seat. "You always tell *me* to be careful, and *you're* the one who's always managing to crash into something—"

"I didn't crash into anything," I protested. "Somebody attacked me and tried to send me over the cliff. And when I fought back, the person tried to suffocate me in the snow."

"*What?*" cried Tom, Arch, Todd, and Gus in unison.

And so I told them what had happened. No, I told them, I didn't know if it was a man or woman, and no, I hadn't seen the person, nor did I recognize the voice.

"Ow-wow!" I cried. Thousands of bees were stinging my fingers and cheeks simultaneously. No, wait, I was getting the feeling back in the parts of my skin that had been exposed. "Agh!" I shook my hands free of Gus's ministrations, then wagged my head from side to side. The neck muscle injured this morning protested. Another wave of dizziness rolled over me, and I suddenly realized that my chest and back both hurt like hell.

"Aunt Goldy," Gus said gently, "I hope you're going

to be able to take it easy for a couple of days, and really not do any catering—"

"Forget it!" I hollered, with more heat than I intended. "Sorry, Gus, it's just that I can't."

"Or won't," Arch muttered from the front seat. Tom shook his head.

What I didn't say to them was that I didn't need to cater so that I could help Julian, who was perfectly capable of running the MacArthurs' lunch without me. Nor was I going to continue because I needed the money or even because I was worried about pleasing my clients.

No—I was going to continue to do my job so that I could find out who had killed Drew Wellington and Larry Craddock, because now I was *really pissed.*

An hour later, when we'd arrived at Lutheran Hospital—now called something else that I could never remember—a very nice Indian doctor came into the cubicle with Tom and me and began to poke, prod, and examine.

"Do you know how long you were in the snow?" he asked.

"Not long," I replied. "Twenty minutes, tops. It's a bit fuzzy, though, because I think I passed out. The person tried to suffocate me."

The doctor tsked. "You are very lucky your lungs were not harmed. You are also lucky not to have frostbite," he announced.

"I'm fine," I declared, although in truth, I ached from what was now the third bust-up I'd had that day. Which had been worse, crashing Marla's car, rolling to the creek bank, or being assaulted at a ski area? I'd have to think about that one.

"Perhaps you will not do skiing now, eh?" the doctor asked as he tapped my knees to check reflexes. "It is a very dangerous sport." Apparently satisfied that my feet could kick on command, he stood up straight. "You must not do anything strenuous, that requires the use of your arms and legs now, eh? For the next couple of days. You do understand me?"

I exhaled, looked down at my lap, and shook my head.

"Mrs. . . ." He consulted the chart. "Mrs. Schulz? You do understand me? Tomorrow you will hurt very much."

"Doc," said Tom as he helped me off the exam table, "don't even try."

21

The next morning the doctor was proved right. I had a hard time taking a deep breath, and my muscles hurt something awful. In fact, I groaned so loudly getting out of bed that I woke Tom.

"Goldy, what are you doing?"

"Getting up."

"Oh, no, you're not."

Outside, a lone streetlight shone in the darkness. Our room was chilly, despite the fact that the heater had begun the clicking noises it made when it came on. The green numerals of the digital clock glowed brightly, indicating the time was exactly six o'clock. Oh, how I wished the solstice would just get here and then be over so we could start the upward climb to summer.

"I turned off the alarm." Tom's voice was warm and comforting. "I really hoped you'd sleep. Didn't you take those painkillers the doctor gave you? You should take another one."

On my night table, Tom had put a glass of water and the brown bottle from the doc. I shook out a pill and downed it. "Okay, med administered. Now I'm going to go take a shower." I hesitated. "Sorry I'm not in a better mood."

"It's not like you don't have an excuse, Miss G."

"Actually, I think the tumble down the hill in the morning was worse than the face-plant in the snow in the afternoon."

Tom sat up on the edge of the bed. "Well, Calamity Jane, I'm not surprised. If we could just dangle you in front of the killer, maybe we could catch this guy. By the way, I'm staying home with you again today."

"What was that you just said? *Oh, no, you're not.* Anyway, Tom, I want you to go into the department so you can figure out what's going on. You, *we* must be getting close to something, if people are going to the trouble to follow us and heave me into the snow. And anyway," I added, "I have to do this luncheon with Julian, or Hermie MacArthur will go nova."

"Julian is very worried about you, by the way. He already called Grace Mannheim to come help. She wants to, but isn't sure she can make it." He chuckled. "You're not going to believe this. She asked to speak to me, said she wanted to know when she could get into—wait for it—Drew Wellington's house!"

I stumbled off to the shower. "You should set a trap over there."

"We would," he called after me, "if a) it weren't so dangerous, and b) we wouldn't be afraid of getting the wrong person. Wait a minute." He ambled into the bathroom behind me. "At least let me wash your hair so you don't lift your hands over your head and pass out on me."

I was too tired to protest. The hot water did not feel quite as wonderful as I thought it would, and I was still having trouble taking a deep breath. But when Tom's large hands massaged my scalp, I began to feel better— *much* better. I especially liked the part when he brought his warm body right up next to mine, to begin the rinsing.

"This is really nice," I murmured as I clasped him around his warm, muscular middle.

"If you let me stay home," he said over the water, "Julian could do the luncheon, and you and I could spend the day in bed."

"Why not just have a little fun here?" I asked.

"I'm not sure you're up to it."

"Did you lock the bathroom door?"

And so we made love in the shower. By the time I collapsed, panting and laughing, onto the mat outside the shower door, my lungs still ached.

But I felt healed.

"I'm going to make a breakfast that you are going to adore," Tom announced as he toweled off.

"You're the best." I tried again to take a deep breath and finally succeeded. The band of pain around my chest had eased.

"I'm sure Julian's already got your espresso machine going." Tom pulled on his work clothes: dark pants, a white shirt, and a sweater the color of oatmeal. "And by the way, I'm going to tell Big J not to let you out of his *sight* today."

"Where's Arch?"

"At the Vikarioses. They came and got Todd and him last night, after you'd crashed. Now that school's out for the holiday, I imagine those three boys will be inseparable. Anyway, Arch says he'll call us when he wants to come home." Tom hesitated. "Have to say, Miss G., you were a little hard on the kid yesterday. He was just worried about you, trying to help."

"I was hurting. But okay, I'll call him." I gave Tom a pained look as I suddenly felt suffused with guilt. "Can I get him something extra for Christmas?" Tom and I had already gone on a fun-filled shopping trip for Arch . . . in early October. It was hard enough being a caterer over the holidays, and I'd learned that I couldn't shop in November and December.

Tom shook his head. "No need, I'm certain. He just wants to be reassured of your affection."

"Well, he always has plenty of that."

"I know that, and you know that, but sometimes a kid needs to be told, even if he *does* pull away from all your hugs." He smiled, and those sea-green eyes made my heart go pitter-pat, even though we'd just had one of *those* showers.

"She appears!" **Julian** cried, when I entered the kitchen.

"Knock it off, I haven't had my espresso yet."

"Coming right up." He set aside the tool he'd been using to remove the zest from a pile of lemons, put a demitasse cup under the espresso machine's doser, and let 'er rip. I looked over his preparations for the persillade that would coat the lamb chops. If we calculated correctly, the chops would come out at the same time as the Prudent Potatoes au Gratin.

Which reminded me. "Let me start on the second pan of potatoes. Where's my mandolin?" When Tom and

Julian began to mutter discouragement, I said, "It's an easy enough job."

"Drink this first," Julian ordered as he placed a dark, crema-topped double espresso onto the kitchen table. I sat as bidden and took my first sip of much-needed caffeine. Zing! I'd be able to cater two parties!

Tom stopped what he was doing, which looked as if it involved mushrooms, and rummaged in the cupboards until he located my mandolin. Julian, meanwhile, stopped working on the persillade and began peeling the potatoes that I would be slicing.

"Guys!" I protested after taking another slug of espresso. "I can do my own prep work!" This was followed by more grumbling from the two of them, so I let go of it. I remembered what Tom had told me: that I'd been too hard on Arch when he'd just been worried about his mom.

Tom then told me to sit still, he almost had the breakfast ready . . . which I did. A few moments later, he insisted that Julian take a chair, too. In front of each of us, he placed steaming dishes of perfectly shirred eggs topped with sautéed wild mushrooms and chopped fresh chives. By the time I'd finished diving into that, I had just about forgotten the horrid previous day.

"If anything develops," Tom said as he donned his coat, "I'll call. In the meantime, would you see if you can stay out of trouble for one day?"

"Absolutely," I promised.

"Julian," Tom warned, "don't let her have the keys to the van."

"No way." Julian's dark eyes looked severe, and if I hadn't known that he, too, was concerned about my welfare, I would have given him the kind of reply I liked to think of as *raspberry tart*.

Once Tom was gone, I began to make short work of the potatoes with the mandolin.

"You sure you're okay with that?" Julian asked.

"Actually, I still have no sensation in my fingers. So if I cut a couple off, I won't feel it."

"Boss!"

"Yeah, yeah." I noticed he had finished the persillade and was packing it up. "Are you going to chop the sage for me? I'll do the Gruyère."

"Tom told me to do both."

"You want to keep your job, you won't coddle me." I marched into the walk-in and nabbed the cheeses and cream.

Julian groaned, but acquiesced. He knew on which side his brioche was buttered.

We arrived at the MacArthurs' house just before ten, and by that time I was on my third espresso. Between the caffeine and the painkiller, I felt ready for anything. But in truth, I was not prepared to face both Elizabeth Wellington and Father Pete when Julian pulled the van into the MacArthurs' driveway.

"What are they doing here?" I asked Julian.

"Believe me, boss, unless they came two hours early to tell folks where to park, I haven't the foggiest notion."

Elizabeth looked contrite; she would not even meet my eye as Julian and I exited the van. Instead of sporting her usual angry red, she was clothed in a modest gray wool pantsuit, pale pink makeup and lipstick—and pearls. Was this the outfit of repentance? Somehow I doubted it. Father Pete nodded a greeting while I wondered if *he* would be coming to the luncheon, to be Elizabeth's spiritual crutch. Man! Catering could get complicated.

"I'll start bringing the boxes in," Julian whispered. "You can go meet with the welcoming committee."

"Thanks a bunch."

"Goldy," Father Pete said as I walked toward the two of them. "Elizabeth has something to say to you. She wanted me here for emotional support. Actually, I want to help both of you."

Really? If Elizabeth was going to confess to poisoning and stabbing her ex-husband, or bashing Larry

Craddock's head and drowning him, we were going to need a lot more than a priest and a caterer to make *me* feel comfortable. We were going to need law-enforcement-type people, preferably with firearms, just in case.

"I called Father Pete," Elizabeth said, "because I felt so embarrassed about yesterday."

"Oh, well, then. You can pay the bill when it comes from Lutheran. Emergency-room care? Maybe a couple thou."

The old Elizabeth came back in a heartbeat. Her dark eyes flashed, and she bunched her hands into fists. "What are you talking about?" One of those icicle-style shivers plummeted down my spine.

"Now, Elizabeth," Father Pete cautioned.

She swallowed. "I truly do not know to what you are referring."

"I have work to do," I said, still defiant. "And I'm getting cold out here. If you pushed me into the snow yesterday afternoon, then it would be helpful if you turned yourself in to the sheriff's department, instead of running to the church for cover. Even the bishop can't help you beat the rap for assault, I'm afraid."

Elizabeth turned to Father Pete. "This is like yesterday. I have no idea what she's talking about. I think we should leave."

Father Pete's voice was even more gentle than usual. "Why don't you go ahead and tell her what we talked about? Goldy doesn't know what that is."

Elizabeth faced me, her face and body stiff. "I am sorry I was so rude to you yesterday. I was upset about Patricia Ingersoll, who reminds me of the terrible time I had with Drew. I apologize for taking it out on you."

"Hey, guys?" Julian called from the door that entered the kitchen. "Why doesn't everybody come in and talk? Chantal has made some banana cupcakes that she wants us to try. Marla's already here, and Mrs. MacArthur said it was okay for us all to visit." When we didn't move, he said, "It's sure a lot *warmer* inside!"

"Goldy, would you just give Elizabeth five minutes?" Father Pete rubbed his hands together, as if to indicate that we wouldn't freeze in that short a time. "If you can focus, you might be able to answer some of those questions you've been wondering about."

What was *that* supposed to mean?

"Yo!" Chantal called from above us. "Doesn't anybody want my cupcakes?"

Just after Father Pete replied that yes, he thought cupcakes would be a great idea in a few minutes, I saw something. It had nothing to do with the welcoming committee, as Julian called them, but with the house next door. Like the MacArthurs' mansion, the enormous residence took up most of the lot on which it was situated. But the place was supposed to be empty, the owners gone to Florida. And yet I'd caught a glance of a face at a window.

My heart turned in my chest. *Sandee.* It had to be Sandee. Was I being paranoid? I didn't want to look again, because I didn't want to scare her off. Not yet. As I trod up the stairs to the MacArthurs' kitchen entrance, it took all of my willpower not to turn and check if the face was still there.

I was desperate to find out if it was Sandee. But I knew Tom would never speak to me again if I tried to sneak into that house next door. I sighed.

In the kitchen, Julian was doing an efficient job unwrapping the lamb chops and placing the dishes of potatoes au gratin on the center island until it was time for them to heat. Chantal was keeping up a monologue of flirtatious banter, which Julian was very good-humoredly abiding. I didn't know which car Marla had driven over in, but when she saw us enter, she came over and gave me a long hug. I stood by the repaired kitchen window, keeping an eye on the house next door.

"Girlfriend!" Marla cried. She held me back to assess me. She wore a red cashmere sweater and skirt, as well as a double strand of emeralds, and she looked positively twinkly. "Why don't you come into the kitchen and stay awhile?"

"I'm just going to stand here," I replied. "But listen, you look great."

"I called last night, but Tom said you'd gone to bed. He said you had a mishap."

"Actually, I had several mishaps."

"Besides wrecking my car? Do tell."

"I will, just not right now."

Meanwhile, Chantal nabbed her plate of cupcakes and brought them over to us.

"I made these myself," the teenager said of the misshapen lumps, each of which boasted a good half inch of frosting.

"Try one," Marla encouraged. "I've had two, and I'm going to be on a sugar high until lunch."

Julian stopped what he was doing and washed his hands. "Okay, how many coffees and how many teas?"

While he moved around fixing drinks I ate the cupcake and glanced occasionally at the house next door. The cupcake was like wet clay; when the clay hit my stomach, it turned to lead. Not only that, but in the warmth of the kitchen, I again had trouble getting a deep breath. After grabbing two coffees, Marla came over and murmured in my ear: Was I all right? I nodded. But really I wasn't; I ached. And I did have several questions.

Was that Sandee next door? If Elizabeth Wellington didn't push me into the snow, then who did? And anyway, where was Grace Mannheim? If we ever needed her help, now was the time.

Elizabeth licked her fingers and thanked Chantal, for which I gave her points. Marla, who was on her third cupcake, thanked her, too, as did Father Pete and I. Chantal, beaming, went back to regaling Julian with a culinary narrative that, I gathered, did not end with nearly as much success as her cupcakes.

Marla sipped her coffee and watched me with a worried expression. Elizabeth, in the meantime, was starting to tell her story. What had Father Pete said? If I focused, I'd get answers to my questions. Once again, I was very doubtful. But I forced myself to concentrate, wheezing lungs and all. Marla, ever curious, snuggled in next to me. Where was Hermie? Getting dressed, I hoped.

"The whole thing with Patricia," Elizabeth said in a low voice, "just always sets me off. I'm sorry Drew is dead, or at least I think I'm sorry, but actually, he died to me a long time ago. I know that sounds cruel"—she took a deep breath and looked to Father Pete for support—"but it's reality."

I waved this away. "Elizabeth," I said, "right after I talked to you at the ski resort, someone attacked me, tried to hurt me and threatened me, someone I never got a good look at. If it wasn't you, which I'm guessing now is the case, then there's really no need for this."

"You were attacked?" Marla squealed.

"Marla, Goldy, please." Father Pete again.

"I did not attack you," Elizabeth went on. "And I don't know who killed Drew. But I think I know *why* he might have been killed. I told the police all this, but they seemed not to be interested. I mean *why* someone would murder him, in a very general sense." She took an emboldening breath. "I called him shrewd Drew. He never became involved in anything—any case, any business deal, any relationship—that he couldn't win. You've probably heard about how he insisted on getting half my inheritance."

"I think I picked something up. A rumor." I tried to make my face look blank, since of course I was not *supposed* to know the details of what Tom had told me.

In the background, I heard Julian say, "Actually, Chantal, I probably shouldn't come look at your room." Oh Lord. "But I can teach you to prep these lamb chops, if you want." Chantal murmured something, and Julian replied, "I'm a vegetarian, too. But a job's a job." Then Chantal started up again with her bright patter, and I could tune her out while I tried to concentrate on what Elizabeth was saying.

"Before I deeded half my inheritance over to him," she was saying, "he wouldn't stop talking about how he was going to save the world from the bad guys. What was I doing? he demanded to know." She stopped to dab her eyes. "Well, I was trying to save the world, too, by raising money for worthy causes. Drew, though, after I gave him the money he used to buy that Aspen bungalow—probably has a billionaire living in it now—just did whatever he wanted. And unfortunately, what he wanted wasn't me. So then I hoped he would change. I kept hoping and hoping. All right, I was drowning in denial, and I don't mean the river in Egypt, as they say. Plus, I admit it now"—here she looked to Father Pete for support—"being Mrs. District Attorney gave me a platform, a cachet, and I could be more effective, I thought, in that role. So I put up with him acting as if he wasn't married . . . until two things happened. He drove drunk with that young girl in the car."

Here Elizabeth's tears became a torrent, and she stopped talking when she took a tissue from Marla and honked into it. I *so* wanted to get back to catering the party, especially since Elizabeth had told me nothing I hadn't already learned.

"And he lied about it," she said, sobbing, "and tried to get it covered up so he'd be reelected. As soon as I found out the truth, I filed for divorce. But somehow that didn't come out until after he'd lost the election, so it looked as if I'd kicked him when he was down. But I didn't! Actually, in hindsight, I remembered how he'd asked and asked my mother how she was feeling when we'd first gotten married. She was a smoker, and my dad had already died. Then I realized, know what? Right from the beginning, I believe he went out with me, and then married me, because he knew I was the sole heir to a good chunk of money, and that my mother wasn't long for this world. Ooh . . ." and then she trailed off in another fit of crying. Father Pete patted her back, and Marla and I exchanged a look: *How long, O Lord?*

Hermie saved us. "Elizabeth! Come help me figure out the place cards, would you, darlin'? Marla, do you want to come, too? No? Oh, Elizabeth, is this your priest friend? Is he coming to our party?" Her voice became sharp. "Chantal, come out of the kitchen, you're bothering the workers."

"She's not bothering—" Julian began. But even his niceness could be quashed with a chilly look from a hostess, and the glance Hermie gave Julian was straight from the Arctic Circle.

Almost as soon as they left, I wished I'd been nicer to Elizabeth. Oh, why couldn't I feel guilty when I was acting bad, instead of later? These days, I seemed to be getting as uncaring as some of the mean wealthy folks I catered to.

Which reminded me. While Marla chatted with Julian, I pulled out my cell and put in a call to Arch. I got his voice mail, probably because he was already catching air over at Regal Ridge. I told him I was sorry I hadn't been nicer the day before, when I was attacked. He was great, I added, and I appreciated his concern, even if I didn't always show it properly. If he hadn't found me, I might have been hurt far worse. He would always come first in my heart. By the time I pressed End, I was swallowing sobs— which was a message Arch wouldn't love. Oh, well.

"Goldy!" Hermie again. It was getting to the point where I wasn't sure I actually wanted to do any more catering for her.

"Hermie," Marla interjected, "Goldy's busy—"

"Yes, Mrs. MacArthur?" I said quickly.

"My daughter wants to go to the movies with your *assistant!*" Hermie gave Julian an accusing glare.

Chantal would be lucky to get Julian, I thought, but said only, "Oh, we never, ever fraternize with clients. It's strictly forbidden. We never do it."

"Never," Julian repeated, trying not to smile.

"Well, I should certainly hope not. Chantal is just a girl, and she's destined for better things."

"Mrs. MacArthur," I said quickly because I thought Julian might start laughing, "who lives next door to you?" I pointed out the repaired window.

"Why, the Upshaws. They're in West Palm for the winter. Why do you need to know?"

"I was confused, I apologize. The other night, everyone was saying what a magnificent hostess you are, the best one on the street. I thought it was the Barclays who said it—"

Hermie proudly lifted her chin, as susceptible to flattery as the next person. "Well, they probably did say it. The Barclays live on the other side of the Upshaws." And with that she swept out. Thank God.

Suddenly I felt dizzy again. When I grabbed the center island, Marla squawked and tried to catch me. Julian cried that I should get on the floor, right now, before I landed on it. Marla lowered me to the wood planks, and I thanked her.

"You should have stayed in bed," Julian said from above me. "I'm practically done with the work for this party. You didn't need to come and put up with all that baloney."

"You're the one she was insulting."

"I care!"

His favorite line. I said, "I just need to sit down for a minute."

Marla obligingly brought over a stool. At my request, Julian put it next to the brand-new window.

"Now, I've got to go check on the table," Julian warned. "And I don't want you to get up. The food's done. Are you okay here with Marla?"

"I'm fine," I said, with my gaze never moving

Marla asked, "What are you looking at? Or should I say, *What are you looking for?*"

"Just keep an eye on the house next door, would you? See if you see anyone at the windows."

The two of us stopped talking and kept a sharp eye on the Upshaws' place. In the silence, I ran everything Elizabeth, Tom, Neil, and Marla had told me about Drew Wellington through my brain.

He'd been an unfeeling, manipulative, stealing cad, that was certain. And he'd been a lawyer. Go figure.

But it was something that virtually every one of these folks had said that was sticking in my mind. Drew had felt *entitled* to steal maps. He'd felt *entitled* to betray Larry, because Larry lost his temper easily and didn't deal well with people—he wasn't the smooth talker Drew was, anyway. Drew had felt *entitled* to swindle Smithfield MacArthur, because he was very rich, but not a very smart collector. He'd felt *entitled* to half of Elizabeth's inheritance.

Something was nagging at me, and I couldn't think of what it was. Somewhere in all the verbiage that had been slung around in the last two days, and especially in Elizabeth's story, there were nuggets of information I had not known before.

Before I could extract the nugget from the depths of my cerebrum, a car rolled down the MacArthurs' driveway. More guests were arriving, but I wasn't watching them. Just as the car came to a stop, that same face appeared in the window across the way, sending that same shiver right through my body.

So, I was going to get answers to what I was looking for, eh, Father Pete?

I just had.

22

Before you could say "snow," I'd grabbed my jacket and plunged through the door that led from the kitchen to the out-of-doors. Marla called after me, but I ignored her.

The night Larry Craddock and Neil Tharp had been fighting in the MacArthurs' driveway, what exactly had been the last thing Larry had said? I remembered now.

Then go ask the girl! You stupid dumb bastard! Force her to give it to you before I kick your butt over this cliff!

Go ask the girl, indeed. Only someone hadn't wanted the girl to be asked.

It was my guess that the sheriff's department hadn't been able to find footprints at the Upshaws' place because it had been snowing too hard to register any. Yet this was where the snowball had come from all right, with a knife inside, too. I was willing to bet the knife belonged to the Upshaws, and had been used in a spur-of-the-moment attempt to get rid of Larry and Neil. Which it had.

I traipsed through the snow to the Upshaws' garage, got up on tiptoe to look through the garage-door window, and saw just what I'd expected to see. Well, I wasn't going to risk Tom's wrath and try to sneak into the house.

I marched up to the front door and started banging. "Hey, Sandee!" I shrieked. "It's your haircutting client!"

Of course there was no answer, and I didn't expect one. But if I raised enough of a ruckus, I knew she'd come to the door rather than risk security-conscious neighbors calling the sheriff's department. And if she decided instead to take off in Father Pete's old green Volvo station wagon—the one I'd seen in the garage— the department already had the make, model, and plate, and it would only be a matter of hours before she was picked up.

"Sandee!" I screamed again. I peered through one of the wavy-glass side windows, but saw nothing. "You don't have to come out! Just come to the door!"

"I have a shotgun pointed right at your head," came the icy voice from inside. Sandee Brisbane.

Bull, I though . . . but I moved a few steps to the right, just in case.

"Great thing, surveillance cameras," came the same voice. "I can just change my aim."

I started moving from side to side while I talked. The guests arriving at the MacArthurs' house probably thought I'd gone crazy, a caterer in an apron and a jacket, too afraid to go to the place next door and borrow a cup of sugar.

"I can guess why you came," I called. "Vix's mother, Catherine, contacted you, didn't she? After the incident involving the booze, the nightie, and the police. You'd let your relatives know you were alive, didn't you? You gave them some way to get hold of you in an emergency. And Catherine was just so upset, she needed to talk to the young woman who cared so much for her daughter. But instead of being reassured, imagine how surprised Catherine was when you came out of hiding, all in the service of taking care of your niece. How'm I doing so far?"

There was no answer.

"You sent threatening e-mails to Drew Wellington, right? Telling him to keep his pecker in his pocket and move away. But he didn't go anywhere, did he? He wasn't frightened, he just went to the cops about it. So you became more bold in protecting your assets, as you call Vix. Didn't you?"

"I didn't hurt that asshole. I just wanted to warn him in person."

"And how'd that work out? Did you see who killed him?"

"I saw a bunch of people, but once Wellington slumped over, I didn't want to stick around. I raced out the library's emergency exit, 'cuz somebody had already opened it. The end."

"Did you just want to warn Larry Craddock, too?"

"Oh, Goldy, will you stop talking, please?"

Instead, I raised my voice a notch. "Did you try to warn Larry Craddock? To keep away from Vix?"

"Yes! But he was already dead. Now get out of here!"

I tried to make my tone conciliatory. "Look, Sandee, if you turn yourself in—"

"What do you want, Goldy?"

"I want you to leave Neil Tharp alone. I know he was there when Larry and Drew did that thing with the girls—"

"Bye, Goldy."

"Sandee," I tried again, "you're lost. You need help."

"I'm allowed to protect Violet!"

"Let her parents protect her."

"I know a teenage boy whose mother won't be able to

protect him if she doesn't go back to her van and take off. You got it? The shotgun's pointed right at your head. I'm going to count to three. One."

"Sandee, stop!"

"Two!"

Dammit to hell. I stomped off the Upshaws' porch so fast, I fell in the snow. Pain shot through every pore of my body. But at least Sandee Brisbane didn't shoot.

Once I'd painfully raised myself to my feet, I began to shuffle back to the MacArthurs' house. And then Elizabeth Wellington's words that I'd been searching for came to mind: *Somehow that didn't come out.* She'd been referring to her filing for divorce from Drew Wellington. I was thinking along similar lines.

Who had the power not to have something come out? And who had the power to find out about the results of a court case just *as* it came out? Of course, it wasn't exactly legal or ethical to do either, but Drew Wellington didn't exactly act legally, or ethically, or even nicely.

He acted entitled.

I needed to call Tom about Sandee, though by the time the police came for her, she'd probably be long gone from the Upshaws' house. And now I really, really wanted to go down to the Furman County Courthouse to find out if what I was guessing was true. I should wait, I should let Tom handle things, but I'd been the one plastered into the snow and nearly asphyxiated. I refused to be scared anymore. Julian could handle the luncheon; he'd already insisted. Unfortunately, I was unable to just go get my van because Julian had the keys, and there was no way he would give them to me. I would have to find a way to the Furman County Courthouse without using my own vehicle.

But don't worry, I imagined myself saying to Tom . . . *I'm not going to get entangled with a killer. I might, however, steal a car.*

"Mrs. Munsinger!" I called as Louise Munsinger drew to the top of the MacArthurs' driveway in her silver Cadillac DeVille. "I'm doing the valet parking for the MacArthurs. May I take you down to the sidewalk?"

"I don't have any money for a tip." But she moved over to the passenger seat anyway.

"That's all been taken care of by the MacArthurs," I assured her as I slid behind the wheel. "But you'll have to leave your cell phone with me. That's what the other guests are doing. Then you can call your cell from inside the MacArthurs' house, and I'll come pick you up."

Louise said, "Well, all right." She drew her cell right out of her purse and handed it to me. I drove to the MacArthurs' sidewalk, jumped out of the car to open Louise's door for her, and watched in delight as she trod down the path.

I didn't know what Louise Munsinger thought of my next move, rolling down to the end of the driveway, turning around, and taking off. And I certainly didn't intend to wait and find out.

On my way down to the Furman County Courthouse, I tried to call Tom on Louise Munsinger's cell phone. When I got his voice mail, I informed him that Sandee Brisbane was staying inside the Upshaws' house, next door to the MacArthurs' place, in Regal Ridge. I'd just had a chat with her, I added, and she insisted she hadn't killed Drew Wellington. She *had* been stalking him, though. It was a long story, I concluded. I could imagine Tom shaking his head.

Inside the courthouse, the person I needed to talk to first was the clerk of the court. Harriet Taub was a nice woman, older, with gray hair, a winter-white suit, and a tinsel corsage that you just knew had been given to her by office workers. The kind of bribery I was thinking of was not of such a sweet variety.

I knew Mrs. Taub, as she told me to call her, had to look something up, either by name or case number. I didn't have a case number, but I had a name.

So Mrs. Harriet Taub tapped computer keys until she had a hit. As I suspected, the judge had made his decision in *Ingersoll v. Ingersoll* just four days ago, on Thursday, December 14. Mrs. Taub directed me to the clerk of the division that had handed down the ruling: Division One.

Miss Ginnie Quigley, the Division One clerk, was an almost pretty woman, just the wrong side of thirty. When she smiled, she showed yellow, crooked teeth. She wore her dull brown hair long, and the black suit she wore in an attempt to make her look slender only made her pale face look as if it was floating somewhere above her body. She was not wearing a corsage. But I was sure Drew had told her she was beautiful, that she was his special friend. And no doubt she'd believed him.

I introduced myself. "Oh," Ginnie Quigley said with a huge smile, "Tom's wife! He's so sweet."

"He's not going to be sweet to you when he finds out what your relationship was with Drew Wellington."

The smile faded. Ginnie Quigley swallowed, then licked her thin lips. "Uh, Drew's dead."

"I know. Now please tell me when you let him know

the decision in the Ingersoll case, or I'll call Tom down here right now."

Ginnie Quigley didn't hesitate to tell me she'd called Drew as soon as the ruling was in: Thursday evening, December 14. And yes, she'd told him what the ruling was.

You ordinarily did not see a woman wearing a caterer's uniform and a winter jacket racing through the courthouse to the side where the sheriff's department was housed. But these were extraordinary circumstances. Or maybe somebody was already calling up to Tom's floor to announce in a jaded voice, *Tell Schulz his wife is here.*

"No, he's not around," the staff sergeant told me when I arrived, out of breath, at his desk.

"I have to know where he is. It pertains to one of his cases, and is very, very urgent."

The sergeant didn't care how urgent anything was, he had to confer with superiors before telling me even the smallest factoid.

Finally he faced me. "They pulled the detail off Drew Wellington's house a couple of hours ago. Officer Schulz has gone back up to Aspen Meadow with his team, to do some more investigating."

"*Where* in Aspen Meadow is he?"

"You have a cell? Why don't you call him?"

★   ★   ★

Which was exactly what I did. But either Tom wasn't answering or he wasn't getting reception. *I won't do anything,* I told myself. *I'll just go where I know Patricia is. I know what she wants, and she'll be waiting to go in and get it. She wants what she thinks she's entitled to.*

I couldn't have figured any of this out, and I believed I was right, hoped I was right, without Elizabeth Wellington's feeling she had to clear her conscience. As I gunned Louise Munsinger's Caddy back up the interstate, I remembered how perplexed Elizabeth had said she'd been, that her filing for divorce had not been announced until after her then-husband had lost his reelection bid.

Drew Wellington knew how to manipulate people; that was how he'd gotten either Ginnie Quigley or some other minor bureaucrat to sit on Elizabeth's divorce filing. But the Furman County Sheriff's Department hadn't been quite as tractable, and the news that Drew Wellington had been arrested for a DUI, which he'd then tried to have hushed up, had outraged voters enough to shoo him out of office.

Undaunted, he'd sold the house in Aspen, made a bundle, and rented a big place in Flicker Ridge. He'd also used the rest of the money he'd made to set himself up in map dealing. And he'd chosen a mentor, Larry

Craddock, who was just difficult enough to deal with that he knew stealing Larry's clients would be no problem. All he had to do was undercut Larry's prices . . . which was easy enough if you stole some of the maps you sold.

Drew must have realized his world might collapse someday, but he probably figured that the worst that could happen would be that he'd have to pay back some of his clients. Or maybe he hadn't figured that at all, I thought, as I made the turnoff for Aspen Meadow. But still, he'd wanted some insurance.

And then that insurance had fallen right into his lap, with Patricia Ingersoll asking, *asking* to be introduced to him. Drew knew he was handsome and able to charm . . . he just didn't figure that Patricia thought she was equally good-looking and charming, and searching for some insurance herself, in the form of a wealthy person who might be her safety net.

Patricia had been in a drawn-out probate battle with her deceased husband's daughter, Whitney, for over a year. But what if she lost, she probably wondered, and had to forfeit everything except the money Frank had left her in an insurance policy? She needed a fellow with financial depth, and that was why she'd searched out Drew Wellington, whom she'd thought had all kinds of money, because that was the way he lived.

Things had gone her way for a while . . . Aspen Meadow's impossibly gorgeous, fabulously wealthy couple had seemed to be in love.

But then the ruling had come in on *Ingersoll v. Ingersoll*. Patricia had lost, as well she should have. Alerted to the decision by an obliging Ginnie Quigley, Drew had dropped Patricia faster than you can say "Bye!"

So there Patricia was: instead of having everything she wanted—the two houses, the big money, the gorgeous guy—she had nothing. But she did have a chance for *one* thing: revenge. And she'd wanted that revenge to be full and *sweet*. So she began to think—how can I get that kind of vengeance?

She had that final night with Drew. She'd acted cavalier, perhaps . . . Let's just have one last fling, for old time's sake. I didn't know how she'd put her hands on cyanide and Rohypnol, but maybe she'd always kept them in reserve, just in case things didn't work out. Anyway, law enforcement was better at figuring out that kind of thing than I was. Patricia knew about Drew cutting maps out of books . . . with his propensity for hubris, he'd probably shown her how he did it. But if she threatened to expose him, that wouldn't be enough to get the vengeance she was imagining.

I interrupted my reverie long enough to call Tom, and again got his voice mail. Urgent, I said. Meet me at Drew Wellington's house.

This was Patricia's plan, I thought as I turned into Flicker Ridge. Put a very small amount of Rohypnol into Drew's flask, just so he would feel so drunk that he'd need the coffee she knew he always took into the library. Pour the cyanide into Drew's coffee when she filled his thermos at the beginning of the day. Make sure she was seen in the morning by the nosy neighbor. Agree to meet with one of the Losers members for an alibi, and bring a few books for the book sale. Get to the library early enough with an X-Acto knife, maybe one just like the ones she used at home, but not one *from* home. Watch and wait, and when the Rohypnol took effect and Drew couldn't fight back, when he'd slugged the poison-laced coffee, stab him with the X-Acto knife. That way, it could look as if a disgruntled dealer, or maybe an angry collector, had used the same weapon on him that he'd used to steal maps.

Then she slipped out the emergency exit so she wouldn't be taped by the surveillance camera out front.

Patricia wanted desperately to have everyone but her look like a murderer. She'd told me about Neil, about Elizabeth, about Smithfield . . . and she knew I could easily find out about Larry and some more of Drew's disgruntled clients. And if none of those worked out, she even had the perfect suspect to offer up to the police for the murder. For nearly a month, Drew Wellington had been receiving threatening e-mails, e-mails he'd asked the sheriff's department to investigate, e-mails that had come from public libraries. Patricia had spotted Sandee lurking around Drew and had recognized her. She knew Drew had taken a public stance on Sandee's case, criticizing the police for letting her get away. Even if Sandee herself was never caught by the cops, a mysterious stalker who had it in for Drew made for a much better killer than a grief-stricken fiancée.

But then she'd started miscalculating. She'd miscalculated Whitney, for one, who was not satisfied with merely winning the expensive legal battle with her father's widow. When one of Whitney's Aspen Meadow spies had let her know that Patricia's boyfriend, Drew Wellington, had been found dead in the library, Whitney had called in a false tip to the cops about Patricia, hoping her nemesis would somehow dig herself a hole.

And it had almost worked, because Patricia *had* killed Drew. She *had* driven away from the library in her X-5, as Whitney had anonymously reported to police, and there *was* an X-Acto knife with blood on it in Patricia's house. Only the weapon the police had found hadn't had

Drew's blood on it; it had only a little bit of Patricia's. And with nothing but a report of a vehicle half the rich folks in Aspen Meadow drove . . . that wasn't enough to keep someone behind bars.

As extra insurance, Patricia had called Brewster Motley and told him to meet her at my house so she'd have an excuse to come over. Then she'd begged me to help her solve the case, and she'd begged again when I'd visited her in jail. She must have assumed I'd be so terrified at the prospect of the Jerk's killer running around loose, threatening my son, that I'd do everything in my power to chase Sandee down.

Which left Patricia free and clear, once the police finished their investigation. I was more than willing to bet she still had the Rodin drawing that she'd hidden in a place Drew had told her about. She could sell the drawing quietly on the black market and make a bundle from it. Now that Whitney had won her lawsuit, she knew she had no hope of retrieving the Rodin from Patricia by the usual legal means. So she had sent in Grace to search for a way to get into Drew's house to look for it. But Grace wouldn't have had any luck, because the police had had their detail on the place until the past hour.

Why had Patricia killed Larry Craddock? I mused as I gunned Louise's Cadillac up the interstate. Greed and fear. Drew had had three maps on him when he'd gone

into the library on Friday, December 16. He'd offered
two of them, the less valuable maps of Nebraska and
Texas, to Larry as a peace offering, but Larry had smelled
a rat . . . and had gone to check if the maps had been
reported stolen. Drew, maybe already drunk or feeling
the effects of the Rohypnol, must have hidden the Nebraska map in his coat pocket so that Patricia, in her
hurry to get out the library's emergency exit, had overlooked it. But the Texas map and the very valuable one
of the New World that Drew had planned to show to
Smithfield—those two she took. Probably she'd tried to
sell the Texas map to Larry. No doubt he'd immediately
recognized it as one of the maps Drew had tried to sell
him right before he was killed. So Larry had been one of
Patricia's victims, too. The map floating down Cottonwood Creek was a casualty of that particular encounter.

Why had Patricia followed us from her house yesterday, then mashed me into the snow? Because she'd sensed,
by my bringing Tom to interview her, and by my taking a
not-surreptitious-enough look around for the Rodin, I no
longer fully trusted her story. And then she'd seen me
talking to Elizabeth. Patricia feared I might confront
Elizabeth about that Heart Association fund-raiser.
Which I had. And Elizabeth Wellington had been right to
act confused, to say, "I don't know what you're talking
about." Because Elizabeth hadn't *had* a luncheon fund-

raiser for the Heart Association; it was just something Patricia had made up on the spur of the moment, when we'd asked her what she needed from the house, and she'd said she needed her green dress. When Patricia, who'd undoubtedly hustled fast down to the RRSSA so she could sit in the parking lot and wait for me, had known she could get caught in a lie . . . she'd probably figured it was time to try to scare me off.

I knew why she had to have her green dress. Or at least I suspected. And when I drove up to Drew Wellington's house, and saw Tom leading Patricia Wellington out in handcuffs, she was indeed wearing a long, floating dress of lovely dark green.

I rolled down the Caddy window. "Don't let her out of your sight with that dress on!" I shrieked at Tom. "I'll bet there's a Rodin drawing in the hem!"

"Shut up, you!" Patricia shrieked at me. "I wish you could have some of what's in this dress!"

Tom handed Patricia off to an assistant and walked over to me. Instead of congratulating me on cracking the case, he said, "Miss G.? Whose Cadillac is this?"

Tom drove Louise Munsinger's car back to the MacArthurs' house—with a police car escort—parked it in the driveway, and gave Julian Louise's cell. The luncheon, thank God, was still going on, with Grace Mannheim helping. When Tom had told Julian what I'd been up to, Julian had just shaken his head.

Tom also told me that Sandee, as I suspected, was long gone. At least she'd had the decency to leave Father Pete his Volvo, with the keys inside.

Later, Tom told me the whole thing had actually been my idea: to make it look as if the detail had been pulled off Wellington's house when Tom was inside with his team, waiting for a killer. He said if I'd shown up ten minutes earlier, he'd have had to shoot me, just to shut me up.

The Rodin drawing was indeed in Patricia's hem. She wouldn't have wanted to risk having Whitney or anyone else find it in her house. I did get to see a photograph of the drawing, one of the studies for the *Gates of Hell*. Father Pete, I thought, would love the irony.

There was also, in Patricia's hem, a small bottle of someone else's prescription for Ritalin, and—surprise!— a plastic baggie of Rohypnol. She'd been able to slip that small dose into Drew's flask while he was showering, then push the tiny bag back into the loosely stitched hem of her dress, where, she had correctly surmised, no investigator would look . . . until she lost her cool and told me she wished she could give some to me.

Later, a witness came forward with a description of Patricia's car, with the correct license plate number, that the witness said had been parked near the place in the creek where Larry Craddock had been killed on Sunday morning. Finally, sheriff's-department investigators used a bloodhound to find the missing X-Acto knife handle, which had traces of Drew Wellington's blood on it, as well as a small bottle of cyanide, buried at the far end of Patricia's yard, under a foot of pine needles and another foot of snow.

But nowhere in Patricia's house, and nowhere in her yard, and certainly in none of her hems, was there any map of the New World.

Eight days later, Roberta Krepinski called and said there was going to be another staff and volunteer breakfast at the Aspen Meadow Library, only this time, Tom and Arch and I were to be guests. Roberta, Hank, and all the other worker bees were very happy to provide a potluck, and to treat us like royalty. Neil Tharp and Elizabeth Wellington came together. Neil had called me and shyly announced that the library function would be their second date, and could I make something special? I had obliged by concocting a toffee, date, raisin, pecan, and chocolate-chip bar that I'd dubbed Got-a-Hot-Date Bars.

"You won't need any Rohypnol with this," I said as I passed Neil a wrapped packet of the bars.

"That's not funny, Goldy," he replied, but he smiled.

The MacArthurs were in attendance, and Smithfield beamed with pride while loudly relating that his very own caterer had been instrumental in finding the killer. Julian and I exchanged a glance. Tom managed to leave the room before he burst out laughing.

There was only one fly in the ointment of happiness, however. The Special Collections of Stanford's Green Library was still missing its map of the New World, from 1682. Patricia had been offered all kinds of incentives to tell the police where it was, but she swore she'd never seen it. Private investigators hired by Stanford had cooperated with the police in searching both residences, and the map was in neither. If the map was in neither Patricia's nor Drew's house, Neil Tharp insisted, then Drew *must* have had it with him when he'd come into the library that Friday.

The librarians had followed what Smithfield MacArthur and Neil Tharp had told them, that map smugglers had not only hidden maps in clothes, but inside the jackets of other books. The librarians, investigators, and volunteers had started with the atlases and gone through every single library book, checking behind the jackets and within the pages, to no avail. When books that had been checked out over the weekend were called back in, those were checked, too—but there was nothing in them, either. The librarians had somberly reported that the map was not to be found.

Our library holiday party went on for hours. Exhausted, and finished with serving, I finally decided to rest in front of the reading-room gas fire. I smiled at Arch, who was there with a group of pals from the Christian Brothers High School. He grinned back. He'd accepted my apology and told me please not to tell him all the time that he should be careful. *I* should be more careful, he said. I told him I would if he would be less messy. He'd said, "Deal."

"Arch," I said suddenly as I stood up from the hearth. "Can you come help me with something?"

He said, "Oh, Mom," but followed me anyway.

"Just indulge me," I said.

When we were up at the front desk, I asked Arch to walk in front of the security camera, but not to stop at the circulation desk.

"Where am I supposed to go?"

"Just act as if you're half drunk," I said, thinking of how Drew Wellington had acted on the surveillance video, when he'd probably already begun to feel the Ro-hypnol. "You're stumbling around, but you want to hide something."

"Mom, I feel stupid."

"There are no girls here, so you're fine. Where are you going to go? Keep walking," I told him as he passed me, reeling.

"I'm going to go out this door," he said, pointing to the entryway to a hall that led to the back exit/entrance, the same one I had used to bring supplies into the library that fateful Friday evening.

"Yes," I said, "exactly. Let's go." We pushed through the door and walked down the hall. The librarians had brought their goodies in this way today, and the air was still cold.

"What are we looking for?" Arch asked.

The first room was used for storage, and it was completely empty except for some fans used in summertime. The door at the end of the hall, I knew, led to the staff kitchen and lunchroom. In the middle was the room where the books for the used-book sale were stored. There were about a hundred volumes on the shelves, all accumulated in December.

"Arch, help me go through these volumes, would you?"

"Every one of them?" he replied, incredulous. "But I

already know what's in these books. Some of them are mine, or they were."

"You don't have to look in those, because we didn't bring them to the library until Sunday, but everything else we have to search. We're looking for a map, a valuable one," I replied as I pulled the first stack carefully off the shelves and began checking for something tucked behind the jacket, or in the pages, or someplace else where Drew Wellington might have hidden something. He might have thought he was getting drunk, or someone was trying to drug him, to steal his maps. He may have thought, *I'll hide this and find it later.*

After we had worked for about ten minutes, Tom became concerned and corralled Julian, and the two of them came looking for us. Soon the four of us were working in earnest.

"*Mare occidentalis,*" Arch announced triumphantly as he unfolded a large piece of vellum. "That's Latin for Atlantic Ocean. Wow, look at this thing."

Our Christmas was quiet, which was just the way we wanted it. Marla was with us, and Julian had insisted on bringing Grace. So maybe it wasn't that quiet. I can't even remember what each person received, except that Stanford University sent every one of us shirts with their logo, and said we could all come out to visit, at their expense, whenever we wanted.

Tom said, "That's real nice, but I'd rather just stay home." We all agreed.

About a month into the new year, I received a postcard. On the front was a map of Brazil. I got online to check out the Portuguese text, handwritten by—I guessed—a twenty-two-year-old former stripper:

"No hao perdida."

"I am not lost."

The card was unsigned.

Brazil will not extradite murderers back to the United States.

Acknowledgments

The author would like to acknowledge the help of the following people: Jim Davidson; Jeff, Rosa, Ryan, and Nicholas Davidson; J. Z. Davidson; Joey Davidson; Sandra Dijkstra, my hardworking agent, along with her outstanding team; Carolyn Marino, my fabulous editor; Michael Morrison, Lisa Gallagher, Dee Dee DeBartlo, Lucinda Blumenfeld, Wendy Lee, and the entire brilliant team at Morrow/HarperCollins; Kathy Saideman, for her usual helpful readings of the manuscript; the entire excellent staff of the Evergreen branch of the Jefferson County Public Library, Evergreen, Colorado; Bryan Streelman, Esquire, Golden, Colorado; Diane Barrett, Esquire, vice-chancellor of the Episcopal Diocese of Colorado; Shirley Carnahan, Ph.D., senior instructor in the humanities, University of Colorado; Patrick N. Allitt, Ph.D., professor of history, Emory University; Curtis and Alana Bird of the Old Map Gallery, Denver, Colorado; the following writer friends, who supplied ongoing support: Jasmine Cresswell, Julie Kaewert, Emilie Richards, Connie Laux, Karen Stone, and Leslie O'Kane; the superb caterers John William Schenk and Kirsten Schenk of Littleton, Colorado, and our wonderful new caterer in Evergreen, Ed Neiman; and as always, my extraordinarily helpful source on police procedure, Sergeant Richard Millsapps, Jefferson County Sheriff's Department, Golden, Colorado.

Recipes in *Sweet Revenge*

Chicken Divine

Chuzzlewit Cheese Pie

Prudent Potatoes au Gratin

Stylish Strawberry Salad

Bleak House Bars

Unorthodox Shepherd's Pie

Deep-Dish Cherry Pie

Got-a-Hot-Date Bars

Piña Colada Muffins

Door-Prize Gingerbread

Chicken Divine

2 cups buttermilk
1 cup whipping cream
1 tablespoon kosher salt
1 tablespoon granulated sugar
4 pounds (about 5 pieces) skin-on,
    bone-in chicken-breast halves
additional sea or kosher salt
freshly ground black pepper
¼ cup dried tarragon

In a large nonreactive or glass bowl, mix together the first 4 ingredients and stir until dissolved. Rinse the chicken under running water, pat it dry, and then place it in the buttermilk mixture. Make sure all the pieces are completely submerged. Cover the bowl with plastic wrap and place the bowl in the refrigerator overnight.

When you are ready to roast the chicken, preheat the oven to 400°F.

Drain the buttermilk mixture from the chicken and discard the buttermilk mixture. Rinse the chicken under running water and pat it dry with paper towels. Grease a 9-by-13-inch glass pan and place the chicken, skin side up, in the pan, being careful not to crowd the pieces. Sprinkle with salt and pepper, to taste. Crush the tarragon between your fingers and sprinkle it evenly over the chicken.

Bake for 35 to 40 minutes, until a meat thermometer inserted into the thickest part of the chicken reads 160°F. Immediately bring out of the oven and serve.

MAKES 4 TO 5 SERVINGS

Chuzzlewit Cheese Pie

2 cups half-and-half

4 ounces (1 stick) unsalted butter

½ cup all-purpose flour

1 teaspoon baking powder

½ teaspoon sea salt

¼ teaspoon cayenne pepper

2 teaspoons Dijon-style mustard

8 large eggs

½ pound extra-sharp Cheddar cheese,
   grated

½ pound Gruyère cheese, grated

In a small saucepan, heat the half-and-half over medium-low heat until very hot but not boiling. Remove from the heat. In a large saucepan, melt the butter over medium-low heat, add the flour, and whisk a couple of minutes, until it bubbles. Slowly add the half-and-half, whisking constantly. Cook and stir this cream sauce until it thickens and is very smooth. Remove from the heat and set aside, stirring frequently, until cool enough to touch with your (clean) finger.

Preheat the oven to 350°F. Butter a 9-by-13-inch glass baking pan.

Whisk together the baking powder, sea salt, and cayenne pepper. Stir this mixture into the cream sauce along with the mustard. Whisk until smooth. (Do not reheat.)

In the large bowl of an electric mixer, beat the eggs well, until they are frothy. Keeping the beater going, slowly add the cooled cream sauce and beat on low speed until completely combined. Toss the cheeses together, then thoroughly stir them into the egg–cream sauce mixture. Pour into the prepared pan. Bake for 40 to 45 minutes, or until the pie is puffed, brown, and set in the middle. Serve immediately, as the pie deflates as quickly as a soufflé.

MAKES 8 LARGE SERVINGS

Prudent Potatoes au Gratin

½ tablespoon unsalted butter

1 tablespoon olive oil

1 large yellow onion, trimmed, peeled
   and very thinly sliced
   (approximately 2 cups)

4 pounds russet potatoes

½ pound Gruyère cheese, grated

½ pound Comte or Fontina cheese,
   grated

½ cup freshly grated Parmesan cheese

1 tablespoon finely chopped fresh sage

1 teaspoon coarse sea salt or kosher
   salt

½ teaspoon freshly ground black
   pepper

2 cups heavy cream

Butter a 9-by-13-inch glass baking pan.

In a large sauté pan, melt the butter with the oil over
medium-low heat, then add the onion. Cook over low
heat, stirring frequently, until the onion is very limp
and has caramelized without burning, 15 to 25 minutes.

Be sure to cook until the onion has completely changed color.

Preheat the oven to 375°F.

Scrub the potatoes under running water, then peel them. Slice them thinly. Toss together the grated cheeses. Place a layer of sliced potatoes in the prepared pan, followed by a scattering of the cooked onions. Sprinkle on a layer of cheese, then sprinkle on some of the sage. Continue to layer until you have used up the potatoes, onions, cheese, and sage. End with a layer of cheese.

Stir the salt and pepper into the heavy cream and pour it slowly all over the potato mixture so as not to disturb the cheese topping. Bake in the middle of the oven for about 1 to 1½ hours, until the potatoes are very tender and the top is golden brown.

MAKES 8 TO 12 SERVINGS

Stylish Strawberry Salad

1 head baby romaine, washed, patted or spun
    dry, and carefully separated into leaves
2 cups fresh strawberries, washed,
    hulled, and cut in half
3 tablespoons best-quality sherry
    vinegar
1½ teaspoons Dijon-style mustard
1½ teaspoons minced shallots
2 tablespoons granulated sugar
¼ to ½ teaspoon sea or kosher salt
¼ teaspoon freshly ground black
    pepper
6 tablespoons best-quality extra-virgin
    olive oil
2 avocados, peeled and sliced at
    serving time
additional sea or kosher salt
additional freshly ground black pepper

Prepare the lettuce and wrap it in a clean dry cloth
towel. Refrigerate until serving time.

Prepare the strawberries and set aside.

Whisk together the vinegar, mustard, shallots, sugar, salt, and pepper. Then, whisking constantly, drizzle in the oil until the mixture emulsifies. Set this vinaigrette aside.

Just before serving time, prepare avocados. At serving time, divide the lettuce among four plates. Arrange the strawberries and avocado slices (each person gets ½ avocado) on top of the leaves. Shake the vinaigrette and ladle a few spoonfuls onto each salad. If desired, sprinkle a tiny amount of salt onto each salad, then follow with a few grinds of black pepper. Serve immediately.

MAKES 4 SERVINGS

Bleak House Bars

¾ cup pecan halves

8 ounces (2 sticks) unsalted butter, at
    room temperature

½ cup dark brown sugar, firmly
    packed

2 cups all-purpose flour

¾ teaspoon salt, divided

14 ounces (1¼ cups) sweetened
    condensed milk

18 ounces (3 cups) semisweet
    chocolate chips, divided

8 ounces cream cheese, at room
    temperature

⅓ cup granulated sugar

1 large egg

½ teaspoon vanilla

½ cup seedless raspberry jam

In a large sauté pan, toast the nuts for about ten minutes, until they are slightly brown and emit a nutty scent. Remove them from the heat, cool, and coarsely chop.

Preheat the oven to 350°F. Butter a 9-by-13-inch baking pan.

In the large bowl of an electric mixer, beat the butter until it is very soft and creamy. Keeping the mixer on medium speed, beat in the dark brown sugar. Remove the beater from the bowl and scrape it. Stir the flour, ½ teaspoon of the salt, and nuts into the butter mixture until very well combined. Measure out 2¼ cups of this mixture and set the rest aside. Wash and dry the bowl and beaters.

Press the 2¼ cups of butter mixture into the bottom of the prepared pan. Bake for about 10 minutes, or until the edges are golden brown. While the crust is baking, combine the condensed milk with 2 cups of the chocolate chips in a heavy saucepan. Cook, stirring, over low heat until the chocolate is melted. Remove the crust from the oven and immediately pour the chocolate mixture over the hot crust.

In the large bowl of the electric mixer, beat the cream cheese until it is very smooth. Add the granulated sugar and beat once more until smooth. Finally, add the egg, vanilla, and remaining ¼ teaspoon of salt and beat until very smooth. In a small bowl, stir the jam until it is smooth.

Now you are ready to make the rest of the layers. Sprinkle the remaining butter-nut mixture over the chocolate. Using a soup spoon, ladle the jam evenly over the butter-nut mixture. Using another soup spoon, ladle the cream-cheese mixture over the jam layer. Finally, sprinkle the remaining cup of chocolate chips over the cream cheese.

Bake for 30 to 35 minutes, or until the cream-cheese layer is set and no longer liquid in the middle. Cool on a rack.

MAKES 32 BARS

Unorthodox Shepherd's Pie

2 pounds lean ground beef

2 cups chopped onions

2 cups chopped celery

2 tablespoons olive oil

¼ cup plus 1 tablespoon all-purpose
  flour

2 cups chicken stock, preferably
  homemade

2 teaspoons dried thyme, crumbled

½ teaspoon dried rosemary, crumbled

1 teaspoon sea or kosher salt, or to taste

¼ to ½ teaspoon freshly grated black
  pepper, or to taste

1 cup frozen baby peas

1 cup frozen baby corn

4½ pounds russet potatoes

1½ cups half-and-half

1 cup grated Gruyère cheese

½ cup freshly grated Parmesan cheese

additional sea salt, to taste

additional freshly ground black
  pepper, to taste

> 2 ounces unsalted butter (½ stick), cut
>   into bits
> paprika

In a very large sauté pan, sauté the ground beef, onions, and celery in the oil over medium heat until the beef is browned and the vegetables are limp. Add the flour and stir for 2 to 3 minutes, until the mixture begins to bubble. Slowly add the chicken stock. Stir until completely combined, then stir in the thyme, rosemary, and salt and pepper. Cook and stir until the mixture is bubbling and thickened. Stir in the peas and corn and set aside.

Bring a large quantity of salted water to boiling. Peel the potatoes and drop them into the water. Cook for about 40 to 45 minutes. In a small saucepan, heat the half-and-half until it is steaming, but not boiling.

Preheat the oven to 350°F. Butter two 9-inch deep-dish pie plates. Grease or line a baking sheet.

Remove the potatoes from the heat, drain, and place them in the large bowl of an electric mixer. Begin to beat the potatoes on low speed, slowly adding the hot half-and-half, the cheeses, and the additional salt and pepper.

Place half the beef mixture in each of the prepared pie plates. Place half the potato mixture on top of the beef. Scatter half the butter bits on top of each potato mixture. Sprinkle generously with paprika.

Place the pies on the baking sheet and place them in the oven. Bake for about 45 minutes, or until the potatoes are browned and the pies are completely heated through. This goes well with a fruit salad.

MAKES 8 LARGE SERVINGS

Deep-Dish Cherry Pie

Crust:

3½ cups all-purpose flour

1 tablespoon plus 1 teaspoon
confectioners' sugar

1 teaspoon kosher salt

1½ cups (3 sticks) unsalted butter, cut into 1
tablespoon pieces and chilled

¼ cup plus 2 tablespoons chilled lard or
vegetable shortening, cut into 1-tablespoon
pieces and chilled

½ cup plus 1 to 2 tablespoons iced springwater

2 egg whites, kept in separate bowls and lightly
beaten

additional granulated sugar or crushed sugar
cubes

Filling:

2 cups granulated sugar

¼ cup plus 1 tablespoon cornstarch

1 cup reserved cherry juice

4 cups canned sour pitted cherries
(contents of 2 cans, drained, juice
reserved)

    1 tablespoon melted unsalted butter
    1 teaspoon freshly squeezed lemon juice

To make the crust: In a large bowl (or the bowl of a food processor fitted with the metal blade), whisk together the flour, sugar, and salt until thoroughly combined, about 10 seconds.

Drop the first 8 tablespoons of chilled butter on top of the flour mixture, and cut in with two sharp knives (or pulse in the food processor), *just* until the mixture looks like tiny crumbs. (In the food processor, this will take less than a minute.) Repeat with the rest of the butter and the lard or vegetable shortening in batches, keeping the unused portion of fat well chilled until it is time to cut it into the flour. The mixture will look like large crumbs when all the butter and lard has been incorporated.

Sprinkle the water over the top of the mixture and either mix with a spoon or pulse until the mixture *just* begins to hold together in clumps. If the mixture is too dry to hold together, add the additional water until it does. Divide the mixture in half and place each half into one of two 2-gallon zipped plastic storage bags.

Pressing very lightly through the plastic, quickly gather the mixture into rough circles in the center of each bag. Refrigerate the bags of dough until they are thoroughly chilled.

When you are ready to make the pie, preheat the oven to 400°F. Have a rimmed cookie sheet ready to place underneath the pie.

Remove one of the bags of dough from the refrigerator. Unzip the bag, then quickly roll out the dough (still in the bag) to a circle approximately 10 inches in diameter. Using scissors, cut the plastic all the way around the bag and gently lift back one side of the plastic. Place the bag dough side down in a 9-inch *deep-dish* pie plate. Gently remove the remaining piece of plastic so that the dough falls into the plate. Trim the edge of the crust. Gently line the crust with parchment paper and weigh down the crust with rice, dried beans, or pie weights.

Bake for 10 minutes. Remove from the oven and remove the parchment with the weights. Brush the bottom and sides of the crust with one of the beaten egg whites.

Return the crust to the oven to bake for 10 minutes more. If the edge begins to brown too quickly, it can be covered with pieces of foil until the crust is baked. Remove the crust from the oven and allow it to cool slightly while you prepare the filling and the top crust.

To make the filling: Combine the sugar with the cornstarch and stir until well mixed. Stir in the reserved cherry juice. Place in a medium saucepan and cook this mixture over medium heat, stirring frequently, until the mixture thickens and bubbles; cook a minute or two longer, until the mixture begins to clear. Remove from the heat and add the cherries, melted butter, and lemon juice.

Place the cherry mixture in the cooked crust. Remove the second chilled bag of pie dough from the refrigerator. Prepare the dough repeating the process for the first crust to make a top crust for the pie. After cutting the plastic, gently lift the plastic from one side of the dough. Center the bag, dough side down, over the cherries and gently remove the remaining piece of plastic. Press the dough around the edge of the baked crust to seal the 2 crusts. Cut slits in the dough to create vents. Brush the top crust with the second egg white. Sprinkle the additional sugar or crushed sugar cubes lightly over the top. Place the pie onto a rimmed cookie sheet before it bakes.

Bake for 40 to 45 minutes, or until the crust is browned and juices are bubbling out of the pie. Place the pie on a cooling rack for at least 2 hours, so the pie can set. Serve alone or with best-quality vanilla ice cream.

MAKES 12 SERVINGS

Got-a-Hot-Date Bars

1 cup whole pecans

½ cup chopped dates

½ cup raisins

2 tablespoons buttermilk

2 cups all-purpose flour

¾ teaspoon baking powder
    (high altitude: add ½ teaspoon)

½ teaspoon baking soda

½ teaspoon salt

8 ounces (2 sticks) unsalted butter, at room
    temperature

2 cups dark brown sugar, firmly packed

2 large eggs

1 teaspoon vanilla extract

1 cup semisweet chocolate chips

1 cup almond brickle chips (Bits O' Brickle or
    Heath Toffee Chips)

Preheat the oven to 325°F. Butter a 9-by-13-inch pan.

In a wide frying pan, toast the pecans over medium-low heat, stirring constantly, until they begin to turn a darker brown and emit a nutty scent, about 10 minutes. Immediately remove the pan from the heat and turn the pecans out on paper towels. When they are just cool enough to touch, roughly chop them. Set aside.

In a small saucepan, place the dates, raisins, and buttermilk. Bring to a boil over medium heat, then immediately remove the pan from the heat and turn the date mixture into a shallow bowl to cool. Set aside.

Sift together the flour, baking powder, baking soda, and salt. In the large bowl of an electric mixer, beat the butter until it is very creamy. Add the brown sugar and beat well, until the mixture is light and fluffy, about 3 minutes. Add the eggs one at a time, beating well after each addition. Mix in the vanilla. Using a wooden spoon, stir in the flour mixture, date mixture, nuts, chocolate chips, and almond brickle chips, stirring only until combined. Turn the mixture into the prepared pan and smooth the top.

Bake in the middle of the oven for 35 to 40 minutes, or until a wooden toothpick inserted into the middle comes out clean. Cool on a rack. When completely cool, cut into 24 bars.

MAKES 2 DOZEN

Piña Colada Muffins

1 cup dried pineapple

additional 12 pieces of dried pineapple, for
 garnish before baking (about 6½ ounces
 pineapple, total)

1 cup dark Jamaican rum, optional

2 cups all-purpose flour (high altitude: add 1
 tablespoon)

1 teaspoon baking powder

½ teaspoon baking soda

¼ teaspoon salt

6 ounces (1½ sticks) unsalted butter, at room
 temperature

1 cup granulated sugar

2 large eggs, at room temperature

1 cup dairy sour cream

1 teaspoon vanilla extract

¾ teaspoon finely minced orange zest

¾ cup sweetened flaked coconut

Place the pineapple in a small saucepan and pour the
rum over it. If you are not using the rum, pour in 1 cup
water (preferably springwater). Bring to boiling, then
allow the pineapple to cool in the liquid for about 30

minutes. Drain the pineapple. (If you are using rum, after draining, either discard it or reserve it for another use.) Pat the pineapple dry with paper towels, reserve 12 pieces, and roughly chop the remainder and set aside.

Preheat the oven to 350°F. Thoroughly butter the *top* of a 12-muffin pan. (This is to ensure easy release of muffins after baking.) Place paper liners in the 12 muffin cups.

Sift together the flour, baking powder, baking soda, and salt. Set aside.

In the large bowl of an electric mixer, beat the butter on medium speed until it is very creamy. Gradually add the sugar and beat well, until the mixture turns light. Add the eggs, one at a time, and beat until the mixture is well combined. On low speed, mix in the sour cream, vanilla, and zest until completely combined. (Mixture will look curdled.) Gently stir the flour mixture, pineapple, and coconut into the butter mixture, stirring only until completely combined. (Batter will be thick.)

Using a ½ cup measure, measure a scant ½ cup batter into each paper liner. Top each muffin with a reserved piece of pineapple. Bake for 15 to 20 minutes, or until the muffins are puffed, golden brown, and a toothpick inserted in the center of a muffin comes out clean. Gently remove muffins from pan. Serve hot or at room temperature.

MAKES 12 MUFFINS

Door-Prize Gingerbread

Baking spray that includes flour (to be used to
  prepare pans)
4⅔ cups all-purpose flour (high altitude: add ¼
  cup plus 2 tablespoons)
2 teaspoons baking soda
2 teaspoons ground ginger
½ teaspoon ground cinnamon
¼ teaspoon freshly grated nutmeg
⅛ teaspoon ground cloves
¼ teaspoon salt
½ teaspoon freshly ground black pepper
4 sticks (1 pound) unsalted butter
2 cups unsulfured molasses
2 large eggs
2 cups sugar
1½ cups boiling springwater
1⅓ cups sour cream
1 teaspoon freshly grated gingerroot
3 tablespoons orange juice (high altitude: add 3
  tablespoons)

Preheat oven to 350°F. Take out three 8- or
9-cup nonstick castle molds and baking spray, but do

not spray pans until just before batter is to go into the oven.

Sift together the flour, baking soda, spices, salt, and pepper. Melt the butter with the molasses, and set it aside to cool.

Using the paddle attachment of an electric mixer, beat the eggs with the sugar until they are very thick and almost white. Add the butter mixture and beat on low speed, just until combined. Add the flour-spice mixture, and beat on low speed, just until combined. Using a rubber spatula, scrape the sides of the bowl and the paddle attachment, and stir well, making sure all the ingredients are well combined. Add the boiling water, sour cream, gingerroot, and orange juice, and beat 3 minutes. Scrape down the sides of the bowl and the paddle attachment, making sure all the ingredients are well incorporated.

Spray the 3 castle molds with the baking spray until every surface inside the molds is completely covered. Immediately pour the batter into the molds, dividing it evenly. Bake for 25 to 30 minutes, and check with a toothpick to see if the gingerbread is done. If necessary, allow another 5 to 10 minutes for the gingerbreads to bake, until a toothpick inserted into the middle of each gingerbread comes out clean. (You may also bake the gingerbreads on convect, checking after 25 minutes.)

Cool the gingerbreads on racks for 20 minutes. Carefully invert them to unmold on greased racks. Cool completely, then carefully slide onto serving plates. Decorate as desired, and serve with best-quality vanilla ice cream.

MAKES 3 GINGERBREADS; EACH GINGERBREAD MAKES 4 TO 6 SERVINGS